THE GIRL
IN THE
POLKA-DOT DRESS

GUY COTE

World Castle Publishing, LLC
Pensacola, Florida
Copyright © Guy Cote 2024
Hardback ISBN: 9798891261082
Paperback ISBN: 9798891261099
Paperback ISBN: 9798891260221
eBook ISBN: 9798891260238
First Edition World Castle Publishing, LLC, January 2, 2024
http://www.worldcastlepublishing.com

Licensing Notes

Cover: Sentimental Art, Chris Turley
Editor: Karen Fuller

"I'm afraid there are guns between me and the White House."
Senator Robert F. Kennedy
(April 1968)

For my Dad, Roland A. Cote. The English language is incapable of providing all the words and phrases I need to convey how much I appreciate all you've done for me.

PROLOGUE

Ambassador Hotel, Los Angeles, California. June 5, 1968

He's been working extra hard at an exhaustive pace to catch up, but some people just can't forgive his tardiness. They expected him – they *begged* him – to be the first to volunteer to correct the mistakes of the current leadership. He dragged his feet, trying to work with the leadership. It wasn't until others stepped forward and gained support that he finally announced his intention to dethrone the sitting king. As a result, they've labeled him *Bobby-come-lately*.

But they can't deny his passion. He speaks from the heart about matters that touch him deeply. "Some men see things as they are and ask why," he says on the campaign trail. "I dream of things that never were and ask why not." He offers hope, showing the people what greatness can be. He wants everyone to enjoy the fruits of prosperity, not just those already enjoying them. His message resonates with a bitter, divided populace, and they're starting to reward him for it. Tonight is his biggest victory thus far. The people in the Golden State elected to follow *his* path to a bright tomorrow, leaving behind a decade of troublesome yesterdays.

The celebration of his Golden State triumph is a modern-day jubilee with streamers, banners and balloons, cameras, microphones, elation spilling from the liquor lubricated lips of interviewees. His adherents are so numerous, so enthusiastic, and so eager to touch him he has to detour through a kitchen in order to announce his victory to a waiting media. Cooks, servers and busboys mix with supporters clustered in front of him and an excited throng behind him. He shakes enough hands to chafe his skin. He smiles at dozens of faces. He says "Thank-you" so often it becomes an involuntary response. He thinks of his wife, three months pregnant and fifty feet behind him – big professional athletes shielding her from the press of the people. He hears cameras click and stoves sizzle, the ringing melody of cutlery tapping against metal tables.

Supporters chant, "All the way with RFK." Well-wishes come in a variety of volumes. Wherever he looks, he sees the marginalized and the celebrated, rich and poor, young, old and middle aged. His diverse followers weep with joy, believing in him alone. He'll never say it, but he knows he's finally stepping out of the long shadow cast by his beloved, martyred brother.

He catches the rich aroma of beef wellington as it bakes. Ladies' perfume and men's cologne mingle with the smells of sweat and alcohol. A kitchen porter shakes his hand, saying, "Mucho gusto." His other hand goes to a busboy.

The hotel maître d' pulls him. "Let's go, Senator."

He turns to his right as a bushy-haired young man little more than five feet tall, springs before a girl, reaches around the maître d' and thrusts his hand forward. But the man isn't offering his congratulations. Two quick pops explode from his fist, accompanied by fire-bursts.

He jumps. His hands fly to his face. He staggers back on rubber legs, falling into a fluid crowd. Rapid pops follow, as if someone lit a string of firecrackers. People scream while others are unable to move. Some rush to help him. Some swarm the shooter. Sinking to the floor, the last thing he sees through a sea of desperate faces is a flowing white dress with black polka-dots moving away from him, quickly out of the kitchen.

CHAPTER 1

Los Angeles, California. 2018

"To Mr. Caron," yelled one of the investigators. "Slashed tires and harassing calls in the middle of the night couldn't stop him from bringing in today's verdict." Most seconded his toast, but some chuckled uncomfortably at his understatement.

Frank Caron raised his mug. "Slashed tires and harassing calls – if only." He read the room, which contained more than forty legal professionals toasting his success. He hardly knew most of them. "We got him this time. We really got him."

People tipped their drinks to their lips. It wasn't every day Los Angeles County notched a victory as great as this one. It deserved more said about it. It really did. But as the crowd divided according to social interests, he figured he'd let them get to exorcising their workplace demons. It was better for everyone that way, including him.

Propriety dictated he stay even though he was long past his days of drinking more than one or two. He checked his watch – a Citizen, two hundred bucks four years ago, and it still kept good time. What it told him was *you can only give propriety another fifteen minutes, tops. Start planning your escape.* A legal assistant caught his attention from a nearby table. The kid had a dramatic way of mesmerizing a cute intern with a harrowing tale of the Calessi mob. Frank would've laughed if the kid's story allowed for it, which it didn't. There was nothing amusing about Vincent Calessi and his thugs. Fortunately, today's verdict – Frank's victory – meant scary stories would be the only horrors Calessi would visit upon the city of Los Angeles from now on.

"Happy with yourself?"

Is it obvious? He turned to see Rip Reed, a compact yet muscular black man, weave through a small group to join him. He hailed a waitress. Swamped as she was, she gave him priority. "Blueberry beer. One." He already had a drink, so…he smirked as Rip's eyebrows pushed wrinkles up his considerable forehead. "Your testimony turned the trial. I owe you."

A shake of the head and Rip settled onto a stool. "You got the warrant for the phone tap, but – yeah. I'm out of the shadows now. For that, you owe me more than a girly drink."

"I'm out of the shadows, too, for now."

"What prosecutor would rather negotiate plea deals than face baddies in court?" asked Rip. "Never heard of such a thing."

"We can't all be Elliot Ness."

"You can when you want to be. That's just been proved."

"Give them another celebrity murderer or serial killer, and they'll forget about me. I can get back to negotiating. I never understood why I got this assignment in the first place."

Noise near the front door made Rip peer for a better view. He seemed a little too anxious, like he expected to see something.

Frank also looked but found nothing of note. He dropped a glance on his Citizen – seven minutes burned. He didn't see the waitress return until she set a blue beer before his companion.

Rip perked up, but it had nothing to do with the drink. "That's the least he can do, congratulate you in person." He pointed to the front door. "You might've got him re-elected."

"What?" Realizing who had just entered the pub, Frank felt a sudden compulsion to gulp down his drink. It wasn't enough, so he did the same to Rip's fruit beer. Girly for sure – too sweet for a beer, but that was all the notice he gave it. "What's he doing here?" It was a useless question, already answered. His friend pulled him toward the entrance, and he didn't resist, mainly because he had the presence of mind to know how it would look. For five years, he'd labored in the obscurity of the

District Attorney's Office without ever having met the district attorney. That wasn't all that unusual. There were over eleven hundred deputy district attorneys in Los Angeles County, and only a handful – no more than fifty – worked closely with the man in charge. And unlike most prosecutors who entered the DA's Office after law school, Frank spent nearly twenty years defending individuals the DA sought to punish. That hardly made him someone the district attorney would invite to eighteen holes at his country club. And that begged the question, for the umpteenth time, why did he get this assignment?

People put their phones on camera, aimed them at the man. They didn't do that to Frank after he won the case, so who really won the case?

They may not have ever met, but Frank had seen him from afar or on television and in the papers countless times. He seemed to be everywhere at once, ruling over Southern California's legal system. *Time* magazine called him "America's District Attorney", and other outlets like the *L.A. Times* praised him thirty times for every one they criticized him. It didn't hurt that he had everything Frank didn't: movie star looks, an adorable young family, charisma, wealth, and at forty-two, he was a decade younger than Frank. His real magic, however, was an unprecedented string of high-profile legal victories for which he claimed credit.

Frank remembered his watch – not sure why with all this excitement, but it confirmed his suspicions. He was now officially late, even if he abused the speeding laws. *Shit.*

Rip didn't stop until he put his friend face-to-face with famed Los Angeles County District Attorney Marco Diaz. The great man smiled perfectly, offering Frank his hand. "It's a pleasure to finally meet you after weeks of watching you."

"Uh – you've been watching? Of course, you have. Why wouldn't you? I mean –"

Mr. Diaz tightened his grip. "Better late in your career than never, huh?" His golden brown eyes shifted to Rip. "Good to see you again, Ripley."

"You too, sir."

"Glad I took your advice on this one." The DA gestured to Frank with a nod of his head.

His umpteen questions answered with that one line, he looked from Rip to Mr. Diaz, back and forth. All he could manage to say was, "I gotta go." And he put action to his words.

#

Other hypnotists tried to get the old woman to this point, but resistance from the subject made their task impossible. Sasha Frye built a bond with her over six weeks, four times a week. She also added a personal touch, exhuming the four-carat diamond ring she buried in her jewelry box, wearing it on her right hand and casually waving it before her subject – a tribute of sorts to her professional forebears and their swinging gold watches. The ring no longer burned her finger as it once had. Four years cooled the metal quite a bit. That didn't mean she enjoyed wearing it, especially given the other personal touch that helped her facilitate this hypnosis. She was involved with the subject's son. It wasn't a big romance, not yet. It was mostly physical. But it broke down the family's resistance to hypnosis. What family? It was essentially the son. Her coupling with him was a factor. She didn't believe it was *the* factor, but it helped convince him to allow her to treat his mother.

She'd never used her looks, her sex, to get her any such advantage before – not really. This was something she couldn't pass up, so she *may* have turned up the heat just a notch when she proposed hypnotizing his mother. She didn't seduce him. It was all in service to the old woman anyway. She was an ideal candidate for rementia, which was the use of hypnosis to reverse the symptoms of early-stage dementia. She read about it, even took a course on it at the San Luis Obispo Institute of Wellness. Of all the residents she dealt with, Charlotte Caron was most in need of this treatment.

She watched Charlotte's eyes move REM-style under their lids. That was significant because the poor woman had a stroke some years past that damaged the motor skills of her left eye. It was a lazy eye that often acted independent of the right. It was a peculiar but not unheard of debilitation. Perhaps hypnosis could improve her muscle coordination as well as her concentration, relaxation and socialization. She brightened as she considered that possibility.

The safe place in Charlotte's imagination was bright with vibrant colors. It was where she felt free and unrestricted by age or infirmity, where she could walk through tall grass. In real life, that wasn't possible because she was mostly wheelchair bound. "That's right," she told her. "Your place is fun and colorful. The grass is long but soft. It gently strokes your bare legs as you walk through it. You feel the whispering breeze and the warming sun."

She had to be careful. Their last session revealed a darker imagination in which Charlotte envisioned beasts devouring children and fire ravaging villages. With images like that in her subconscious, she could see why the woman seemed so troubled in her waking life. "Tell me about the water. Do you see a lake or a stream?"

The room had thick walls in the back, and the front, but the one separating them from the nearby storage closet was thin with a large window. She heard a door open. She heard shuffling, and things moved around to accommodate someone entering the closet. He was late, but she didn't show her annoyance. She was a professional. Why was he late, though? Really? His trial was important, but the news said it ended hours ago. He should've been here when they started.

"It's a river," said Charlotte. "It's by a horse farm, and the horses drink the water."

"That's right. Beautiful horses drink from the river. Is the water fast or slow moving?" She saw the curtains behind the storage room's window slide open. Frank eased into the chair she left for him. He mouthed the words *I'm sorry*. That made her look away, but the sight of him remained imprinted on her retinas. He had strong shoulders and thick arms for a man who didn't exercise much. When his arms encircled her, she felt as protected as a cat in a cardboard box. It was a strange analogy, she knew, but that was how she felt. And a cat in a box could lash out at any threat coming at it from the front. His hair was sandy blond with no noticeable gray. His eyes were clear and blue – abnormally blue. His nose was his most notable feature. It was wider and larger than most, like the swollen beak of a boxer a day after a fight, but she thought it was as cute as hell. He was also smart. At her age, in her forties, she'd come to realize how attractive that quality really was.

"The river is slow now," said Charlotte. "And it's shrinking. Fish can't jump because they'll land on rocks and flop around till they die. Plants are withering. The dirt is dust."

She tried not to seem alarmed, but unpleasantness was once again invading the woman's vision. It was how her last dark imaginings started. And from there, they turned rapidly traumatic.

#

Frank owed her an apology. He planned to be there on time, but the district attorney…hmm. What was he supposed to make of that? Nothing, he hoped. *Congratulations. You gave me another notch on my victory belt. See you around.* The question he now faced was to whom did he owe the apology, Sasha or his mother? That really didn't require an answer. Whenever he tried to prepare Charlotte for one of her sessions, she acted as if she didn't want him there. He already told Sasha he was sorry, but she missed it. The award had to go to Sasha.

The apology he'd like to give her would be one they'd both enjoy. He loved the thrill of a new relationship. The exploration was the best part, anatomy and personality-wise. Of those two the physical exploration had always been his favorite. But lately, the need for an occasional bump from a little blue pill pushed forward his preference for personality. Not that Sasha didn't have both in spades. She looked exotic: half-Hispanic and half-Irish-American. He loved her almond eyes, mocha skin and wavy auburn hair. She had more curves than the PCH. She was also honest, direct like him, and he perceived in her a selfless spirit. Where he had to work at that, it seemed she did not.

He heard her tell Charlotte, "You're seeing the changing of the seasons when rivers dry to a trickle only to run heavy later, after the mountain snows melt. It's glorious nature."

Is she implanting imagery into Mom's vision? After she pitched using hypnosis to treat Charlotte's early dementia, he did some research of his own. Hypnosis often got a bad rap because people associated it with parlor tricks like convincing someone they were a chicken. But a good hypnotist could bring subjects to a peaceful state of mind where they worked on their issues. That convinced him it'd be good for his mother, who long dealt with the issue of extreme pessimism, among other things. Oh, and the hypnotist, *she* convinced him.

"There's no snow in the mountains." Charlotte's eyes appeared to move in unison beneath her eyelids. "I can't see the sun behind the black clouds in the sky."

He leaned closer to the window, almost touching it with his nose. He hadn't seen his mother's eyes move in synchronicity in years. That alone was real progress.

"Storms are cleansing," said Sasha. "Winds are cool, and rain brings life to thirsty plants. Can you feel the joy in the trees as nature gives them a shower?"

In addition to uncoordinated eyes, the stroke put two faces on his mother. She had control over the right half of her face, but the left was often slack and useless. Watching through the glass, he could see the right half of her face twisting as she tried to experience what her hypnotist described for her. But she didn't appear able to. It was like a succulent fruit dangling just out of her reach. He recognized the expression from the many times she wore it when he was younger. She never seemed capable of getting what she wanted, and the torment of longing gave her an *I don't care attitude* that showed in her mismatched wardrobes and unmanaged Einstein-like hair. It was tough for him to have sympathy for her when she was like that, but he was trying.

"There's no wind," said Charlotte. "It's hot. The mob is making me sweat. There won't be rain because the black clouds are for *him*. He creates the clouds. He lives in them."

Her *mob* reference caught his attention. He'd been deep into it for months, studying every aspect of it in preparation for the Calessi case. But he never discussed it with his mother or Sasha. He couldn't imagine why she'd mention it while under hypnosis. And who was the *he* she emphasized? A lot of people ruffled her feathers over the years. For the longest time, he thought of her as perpetually pissed. Yet he couldn't think of anyone who burrowed so deep into her subconscious that they'd come out during hypnosis, and in association with the mob.

"Somebody *is* there with you," said Sasha. "I am with you."

He knew that was her way of being affirmative. Hypnotists had to stay positive for the mental health of those they treated. He appreciated and admired her for it. He really did.

"Not you," said Charlotte. "*Him.*"

His mother didn't point at or acknowledge him, but it felt like it with the way she said that last word. It brought to mind the thing he did for which she never forgave him. That thing was always there, like the sick stench of skunk he could never wash off.

"Who is in your safe place with you?" asked Sasha.

Don't ask her that. He'd done his research on hypnosis, but he wasn't a researcher. That was what he had Rip for. Could hypnosis make his mother tell Sasha what he had done? Was that, in fact, what Charlotte was now talking about?

The slack side of his mother's face appeared to be rejuvenated by the struggle over whether or not to name the man in her subconscious. It was another extraordinary development, one that would have excited him but for the fact that *he* was the man in her subconscious. If Sasha heard the truth, she'd want nothing to do with him. As fond as he was of her, he worried more about how the revelation would impact the rest of his life. He wanted to ease his mother through her final years. It was the right thing to do. He didn't want her to spill the secret of which he was most ashamed. He didn't want her to shatter his hermit crab shell.

He had to shut her up. But if he tried to enter the hypnosis room from the hall, he'd be too late. He could beat the glass until Charlotte awoke. That wouldn't be good for her because people were supposed to ease out of hypnosis carefully. For those like his mother who were physically frail, a traumatic awakening could be truly detrimental. He raised his hands anyway. It was a risk he'd have to take. He was about to hit the glass when he heard her say, "The senator's killer is in my safe place." He froze. With arms upright, his reflection in the glass resembled someone surrendering to the police.

His mother's eyelids flew open, but only the whites of her eyes showed. She looked possessed, and her hands moved before her as if shaking out some sort of fabric. "I don't like this dress," she said. "But I have to wear it for him to die. And Robert Kennedy *must die*. Polka-dots are ugly."

CHAPTER 2

Redondo Beach, California. Early August 1965

Charlotte Remy lifts long false lashes to see her candy stripe mod dress hanging untouched in the closet. All week she looked forward to wearing it out on the town, but when Pete stepped out of the shower smelling of Ivory and glistening damp, that was it. He lays beside her now. Gaps in the window blind allow tiger stripes of sunlight to fall onto his nude body. These are the crazy days of her cycle. She inhales his aroma. She wants to taste his tongue and feel his scruff rub her face red. She loves his coarse hands exploring her body, which prickles to his touch. How can she make plans to dress up when all she wants to do is get naked with him?

He rolls onto his back. A sliver of daylight falls upon his face, fluttering his eyes open. They're aqua green, and they seem lost until they find her. "That was a fun night."

She touches his stomach, feeling hard muscles beneath the carpet of dark hair that forms a happy trail leading to…. "We can make it a better morning." Her fingertips walk down the trail.

"Shit!" He bolts out of bed as if ejected by the mattress springs. His eyes are on the bedroom clock while hers are on his clock, which shows their moment shrinking away with each passing second. It wouldn't take her thirty seconds to get him ready again, but he spins, denying her access, and he charges the bathroom. "They'll can me if I'm late again."

She hears the shower start. He won't climb into it for a

minute or two. The rust has to work its way out of the water, and it takes a while to warm. She's struck by the peculiarity of events unfolding, opposite of how they did last night, when he came out of the shower to change their plans. She looks back at the dress. She can hear it ask, *was it worth it?* Her response is to exhale. She flops back onto the mattress. The sweat generated by last night's row seeped back into her pores as she slept, but she can feel it returning now – this time uncomfortably.

Pete pokes his head out of the bathroom, white cream covering his scruff. "We can have another go tonight if I'm not too tired." He smiles. "It ain't easy keeping up with you, Char."

#

They're peddling the best dope in Brentwood, but it will take a lot of it to numb Charlotte's hormones. *Whore moans.* She chuckles. She wouldn't really call herself that. If a guy can have a celebration when he gets it, why can't a gal? They don't talk like that back home in Nebraska. She sucks another toke of Brentwood, holds it in then lets it out slowly. But they do here. *Thank the stars for liberation.*

Sun, sand and surf, she stumbles onto the beach. Her sandals trip her up – she's blaming them anyway. The crowd du jour is over by the pier, but she's looking for the beach bunnies. They're hard to find in a Brentwood haze.

"Chica! Chica! Got a spot for ya here, Chica."

She doesn't bother to look back. She knows it's the Chicanos shouting from the hood of their bean wagon. It's what they always do. *What white chick gets hot over that?* They're slimes. Fortunately, they avoid the sand, like it'll dry up all their grease or something. She's safe among her kind. And there they are. She counts six – no, eight. Nine. She sees ten. Ten beach bunnies hopping in and out of the crowd. She knows half of them, her favorite being Beverly, whose heavy assets make her the most recognizable. She doubts the girl has ever worn a bra. They probably don't make them in her size.

The Chicanos try again. "Don't take away that hot box. Bring it on back here."

Brentwood comes to her rescue once more. It smokes her lungs, fogs her head and, most importantly, pushes the spics way, way behind her. The nearer she comes to the pier crowd, the louder their entertainment becomes. Sometimes it's a traveling troubadour. Other times it's a peddler of the latest hip narcotic. Today's entertainer appears to be a beach barker.

"Cha Cha, where've you been?" Beverly is a blur until she appears inches from her face. "Whoa, your pupils are – good morning to you. You gotta hear this one. Matthew Whalen is his name, up from Venice." She drags her into the belly of the crowd. More faces come in and out of view. Some are bunnies. She recognizes Mitzi and Louise, Sally, and *what's this one's name?* She knows other people besides the bunnies. They're regulars around here, all doing what they do best, which isn't much.

A voice comes at her louder than the other human-made noises. It's smoky with a mysterious quality. "Every great religion is born out of something else," it says.

The dope makes processing the barker's words harder than digging his tone. When she finally understands him, she realizes he's not serving what she's ordering. *He's a preacher?*

"Where're you going?" asks Beverly. "Give him a chance. He's brilliant."

"I left religion where I left my straight hair and drab threads."

"Look at him." Beverly pulls her past a few listeners to a better spot in the sand. "He's like Tab Hunter with dark hair."

She finds the barker as out of focus as everything else, not immediately in front of her. But she does see a nest. It sparkles with the light of a thousand fireflies. She's mesmerized by its glitter among strands of…*is that hair? What am I looking at?*

The barker changes his voice. No longer beguiling, he sounds like a southern minister. "But brothers and sisters, I didn't come to dish about gods and religions."

Beverly laughs at her. "It's a beehive, Cha Cha. We should give you one." She pats the wildest strands of her runaway hair. "Tame this tumbleweed."

It's a beehive hairdo, of course. "I hate that freaky style." A step to the side takes her out from behind the girl with the tall hair to give her a direct view of the barker. "He doesn't look like Tab Hunter."

"Of course he does. Check out those sky blues."

He's twenty or more feet away, so she can't tell the color of his eyes any more than she can make sense of what he's saying. She shuffles closer, but the damn sand fills the space between her feet and her sandals. She crouches unsteadily to unstrap her footwear.

The barker says, "I'm here to talk about rock 'n' roll."

She looks up, and she falls on her ass. Once again, she can't see him, prevented by those standing before her. But he's now more interesting than he had been. People like him are called beach barkers because they wander from Baja to San Francisco, making social commentary and espousing political philosophies. They say they're penniless truth-tellers, but they get bread (and hanky-panky) from lonely widows or the neglected housewives of workaholics. It's cool, though. Everyone's got to get by one way or another.

"Like religion, rock 'n' roll has a pantheon of gods," he continues. "I choose to worship The Animals. *The House of the Rising Sun* is as timeless as the scriptures."

It's not easy when the ground is a seesaw, but she manages to stand on her own. She weaves through the crowd, bumping into human obstacles. She smells patchouli. She inhales the aroma of salty seaweed. She looks back at Beverly, who has lust in her eyes – directed at the barker. If he's willing, she'll give it to him. Bedding itinerant speakers is her thing. "You think every guy with blue eyes is Tab Hunter, and you'd just love to get your hands on Tab's tab." She laughs at her own wittiness, but Beverly is too far away to hear her.

The barker continues, "Think of your favorite song and how you connect with it, affecting your mood and making you feel happy or sad, melancholy or keyed."

She hears him more clearly now, and she understands him

more easily. The body odor of a nearby man smells like stagnant seawater, and she cringes away from the olfactory assault. An abrupt escape to the right puts her only feet away from the barker. And whoa, where does her breath go? She sees his eyes shining like sapphires against the backdrop of his tan face. They're a deeper blue than Tab Hunter's. His hair is midnight black. Dark hair and the bluest of blue eyes make for a striking combination. His teeth are straight and perfectly white. He can't be more than four years older than her, which would put him at twenty-five.

"Like all great movements, rock 'n' roll sprang from something else," he says. "Its ancestors are folk, blues, gospel and jazz. It marries poetry with melody. It's beat and words."

She's even digging his duds: a green and gold kimono imprinted with mystical symbols. His black chest hairs wave at her from behind the kimono's fold. He wears his feet naked in the sand. She looks down at her own bare feet then returns to his face. He's a New Age Jesus.

"Leaders back east in the D.C. are deaf now." He smiles snowy white. "But our music will weave its magic in the hearts and minds of all. They *will* hear it. It'll be our legacy."

Someone next to her – she doesn't know who, and she doesn't care – parrot's "our legacy" back to the barker. Others shout out too. She gets the vibe they're feeling. It's not just his messiah-like appearance, though that's a big part of it. It's the meaning of his words. They pertain to a situation she's been pushing out of her mind with the help of narcotics, a carefree beach lifestyle and frequent sex with Pete, the latest man with whom she shares a bed. The situation is that of her brother. Where she traded ho-hum Nebraska for the California sun, he fled their upbringing disguised in Army green. The old men who run the country decided to send this fresh recruit to a place called Viet-Nam. She doesn't know much about it, and no one has given her a satisfactory explanation for why he's there. Her rents back home are no help. She's spoken to them once since leaving eighteen months ago, and she heard them say they didn't need to know why he went overseas. He was a representative of Uncle

Sam. For that, they were proud, unlike how they felt about her.

"We're on the cusp of a revolution," says the barker. "The songs of our generation will show everyone the way."

What is *the way?* His hypnotic eyes have her in a trance-like hold, but he's got to give her more. *What kind of revolution? With guns and tanks? You'll lose me if it's that.*

The barker pauses dramatically. His action affects the people around her in different ways. Some fidget anxiously. Some hang on the soundless air around him. They seem unwilling to breathe for fear of missing his next statement. Others mumble questions to each other. A few outright ask him for answers. Seven or eight people walk away impatiently, unsatisfied. She wishes she could dissolve her Brentwood fog. He raised issues that require consideration from a sober mind. Finally, with people at the outer limits of their patience, the barker lifts his arms heavenward. "Revolution will come," he shouts. "But only if we spread the message of our gods. I encourage you all to find enlightenment in the lyrics that speak to you. We will change the world, and we will do so as rock 'n' roll evangelists."

Sometime in the course of him making his final plea, her jaw dropped open – undoubtedly an effect of her inebriation, but she's not aware of it until Beverly closes it for her, chuckling as she does so. "That's it?" she asks her. "You said he was brilliant."

"He looks brilliant. You might want to –" Beverly pretends to wipe drool off her friend's lower lip, and she gestures, as subtly as possible, to the man approaching behind her. He's a big man, marching hastily – two reasons for people to move out of his way.

It takes a few moments for her dopey eyes to recognize the man as Pete. In that time, he closes the distance to arrive before her. He doesn't look as good as he did the last time she saw him, without any clothes. But his mechanic uniform is clean, unlike how it usually is after a shift at work. He still smells of soap. His hair is neat. The expression on his face is miffed – not quite angry and not quite sad, but entirely off-put. "I told you what they'd do if I was late," he says.

His words, like his appearance, don't immediately register

with her. When they do, she recoils defensively. "That's not my fault."

"I didn't say it was." Slowly, his miffed expression dissolves into a frown, which further melts into a mischievous smirk. "At least I'm not too tired now."

She tilts her head. She raises her eyebrows. The tingle inside her says she hasn't smoked enough to numb her hormones after all.

Pete's aqua greens shift to the barker, who tries to weave through the press of people while answering questions raised by his speech. "What's his bag?"

She takes him by the hand. It's a strong hand, one she associates with pleasure. "Nothing but hot air."

CHAPTER 3

2018

Frank felt like a suspect who was about to beg the judge for leniency. Mrs. Chalker, the DA's secretary, told him nothing. She barely looked at him. It didn't matter that people passing him in the Justice Building congratulated him on the outcome of the Calessi trial. He received a summons from the great man, and from that, he couldn't escape. It came only hours after his mother's hypnosis-driven confession. The two *had* to be related. It cut him deeply to think Sasha took it to the DA, but who else could it have been? No one else was there.

That didn't mean he'd show up unprepared. In his hand, he held a statement issued by the U.S. Justice Department, which read *in certain limited cases, the use of hypnosis can be an aid in the investigative process [but] is subject to serious objections and should be used only on rare occasions. [It] must be thoroughly checked as to its ultimate accuracy and corroborated.* His preparation didn't stop there. He learned twenty-eight states went so far as to adopt a per se rule of exclusion for hypnosis-derived statements. He was also ready to argue that courts throughout the country almost uniformly rejected as inadmissible the out-of-court statements made by suspects or witnesses while under hypnosis. It wasn't a slam dunk, but given this district attorney's tendency to bring to trial only those cases he felt confident in winning, he hoped it was enough to dissuade Marco Diaz from looking into his mother.

Mrs. Chalker said, "The district attorney will see you

now."

He stuffed the hypnosis admissibility paper into his pocket and walked past the secretary. What he entered was a room more lavishly appointed than the county's budget allowed for. An oriental rug lay over a light oak floor. A tufted brown leather couch sat to the right, behind which stood industrial shelves with butcher block wood. On the shelves, hand-carved marble bookends held in place a collection of law books. The walls were gunmetal gray, supporting original and expensive artwork. The back wall accommodated a tinted window with a commanding view of the city's many buildings and busy thoroughfares. Most peculiar of all, a marble bust sat on a matching pedestal to the right of the kitty-cornered desk. It depicted an old man with a beard.

The DA glanced up from the laptop upon his desk to see Frank scrutinizing the bust. "That's Moses, the great law giver. He helps to remind me what we're doing here. Not that I need reminding when I have prosecutors like you on my roster. Have a seat."

Frank took one of two tufted brown leather chairs situated before the desk.

"Where do you see yourself next year at this time?"

Is that a trick question? Where he saw himself depended upon what this man did in regards to his mother. He glanced again at the stone head of Moses, buying time before responding. *Ever heard of the separation of church and state?* He turned back to the DA. "I was thinking of taking time off."

Mr. Diaz returned his eyes to his computer. "You have a careful résumé here."

And my mother's past threatens everything. Do you think I don't know that?

"Nineteen years as a defense attorney and…let's just say for you the courtroom has been a foreign land. You've been more aggressive as a deputy DA, but you still prefer misdemeanors over felonies. You've only notched three major convictions for us, including this one."

He cocked his head. He'd heard the district attorney could be wily, but the man seemed more interested in belittling him than manipulating him.

"Of course, prosecutors rarely pick their own cases, but we become known for certain things around here. Until recently, you were known for…I'll call it the *lighter fare.*"

"If Vincent Calessi is light, I'd hate to see heavy."

It took a moment before the DA laughed, and when he did, it wasn't genuine. "I assigned you that case personally on the recommendation of your investigator."

He'd already figured that out based on their exchange in the pub. What he didn't know was why Rip advocated for him. He thought it better not to ask until he got more information.

The DA scrutinized him the way he scrutinized the Moses bust. "So…you win the Super Bowl, and you tell me you're *not* going to Disneyland?"

He'd been through enough negotiations to know it was time to stop dancing around the subject – if they had in mind the same subject. There was only one way to find out. "Something recently came up in my personal life. The leave of absence is so I can attend to it."

That brought a change to Mr. Diaz – a more inquisitive and, for Frank, a more uncomfortable one. After a moment, he said, "I can't let you do that."

"Excuse me?"

The DA exhaled for effect. "You're my media darling, for now anyway. How's it going to look if I sideline or –" He looked him over, smirked. "Put you out to pasture?"

His eyes grew wide. The good news was that his mother's confession didn't appear to be the subject. The bad news: his age was. "That's the second time you've referenced that."

"Your next assignment will come down within a week. Until then, take a few *personal* days." Mr. Diaz went back to his computer. Apparently, the meeting was over.

#

Sasha sat alone in her office at the Brookside Retirement Center.

She drew the blinds, but through the slats, she could still see people passing by in the hallway. Before her, on the computer, a cursor pulsed in expectation of her typing in the message section of the San Luis Obispo Institute of Wellness website. Short of driving all the way out there, it was her only option after leaving three phone messages. The certificate awarded after she completed her studies at the Institute hung in a frame on the wall behind her. She didn't want to look at it.

She started tapping the computer keys. *I'm a recent graduate of your hypnotherapy program. I left messages. I really need to speak to Dr. Greenfeld, Dr. Sprague or Dr. Floyd. If they're too busy, I'll welcome a call from anybody, really. I need to talk –* She stopped typing. "That makes me sound like a push-over." She erased it, but not all of it. She picked up again after *I left messages.* She added *I have a legal problem. It might become YOUR problem. Using hypnotherapy techniques you taught me, I got a patient to divulge a deep and very dark secret.* Again, she paused. They'd say Charlotte was a subject, not a patient, something to be studied. Forging ahead with the message, she typed, *she admitted to being a part of the conspiracy that killed Robert Kennedy.* "No!" Her hand jumped up to the backspace button, using it to delete the line faster than she had created it. "Only a moron would put that in writing."

She stopped again, watching the cursor blink impatiently. A glance at the window and the people behind it made her shiver. What would happen if anyone found out what she got Charlotte to admit under hypnosis? She hadn't spoken to Frank yet. He bolted after she woke his mother. She called him, but he didn't answer. She called him twice. She was starting to feel like a pariah with no one taking her calls. But she decided to delete the message anyway.

#

The thoughts swirling in Frank's head consumed him to such an extent he didn't realize he'd walked out of the Justice Building until he was in the middle of the parking lot, the sun flashing in his eyes. Then it occurred to him, "Y'know. He never congratulated me." He turned, looked at the building that showed him its indifference.

He resumed his trek through the lot. And his head returned to its thoughts about his mother, Sasha and his job. He could at least be thankful Sasha didn't say anything about it to the DA. He could answer her calls now, he guessed.

It didn't take him long to find his car, a five-year-old Camry. That was mainly because it had a six foot six, 360lb man leaning against it. His stomach dropped as the man walked toward him. He had this feeling whenever he saw him, which wasn't often. And his anxiety had nothing to do with the man's size, muscles, many scars or the foolish King Kong tattoo on his neck.

"Hello, *Dad*."

It was that – the disdainful tone with which he addressed his father.

"They said you'd be here."

He had no idea who *they* might've been, but he knew his son was uncannily resourceful. He always had been. If he wanted to find you, you'd be found. "What do you want?"

"Trevor Blackburne, my name. I assume you forgot it because it's not anywhere on the emergency call list at Nana's nursing home. And she's been there three months."

"Two."

"I chipped in on the deposit three months ago."

"I didn't ask you to contribute anything." His son was so large he blocked the path between vehicles, so he had to take a detour route to reach his Camry. "She's my responsibility."

"Responsibility." Trevor laughed. "That's a new one for you."

"I'm not doing this with you again." He unlocked his car. "I'll put you on the list."

Trevor followed him to the car. "I got a call this morning from her hypnotist."

He stopped short of climbing into the car.

"How did she know to call me if I'm not on the list?"

"What did she say?"

"You knew they were hypnotizing her? They need

permission to do that."

"What did Sasha tell you?"

"Sasha...sounds like a stage name."

He climbed into the vehicle and shut the door. He missed putting the key into the ignition because Trevor pushed hard on the hood, making the car bounce. Frank threw the door open, and he jumped out. "You still owe me for the last car you wrecked. You want to do it again?"

"That wasn't your car." Trevor stared as if daring him to challenge his statement. "Your hypnotist friend told me Nana went to a dark place, and she wasn't qualified to deal with it."

"That's all she said?"

"Is there more?"

"She hypnotized Charlotte to help with her dementia. I don't know anything else."

The thick, calloused skin of Trevor's brows folded skeptically. "She deserves for you to call her mom. She earned that." He turned and walked away. "I'll see ya soon, *Frank*."

CHAPTER 4

Redondo Beach, California. Mid-August 1965

Charlotte can't actually hear it, but she thinks she can. Innocent people shriek amid the pop, pop, pop of gunfire. Rioters shout out in anger as they shatter glass. Flames roar like a howling wind. Never ending sirens scream at the mayhem. The Watts riot is sixteen miles away, but it has her teetering on the edge of reality. The boob tube only makes things worse. She has it on for companionship and to hear the special bulletins with which they keep interrupting regularly scheduled programming. She needs the companionship because Pete took off yesterday on orders from the lieutenant governor, who sent National Guardsmen to assist the cops in Watts. She never wanted to be Johnny Law's girlfriend, but it's the only job he's been able to hold with any consistency. At least he's not in Viet-Nam with her brother.

She's been hiding inside since he left, but she knows the beach is quiet. Even Luigi's Italian Eatery, where she trades her hours for tips, is closed. Anyone with any sense at all fears the chaos in Watts will spill over to here. If her favorite pillow was alive, she would've squeezed it to death by now. It provides small comfort as she hugs it while watching KNXT's *The Big News* on the tube. It's a complete broadcast, more in depth than the special reports. But the footage it shows is downright horrifying: buildings burning in black and white, people throwing flaming bottles and shooting their guns. Who burns and loots their own community? Only animals shit where they eat, and the dirty ones at that.

A fist strikes the door, and her eyes grow wide. Does the knocker know she's alone? The door is triple locked. If she turns up the television, will the knocker think anchorman Jerry Dunphy is in the house with her? It's worth a try.

Rap, rap, rap on the door.

She cranks up the TV dial, but her timing is poor. A commercial for *Lucky Strike* smokes replaces the anchorman. Two middle-aged squares appear on the tube dressed in suits and hats. One says to the other, "Show me a filter that really delivers taste, and I'll eat my hat." That won't fool anyone. She looks back, and she sees a human shape move behind the tie-dye sheet that covers the window beside the door. He's trying to peer in like a Peep-Tom. She rushes to the wall phone and picks up the receiver.

The newscast returns to the television with Jerry Dunphy saying, "Where are our elected officials? Snipers are shooting at helicopters, police, National Guardsmen and innocent civilians. Where is Governor Brown? Arsonists are burning small businesses and chain stores. Where is Mayor Yorty? Looters are running loose in the dark. Where are our city councilmen?"

She realizes there's not a soul out there she can call. If the public officials are running scared, who in Redondo Beach would dare come to her aid? She hears five more thumps amid the noise of the news. It'd make more sense for her malicious visitor to break the window than beat on the door, but no one ever accused rapists of having brains.

Anchorman Dunphy continues, "Governor Brown is in Europe, according to his office, ostensibly on a speaking tour. Mayor Yorty appears to be on a speaking tour as well. Yesterday he was in San Diego while Negro youth in Watts were throwing Molotov Cocktails. Today the mayor is in San Francisco as six buildings in Watts burn simultaneously."

She remembers Pete saying Watts is like New York, Philadelphia, Chicago and Jersey City. Black rioters are on their way, spreading their destruction across the country. It's nice that he wants to protect decent Americans and stop the spread, but she needs him here with her. Now.

"I know you're in there. I see you moving."

She freezes – too late, though. He's already seen her.

"Of the fifteen city council members," continues the anchorman. "Only eight are present to deal with this crisis. Councilman Tom Shepherd is in charge. The seventy-seventh police division is overwhelmed. There is talk that the National Guard won't be enough."

The visitor knocks again. "Charlotte –"

"I don't have any dough." It's all she can think to say, but what's really got her freaked is *he knows my name.*

"Charlotte," he says again. "It's Matt Whalen. I'm worried about Beverly. She went to Watts. Can I come in?"

Beverly went where? Why? But – Matt? The barker from the beach? She's only seen him three times, spoke to him once. Why would he come here? She gingerly approaches the door, as if walking on hot coals. She lifts the tie-dye sheet to look out. Yeah, it's him. He's decked out in a blue suit, light blue shirt and a thin black tie. He looks dressed for a job interview. But his eyes are bugged. He's sweating like a hog in a slaughterhouse. One – tentatively, two, and then the third, she releases the locks. She opens the door a crack. She'll throw her weight into it and shut it with a slam if she has a reason to do so.

He stands there, giving her no reason. He seems as frightened as she actually is. His blue eyes are red with black crescents beneath them. He has the stubble of several days. His hair is unkempt in defiance of his formal attire. "I told her not to go, but she has a friend there. Wanda. Do you know Wanda?" The air smells of smoke, and there appears to be a thin veil of it surrounding him. "Hell is coming our way," he tells her.

What she doesn't add to his comment is that his bark on the beach two weeks ago was a bullseye. Mayor Yorty, Governor Brown and the other old men running things don't give a rip about them. Pete may become a casualty of this new race war. And Beverly – her heart has always been bigger than her brain

– she might become a plaything for the enemy over there. All the decent folk need to stick together. She opens the door wide enough for him and him alone.

He accepts her invitation and enters her home.

She shuts it with a slam. As she reapplies the locks securely, with haste, her chest rubs against his, their faces inches apart. She barely knows him, but with the television rattling the walls with its end of their world broadcast, what does it matter?

#

2018

"Come in."

Sasha dragged herself into Glen Pierce's office. It didn't smell musty because the cleaning service did its job, but it *looked* musty. He even had metal filing cabinets with a fax machine sitting atop one of them. He glanced up from his paperwork. She selected one of the chairs before his desk. "I fucked up."

"I know."

Her face formed a look of surprise, but her mind answered him with *I highly doubt it.*

"Mrs. Abernathy, Mr. Brown, Mr. Lewis, and old Thelma Erving won't stop talking about how you canceled their bitch session."

Oh, that. She couldn't help but correct him. "It's group therapy."

He waved his hand dismissively. "Point is you've been holed up in your office since spending quality time with your boyfriend and his mother. What happened? Did she have enough of you tinkering with her noggin?"

She inhaled deeply, holding her breath as well as her tongue.

"I told you," he continued. "It doesn't work – maybe for professionals who have to untangle convoluted heads, but not here. We have simple seniors looking to live out their twilight as peacefully as we can make it for them."

"I own as much of this place as you do. When you decide to step down –"

His white eyebrows leaped up his forehead. "My plans don't include retirement. That's a promise I gave your dad before –"

"I don't want to talk about my dad."

That took some of the edge off his scowl. After a moment, he spoke with a slightly softer tone. "How do you propose we fix your fuck up?"

She considered apologizing – wouldn't do it, of course. Her dad was a touchy subject: a great friend and a good partner to Glen, but he was a condescending and judgmental father to his only child.

In the hesitancy of her reply, they both heard noises in the hallway. It sounded like an argument with one voice growling like a bear with a throat cold.

"What's that?" Glen stood, but his two hip surgeries made that a slow process.

The deep voice continued in the background, but someone with a familiar Asian accent came closer, speaking rapidly. A moment later, Carolyn Tanaka, head of housekeeping, opened the door without knocking. "Sorry. Sorry. There is a real big man at the desk. He is very big with a tattoo of a monster on his neck or something like that. He is not a happy monster."

Glen moved awkwardly, using his desk for support. "These relatives of residents –."

"No." She shot out of the chair, but she stopped to look at Carolyn, tilted her head.

"Sorry." The housekeeper left the office, closing the door behind her.

"He's here because of my fuck up." She looked between the blinds, out the window, but she couldn't see anything. "The problem isn't that Mrs. Caron's hypnosis wasn't a success. It was too successful. I need to tell you what crime she admitted to being a part of." The voice outside sounded louder. "But right now, I have to deal with him."

Glen's scowl now twisted with confusion.

She hated to leave the old man like that, but another

outburst from their visitor in the hallway made her rush out of the office. *Holy shit!* She stumbled back. He was Frank's son, but his last name wasn't Caron. It was Blackburne, his mother's last name. He looked like something Hollywood created with CGI technology. She immediately regretted reaching out to him when she should've first spoken to his father. But what could she do? Frank didn't want to talk to her.

CHAPTER 5

February 8, 1969

He looks like a clueless teenager, not what he really is: a killer awaiting a death sentence in a maximum-security prison. People think he's Mexican, or possibly Cuban, but he's from the other side of the world, a member of a tormented race. In his country, parents often vanish, and male role-models have short life expectancies. His homeland is a man-made hell that once left him crying in the dust while fighter jets rained destruction all around him.

He's now two decades removed from those horrors. A peace-loving religious group known as The Society of Friends transferred him from Palestine to the golden state of the wealthiest nation on earth, giving him a chance to become anything. So why did he shoot a man trying to bring peace to a war-torn world? He wishes he knew. He *really* does.

A son of Zion named Dr. Bernard Diamond thinks he can probe the young man's mind the way a Saudi sheik drills for oil. The Jew has the kind of pedigree Americans love: professor of law and psychiatry at the University of California at Berkeley and a specialist in criminal law as applied to the mentally ill. But he knows nothing about what makes a Palestinian tick. Jews are only interested in slaughtering Arabs and stealing their land.

The day before their session, the prisoner told an investigator he was fooling Dr. Diamond by pretending to be "asleep". To prove his point, he said he'll lift his middle finger off his lap while "under hypnosis" and wave it as a sign that he's faking. But as the session progressed, his finger never rose. It strained and quivered. Nothing more.

The prisoner awakens with a shiver and a smile, confident his middle finger proved his manipulation of the prestigious psychiatrist. He gives the investigator a wink.

Dr. Diamond cups a handkerchief over his nose and blows.

Realizing the chill in the cell has more of an effect on the doctor's sub-par immune system than on his own, the prisoner climbs the bars. He'll *show* them he's physically superior. "Oooh. Oooh," he says. "Ahhh. Ahhh." He swings his legs side to side. "Ahhh. Ahhh. Ahhh."

The investigator's jaw drops while the psychiatrist returns his handkerchief to his pocket and asks, "Why are you climbing the bars?"

He drops into an upside-down hanging position, feet between the bars. "Exercise."

Dr. Diamond presses the stop button on a reel-to-reel recorder. He pushes rewind and the tape rotates back to counter number 3872. He stops it, pushes another button. The machine plays back his voice. "When you wake up, I'll blow my nose, and you'll climb the bars of the cell and act like a monkey. You'll think you're exercising and not know that I told you to do this."

The young man feels life ooze out of him. His legs quiver and will soon release him from his upside-down hang. He'll fall into a heap before the psychiatrist and the investigator – a worthless embarrassment of himself and his people. A vein in his forehead swells like a snake engorged on his shame. The Jew just revealed his most painful secret: he's crazy.

#

2018

Frank looked up from his notes. The young inmate he read about (actually re-read about for the seventh time) now sat before him as an older inmate. He was compact with hair more salt colored than pepper. Orange prison garb covered his frame. The state designated him inmate B21014, but the world knew him as Sirhan Bishara Sirhan. His thin lips formed a line that made him look annoyed. A half century of watching murders, beatings, and prison rapes painted a film over his dark eyes. He may have grown older, but that didn't make him harmless. His gun shattered millions of dreams. In killing Robert Kennedy, he handed the presidency to Richard Nixon, whose lies plunged America into the constitutional crisis known as Watergate – *our long national nightmare.* He reportedly enjoyed his violent reputation. "They can gas me," he once said. "But I'm famous. I achieved in one day what it took Robert Kennedy all his life to do." He received the death penalty for his crime, but five decades later, he was still alive because the state commuted his sentence to life behind bars. He appeared before the parole board fifteen times, rejected every time.

The air conditioner blew its cold from a ceiling vent onto the back of his head, but Frank still sweated before the convict. He was America's most notorious living assassin, and securing this interview at the Richard J. Donovan Correctional Facility was no minor accomplishment. It was in San Diego County, usually out of the jurisdiction of prosecutors from Los Angeles County, but the warden owed him a favor for some plea-bargaining he did for his nephew a decade ago. He never could've imagined then how he'd collect on that favor now. He cleared his throat. "I'm Frank Caron."

"They told me."

"Do you remember climbing your bars like a monkey? I'm talking about your session with Dr. Diamond, dated February 8, 1969."

"I know about you."

Frank guessed he saw news coverage of the Calessi trial. "I want to understand your session with Dr. Diamond. Why did you act like a monkey?"

"That was a long time ago."

He returned to his notes, flipping to a highlighted passage. "After meeting with you eight times in your jail cell for a total of twenty-five hours, Dr. Diamond wrote, 'He claims to be ready to die in the gas chamber for the glory of the Arab people. However, I see Sirhan as small and helpless, pitifully ill.'"

Sirhan fidgeted. He looked at the papers on the table and Frank's phone beside them.

He kept reading, aware of the inmate's reaction. "'With a demented, psychotic rage, out of control of his own consciousness and his own actions, subject to bizarre, dissociated trances in some of which he programed himself to be the instrument of assassination, and then, in an almost accidentally induced twilight state, he actually executed the crime, knowing next to nothing as to what was happening.'"

"Do you know how many times I've heard those words?"

"Dr. Diamond diagnosed you as an ill young man who put himself into a trance in order to assassinate Robert Kennedy."

"His opinion. Why are you asking about this?"

"You refused to allow your lawyers to use the insanity defense because you didn't want anyone to think you were crazy."

"My lawyer was corrupt."

He knew all about that, having read the extraordinary story of Grant Cooper, Sirhan's lawyer, in 1969. While defending Sirhan, he also defended infamous mobster Johnny Rosselli in a card cheating scandal. During Sirhan's trial, the feds put Cooper under indictment for illegally possessing grand jury paperwork in the Rosselli case. "I'm not here to talk about Mr. Cooper."

"You're here to talk about – what? Are you writing a book? Everyone wants to get famous with my story. But you're already famous. They're calling you *the mob prosecutor*."

"I'm not writing a book."

Sirhan's eyes narrowed with skepticism. Again, he looked at the phone.

"You were diagnosed paranoid schizophrenic –"

"Do you know Paul Schrade?"

"I know *of* him. He was one of five people you wounded when you shot Kennedy."

"Paul Schrade told the parole board I didn't kill Robert

Kennedy. He said he forgave me for shooting him and the others."

He read so much in a short time preparing for this meeting, but what he read about Mr. Schrade stuck with him. A union leader in the fifties and sixties, Paul Schrade, became a Civil Rights activist who knew Cesar Chavez and marched with Martin Luther King, Jr. He was also a close friend of Bobby Kennedy. At the age of 91, he appeared at Sirhan's fifteenth parole hearing. He testified Sirhan was a deliberate distraction while a second gunman fired the fatal shot into the back of RFK's head. And he gave the parole board a letter authored by RFK's son, Robert F. Kennedy, Jr., in which he beseeched the U.S. Attorney General to re-examine the assassination. The AG denied his request. "That doesn't mean the State of California has forgiven you."

Sirhan's nostrils flared. His back went rigid.

"Dr. Diamond said you have no memory of killing Kennedy because you were in a state of deep self-hypnosis. How did you do that?"

"'I forgive you for shooting me but knowing that you did not shoot Robert Kennedy.' That is word for word what Paul Schrade said to me. I memorized it. I will never forget it."

"I read you were into the occult. I believe it was the Rosicrucians. Did you learn self-hypnosis from them?"

Sirhan threw his fists against the table, producing a slam that made Frank shoot his chair backward. "Paul Schrade was there. You need to listen to him."

He kept his distance, glanced at the tabletop. His papers remained. So did the phone, though the impact bounced it closer to the edge. "All anyone needs for self-hypnosis is a mirror. The Ambassador ballroom was lined with mirrors. You consumed four Tom Collins at the bar. There were more mirrors behind the bar. Did alcohol help with the hypnotism?"

Sirhan's eyes appeared bloodshot where they hadn't a moment earlier.

"If forgiveness is what you seek – like what Paul Schrade gave you – then you need to give the state what it wants."

"You came here to get a confession?"

"The state wants you to show remorse. You widowed his pregnant wife. You left eleven children fatherless." In fifty years, no one got a murder confession from Sirhan, but he didn't need one. Hypnosis was his angle, self-hypnosis, to be exact. If Sirhan hypnotized himself, as Dr. Diamond believed, then it didn't matter what Charlotte or anyone else did or didn't do that night.

"I can't regret what I don't remember doing."

"You don't remember doing it because you were under a self-administered hypnosis. Surely you can remember doing that."

"You think I can remember hypnotizing myself? You don't know how it works."

"Tell me."

Sirhan looked at the room's two-way mirror. He leaned forward and spoke as if he knew the phone on the table was set to record mode. "The girl in the polka-dot dress hypnotized me."

He didn't expect him to go there, and he lost his breath as a result. He floundered for a few seconds, and he also looked at the mirror. He had no reason to believe anyone was behind it, but what if the warden told Marco Diaz of this meeting as a professional courtesy? Surely the DA would want to eavesdrop. *Well, since he raised it....* "You, uh, you said you had coffee with a girl wearing a polka-dot dress. It was the last thing you remembered before waking up to men hitting you, saying you shot the senator."

"That's right."

"You got drunk at the bar - or heavily buzzed." He raised his voice for the benefit of anyone listening from behind the mirror. "You wandered around the ballroom while everyone waited for Senator Kennedy to make his victory speech. You saw a pretty girl in a polka-dot dress drinking coffee and decided to join her, probably to hit on her. The wall behind her had mirrors. In their reflection, you finished a hypnosis you started in your mirror at home and continued when you were at the bar, staring into another mirror. The girl walked away, but you were too far gone to remember it. You were fully hypnotized and ready to kill."

Sirhan's eyes again went to the phone. And he stood with the speed of a younger man.

"We're not done."

The prisoner said, "Guards."

A guard opened the door, causing Frank to wonder why he heard Sirhan's summons but not the slam of the table, which was much louder. He turned to the mirror, but all he could see was the reflection of Sirhan walking to the door with two guards now escorting him. "You can either admit to me you hypnotized yourself, or…you think you seemed crazy before. I can make you look like a fool."

Sirhan spun. He scoffed. Then he looked around. "Legally speaking, I'm not guilty of anything. It's not that I'm making light of it. I'm responsible for being there." A distant look crossed his face, as if he gazed back through time. "I should have never gone there that night. All I ever wanted was to be a jockey. I was good at it. I loved the horses. The horses loved me. Sometimes I still hear the squishing sounds of their hooves in the damp mud. I smell the hay. I feel their coarse hair."

He watched Sirhan linger with that contemplative, far-off stare. The material he read last night covered the convict's affinity for horses. He had some skills, and he was the right size to be a jockey. If only he had stayed at the stables that night. *If only* he admitted to hypnotizing himself before the shooting. In either case, it wouldn't have mattered if Charlotte wore a polka-dot dress to Robert Kennedy's reception. And Frank wouldn't be in this position.

#

Sasha invited Trevor into the parking lot. It was a strategy her dad taught her years ago when confronted by family members upset over the nursing home's policies, prices or whatever else. But her dad had never dealt with something like this. And Trevor led the march outside.

He spun around on her. "What bullshit operation are you running here?"

She glanced at the potholes and the loose rubble around them. She didn't think that was the *bullshit* he meant, but she was sensitive about it. Repaving the lot had been on her agenda for months now. Unfortunately, there wasn't enough money in the budget.

"I can have you shut down. I have experience in that area."

"What is it you want, Mr. Blackburne?"

"Let's start with the secret you and Frank are keeping."

Her stomach did a somersault. He knew there was a secret, but he didn't know what it was. So…Frank didn't tell him. She saw Glen hobbling out of the main building. The geezer was too stubborn to use a walker and still macho enough to think he could protect her.

"I'm thinking it has to do with that dark place you took Nana to." He studied her like a predator appraising the movements of its prey. "I can see by the look on your face I'm right."

"Charlotte talks about you. I thought you should… hypnotherapy has been shown to improve cognitive abilities, motor skills. It can improve the overall quality of life for people with your grandmother's limitations. But I can't treat her anymore. I called to let you know."

"You told me that already."

"It's all I have to say. If you think there's something more, ask your father about it."

The huge man stalked toward her. "The deputy district attorney who locked up Vincent Calessi? You want me to ask him?"

She nodded, taking a backward step for every one he advanced. That led them back toward the building, the crowd inside looking out, and Glen.

"He doesn't have time for anyone. His mother is his inconvenience."

"He's been very supportive of our sessions."

His eyes wandered over her, now even more like a predator. "I came here thinking you were his favorite stripper or something. Maybe I'm right."

It was her turn to advance. "I'm a professional hypnotist."

He didn't move back. "They said you managed this nursing home."

She had to stop, or she'd find herself chest to navel with him. "I'm an owner of this facility and a hypnotist. I'm trying to treat those residents I think can most benefit from it."

He shrugged. "Frank pawned me off on his mother when I was little even though he claims she was a shitty mother – the shittiest, he'd say. I didn't see him again till I was in juvie. It was a quick visit. He offered to represent me four years later when I was arrested, but Nana took care of it like she always did. Now he's this supportive son letting you play around in his mother's deteriorating mind? See why I'm suspicious?"

"You should talk to him about this."

Glen shouted, "Sasha?"

She turned and saw the old man approaching unsteadily. It was the last thing she needed. This behemoth could give him a heart attack just by raising his voice.

"*You* should tell me what you two are hiding. I know Nana goes dark. I saw it many times growing up. You know what sets her off most? You wanna guess?"

"Frank?"

"There's a history there even I don't know. What I do know is she's got good reason not to trust him. Me too."

She heard the scrape and scratch of rubble kicked up by Glen's shuffling, and she thought of what would happen if he hit a pothole. She guessed him to be ten or twelve feet behind her. If he overheard their conversation, what would he think of Frank? He wasn't her father, but in her father's absence, she kind of… she sort of…she cared what he thought of a guy she was…what was it that she and Frank were doing?

"So," said Trevor. "If I can't hold him responsible for what happens to Nana in this place, I can you."

She estimated Glen was now seven feet behind her. Trevor was two feet in front of her. They each deserved to know what horrible secret Charlotte revealed through hypnosis, but she only felt obligated to tell one of them. She pulled out her phone and placed a call.

It wasn't even two rings when Frank answered. "Sasha. I've been meaning to call, but now is not a good time. Can I –"

"Your son is here, very upset. He thinks you're lying to him about something."

"Trevor? What's he doing there?"

"You two need to talk." She hung up. It felt good to do that after he'd been avoiding her. She left Trevor too – not so much out of fear but because she was over what he had to say about his father. She crossed the distance that separated her from Glen. Speaking to him in just above a whisper, she said, "Mrs. Caron admitted to being one of Robert Kennedy's killers. And that's her grandson." He had good hearing for an old man. And with the color draining from his face, she knew he understood the implications of what she said. Trevor's phone rang behind her, which put one more item to the list of what she knew. Frank was on the other end of that call.

CHAPTER 6

Frank didn't want to deal with Trevor's aggressive curiosity or set his story straight with Sasha until he had first gathered all the information he needed. It was the prudent, lawyerly way of doing things. That was why he sent the recording of Sirhan's interrogation room interview to Ripley Reed. He was his confidante, to a certain extent, and the best investigator he knew. When Rip suggested they meet at the former site of the Ambassador Hotel at nine thirty at night, he raised an eyebrow over the choice of location, but he showed up fifteen minutes early anyway.

Robert F. Kennedy's 1968 murder in the Ambassador Hotel's kitchen pantry began the property's long decline. It coincided with a rise in poverty, illegal drugs and gang activity in the area. The hotel closed to guests in 1989 but allowed television and motion picture filming as well as private events for the next decade. Despite preservation efforts and much litigation, the city began demolition of the hotel in 2005, finished the work in 2006. Three years later, The Robert F. Kennedy Community Schools opened on the site with a staggering construction cost of over half a billion dollars. An important part of the new complex was a pocket park dedicated to the ideals championed by RFK. Facing the bustle of Wilshire Boulevard, Robert F. Kennedy Inspiration Park provided a tranquil setting for peaceful reflection.

Frank took the time he had to read the RFK quotations on the park's monuments. He identified with one in particular: *Each time a man stands up for an ideal, or acts to improve the lot of others, or strikes out against injustice, he sends forth a tiny ripple of hope.* He liked to think the passage applied to him because he left the defensive side of the law and became a prosecutor so he could improve the lot of others. But it was the part about injustice that most stuck with him. Injustice was the assignment of guilt to someone who was innocent. Was his mother innocent of what her own memory confessed? They had their issues, but he couldn't imagine her participating in an assassination. Would he defend her if she did? Would he prosecute her? Would he be able to abstain altogether and leave her fate to the courts?

"People today don't know what it means to sacrifice for what you believe."

He turned to see Ripley – *barely* see him as he was a black man wearing a dark shirt with dark pants at night. "You should carry a flashlight."

"Afraid I was a ghost?"

"This place is full of them. I remember they demolished the hotel." He gestured beyond the monuments and a manicured park to the six-story school building. "I forgot about all this."

"The Ambassador had to go." Rip looked at the oversized close-up of RFK etched into one of the monuments. It depicted Kennedy with a smile, but it was a sad smile with compassion in his eyes. "It wasn't the killing of a man so much as it was the death of a movement."

He nodded. "I grew up in the seventies – bell-bottoms, sideburns and fucking Nixon. All anyone ever talked about was how we wouldn't be in this mess if we still had the Kennedys."

"You could say he was the last politician who actually cared about the people rather than just trying to look like he cared."

Frank went to the stone steps on the side of the park. His waist had grown a bit too thick lately, so sitting was preferable to standing. Rip joined him, but he had the body of a lacrosse player with no great need or desire to sit. "So…the recording?"

Rip took some time with his answer, finally saying, "In

an address to the nation when he was president, JFK called Negro Plight 'a moral issue as old as the Scriptures and as clear as the American Constitution.' For him and his attorney general brother, it was an intellectual matter. That changed in November of 1963. Bobby became passionately empathetic after his brother's assassination. The struggles of the disenfranchised became his struggles. He visited slums and consulted the poor. After Dr. King died, Bobby was all we had left. Then they took him."

"I know."

"You didn't hear me. I said *they* took him."

He turned to see his friend as serious as he'd ever seen him. "You don't believe what Dr. Diamond said about Sirhan self-hypnotizing?"

"Why did you go there? I don't remember you ever mentioning Bobby or his killer."

"I admire Bobby Kennedy."

"Like Elliot Ness?" Rip stood and stretched. "Let's walk." He led him to the Ripple of Hope display. "Marco barely knew your name when I first mentioned it."

"Is this a mentor/protégé thing? I'm older than you, remember?"

"How long have we known each other? Have I ever –"

"Pestered me to ask out a girl I wasn't interested in? Convinced me to buy a motorcycle when I didn't have a license? Talked me into giving up my practice to become a prosecutor?"

That brought a laugh, breaking Rip's seriousness.

"I was fine where I was."

"You only thought you were. Do you know how many investigators the DA put on Vincent Calessi and his guys? Probably twenty of us, but I hit the motherlode when I looked into the 5150s. Who'd have thought the Calessi mob would encourage the violent homeless to distract law enforcement while they committed their crimes?"

"Me."

Rip nodded. "You. When Marco asked me which prosecutor I thought should get that assignment –"

"This DA doesn't ask for recommendations. And the only opinions he likes are his own."

"Would you agree I've always had your best interest at heart?"

"I nearly killed myself on that Harley."

Rip glanced around the park. "There's a line from the poet Dante that John and Bobby Kennedy often quoted. You could say it was their mantra. *The hottest places in Hell are reserved for those who in times of moral crisis preserve their neutrality.*"

"What does that have to do with anything?"

"Damn, man. You want me to spell it out? You spent your life taking the path of least responsibility to avoid being the cause of another calamity. Your fault or not, she's a long time gone. I pitched you to Marco because I figured it was time you realized your potential. And you know what? I was right. Other prosecutors tried, but it was *you* that got the conviction."

Frank's eyes flashed wide only to shorten as his eyebrows folded. "That wasn't your call. If I want to avoid making life or death decisions, it's on me." He took it to one of the nearby benches. Now more than ever, he felt he should sit.

Rip joined in his relocation but remained standing. "Is that why you visited Sirhan Sirhan in prison? To avoid life or death decisions? They don't come much bigger than that case."

Ready as he was for them to keep talking about *she's a long time gone*, Frank couldn't hide his relief over Rip moving past it. It took a bit of refocusing for him to get his thoughts back to the original purpose of their meeting. "I'm looking for your take on it," he finally said. "Sirhan denied hypnotizing himself but claimed to have no recollection of the event. Dr. Diamond agreed he had no memory of it."

"I don't think that doctor got it right in sixty-eight, but you should leave it alone. Even if you could prove the assassin had accomplices – and they'd all be dead by now – retrying the Kennedy case would never get past the DA, to say nothing of a grand jury. Pepper and Dusek already went that route."

He didn't think of that earlier, but he remembered it now

that Rip mentioned it. William Pepper was a lawyer famous for winning a civil case in which a jury decided there was a conspiracy in the murder of Martin Luther King, Jr. A dozen years later, he teamed up with New York attorney Laurie Dusek to petition the courts to re-examine the other infamous 1968 assassination: the slaying of Robert F. Kennedy. The Los Angeles District Attorney (Marco Diaz's predecessor) strongly opposed their filings, and the U.S. District Court ultimately rejected them. The mainstream media paid it little attention. Since most of their coverage came from conspiracy-prone websites, the lawyers failed to generate enough public support to move the court in their favor. "What makes you think I want to go the way of Pepper and Dusek?"

"You're a prosecutor, and they're defense lawyers, but forgetting that, I can't see why else you'd want to interview Sirhan. He said you wanted to write a book. Is that it?"

He laughed. It was the most effective way, he thought, to dismiss the suggestion. "I just wanted your take. That's all."

There was no way Rip bought that. But rather than push, he took an empty seat on the bench beside him. "Vincent Calessi has a whole army of lieutenants ready to fall. Let's go after them. Why be a one-hit wonder when you can have a string of chart toppers?"

The take he really wanted from Rip was what he thought about Charlotte's hypnosis-derived revelation. But telling the truth would make his friend an accessory if there was any attempt to cover it up. In this case, the old adage was best: to keep a thing a secret, you must limit who knows about it. That brought him back to Sasha and what he should do about her. As Rip looked at him, still waiting for his answer, only one response came to his mind. "A chart topper has more to lose than a one-hit wonder."

#

Sasha couldn't reach Glen. She didn't bother to try last night. The look on his face when she told him about Charlotte convinced her to give him some space, but he hadn't yet shown up for work. It was now mid-afternoon. His wife said he left home this morning as usual, so where was he? That would have to wait, however. The other man who'd been avoiding her was now on the premises, visiting his mother.

"Good afternoon, Ma'am." Carolyn Tanaka looked at her the way most of the staff looked at her since her encounter with Trevor: like a battered woman in need of their sympathy. It reminded her of how she felt six years ago when her husband cheated and everyone and their mother treated her like she was as delicate as a porcelain cup. "Mr. Caron is –"

"I know. Thank you."

"Oh, okay." Carolyn looked like she wanted to get back to her chores but do so in a tactful way. "He is...I believe he is a good man."

"So do I." And that was true despite what his son said. There were two sides to every story. Charlotte resided in the last room on the right, the end of the hall. As she made her way toward it, she thought of something else his son had said. *He'd better not be the strip club type. He doesn't seem to be, but – he isn't.* Six years ago, it wouldn't have bothered her as much, but that was before her ex's infidelity started with visits to the Pussycat Pavilion.

The door was open an inch or so, not enough for Frank to notice if he didn't look for it. He wasn't a frequent enough visitor to know the handle often needed a hip check to lock shut. It was another item for her to add to the repair list. But it gave her an opportunity now. Maybe she could eavesdrop *just a little.*

"Why don't you put up some pictures?" Frank asked his mother.

Charlotte replied, "People in pictures watch me."

"A few personal items might make you feel more at home." His voice lightened with a touch of humor. "I'm not asking you to bring in a pinball machine."

Sasha knew that story. He told it to her when she asked him why he had a pinball machine in his dining room. It was a KISS game, manufactured in 1979. He said his parents reluctantly let him get it because he was an obsessive fan of the band. In those days, distributors tried to keep games out of homes because private ownership meant less revenue for arcade operators. It was Charlotte who found someone willing to break the distributor's code and make a private sale, but the man agreed only if young Frank could beat him on the game. The part of the story she liked the most was how Charlotte coached her son to win. She imagined it was a great bonding moment between them. And she recalled him saying his mother *really* wanted him to win - like she wanted to teach the distributor some sort of lesson.

"It was one thousand eight hundred and ninety-five dollars." He laughed. "I remember the price because it took over a year to save for it, and Dad still had to kick in half."

"You don't want to talk about that," said Charlotte. "What did you come here for?"

Sasha took a stutter-step closer to the door jamb.

"Alright, Mom." Frank exhaled audibly. "When you were hypnotized –"

"I don't want to talk about that."

"You said something. As a prosecutor, I can't pretend you didn't say that."

Should I go in? Usually, average people in typical sessions couldn't recall much of what they experienced while under. But Charlotte's dementia and the way Sasha hypnotized her because of it made recollection more likely. *I have to go in there.*

"Get out," said Charlotte.

She stopped where she was, a step shy of entering the room.

"You said –" Frank hesitated, wrestling with his choice of words. "You mentioned a crime from 1968. It was a big one, and the way you talked about it, it sounded like firsthand information. Do you know what I mean?"

"Where's my big boy? T-dog won't let you harass me like this."

"I didn't tell Trevor – nobody calls him T-dog anymore. I didn't tell him what you said. Only three of us know: you, me and –"

Sasha had the feeling someone else had their ears open.

Looking into the hall, she found her feeling confirmed. Glen stood with a paper in his hand. She always heard him approach, especially indoors. How did she miss it this time?

He offered her the paper. "The librarian helped me print this from a website. I had to fill out a questionnaire first, but no matter." He lowered his voice, but it was still louder than it should've been. "There was a girl police wanted to question over Bobby Kennedy's assassination. Witnesses described her, but no one ever found her."

Her jaw dipped open. She looked at the paper with its title, *The Mystery of the Girl in the Polka-Dot Dress*. The web address at the bottom of the page wasn't from any mainstream news source she recognized. "You went to the public library?"

"Don't know where else to find a librarian. I can't do a computer."

She put her arm around his bent shoulder, trying to steer him away from the door and back down the hallway. "What did they ask you in that questionnaire?"

"Sasha."

She spun around, finding Frank a step outside of his mother's doorway. His left arm extended across it, braced against the frame as if barring anyone from entering or escaping the room. The look on his face went beyond disappointment, bordering on recognition of pure betrayal. She knew he heard everything Glen said.

CHAPTER 7

Redondo Beach, California. January 1966

Charlotte has been having strange thoughts, the latest being that if her customers could see her naked, they'd run from the restaurant. She has veins in her legs where they'd never been before. Her ankles and feet are swollen. She has pinkish red blotches on her skin. Her hair and nails are growing so fast she sometimes thinks she's becoming a werewolf. Her boobs are bigger, which is nice, but so is her belly, which isn't. And she's been irritable.

"Onion and anchovy," says Ben, the chef with a belly bigger than hers. "Table seven."

That's Matt Whalen's table. He's been coming in often since the summer, sometimes twice a week. She tries not to talk to him much until after her shift, and even that she limits so he won't get too attached. After all - she completes the thought by touching her belly.

Luigi's Italian Eatery is a bit hoity-toity for a pizza joint. The walls are garnet with paintings of estates in the old country. The draperies are gold. The lighting is dim. The only thing that makes it less hoity-toity is the television Luigi watches in the kitchen, out of view of the customers. He bought it after the Watts riots, claiming it will inform him if darkies rise up again. He doesn't like it when servers run each other's dishes because he thinks it confuses customers. But Matt's server, Karen Templeton, is busy, and the order is piping hot.

Matt doesn't act surprised when she brings his order. "Take a load off."

"I can't."

He pulls a slice from the whole, twirling tendrils of cheese with his fork. She may be at work, constantly smelling and handling food, but her stomach grumbles at the way he prepares the pizza. He sets it on a plate and slides it before her. Damn her body's metamorphosis. She's always hungry, more so when he's around. Why is that?

"Anchovies are good for the baby."

She sees Karen Templeton in the server station with her arms folded. "I have ta go."

"What does the doctor say?"

"What doctor?"

"You don't have a doctor?"

One little bite, and I'll make it quick. She looks around, except at Karen, and she indulges her eager stomach. "My mom gave birth five times. Never once saw a doctor."

"You told me you have three siblings."

"The last was stillborn." It's good. One bite isn't enough, so she takes another.

"Aren't you worried?"

"Are you?" *Where did that come from?* She puts her hand over her mouth, still chewing.

"Me?"

Who have you been shacking up with? Barkers hardly ever stick around. As much as she wants to, she doesn't voice her thoughts – mainly because of the transformation his face makes as he looks behind her. She twists around, and there's Pete. He's pissed, smells of sweat, and he wears oil smudges on his mechanics' duds. "What're you doing here? Your shift doesn't end –"

"A man doesn't cavort with another man's woman – 'specially in her condition," says Pete. "Unless he's a snake."

"Why aren't you at work?" From the corner of her eye, she sees Julie Montlebaum, the other waitress, sheepishly approaching.

"Uh, Luigi wants you," says Julie.

"Been hearing things about your friend here, Char," says Pete. "Things I don't like."

"He's a customer."

Pete's eyes drop to the pizza. "I think I'll stay. I like anchovies. They're good for you."

"Ahhh." She grumbles, heading to the kitchen. She's actually glad to be removed from the situation, but she doesn't appreciate the bitch-girl once over Karen gives as she passes her.

"What-a you doing?" asks Luigi from his perch on a fold-up chair in front of the TV. "No poaching tables."

"His pie was getting cold." The television steals her attention as it shows Chet Huntley from *The Hunter-Brinkley Report*. He's standing before a screen which shows buildings burning and Negro boys throwing flaming bottles at white people. It's Watts. Or maybe it's one of the country's many other race riots.

Karen enters the kitchen, asking Luigi, "Did you see her eat the customer's food?"

She turns up the volume – partially to drown out Karen but mostly to hear the news. "American leadership is schizophrenic on the issue of Negro violence," says Chet Huntley. "In some cities, the authorities answer with force, firing water cannons and rubber bullets. Elsewhere civic leaders arrest agitators before they can incite their followers."

"When do I let you eat with customers? Turn it down." Luigi reaches for the television.

Julie yells from the restaurant area. "Luigi!"

Matthew and Pete are in each other's faces, leaning over the table between them. "This is a new age," says Matt. "Get with the program or crawl back into your cave and let us change-makers do our thing."

Pete glares at him. "My girl is not *your program*."

"Is she saying that, or are you?"

"Her oven's cooking my bun. That's all you need to know."

Even with the boob tube at high volume, she can hear them

from the kitchen, as much as she doesn't want to. She, like most everyone else she knows, has been on edge over the upsurge in racial violence since Watts. Pete and Matthew's argument isn't important – not when she needs to know what kind of world her kid is about to enter. Huntley reports, "The one voice in Washington that appears to have the attention of both blacks and whites comes from the junior senator from New York, Robert Kennedy."

Luigi stumbles out of his chair. He doesn't do that without serious motivation. Grabbing her arm, he pulls her toward the dining area. "Get your Casanovas outta my restaurant."

She resists, trying to see Robert Kennedy address a Negro crowd on the television. "Ghettos are a fact of life," says Kennedy. "They aren't going away. But they can be made safe. They can be made livable. Black leaders need to stop blaming others for their problems. They need to make the hard and sometimes unpopular decisions that come with responsibility."

"That's right," she tells the TV. "Responsibility isn't rioting. It's getting a job."

"*Your* job." Luigi points at Pete and Matthew, who still argue. "*Your* responsibility."

She thinks of correcting him, touching her belly. *This is my responsibility.* But she can't explain it to him. He's a man, and he's an employer who never shows any consideration for her condition. She finds her thoughts interrupted by gasps and shrieks coming from the dining area. She hears a table overturn. She peers in, and she sees Pete clutching Matt by the shirt collar.

"You – no more." Luigi gives her a shove toward the dining area. "You take them with you and don't come back. None of you." Her balance hasn't been good lately, and his push is all it takes to make her stumble. She reaches for Karen, but the bitch steps out of her way. She turns sharply to the right, trying to avoid a fall, but she smashes her belly into the counter. Pain shoots into the most precious part of her body. She wails and sinks to the floor, clutching her stomach.

Pete and Matt must've heard her because they abandon

their squabble and rush to her. They reach her in record time – one on her left, the other on her right. Heat from the kitchen, the confusion of those around her, and the overbearing aroma of cooking sauces, spices and cheeses: all she wants to do is get out of there, as Luigi wishes. But she's afraid to move for fear of what she might've just done to her unborn baby. She looks around helplessly, not knowing what to do.

#

2018

The TV was off. The lights were on. Frank's eight-year-old shepherd Tippy lay on the floor, watching him work through the papers sitting atop his coffee table. There were more papers in a box between the couch and the recliner. Rip may have been against him re-litigating the RFK case, but that didn't stop him from delivering hundreds of pages of research without being asked for it. The speed with which he produced it said the RFK case had long been his obsession. If not, how else could a county investigator access so much research so quickly?

Rip's change of heart would take some figuring out, so in the meantime, Frank decided to look into the girl in the polka-dot dress. Over a dozen witnesses mentioned her in connection to the assassination. A knock turned his head to the door, and Tippy threw up a bark. She sprang to her feet. Another knock made her bark again. "Who is it?"

"Frank, it's me."

"Oh, shit," he muttered.

"I heard that."

Tippy's heavy tail wagged in recognition of the voice on the other side of the door, and she swayed excitedly from side to side, waiting for him to open it.

Sasha met him in the doorway. She was as gorgeous as always with yellow heels, a black mini-skirt, and a light-yellow top unbuttoned so as to be comfortable for her and, he guessed, appealing to him. "Can I come in?"

He opened the screen door for her.

"Ah, Tippy. Loveable Tippy." She lowered to a crouch,

wrapped her arms around the dog's neck and hugged her like they hadn't seen each other in years. When she stood, she had strands of fur clinging to her top as if unwilling to let her go.

Why does Tippy have to love her so much? And why does she have to look so good?

"I...uh...we're equal partners at Brookside. I had to tell him."

"You should've talked to me first."

"How?"

He knew he shouldn't have waited so long to discuss Charlotte's hypnosis with her. That made it his fault, but he didn't have to approve of her telling Glen about it.

She took his silence as an invitation into the living room, and she glanced at the papers awaiting his attention. "Preparing another case?"

"I hope not." He approached her. "I've been reading about Robert Kennedy's assassination, particularly what witnesses said about a girl in a polka-dot dress."

Her eyes grew a tad wider.

He picked up the nearest packet. "This is a transcript of an interview between a detective and a witness." He extended it to her. "Peace offering?"

She looked skeptical, but she accepted it. "The witness is Sandy Serrano," she said while perusing the top page. "She was a nineteen-year-old Kennedy campaign volunteer."

"I see you've been reading too."

She smirked mischievously. "Only hours after the shooting, she told NBC News she saw a girl wearing a polka-dot dress run out of the hotel shouting, 'We've shot Senator Kennedy.'"

That smirk was a lot like the ones that resulted in him taking her into the bedroom, but *you read this stuff in the research Glen did at the public library.* He knew he had to let that go.

"How 'bout I read the part of Sandy Serrano, and you –" She wandered over the page. "You can be LAPD Sergeant Enrique Hernandez."

He wasn't ready for that. In truth, he wasn't ready to

discuss any of this with her yet. He did make a peace offering, though, and the sight of her walking to his couch, sitting and crossing her smooth, glistening legs…he joined her on the couch. "I'm sure there's another explanation for why my mother said that."

"Sandy Serrano spent most of the night of the assassination downstairs in the ballroom. It was hot and crowded, so she went out onto the fire escape. The fire escape led up to another ballroom where Kennedy would soon make his victory speech." She looked at him. "I'm sure there's another explanation too. But we're not going to find it without knowing the story."

He couldn't disagree, but her enthusiasm seemed a little too much. She was like an amateur sleuth with a hot lead. He watched her finger with its French tip nail trail down the page until it arrived at a line of dialogue. She tapped the page, her eyes telling him to read it. Her perfume…he didn't know the name, but it smelled like vanilla mixed with those little white flower clusters he encountered on the route when his jogs turned into walks.

"Do you need a boost?"

"What? No." He returned to the page and the line of dialogue she indicated. "Sergeant Hernandez said, *'When you told the police that a girl with a polka-dot dress told you she had shot Kennedy, were you telling the truth?'*"

Sasha read. "'*She didn't say, 'We had shot Kennedy.' She said, 'We shot him.'*'"

"'*Did a girl in a polka-dot dress tell you that 'We have shot Kennedy'?*'"

"'*It was a white dress with black polka dots.*'" She turned to him, and her lips nearly touched his cheek. "Sirhan Sirhan said the last thing he remembered before blacking out was having coffee with a pretty girl wearing a polka-dot dress."

"You know a lot."

She returned to the text, now paraphrasing what she read. "Miss Serrano was on the fifth step of the fire escape when a girl and two guys passed her going up. The girl was in her mid-twenties wearing a white polka-dot dress with a bib collar and a small black bow."

"There could have been dozens of women like that. Polka-dots were a sixties fad."

"She said the men looked Mexican. One was clean-shaven and good-looking with greased black hair, dark pants, a light shirt and a gold sweater. The other was small, maybe five-three, with black curly hair. He was in his early twenties. He looked like he was drunk."

"The second guy was Sirhan."

She nodded. "About twenty minutes after they went into the hotel Miss Serrano heard six loud pops. She said it sounded like a car back-firing."

"I read that part. She said the girl and the guy in the gold sweater ran out of the hotel thirty seconds later. They almost tripped over her going down the fire escape."

"The girl in the polka-dot dress said, 'We shot him! We shot him!' She asked who they shot, and the girl replied, '*We've shot Senator Kennedy.*'"

He stole another glance at her mocha legs, but the serious subject matter of their reading forced him to relocate his gaze. "I have two problems with this."

"Why would the girl in polka-dots admit to a complete stranger that they shot Kennedy?"

"You see it too. Good."

"Have you ever been so excited about something that your mouth got away from you?"

"No."

She looked like she didn't believe him. "They just pulled off something *huge*. She couldn't keep it in. Criminals do stupid things all the time, don't they? It's why they get caught."

"Okay, but the witness said twenty minutes passed between when they entered the hotel and when she heard the gunshots, saw them run out of the hotel."

"Right." She double-checked the papers in her hand.

"In twenty minutes, Sirhan could not enter the building,

weave through the crowd, grab a spot at the bar, catch the bartender's attention, order and consume four drinks, find the girl in the polka-dot dress drinking coffee, become hypnotized, make his way into the kitchen pantry, lay in wait then jump out and unload his gun on Robert Kennedy. It's an implausible timeline."

"Who said Sirhan did all those things?"

"The police in 1969, the prosecution, even Sirhan's defense team."

She lowered the papers to her lap and slid to the right enough to face him while still being only inches from him. "*You* sound like a lawyer on a defense team."

"Do I?"

To his surprise, she stood. She walked in an almost meandering fashion to the bookcase built into the wall. It held law books, history books, photo albums and collectible KISS figurines. She looked at the KISS pinball machine in the other room – her eyes lingering on it. And she turned to him. "Have you ever had a woman live here?"

"Does Tippy count?"

She didn't laugh. "What about Trevor's mother?"

"I thought we were reading the transcript."

"Glen thinks we should look into finding another facility for Charlotte."

That drove his eyebrows up his forehead. "Is that so?"

"I didn't say it's what I want, but –" She looked back at the pages in her hand. "I don't know if you caught on, but the policeman didn't believe the witness."

"Oh, I caught that."

"I have to tell you, I already read this. It was in the paper – it doesn't matter where. Sergeant Hernandez goes on to browbeat this nineteen-year-old girl so much she actually changes her testimony and claims she made the whole thing up."

"Which helps my mother's case," he said. "If there was a case."

"Right."

"You're wondering where I'd go with that." He stood and walked around the table to the center of the room. "Would I pursue the Sergeant Hernandez angle? The witness lied, so there was no girl in a polka-dot dress. Or do I think the police sergeant intimidated her into changing her testimony, and there *was* a girl in a polka-dot dress?"

"That's exactly what I'm wondering."

He met her near the threshold between the living room and the dining room. "I'm wondering what this has to do with you. You want to help my mother, and you *have* helped her. But you told Trevor you can't help her anymore."

"I shouldn't have called him." She touched his arm as a gentle means of apology. "I've been thinking about this. I'm a gifted hypnotist, but I don't have a lot of experience. If I can get Charlotte to talk about that, someone else can too – maybe."

"And you don't think they'll honor the code of therapist/ patient confidentiality?"

She took her time with that, working through her response. Then she said, "There *was* a girl in a polka-dot dress. We know that. And we know Charlotte knows something about it. If it wasn't her, then maybe her repressed memories can tell us who it was. We could finally solve the mystery of who killed Robert Kennedy."

"Before someone else does?"

"We make a good team." She smirked again.

"And we could write a book – *The Definitive Who Killed Robert Kennedy.*"

Her smirk became a question mark, making her beauty a bit less apparent.

He placed his hand over the one with which she held the transcript. It was a symbolic handhold over the documents that could start their partnership, but it felt to him like a sell-out of his integrity with her handling the cash transaction. He took the papers back, though more abruptly than he intended. "I don't want her hypnotized again." Her face froze in shock, but he returned to the couch so he wouldn't have to see it. "I'll move

Charlotte to another facility soon."

CHAPTER 8

Sasha couldn't sit. She stood by the older woman's desk, watching the door and tapping her fingers against her hip. She didn't bring anything but her purse. She could've brought what Glen dug up at the library, or she could've found a copy of the transcript she and Frank read last night. Frank – shook her head. It was all she could do with the older woman sitting nearby.

"Don't be so nervous, Sweetie. He's not a teddy bear, but he's not a grizzly either." The older woman was Mrs. Chalker, the district attorney's personal secretary. "You can go in."

She turned the handle and pushed the door. It was heavier than she expected. The first thing to hit her was the overwhelming masculinity of the room: gray walls, brown furniture and a marble statue of an old man. That was a strange thing to find in the office of a public servant.

The public servant was on his feet, hand extended, wearing a politician's smile, greeting her in the middle of the room. The wall of windows behind him was like a large movie screen with a bird's eye view of the city. "District Attorney Marco Diaz. It's a pleasure." He guided her in a fluid motion to one of two tufted leather chairs before his oversized desk. Only feet before her, he leaned with the back of his legs against the desk edge. "When Irene – Mrs. Chalker – told me who you were, I asked her to carve out some time in my schedule. So how is he?"

"Living in Aruba last I heard, with his mistress." She sat back, nearly swallowed by the plush chair. "She's probably not his mistress anymore."

Mr. Diaz's smile faltered, unsure if it should stay or go.

"I know my ex-husband wasn't any more to you than a political donor – a substantial one. You couldn't have known what a lying, cheating narcissist he was."

He took a deep breath, glanced aside then back at her. "What can I do for you, Mrs. –"

"I go by my maiden name now, Frye. You can call me Sasha."

The district attorney walked around the desk to sit in the chair behind it. He was too tactful to say it, but she had limited time with him now that he knew her visit had nothing to do with a fat campaign donation.

"I'm here about my boyfriend – his mother. Actually, I guess he's my ex-boyfriend now. That doesn't sound good. I come here talking about my ex-husband then my ex-boyfriend."

"Who is your ex-boyfriend?"

"Frank Caron."

"My prosecutor? He's been getting a lot of press lately – more than me." He laughed. Then something dawned on him. "He requested a leave of absence for personal reasons. Whatever relationship problems you're having, I expect him to come to work."

She couldn't help but wonder if Frank had requested a leave so he could spend it with her. She wondered when he requested it, before Charlotte's hypnosis or after. It didn't matter. What he did last night – no, it didn't matter when or why he requested a leave. She fixed her gaze firmly on the DA. "If I have knowledge of a crime and I keep it to myself, does that make me party to that crime?"

"Yes."

"Then I need to tell you, I'm a hypnotist. As a favor to my boyfriend – ex – I was treating his mother. In our last session, I uncovered a repressed memory in which she confessed to being the girl in the polka-dot dress."

"The – who?"

"You can look it up. *Frank's* been looking it up. The night of Robert Kennedy's assassination, witnesses saw a girl wearing a polka-dot dress meet with Sirhan Sirhan before he shot Kennedy. Sirhan himself admitted to having coffee with her. After the shooting, witnesses saw her run out of the hotel with another man. One of the witnesses testified that in her excitement, the girl shouted, 'We shot Kennedy.'."

"She testified *in court* that the girl shouted that?"

"I don't know if it was in court. But I read the transcript, and she said it plain as day."

"And while recently hypnotized – by you – Frank Caron's mother said she was the girl in polka-dots who shouted out a confession while running from the scene of the crime?"

Coming from the district attorney, in that manner, it didn't seem as convincing as it did before she walked in here.

"I'm sure hypnotism has its purpose, Mrs...uh... Ms. Frye. It helped my aunt quit smoking. But the law views it as unreliable. In most cases – especially when hypnotism occurs outside of the courtroom – what someone says under hypnosis is inadmissible. Do you have any solid evidence to support these claims about your ex-boyfriend's mother?"

"I didn't come here as a scorned woman hoping to smear Frank or his family." She paused, wondering if that was true. He hurt her last night. She offered her skills to help him find the truth, and he took it to mean she was some glory-whore looking to write a book. "I'm a *certified* hypnotist. I own and manage a well-regarded senior care facility. I discovered a repressed memory in a patient who happens to be my ex-boyfriend's mother. It's a memory in which she helped to assassinate Senator Robert Kennedy. It's not a fantasy. It's real, whether your law accepts it or not." She stood. It seemed the right thing to do, like adding an exclamation point to the end of her statement. But once on her feet, she didn't know what else to do.

He conveyed nothing with the expression he gave back to her.

"Okay then." She took her first steps toward the door,

feeling sandwiched between the leather chairs and the large desk. He stayed silent as she squeezed out of the sandwich, approached, then passed the statue. It looked creepy with blank, white eyes. *What a weird thing.*

"It took a lot for you to come to me," he finally said. "I appreciate it."

She turned to him.

"I'll look into it," he added. "I promise."

He was a politician, as plastic as a Ken doll, but she believed him. She felt she had to. *Frank's not going to like this.*

#

With his mother waiting in the common area, Frank signed the paper that terminated her residency at Brookside Retirement Center. She had a stroke several years ago and was diagnosed with mental illness, but they never pursued having her declared legally incompetent. Therefore, she *could* override his decision. She wouldn't, though – not today, one of her less than lucid days. They'd been happening more frequently, which further convinced him of the need to place her in the right facility. "Did Sasha come in yet?" He slid the paper back to the receptionist.

"I haven't seen her." The young woman – probably mid-twenties – reached for the desk phone. "Should I page her?"

"No." He gestured to the paper. "Can you email me a copy?"

"Of course. All her meds should be current, but check with Mrs. Watson, our resident pharmacist, before leaving. Will you require any assistance?"

He shook his head. Sasha wasn't merely on his brain. She poked at his heart. Neither said it, but they didn't have to. They were done – their relationship nipped in the bud. It was probably for the best. Then again, what if it wasn't? She was unlike most women he dated. They were all beautiful in one way or another, but she was kind and cared about others like Charlotte, who needed help and compassion. Most people her age, hardened by life, didn't have that.

He found Charlotte in the common area where he'd left

her. But he left her alone, and now she wasn't. Trevor had her bag of belongings slung over his shoulder. He was in the process of turning her wheelchair to take her back to her room. No one else in the area paid them any mind, having eyes on the television, their knitting, or just looking out the window.

He ran up to them. "What do you think you're doing?"

"I can tell you what I'm not doing," said Trevor. "I'm not taking her out of here."

He put himself before the chair to try to stop it, but he should've known Trevor wouldn't have any qualms about smashing him in the shins with the footrests. Stumbling back and bending over to massage his legs, he looked up to see his son actually enjoy inflicting him with pain.

"Let's go, Nana."

"Home?" she asked.

"That's right." Trevor pushed her down the hall.

He limped after them. Having learned his lesson about being in front of the chair, he grabbed the bag on Trevor's back and spun him around. "You don't get it. I *have* to find her a new facility." Then his face turned quizzical. "How'd you know I was having her discharged?"

"I can use a phone," growled Charlotte.

Trevor nodded with his head tilted toward his grandmother. "Let me guess. You had a fight with your hot girlfriend, so you're gonna take your ball and go home. Well, Nana's not a ball. I wasn't psyched when you put her in here, but she needs stability, not moving around." He leaned in on his father. "And there's a secret here I intend to figure out."

"You need to get off that."

Trevor smiled, and he looked so mean when he did it. "What do you know about me that makes you think I'll do that?" He continued pushing his grandmother in her chair.

To keep up, he had to side-step and stumble alongside the chair, progressing down the hall. "They already gave someone her room. This place has a waiting list."

"It should be easy to move a rickety old person out after

they only just moved in."

"Mom, you don't want to live here anymore. You said yourself – do you want to keep being hypnotized? That's what will happen if you stay here."

"I like my group," said Charlotte. "Ebony Abernathy is a hoot. Bucky Lewis is a real swinger. But I don't much care for Nurse Enema. Know what I mean?"

Trevor laughed. He picked up the pace, which made his father do the same. "I'll look out for you now. You don't have to worry about any more Nurse Enemas."

He grabbed his son's arm. It took both hands, and he still didn't encircle the bicep. But he stopped them from going any further. "I was wrong, okay? Hypnotism was wrong for her."

"That's not what you said. It's not what Sasha said."

"It's what I'm saying now." He looked at his mother, facing forward with her hair like a sea sponge atop her head. "You heard it went bad, but you don't know how bad. Leave it at that, and we'll *both* decide where she goes next."

Trevor studied him with the squinting eyes of an appraiser. "I don't think so. I think if I'm here, and you're not, another try at hypnosis might do what Sasha said it would."

He knew it was manipulation. His instincts, refined by years of negotiating punishments for lawbreakers, told him so. And Trevor was a repeat lawbreaker. Instincts, however, were no match for emotions. He saw Trevor in his place: sharing Sasha's excitement over the possibilities of hypnotherapy, working with her to improve Charlotte's quality of life. "Alright. You want to know? As a member of this family, I guess you have a right to know."

"Nice of you to include me in your family."

He grimaced but didn't take the bait. "Your hypnotized grandmother admitted to participating in the plot to assassinate Senator Robert Kennedy in 1968. There, you know."

Trevor had a frozen face and a still body, but his mind probably whirled like a tornado.

He watched his son, trying to interpret his reaction.

Trevor's missteps with the law were nothing compared to his grandmother's possible involvement in an assassination. How would the young man take it? Would it repulse him or excite him? "Now that you know of the crime, you're legally obligated to report it. What are you going to do?"

Trevor looked too stiff to answer him. Only his eyes moved, dropping to his Nana.

"I'm staying here," said Charlotte. "With my friends, and you can't make me leave."

CHAPTER 9

There were respectable entertainment companies in Van Nuys, but as a defense lawyer and now a prosecutor, Frank only dealt with the ones that produced porn content. He had never heard of Aina Sound and Post, so he hoped Rip invited him to one of the Valley's more reputable businesses. "Alright. Why all the mystery?"

Rip replied, "You're going to want to hear this." It was the same thing he said when he first asked to meet him here.

Digging for more would've been futile, and he was still contemplating Rip's odd behavior of late, so he followed his friend into Suite 5. Soft darkness met him, interrupted by multi-colored lights, like Christmas lights, variously blinking. The chamber looked to be about the size of a small living room, though it was hard to see exactly where the walls stood. A lone man sat at a bank of consoles. He had a full beard that looked to be blond (hard to tell with the poor lighting), wavy surfer-dude hair, a white long-sleeve button shirt and a dark bowtie. He spun his chair to face them. "You're on time. I appreciate that."

Rip closed the door. "This is Nelson Kemp, senior audio engineer for film and television. He's an expert in audio forensics."

He folded his eyebrows confusedly, not that they could see.

Nelson half-rose from his seat and extended his hand to Frank, but he spoke to Rip. "Should I play it, or do you want to talk history first?"

Rip settled into one of the room's empty chairs. "Play it."

"Wait. Hold on. If you're gonna play a recording of a crime being committed, then I assume you cleared it with the DA. If you didn't, I shouldn't listen to it."

Rip gestured to an unoccupied chair.

He still wore skepticism in his creased forehead, but curiosity compelled him to sit.

"I did what I could to enhance it," said Nelson. "But this is a fourth, possibly a fifth, generation copy of an original recording that was lost years ago." He pressed a button. The room became filled with a scratchy, somewhat muffled sound pumped in by speakers along the ceiling and in the walls. It was unmistakably the noise of a crowd. Voices competed for attention, and orchestra music played in the background. Glasses clinked, and feet shuffled. There were the scuffing sounds made by objects that rubbed against a microphone.

It's a copy of an original recording that was lost years ago? It sounded old. He even heard someone on the playback use the distinctly sixties word *groovy*. Kitchen sounds began to emerge: sizzling meat, ringing cutlery, instructions given to staff – all in the background. Animated voices were at the fore of the recording, and they derived their enthusiasm from the celebrity they called "Kennedy" or "Bobby." He sat up, throwing a look at Rip. "Don't tell me this is the Ambassador Hotel on the night of Kennedy's shooting."

Rip let the audio speak for itself.

Did he want to hear it? Hell, yes, he did. Did he think he should? Yes, to that too. But why was another question – the sister question to why Rip relinquished all that unsolicited research. As with the research, he figured it was best to take advantage of it when it was offered. He closed his eyes and concentrated on the sounds. The recording was poor, but he could imagine people swarming RFK. He heard a woman say Bobby was "the last hope for a dying democracy". Others expressed similar sentiments though a tad less dramatic. He imagined people weeping happy tears, trying to touch the great man. Someone yelled, "All the way with RFK!" Others predicted a second Kennedy presidency even greater than the first. The recording seemed incapable of capturing all their enthusiasm.

Then a loud pop! People screamed. The microphone making the recording was on the move, hitting things. Bodies bumped into one another, dishes broke, and pots clanged. More pops rapidly followed. It was impossible to tell how many, but they grew louder as if coming closer. Joyous expressions became screams of horror. People shrieked. Someone cried, "Not again! Not Bobby!" Wrestling sounds joined the confusion, along with scuffling and fighting, trays crashing. People shouted to apprehend the gunman. Someone wailed, "Please, God, not Bobby too."

The room turned abruptly silent, like a vacuum in space. He realized Nelson had stopped the playback. His mouth felt dry, words hanging on his lips. It was over so quickly. He wanted to hear more. Then again, he didn't. He saw console lights twinkle, reflecting in the dampness of Rip's eyes.

"I've heard it hundreds of times," said Nelson. "But it still gets me – low quality or not."

"Most major news outlets were there to cover Bobby's speech, so this isn't the only recording from that night," said Rip. "But it's the only one recorded in the kitchen pantry, where the shooting took place."

Nelson nodded. "It's called the Pruszynski Recording, named after the man who recorded it. When the shooting started, Polish reporter Stanislaw Pruszynski was forty feet away from Bobby Kennedy. His reel-to-reel machine was in recording mode. Hearing the first shot, he rushed into the kitchen pantry, where he captured the entire shooting and its aftermath."

Frank asked, "How long have authorities had this tape?"

"The FBI acquired it in 1969, but technology back then wasn't advanced enough to adequately analyze it. They passed it on to the LAPD, who put it in storage. Sometime in the late eighties, it went to the state archives."

"How did you get it?"

"I gave it to him," said Rip.

"How did *you* get it?"

"It's been in the possession of the DA's office since the early 2000s."

He knew better than to get into it in front of the audio technician, but he still had to wonder. Rip was a DA investigator. That was his title. But he wouldn't have access to something like this unless someone high up gave it to him or he stole it.

Nelson continued, ignoring their sidebar. "I'm not the only expert. Phil Van Praag, Wes Dooley, Paul Pegas, Eddy Brixen, and Phil Spencer Whitehead all put it through their tests."

"I don't know those names."

"Phil Van Praag wrote *Evolution of the Audio Recorder*, a respected textbook in the field of magnetic recording. Wes Dooley is a member of the American College of Forensic Examiners. Paul Pegas is his esteemed associate. Eddy Brixen is a forensic audio and ballistics expert from Copenhagen. Phil Whitehead is at the Georgia Institute of Technology."

"Sirhan's gun held eight rounds," said Frank. "If your tests detected more than eight gunshot sounds –"

"Then there was another shooter," said Rip.

He narrowed his eyes on his friend. *Yeah, we're gonna talk.* He turned to the soundman. "How many did they detect?"

"Phil Van Praag identified thirteen gunshots. He wasn't certain of that number, but he was positive it exceeded eight. Dooley, Pegas and Brixen put the number at ten but also identified double-shots."

"Double-shots?"

"Gunshot sounds that are too close together to have come from the same weapon."

"Two guns?"

"No other way to make double-shots." Nelson looked at Rip. "Dooley, Pegas and Brixen identified ten shots *with* double-shots."

Rip addressed Frank. "Four highly respected audio professionals determined two guns fired concurrently on Robert

Kennedy shortly after midnight June 5, 1968."

"Five, including me," said Nelson. "And Phil Whitehead. He also identified more than eight shots."

"Six experts," said Rip.

"Did anyone identify eight or less than eight gunshots?" he asked.

"Phillip Harrison, a forensic audio specialist from England, identified seven shots on the recording with a few indiscernible sounds that could have been an eighth gunshot."

"Let's not forget the other tapes," said Rip. "ABC News, Mutual Broadcasting and Continental Broadcasting all had their audio recorders on."

"But they weren't near the shooting."

"That's right." Rip nodded. "ABC News was broadcasting from the Ambassador Hotel ballroom when Sirhan Sirhan began firing. Mutual and Continental were also nearby."

Nelson said, "In 1982, Dr. Michael Hecker of the Stanford Research Institute performed oscillographic and spectrographic analysis of the recordings from ABC News, Mutual Broadcasting and Continental Broadcasting. He said, 'no fewer than ten gunshots were ascertainable following the conclusion of the senator's victory speech until after the time that Sirhan was disarmed.'"

"You memorized what he said?"

Rip cleared his throat. "This isn't a spontaneous get-together, Frank."

"I've noticed."

"Uh...Hecker," said Nelson. "He had an impeccable reputation, top of the field. Before this, he analyzed the tapes that brought down the Nixon presidency."

"Critics disagreed with him back in '82," said Rip. "They said the recordings weren't made close enough to the shooting to be accurate. The gunshot sounds could've been balloons popping, microphones bumping into things. But in light of what the experts found on the Pruszynski tape, Hecker's findings now add further credibility to a second gunman theory."

He began to feel the full weight of what these men had to say. Their motives – or Rip's motive – notwithstanding, he had to accept that according to the experts (with the exception of Phillip Harrison from England), the audio tapes indicated a conspiracy in the murder of Robert Kennedy. That didn't bode well for his mother.

"Are you alright?" asked Nelson.

"Even with good instruments to analyze it, a scratchy, fifth generation tape can't possibly be conclusive."

"I thought you wanted to launch a second investigation," said Rip. "This recording and those papers I gave you are reasons to do it."

"I never said that. I wanted –" He glanced at Nelson, then he went back to Rip. "We might as well get into it now. You produce hundreds of pages of research so soon after – so soon. And you invite me here to listen to this tape. Why? You warned *against* looking into this."

"He brought you here because I asked him to," said a voice in the dark.

He searched for the source of that voice, whipping his head around. It was like it came from a hovering spirit. Nelson flipped a switch on the nearby wall, and a single light awoke in the area separated from them by a wall of Plexiglass, the performance area. And there sat Marco Diaz before a piano. He dropped his fingers on the black and white keys, producing the abrupt awakening sound of a two octave D flat Major. Slowly, the DA turned to face them.

"Why didn't you tell me why you met with Sirhan?" asked Rip. "I could've helped you."

Why do you *think I met with him?* Once again, things with Rip weren't measuring up. *How could you have helped me exactly?* Staring at his "friend" while wondering what he and the DA cooked up and why, he thought about what brought them all here. It would've taken months, most likely years, for all those experts to analyze the Pruszynski tape. Then it dawned on him. Pepper and Dusek, the lawyers Rip reminded him of in

Inspiration Park. The previous DA would have commissioned the tape's analysis in preparation for the case being brought by Pepper and Dusek. That meant it would've been on Marco Diaz's radar since he first took office. But that didn't explain why they were here now, unless – no, he decided. No. Rip wouldn't have told the DA about their conversation in RFK Inspiration Park, would he?

"You might say the tape we just heard is circumstantial," said Marco. "And you're right. But we now know the whereabouts of a possible conspirator. That changes things."

His stomach dropped. *Sasha.* She *did* tell the district attorney. It had to have been her or Trevor, and he was pretty sure it wasn't the latter. His world just got a whole lot more complicated. And betrayal, it seemed, was everywhere around him.

CHAPTER 10

Redondo Beach, California. April 1966

"It's been hell," says Charlotte. "The mood swings and midnight cravings for weird stuff like oysters in chocolate sauce, but, worst of all, I have dreams I'll give birth to a carnival freak."

"What?" Matthew nearly trips – either from what she said or in avoidance of the severed fish head lying in his path, baking in the sun and staining the pier with its remains.

She's insisting on this pier stroll because sweet things like chocolate sauce repulse her at the moment. She wants to taste salty air. She has a desire to see and smell fish flopping on the ends of fishing lines. "I'm as big as an orca." She hitches her step as a pain – one of the many she's been feeling – threatens to rip her pelvis. She clenches her jaw, pretends not to feel it.

Her charade works because he doesn't seem to notice. "The kid will play linebacker for the Rams. Have you named him yet?"

"It won't be Rosey or Merlin." She isn't a sports fan, but everyone in Southern California has heard of Rosey Grier and Merlin Olsen. "Who says it will be a boy?"

"A boy would be best." He sees annoyance ripple her forehead, so he explains. "Women aren't leaders, and that's what we need right now."

"You should cool your chops."

"I'm worried about the world we'll be bringing your kid into."

"We?"

"Our country's going in the wrong direction. From last year to this year, LBJ raised troop levels in Vietnam by two hundred thousand."

She nods. "My brother is there."

"That number should be more like two million."

She stops and stares at him, too stunned to say anything.

"Johnson is pussy-footing, like Kennedy did. The world is either ours, or it will belong to the reds. Here in America, Negroes want it all. This country will be black, or it'll be white."

Her hard look softens. "Watts *was* scary."

"If something different doesn't come out of Washington, everything will belong to the reds and the blacks. Where do you think that'll leave us?"

"Something different *is* coming out of Washington. Robert Kennedy –"

"Robert Francis Kennedy? He advised his brother to be soft on Commies, and he hasn't gotten any tougher since."

"He's telling blacks to clean up their own backyard."

He looks away, dismissing her statement.

"You think because I'm a chick I can't have an opinion about politics?"

"I like that you have opinions. Beverly doesn't have any that don't come from me first."

"I don't want to hear about her."

He appears to have already moved on from the subject of Beverly, looking at eight men near a sink. One of them rinses his latest catch. "Turn around."

"Why?"

"Before he sees you." He grabs her shoulders to twist her.

She resists, which makes her wince with another sharp pain. Through squinting eyes, she sees that Pete is one of the eight. He has a pole in his hand, its line running into the water. As fast as her awkward body will let her, she breaks free of Matt and rushes up to Pete. She fights through the fishermen and grabs him by the shirt. "What do you think you're doing?"

The surprise that first transforms him dissolves into flashing fury when he sees Matthew. "What are *you* doing?"

"How long has this been going on?"

"That's my question." He snarls as he talks.

"Were you canned? I'm going to have to go back to five-fingering our groceries?"

Pete looks at Matthew. "I told you to keep your mitts off her."

A fisherman says, "Looks like mitts aren't what he should be worried about." He gets chuckles from a few of his buddies.

Matthew steps up beside her, defying the chucklers and Pete. "You steal groceries?"

"Sometimes."

His glare burns Pete. "This is how you provide for her?"

Pete turns it into another nose-to-nose standoff. They're bigger than her and resolute in their mutual dislike, so it's impossible for her to separate them. And the effort blasts an intense heat across her lower back. It's more piercing than the pain she felt before, spreading to her lower abdomen and radiating across her upper thighs. She drops both hands to her belly.

"That's something coming from a bona-fide mooch." Pete grabs for his collar.

She interrupts his reach, but the press of his body knocks her backward. She stumbles as fishermen move in to try to split them up. Their intervention conspires with her excessive weight, awkward body shape and tired legs to dump her on her ass. She lands with rubber boots scrambling around her. She hears voices and sees grimy hands reach for her, but all she can concentrate on is the pain now scourging her abdomen. It isn't like any discomfort she's ever had. She squirms on the concrete, in the blood and guts of disemboweled fish, in the spilled sea water and the crud. "I...I think the baby's coming!"

"Are you sure?" asks Pete. "You said it wouldn't be for –"

"Don't argue with her." Matthew fights through fishermen to reach her. "Can you make it to the hospital?"

"We don't have money for that," says Pete.

"You would if you didn't waste your days fishing."

A wail from Charlotte shuts them up. The baby is coming – here on this grimy pier. Ugly people with bad teeth bend over her. *Is it too much to ask for some privacy?*

"I'll deliver it." Matthew tries to get between her legs.

"The hell you will!" Pete scrambles to beat him to the destination.

On her back, looking over her belly and between her bent knees, she sees her lovers shove each other like bickering children. She wants to scream at them, but – *oh, God* – her bowels dump sloppy diarrhea into her cotton underwear.

Onlookers gasp and gag. *Serves them right for being nosey.* The pain is so overwhelming, and the scene is so chaotic, that all sense of decency has left her. Who cares if she'll be the talk of the beach for years to come? She needs to get through this. One of her lovers pulls her underwear off. She doesn't look to see who. She feels a pressure from within that's so intense she thinks it will explode out of her belly button.

Pete tries to do his part, reaching between her legs.

"Wash your hands," she yells. Another labor pain makes her gasp. She tries to push, but it hurts so damn much. She's feeling light-headed.

While Pete throws his hands into a nearby sink, beneath the faucet, Matthew spreads a newspaper over her diarrhea. Something dislodges within her and escapes out onto the paper.

"Gross," exclaims a boy in the crowd. "It looks like The Blob."

"Get the kids out of here," says Matt. "Everyone leave."

"My baby looks like The Blob?" Other stuff comes out too, but she doesn't lift her head to see. It feels as if she's peeing and can't stop.

"I think I see his head," says Matthew.

Pete returns, muscling his way between her knees. "My hands are clean. Get back."

Matt doesn't give ground. "Did you use soap?"

Pete elbows him, knocking him back.

Her legs are wide enough to wrap around a California redwood, and her insides are escaping between them. Her flesh rips as the expulsion begins. She yells. People yell with her.

"The head is coming." Pete guides the small wet crown. Its fine black hair is matted, coated in slime. "I see an ear, and the eyes. It's beautiful."

Not to be excluded, Matthew pushes him to the left, further opening her leg. Her hip feels like it's going to snap. She screams. Pete yells at him. "Wash *your* hands."

Peering through tear-blurry eyes, she sees that Matthew can't make up his mind. He wants to assist, but he has diarrhea and other filth on his hands. "Wash," she tells him.

Pete says, "Use soap."

"Just ease it out, moron. I'm coming right back."

"The shoulders are out," Pete tells her. "A little more. Push."

A gush of fluid splashes around his hands. Her guess is that it's the stuff that surrounds the baby. Flatulence coughs uncontrollably from her anus. Diarrhea may follow it again, but of greater concern is the obstinate swell of her belly. It should be going down as the baby comes out, and it is – but only a little.

"C'mon, Char. C'mon. It's almost...it's a girl! We have a girl!"

She strains to lift her head. Between her legs, she sees Pete ease the child out and raise it up. A cord stretches from the baby back into her. The newborn is pale, bathed in reddish clear mucus. People tell Pete to spank the babe, clear its mouth. She yells at him. "Don't hit my baby!"

No one seems to have a towel with which to wipe the child, at least not a clean towel. Pete carefully offers her the glistening newborn. He's all smiles but also noticeably uncomfortable holding such a fragile creature. She wants to reassure him, but all she feels is – she doesn't know exactly what she feels. Is it love? Yes. It's love. She extends her arms to accept her new daughter, but another pain squeezes her from the inside as hard as before. Something is wrong. The discharge of afterbirth is not supposed to hurt.

Pete appears as perplexed as her. He can't give her the baby, and he can't move too far from her because the umbilical cord hasn't been cut. "What's wrong?"

Matthew worms his way back between her legs to inspect. "There's another baby."

"Twins?" Pete turns to the fishermen around him. "Can someone hold this one?"

Matt snaps at him. "I can't believe you said that. *You* hold her."

"You're not delivering my child."

Charlotte feels more tearing down there. The second birth is supposed to be easier than the first, but this one is worse. Head #2 is bigger. She doesn't have to see it to know it.

"It's stuck," says Matthew. "You're going to have to push."

"I am!"

Pete tries to nudge him aside. "I got this."

Matt pushes back, knocking him off-balance. Cradling the firstborn in both arms, Pete falls against Charlotte's open thigh. Something pops in her hip, and she screams. The head emerges. "Good." Matthew catches the wet, furry black crown. "Harder."

She's convinced her hip is broken, or dislocated. Her right leg is numb. Unfortunately, her pelvis is not. Her splitting flesh makes wet slurping sounds. She pushes with all she has: lifting her head, squeezing her eyes shut, wailing. Her fingernails dig into the concrete.

"He's got linebacker shoulders," says Matthew. "You *should* name him Rosey."

"No boy of mine is gonna be called Rosey," says Pete. "Is it a boy?"

She yells, but her failing voice makes her sound weak. She sucks in deeply and pushes. She's determined to expel the baby with this effort. Her uterus will probably go with it.

With the passage of its upper half, baby #2's lower half glides out much easier, followed by a gush of blood and clear fluid. "It's a boy," says Matthew. "A boy! You did it, Charlotte."

She drops her head back. She feels different this time. That's the last one. She's sure of it.

"I'm partial to the name Merlin. It begins with M, like Matthew."

Pete growls. "Hand me my boy."

"Is it yours?"

Pete's fist flies out, but it's wet and slippery, grazing Matthew's forehead and sliding off.

The men try to fight as each holds a slimy baby. Cords run from the infants back into their mother through her torn and aching vagina. Each movement of the men causes the cords to tug at her insides. She roars with surprising ferocity, motivated by pain. "Stop!" The physical part of their quarrel abruptly ends, but they still argue.

She's weak and exhausted. But she needs to hold her children – both of them. She reaches with quivering arms. Her voice is once again a croak. "Give me my babies." Passionately disagreeing over names, Pete and Matthew don't hear her. She feels like she's about to go mad. Her babies may still have their cords, but that doesn't mean she'll allow them to become the objects of a paternal tug-o-war. Everything is going to hell: Vietnam, protests, race wars, her lovers always fighting. She can think of only one name that rises above divisiveness, provides answers and shows responsibility. It's the honorable name of an honorable man. Plus, it will shut Matthew up (a woman *can* be a leader), and it will confound Pete. She points at the baby girl and says, "Bobbi" in a voice that regains some of its strength. Pete freezes. Her tired eyes shift to the infant boy. "Francis." Matt becomes as still as his romantic rival. She raises both of her arms and extends them shakily. "Now give me my babies."

#

2018

The looks Sasha got from Carolyn Tanaka and other Brookside staffers said *this isn't right*. She agreed, but she couldn't stop cops from executing an arrest warrant, even if it was for a wheelchair-bound old woman in a nursing home. The look Glen gave her from the doorway of his office was less aligned with the staff. For him, it was about what *she* did. Neither of them came out and said it, but she knew he knew this was her fault.

The guilt of it, along with all the looks, made her run after the cops, through the front doors, out into the mid-day sunlight. Blinking rapidly to expel the glare from her eyes, she caught snapshots of the scene: Charlotte bouncing and squirming as her chair hopped on broken gravel, half a dozen cops surrounding her as if she was a hardened criminal, and Dr. Fitz coordinating the whole operation. At five foot five with a goatee dyed the color of beets, stringy silver hair, and a face partially frozen by excessive Botox injections, Dr. Fitz was a strange looking man. He introduced himself when he handed Glen his credentials as a Yale educated psychologist. The next paper he offered was Charlotte's arrest warrant, signed by a judge *and* the district attorney.

"You don't have to be so rough," she said to a blond cop with frosted tips on his flat-top haircut – a style better worn by boybands of the 1990s. "She needs help, not abusive tactics."

Charlotte yelled like someone being tortured. The police didn't appear to be hurting her, but mentally impaired people didn't perceive things like the unimpaired. To them, roughness meant hostility, and aggressiveness was a form of violence.

"She's scared," she told Flat-top.

"Sasha!" Glen waddled after her, which was his way of running. "She's having a fit."

"Don't be foolish enough to interrupt a court order," Flat-top warned her.

She broke away from the cop to meet Glen. Before she could speak, he said, "I heard from my people."

"Your people?" She watched him form an expression that said *you know what I'm talking about*. And she did know. In spite of her warning to the contrary, he continued to correspond with the conspiracy-minded group he met on the internet. Since he didn't have a computer or know how to use one, she wondered if they communicated by phone or even in person.

"You're on the wrong side of this," he said. "I'm learning

how much the government intimidated, suppressed and silenced witnesses of this assassination. They'll do it again."

"I'm glad you didn't say that when he showed you the warrant."

"We can't stop them, but I called someone who can. We need to hold them up until he gets here." He must've thought she needed him to explain himself because he added, "I may have wanted to move her, but not like this." He pointed to where Flat-top joined the other officers trying to get the old woman into a dark colored van. "Not with them."

"Who did you call?" Another scream by Charlotte turned her head, but she didn't move to intervene. *They're just being a little rough. That's all. This is what's right.*

"What do you think they'll do to her in custody?"

"The district attorney just wants answers." She saw the police succeed in finally separating Charlotte from her chair. They lifted the old woman, who now kicked and tried to scratch them. "She could be the key to finding out what really happened that night."

"The government has never wanted that, but my friends do. They can keep her safe and get the answers you're talking about."

She whipped her head around. "Who did you call?"

"Her son knows how to *legally* stop this."

"You called Frank?" That was the last thing she needed or wanted, and it would only make the situation worse. "I trust the Los Angeles County District Attorney. You should too." She left him with that, running up to the van. She didn't have a plan in mind, and she arrived as Flat-top slid the back door closed. She couldn't see Charlotte or the other cops due to the dark film tinting the windows. She tried to open the passenger door. It was locked. She beat on the glass until it lowered, and Dr. Fitz looked at her from the front seat. Beyond him, she saw a cop in the driver's seat. "I'm her hypnotist. You need me."

It was hard for her to read the doctor because injections largely stole his ability to form expressions, but he appeared to give her comment consideration. She tried to see Charlotte in the van, but she couldn't. It struck her as odd that the old woman, who had been screaming, now made no sound at all. Finally, Dr. Fitz said, "Alright. You can get in the back."

She pumped her fist – not sure why because there was nothing worth celebrating. She spun around to go to the rear of the van, but she stopped at the sight of Frank's Camry pulling into the parking lot. Glen hobbled over to meet him. She wondered for a moment if he was right about her being on the wrong side of this. The Camry skidded to a stop. When she saw Frank leap out of it, she made her decision. And she turned to Flat-top. "We better go – now."

CHAPTER 11

Frank was sure his eyes were bloodshot. He thought he felt the dark circles surrounding them. Each bark from Tippy – and they kept coming – caused his brain to pulse. There was no point in trying to stop her from performing her natural-born duty, so he let her have at it. She raced from window to window, stopping at the door and then on to the next window. There had to be thirty people on his front lawn, representing at least ten news organizations. He knew they'd come, which was one reason he slept not a wink last night. Another reason was Sasha. She looked straight at him then climbed into the van that took Charlotte away. What would they do to his mother? He couldn't trust Sasha to look out for her. That much was clear. And he couldn't get any answers about where they took her.

"They arrested Charlotte. I guess you already knew that."

He turned to find Rip standing in the hallway that led to the kitchen. He gave his friend a key the last time he asked him to check in on Tippy, but it was a decision he now regretted. "All they'll tell me is she's being detained for questioning."

Rip shook his head. "This could've turned out differently if you'd have only told me."

"You need to let that go."

Rip bent over to pet Tippy, who went to him with a wagging tail. "They're expecting you to comment on Marco's press conference."

Frank's tired face produced a perplexed look.

Rip summoned video footage on his phone and brought it to him. "Early morning, during a slow news cycle, the district attorney announces an arrest and a new investigation he's launching into Robert Kennedy's assassination. An investigation he'll take to a grand jury."

He snatched the phone before Rip could offer it. Its screen featured Marco Diaz, all business-like, standing before a bank of microphones. The arrow icon waited for him to press it, but he hesitated. Could not pressing play prevent this nightmare from further unfolding?

#

Sasha didn't know where they were because she spent the duration of yesterday's drive in the far back of the van wearing a blindfold while Flat-top sat beside her to ensure the fold kept her blind. It was dark when they reached their destination. Even with the blindfold removed, she saw little during the brief walk from the van to the building. She knew they were in the country, atop a mesa surrounded by purple-black foothills. She saw a wooden fence, some trees and an outbuilding. Her phone wasn't any help to her here or in the van coming over here. They obviously had a signal blocker in both locations – of course they would.

After a night of separation, she and Charlotte reunited this morning, in the communal area of what appeared to be a ranch. The walls wore multi stained, ship-lap wood dressed with cowboy and Native American artwork. She thought some taxidermy would fit the motif, but she didn't see any. That was probably for the best. The last fifteen hours had been traumatic enough for Charlotte without dead animal heads looking down on her from the surrounding walls.

Charlotte seemed catatonic, sitting in her wheelchair near one of the dark leather couches.

"I didn't give her anything," Dr. Fitz explained. "This is what we call dissociation."

"It might have something to do with the way you removed her from her home."

He looked scornfully at the cops in the bar area, adjacent

to the kitchen. "It might."

Sasha slid to the end of the couch, closer to Charlotte. "I'm here for you, not them. I'll make sure no one treats you bad."

Charlotte's good eye stared ahead while the other leaked down her cheek.

She wanted to wipe away the leakage, but if Dr. Fitz didn't do it, should she? He was trying to decide how much he'd allow her to contribute to whatever this was. She had to take her lead from him. He was Yale trained – no doubt a giant in his field. She could learn a lot from a man like that. Leaning closer to Charlotte, she said, "You can relax with me. We're friends, remember?" That yielded nothing, absolutely no reaction from... *wait*. She looked closer. Her proximity to the old woman showed her something no one else in the room could see. The muscles in the paralyzed part of Charlotte's face quivered. It was like they rebelled against the stoic way the rest of her behaved. She always assumed facial paralysis was absolute. Either Charlotte found a way to overcome the paralysis, or maybe her face had never been paralyzed.

"I think we could use some sweet tea." Dr. Fitz directed his words to Flat-top, who was in the kitchen. "You'll find a pitcher in the refrigerator, glasses in the cupboard."

The cop with the boyband hair didn't much appreciate being turned into a waiter, but he did as Dr. Fitz requested. A lady cop helped him, removing glasses from the cupboard.

"No one here will treat you bad." Dr. Fitz sat in front of Charlotte, on the edge of the coffee table. He reached over, took Sasha's hand in his. "We'll make sure of it."

She could see he expected her to affirm his claim, and she nodded, offering him a smile. But she couldn't get the quivering of Charlotte's paralyzed face out of her mind. She wondered if she should tell him. They were colleagues, weren't they?

"I'd like to talk about the old days, Charlotte. Can we do that?" He didn't get a response from her, and he didn't seem to need one. "I used to be among the Haight-Ashbury crowd. That's a big surprise, right?" He laughed. "I traveled around playing for coins people dropped in my guitar case. I wasn't any good, and my voice was even worse. Bob Dylan, I was not."

His hippie recollections went in and out of her ears. *Are Charlotte's infirmities psychosomatic?* It would make sense if they were. She saw Frank lose patience with his mother more than once. He acted like he didn't believe it when she was disoriented, but then he'd catch himself and try to believe it. It was a bizarre relationship. They both needed therapy, she decided.

Dr. Fitz continued. "Where were you in the sixties? Were you here basking in the California sun? Or were you living it up in Paducah, Main Street, U.S.A.?" He chuckled. "I think you were here. We're a dying breed, you and me – flower power to the end."

She recognized this as therapy 101. The Institute of Wellness taught it: identify with your client in a personal way and ask questions they want to answer. Funny how he got the same training at Yale for a hundred times the cost. Charlotte didn't seem interested in his talk of the sixties. But if she took pains to make her face look lifeless, could this be an act as well?

The policewoman approached them with a hand-carved wooden tray. Three sweating glasses of iced tea sat upon it. She served Dr. Fitz first, then Sasha. She offered the third to Charlotte but got no reaction from her.

Dr. Fitz sipped his tea in an obnoxiously deliberate way. "Mmm. Charlotte?" Once again, she didn't respond. "Maybe she'd like a straw." He reached to take Charlotte's drink for her.

Could you be any more obvious? Sasha's hand flew out, intercepting the drink. Charlotte's tea didn't appear different from anyone else's, but it was, of course. She looked at the four cops sitting at the bar. All had tea, and all raised their glasses to her before drinking. *Oh, brother.* She turned to Dr. Fitz. *You didn't give her anything before? How about now?*

#

Frank stood before the reporters on his lawn without the benefit of a bank of microphones and a podium, which Marco Diaz used in the video. He was also in the unenviable position of getting out the second word to the district attorney's first. Everybody knew the first word, especially when coming from a powerful official, set the tone and usually became the accepted truth for the public. Plus, he was stupid tired after a worry-induced night without sleep. He'd been at it for ten minutes now: answering questions about his mother and why his boss ordered her arrest.

One question stood out because, unlike the others, it came from a female voice that was smoky yet assertive. "How do you intend to free your mother?"

He cocked his head and searched the crowd for the poser of the question. The woman stepped forward so he could better see her from his position on the porch. She had golden blonde hair with platinum highlights and long false lashes over blue eyes. She had the features of an Italian, an extraordinarily attractive Italian. "Who are you?"

"Alex Logan, Serious News XM channel 132." She did *not* have a face for radio. She belonged in front of a camera. "What will you do? The Authorization for Use of Military Force is an elastic document that gives the government wartime authority to indefinitely imprison Americans connected to terrorism."

The back of his mind leaped to the fore as if saying *ooh, ooh, I got this*. That was because it recalled the part of the DA's announcement where he said, "Sirhan Sirhan shot Robert Kennedy as an act of terror to benefit Palestine, his homeland. For that reason, we are able to charge his fellow conspirators according to The Patriot Act, U.S. Code Title 18, Section 2339A – providing material support to terrorists."

"Mr. Caron?"

"There's no fucking way he can do that." The gasps he heard and the stunned faces told him he screwed up – not that he needed to be told. He'd been in the game long enough to know you don't swear like that in front of the press. It turned them into dogs with a bone. "What I mean to say is…cut me a break, guys. I didn't sleep last night because of this."

They cut him no break, shouting over each other, shouting at him. They wanted to know how he could be so sure the DA couldn't do that. They asked if he'd defend his mother. Since he was a former defense attorney, would he seek help from more current, *competent* defenders? The question that most irked him, though, was whether he truly believed his mother was innocent. He didn't answer any of them, directing his response solely to the beautiful Ms. Logan. "The ACLU has been fighting Patriot Act abuses since day one."

That lit them up even more, causing them to speculate that he'd partner with the ACLU to defend his mother. He spun around, leaving them in their speculation, and he escaped back into the house. He slammed the front door, locked it. Tippy met his return with enthusiasm, but his eyes went straight to Rip. "I need you to find out what you can about Alex Logan from Serious News XM Radio."

"Already did."

"And can you put a trace on Sasha's phone?"

"Without a warrant?"

Frank cocked his head to the side. *For what you did with Marco, I think you owe me.* But he wasn't sure if Rip saw it that way.

CHAPTER 12

Sasha stared at the glass of tea resting on an end table beside the old woman, who sat on the couch. They were in the sitting room of one of the bedroom suites. By her calculation, twenty minutes had passed since Dr. Fitz told her to take Charlotte into the suite and *get her to drink it*. Now his voice outside the door indicated his patience was about at its end.

It wasn't in her best interest to snatch that tea from him when they were in the common area. It was an instinctual response. She knew it was laced, and Dr. Fitz later admitted as much in an aside. They dosed it with ibogaine, an alkaloid used by clinics around the world to break opioid addiction. He didn't say more. He probably figured it'd go over her head because she lacked his education and expertise. But the San Luis Obispo Institute of Wellness instructed her better than anyone might expect. She knew ibogaine was a psychoactive drug with psychedelic and dissociative properties. It could ease addiction withdrawal and help to eliminate dangerous drug cravings. For people like Charlotte, who had no drug dependency, it put them in an altered state of consciousness where they might relive memories as if for the first time. He intended it to work on Charlotte like an immersive truth serum. But it had dangerous side effects for someone of her age and with her health history. It could cause seizures, whole body tremors, cardiovascular damage and ataxia, which was the loss of control of bodily movements. Ibogaine had a mortality rate of one in every four hundred and twenty-seven users. Not only did the U.S. government refuse to recognize its legitimacy, it declared the substance illegal.

Dr. Fitz gave her a second chance by sending them into the bedroom suite alone, telling her to make sure Charlotte drank the tea. He didn't have to do that. They could've forced Charlotte to drink it. They could give it to her now as a suppository. It worked that way too, and quicker than if she drank it. She wondered if it was as a professional courtesy that he gave her a second chance. Maybe he saw potential in her. She was, after all, the only hypnotist to get Charlotte to open up. Maybe he wanted to mentor her. That would do wonders for her career…and to think of all the patients she could help along the way.

The knock on the door finally came. She figured it was a testament to the trust he placed in her that it took them this long. Or maybe he wanted to give the drug time to have an effect, assuming Charlotte ingested it, which she hadn't. Not yet.

She couldn't recall ever being so crippled by indecision. She felt hot as she stood between the door and Charlotte on the couch near the tea. They turned up the heat, she recalled, so the old woman would thirst for a refreshing beverage. It caused sweat to glisten on Charlotte's skin and bead on her forehead though she ignored it. That didn't mean she ignored everything. Charlotte looked about with her good eye, showing an awareness of all that occurred.

"Can I come in?" Dr. Fitz asked from the other side of the door.

Charlotte wiped her brow and expelled her breath. She *did* feel the elevated temperature.

It couldn't go on. Sasha had to decide: Dr. Fitz or her conscience. Her conscience claimed she was there to protect Charlotte. Why else did she approach their van before it pulled out of the Brookside parking lot? Why else, indeed? She said she trusted the district attorney. That meant she also trusted Dr. Fitz, who worked for him.

Someone pounded on the door, much more forceful than a knock. "Ms. Frye."

She took two steps toward the door, stretched for the handle. *Why did I lock it when we came in?* That, she realized, was a subconscious decision – instinctual, like grabbing the tea before Dr. Fitz could. What were her instincts telling her to do in this situation?

"Kick it in," said Dr. Fitz.

The subconscious and the conscience were not the same. While everyone had the former, some lacked the latter – serial killers, for example. But most people had both. For her, in this moment, her subconscious and her conscience were in lock step. Knowing what it might do to her, she couldn't let Charlotte consume the drugged tea. *There, decision made.* She turned to her, but – *Oh, no!*

Charlotte drank down the last of the tea, satisfying her thirst. She looked like she didn't want to miss a drop.

A crash and a shattering wood frame, the door sailed open.

Sasha darted to the couch, wrapped Charlotte in a bear hug, and she lifted. The old woman was heavier than she expected. "Help me." She knew Charlotte could walk, though with difficulty. "We gotta go." Charlotte just lagged in her arms as dead weight.

Flat-top was the first one through the door, followed by the lady cop, another cop and Dr. Fitz. All but Dr. Fitz shouted at her, with Flat-top being the loudest. "Put her down."

She dragged Charlotte to the nearest door, which led to the bedroom. It was a matter of feet: her from the door, the cops from her. She was off balance with Charlotte's additional weight, making her fumble with the handle. The voices of three angry cops pummeled her, along with the pounding threat of them running toward her. She heard Dr. Fitz say, "Sasha, don't do this." It was about as clear a warning as she would get: no mentorship if she proceeded.

The door to the next room surrendered to her, opening as Flat-top came to within inches of grabbing her hair. She stumbled through, clinging to Charlotte, but she didn't fall. She staggered. She threw her weight (and Charlotte's) against the door, slamming it on Flat-top's hand. She heard a crack – bones breaking? He roared and pulled back, dragging his flesh against the door pressing into the jamb. It closed with a definitive thud. She knew it wouldn't stay closed. The other cops were already against it, putting all their efforts into opening it. If she could just prop something under the handle to hold it…and there it was: across the bedroom, against the back wall. She saw a vanity with a mirror surrounded by bulbous lights, and a wooden chair accompanied it. If she could get the chair, she could wedge it under the door.

One of the cops on the other side dove against the door, and it flew open, heaving her and Charlotte. Momentum made him stagger into the bedroom, coming at them out of control.

Beyond the off-balance cop, she caught a fleeting glimpse into the sitting room. Flat-top was bent over, clutching his wounded hand. Dr. Fitz was beside him but ignoring him. The doctor stared back at her with a look of pure malice.

She didn't have time to linger on that because the cop that stumbled into the bedroom regained his composure. He reached for them, but Charlotte came to life shockingly, deceptively fast. Hissing like a cat, she raked her nails across the man's eyes. He screamed, hands flying to his face. His writhing blocked the doorway as he bounced from one side of the jamb to the other.

Sasha couldn't stop. She couldn't gape in astonishment or wonder how Charlotte was able to move so quickly and effectively. She had to haul the old woman, who still refused to stand on her own, deeper into the room. In the midst of her wrestling and her struggle, she heard Charlotte speak as if in a cadence, with a thick Northeastern accent. "We ah opposed around the world by a monolithic and ruthless conspiracy."

There was no time for her to consider the old woman's strange words. They had mere moments left to get to the next door. She didn't know what lay beyond it. She assumed there weren't more cops because they would've come in already, but she didn't know. She hoped they'd find an unpopulated hallway on the other side of that door. Maybe they'd find a closet or another room they could hide in until she figured out what to do next.

Charlotte continued. "Its mistakes ah buried, not headlined. Its dissentahs ah silenced, not praised. No expenditah is questioned. No rumah is printed. No secret is revealed."

They hobbled past the vanity – the bed and its furniture accoutrements behind them. Closing in on ten feet from the door, she realized Charlotte felt lighter the more she talked. No longer dead weight, she seemed to put life in her limbs with every word she recited.

Something tackled them from behind – an impact that brought them crashing to the floor, tumbling, bouncing and rolling into the closed door. The female cop was the aggressor this time. She wrestled Sasha, trying to bring her into submission. Charlotte rolled away in the struggle.

She fought the lady cop as best she could, but she wasn't a fighter. She never learned the combat techniques taught in police academies. Her opponent was strong. It wouldn't be long before others came to assist her. She managed to get on top of the woman, and she threw punches. She pulled her hair, loosening her French braid. The policewoman blocked most of her assault, and she hit back. She bucked Sasha off her, but her gun came loose with the effort.

She saw the woman's Mace before she saw the gun. And she grabbed it, aimed it. Only inches from the cop's eyes, she sprayed a direct and potent stream of repellent. The policewoman let out an ear-piercing scream while swatting at the weaponized canister.

Then she saw the cop's gun on the floor beside Charlotte, who reached for it. "Oh no you don't." She leaped off the policewoman, arriving at the pistol only a moment before the old woman. She'd never handled a gun but figured it was better in her hands than in Charlotte's. And it might make their escape easier. How hard could it be to shoot? As the wailing, screaming cop rolled around, trying to wipe the Mace out of her eyes, she pulled Charlotte to her feet. That wasn't easy. The old woman had gelatin for legs. But others would be on them soon. "Let's go."

#

Frank intended to give only one interview on the RFK matter. As he looked around, he wondered if he had made the right choice in picking this show to do it. Alex Logan's XM studio was a bedroom converted to an office in her seventh-floor apartment. The building was nice, but not overly so, upper middle class with a gate and a pair of guards. Her apartment contained the furnishings of a single woman with the means and the desire to live alone. Her only roommate appeared to be a cat named Mittens, who oversaw the interview from atop a climbing post in a corner of the room.

Ms. Logan was a stunner in the comfort of her home, her studio. Her platinum highlights sparkled like polished silver under overhead lights. Her naturally tan skin had a caramel quality. He wished Rip had come with him to be the cold shower he'd need if this interview heated up, which he thought it had the potential to do. But maybe he thought that because attractive women always seemed more attractive to him after he experienced a break-up.

He wore headphones with a microphone attached while sitting on a comfortable beige couch. A wire connected his headgear to a computer on a desk behind which sat Ms. Logan.

She didn't have headphones, but she spoke into a microphone, which also fed into her computer. "Are you saying this is more about you than your mother?" she asked.

They covered most pertinent details of the RFK assassination earlier in the interview, including the actions of Sirhan Sirhan leading up to and immediately following the shooting and the ways in which co-conspirators might have assisted him. They were now on the subject of the current district attorney, his ambitions and why he ordered Charlotte's arrest. "I'm saying Marco Diaz loves headlines. Did you ever hear of another district attorney appearing on the cover of *Time* magazine?"

"Robert Kennedy –"

"He was the U.S. Attorney General."

"Robert Kennedy is a headline?" She spoke with a sultry throatiness that was perfect for radio. Her listeners probably enjoyed it.

"Oh. Of course, he is. The DA wouldn't arrest an old woman with dementia and hold a press conference about it for any other fifty-year-old murder case." He raised his hands in a stop gesture. "Before you say the Golden State Killer case, whose suspect was arrested a few months ago, remember that was a cold, not a *closed* case. We know who killed RFK. We know he acted alone. They closed the case when they convicted Sirhan. It should stay that way. Unfortunately, I'm also a headline."

"You?"

"I agreed to this interview with you, Alex – can I call you Alex?" She laughed in a way that accented the throatiness of her voice, and he took it as permission to proceed. "I don't see you as like other reporters. That's why I'm sitting here with you now." He expected her to like being separated from the pack, but the only thing she showed him was her refusal to fall for a weak compliment. He doubled down. "They're vultures who've been circling since the DA arrested my mother. They don't want truth. They want a story they can build their careers on. They want to resurrect the pain and the shame brought to this city by a martyr's death. They want what the DA wants, but I think you see this for what it really is: a publicity stunt."

"Serious News *is* the name of my program."

She looked like she expected him to continue. Did she think he'd carry the conversation? The first rule of radio was *no dead air*, and here they were with rigor mortis floating between them.

"So…uh…to get back to your question…this is more about me than my mother because Marco Diaz can't stand to be upstaged, especially by someone working for him. He wanted the Calessi conviction to be a feather in his cap – and it is. But everyone is talking about me."

"They're not talking about you as much as you think."

"Tell that to the reporters who tore up my lawn this morning. You were there."

"They wanted a story. We all did."

"And –"

She offered a disarming smile. "This year marks the fiftieth anniversary of Robert Kennedy's assassination. What could be more appealing to reporters and the public than finally solving the mystery and arresting the perpetrators who helped Sirhan Sirhan kill him exactly fifty years later? *That's* the story. My listeners want to know what you're going to do."

"You want to know what I'm going to do about the Los Angeles County District Attorney invoking the Patriot Act to deprive my elderly, mentally ill mother of her most basic rights? I'm not sure. The first thing I need to do is find out where he's keeping her."

"How will you do that?"

He paused, thinking about his latest request of Rip. Putting an illegal trace on Sasha's phone would be in direct defiance of Marco Diaz, who allowed her to participate in Charlotte's arrest and interrogation. If nothing else, it would say on whose side he came down: Frank's or Marco's. So far, Rip has ignored the request. "I think your listeners can help me," he said. "The police can't haul a screaming old woman out of a nursing home and take her to a hidden location without somebody knowing about it. And they wouldn't bring her to a hidden location for any other reason than to give her the Abu Ghraib treatment."

"You think the district attorney –"

"He said it himself in his press conference. She'll be treated as an enemy combatant. Abu Ghraib or Guantanamo Bay, do you think an elderly woman could survive water boarding?"

She inhaled deeply and held her breath for a long moment before turning her head and exhaling away from the microphone. It bought her time to think, but he wondered if it was also because she cared about what he said. "I've been trying to learn what the DA has on your mother, but the arrest warrant only says conspiracy to commit murder. And my sources downtown tell me they don't know any more than that."

"You said the Authorization for Use of Military Force gives the government wartime authority."

"It does."

"When someone is accused of being a terrorist, when the government says they're a threat to national security, do you think their rights of personal liberty, which are supposed to be guaranteed by the 13th and 14th Amendments to the U.S. Constitution, matter?"

"Yes," she said. "If they're a U.S. citizen."

"How much will they matter if she dies under torture before I can get a judge to agree with us?"

"I do have another source," she said. "It's someone with first-hand information about the original 1968 investigation. They say the DA has your mother on eyewitness testimony."

He shot up in his seat, though the couch cushions did their best to absorb him. He had assumed Marco arrested his mother because of what Sasha claimed she said under hypnosis. The DA wasn't foolish enough to think he could build a case around that. He locked Charlotte away in an undisclosed location so he could milk her for information about a deeper conspiracy. *That* would become his case. What nagged him about all that was why a judge would sign her arrest warrant based on something as flimsy as a "confession" under hypnosis. But now – if he could believe Alex Logan – he realized a judge had cause to sign the warrant. Eyewitness testimony was about as good as it could get. "That's not possible." He no longer saw Alex or her cat. The only thing he could see was a new and vexing conundrum. "How can fifty-year-old eyewitness testimony identify my mother *today*?"

#

Sasha patted the ass although it smelled as if it had gone months without a bath. She decided she at least owed it that. Stolen by her from its pen, the witless beast took her and Charlotte down the mesa, away from the ranch house, over shifting and sliding loose-packed earth *in the dark*. It was an unlikely and remarkable escape, really. She had no way of knowing if they were in the clear. They couldn't see more than twenty feet in any direction. She worried that Charlotte's constant repetition of a statement she committed to memory would attract anyone looking for them.

Charlotte dropped *r* off the ends of words and replaced it with *ah*. "We ah opposed around the world by a monolithic and ruthless conspiracy that relies primarily on covert means fah expanding its sphere of influence. Its mistakes ah buried, not headlined. Its dissentahs ah silenced, not praised. No expenditah is questioned. No rumah is printed. No secret is revealed."

Before their escape, Dr. Fitz told her someone put a lock on Charlotte's memories, creating a "mental lock box" deep in her subconscious. If ibogaine was the chemical hypnosis that could open the box, was that why she now recited those words? Why did she start only minutes after drinking the tea when the drug required a half hour to take effect? She watched the old woman recite away while sitting on a white marker stone. Black letters painted over the white declared the name of the dirt road upon which they found themselves: Sloan Canyon Rd.

"…ruthless conspiracy that relies primarily on covert means fah expanding its sphere of influence. Its mistakes ah buried, not headlined. Its dissentahs ah silenced, not praised. No expenditah is questioned. No rumah is printed. No secret is revealed."

They were haunting words, making her wonder what ruthless conspiracy she referred to and why she spoke with an accent that sounded like it came from Boston. The cadence aspect of her repetition was like a speech meant to motivate people. Given what Charlotte already admitted under hypnosis and Dr. Fitz's mental lock box theory, it didn't take much guessing for her to identify whose speech in a Boston accent she recited from memory.

A pair of headlights approached rapidly. She pulled the policewoman's gun out of her pocket. It was either Glen behind the wheel, or it was someone with nefarious intent. After seeing the first Sloan Canyon Road marker a mile or so back, she

Googled the name on her phone. Her search said they were in the unincorporated community of Castaic. She considered herself fortunate to be out of range of their signal blocker. Her phone fluctuated between one and two bars, but it was enough for her to put a call through to Glen. He would've really had to bury the gas pedal to get here so quickly, though. And she never knew him to do that.

"Its dissentahs ah silenced, not praised. No expenditah is questioned. No rumah is printed. No secret is –" For the first time since leaving the ranch house, Charlotte took notice of something other than the memory she kept repeating. Her good eye locked on the car and the person behind its wheel; twenty feet away, fifteen feet. Her back straightened.

The ass made its braying sound, somewhat like *hee-haw*, as the car shortened its distance to less than ten feet away. Recognizing it as Glen's powder blue 1987 Buick Regal, she felt awash in relief. The car was his pride and joy. He drove it to every car show that would have him. But he didn't drive it now. He was in the passenger seat with the window down. The vehicle came to a skidding stop beside her. The driver looked almost too big to fit behind the wheel, though the car was spacious. But she didn't need his size, his scars or his neck tattoo to identify him, even in the darkened night. Her eyes fell on Glen as she wore an intense look of frightened surprise. Her finger caressed the pistol's trigger.

"I'll explain it to you on the road," Glen said.

Trevor disembarked the vehicle on the driver's side. He went to his grandmother and lifted her off her perch, putting a smile on the non-paralyzed half of her face.

Glen added, "You might even laugh."

CHAPTER 13

Frank had to admit Rip came through for him, but everything else seemed suspicious. Rip said Sasha's phone pinged from a chemical warehouse in Redlands. As if that wasn't enough, it was the middle of the night. To his credit, he warned Frank against going alone. To his discredit, he refused to join him, saying it would tip Marco off to what he had done for him.

He didn't know if Sasha was still with his mother. He didn't know if the Redlands warehouse was Charlotte's Abu Ghraib. It seemed odd that the phone would ping now after sending out no signal in the two days since Charlotte's arrest. Or maybe it was that Rip just now decided to honor his request for a trace. He crept toward a large concrete block building because it was the only structure in the area likely to hold his mother. The other structures were shacks with corrugated metal sides or trailers sitting on flat tires. He could also see through grime-caked windows that lights burned dimly inside it. He didn't know what he'd do if he found Charlotte being tortured for information. He didn't have a gun, but he knew the law. He was sure it was on his side. And he knew how to threaten her captors with it.

To his surprise, the door flew open, and Sasha bolted toward him as if the warehouse spit her out. She clutched something. For all he knew, it was a baton she intended to swing at him. He raised his hands defensively and jumped behind one of several motorcycles parked nearby.

She stopped abruptly, looking confused by his actions.

He stepped out from behind the bike. "Do you have Charlotte in there? What are you doing to her?"

"Doing to her? I –" She threw the object in her hand. It opened a tad, fluttering in the air but not so much that he couldn't catch it. It was a roll of papers. She watched him open it.

What am I supposed to make of this? Three pieces of paper, each containing an artist's sketch of a man's face, the pages looked back at him.

"They drugged your mother before I could save her. Trevor's friend drew those off what she said during one of her flashbacks."

He didn't wait for her to say more. All he could think was that they had drugged his mother. What kind of drug? He charged through the building's open door, realizing too late that it probably wasn't his wisest move. A powerful chemical scent slapped his face the moment he entered. He felt it in his eyes and his nose, but his sight adjusted quickly. He saw vats and barrels aplenty. Many of the barrels were metal and coated with rust. Weak lights hanging from the ceiling buzzed with electricity, and shadows covered much of the floor space – 3,000 square feet by his estimation. The gun-toting men he saw milling around gave him pause. Then he saw his mother, sitting and shaking in a wheelchair. One obnoxiously large man watched over her. He didn't appear to have a weapon, and it looked like he didn't need it. And there was Glen Pierce, Sasha's business partner, standing near Charlotte and looking uncomfortably out of place.

No one stopped Frank from running up to his mother. It seemed as if they expected him to. Her shakes were abrupt and sharp, in a herky-jerky motion. "Mom?" He turned to Glen. "What's wrong with her?"

"I told you." Sasha marched through the entranceway. "They gave her something called ibogaine. It's supposed to open up memories, put her in the past and make her relive it."

"Why is she shaking?" He stuffed the sketches into his pocket and grabbed Charlotte's forearms. Her muscles tightened in his grip and relaxed, tightened again.

Glen said, "That drug can have serious side-effects for someone in her condition."

"Like what?"

"It has killed people who have a history of cardiac conditions and strokes." Sasha had a softer expression now, empathetic even. "I've been – we've been – watching her closely."

"My mother had a stroke."

Glen nodded. "If fatalities occur, they're usually within the first seventy-six hours."

"There's also a chance it could exacerbate her dementia," said Sasha.

He wanted to lash out, but where? And at who? Sasha said she saved her, implying she broke her out of custody. If true, he couldn't take her to a hospital. He felt energy coursing through her thin arms, making her muscles spasm. She normally fluctuated between lucid and not-so-lucid moments, but with the drug, he had no way of knowing what went on in her head. Her lips moved. He heard her mumbling, but he couldn't understand her.

"It's been about thirty hours since she drank it," said Sasha. "Too late to expel the drug through vomiting."

"Did you try when it wasn't too late?"

Fire flashed in Sasha's eyes. "I did everything I could."

Then he caught another surprise. It shouldn't have surprised him. He should've figured it out when Sasha told him how the sketches came to be. But he saw it now. Rather, he saw *him*.

Trevor approached with his typically unflappable confidence. "It's good you're here. Now *you* can take what we get to the grand jury, make them leave Nana alone." He went up to his Nana and kissed her forehead. "If this gets too intense, The Bus can wheel you outside."

"If what gets too intense?" He turned to Sasha. "Who are these men?" She deferred to Trevor, who returned to the center of the warehouse. Frank looked back at the big man standing to Charlotte's left. An Italian, he carried a hundred pounds of unnecessary flab on his six-foot frame. Trevor called him The Bus...*The Bus.* Frank's eyes shot wide. Gus "The Bus" Marino was a reputed mobster. He'd seen him in surveillance photos of the Calessi mob.

"Let go ah me," croaked an aged but authoritative voice.

Frank spun around, finding Trevor near a cylindrical vat with a yellow hazard sticker plastered to its side. He also saw an old man with a cane entering from the back of the warehouse under the escort of four tough-acting, Italian-looking thugs. One of the Italians pushed a wheelchair behind him. The old man stopped to strike the chair with his cane. "I ain't in no Special Olympics. Get away."

Trevor stepped up to him. "Robert Kennedy's sister founded the Special Olympics."

The elderly man leaned back to look up at him. Curiosity forced Frank to wander closer, and it felt as if his heart stopped when he saw the man's face: olive skin with liver spots, narrow bone structure, a crooked nose and missing teeth. He blurted out. "That's Joseph Provenzano!" Behind him, the wheelchair bounced as Charlotte squirmed erratically. She made popping sounds with her mouth, like she needed saliva but couldn't produce it. She clearly knew the old man.

Joseph Provenzano was the alleged boss of the largest Mafia consortium in the Southwestern United States. He reportedly united as many as eight, possibly more, criminal enterprises under one umbrella. His empire was said to be so vast and so well-hidden that it reached almost mythical status among law enforcement. "He's supposed to be dead," said Frank. "Everybody thinks he died years ago."

An extra tall Italian emerged from the shadows to join Trevor. He stood six foot eight with broad shoulders and big arms, but his face looked emaciated. "Hello, Mr. Provenzano."

Provenzano strained even more to look up at him. It took a few moments for him to recognize the tall man. When he did, he jerked his cane up and whacked him in the groin. The tall man buckled over, and Provenzano took a swing at his head. But

Trevor caught it.

The tall man wanted to strike back, but a look from Trevor stayed him. And he waddled away. Watching this, Frank guessed at the backstory that brought them all here. Joseph Provenzano was too old to handle the day-to-day management of any enterprise, but he had loyal lieutenants to do it for him. He probably had one or two of these lieutenants poised to seize Vincent Calessi's operation, which Frank rendered leaderless with his recent courtroom triumph. Since The Bus and most of the others in the warehouse appeared to be Calessi, the abduction of Provenzano served them in two ways. It eliminated a powerful threat to their organization, and it gave them something valuable to offer Vincent Calessi's chosen successor. What he couldn't figure out was how Trevor fit into all this and why the mobsters put him in charge. "This is a huge mistake," he told his son. "You don't mess with these people. You don't mess with *him*."

Trevor laughed off the warning. With a push that required no effort on his part, he deposited Provenzano in the wheelchair. "I think you can tell me what I need to know."

As the old man settled into his seat, Trevor seemed to hold all the cards. But the Mafioso assumed a sort of regality in the wheelchair, a king on his throne. "What do you want to know?"

Frank blurted out, "Did the mob kill Bobby Kennedy?" He surprised himself with the question, especially after warning his son about *these people*. He honestly didn't know where that came from.

The old man mocked him with a laugh, but his icy eyes went to the other person in a wheelchair. He studied her for a long moment, and she didn't meet his gaze. "I'll be damned." He wheeled toward her as if no one else mattered. Each rotation of his rolling chair made her more uncomfortable. She squirmed. She quivered. By the time his footrests stopped near hers, Charlotte was a vibrating mess. He took delight in her unease, leaning toward her. "I liked your nose better before you fixed it."

Her tongue swam around her mouth, finally finding its groove. "Its...uh, its mist...uh...mistakes ah buried, not

headlined. Its dissent…its dissentahs ah silenced, not praised."
She pressed her lips so tightly together it looked like they'd burst
from the pressure.

Provenzano glanced at Trevor. "The years ain't been kind
to her."

That inflated the big man, and his fist formed a ball.
Frank rushed forward, putting himself between Trevor and the
mobster. It looked for a moment like his son might hit him, but
Trevor dropped his hand.

"She's been repeating that since she ingested the drug,"
said Sasha.

Provenzano turned to Frank, tapped his nose. "The family
beak don't look so good on you, Mr. Prosecutor. Guess your sister
would'a worn it better."

Frank had been thinking about the strange thing his
mother said with a bizarre accent until he heard *that*. His eyes shot
to Sasha – an involuntary reaction. She didn't learn his dreaded
secret from his mother's hypnotism, as he feared. Would she
hear it now from this old mobster's cracked and black-spotted
lips? How did the old man know anything about him or his sister
unless he knew their mother way back then?

Trevor told The Bus, "Take her out of here." With Charlotte
jerking about and mumbling memorized words, the overweight
mobster wheeled her out the front door.

Provenzano turned his chair with a scoff and rolled away,
speaking over his shoulder. "Like the federal fairy said, there
ain't no mob. That means I know nothin' about who killed the
Kennedy brothers. May they rest in peace."

Frank only asked about one of the Kennedys. Did
Provenzano think their two deaths were related? And the *federal
fairy* was J. Edgar Hoover – a reference to his closet homosexuality.
Hoover and the FBI spent years denying the mob's existence.
It was largely through the efforts of Attorney General Bobby
Kennedy that the federal government took an active interest in
the Mafia. He recalled that from the research Rip gave him.

"It wouldn't do much good torturing you," said Trevor.

"You're almost dead."

"True." The old man didn't stop his chair.

"But I hear your great-granddaughter Marissa is your favorite."

#

A small trolley rode along an I-beam in the ceiling of the warehouse. Frank's interest in the trolley went only as far as what it transported, which was a cylindrical cage that dangled from the bottom of the trolley by a steel cable. A pretty, dark-haired teenage girl was in the cage. Hands bound behind her back, she screamed into a mouth gag.

Joseph Provenzano and his wheelchair were on the top landing of a mobile staircase, eye-level with the cage as it drifted to a stop directly above the cylindrical vat with a hazard sticker. The girl's cage could fit as easily into the vat as a hand fit into a glove.

"This is fluoroantimonic acid." Trevor tapped the vat while looking up at the mobster. "The strongest superacid in the world, it's twenty quintillion times stronger than one hundred percent pure sulfuric acid. Glass, iron, steel, bone, it dissolves everything. The only substance that can contain it is Teflon. But you know that. We stole it from you."

Provenzano growled. "Boy, I will kill you."

"Tell us about Robert Kennedy's assassination."

"I already did."

Receiving a glance from Trevor, the tall mobster (who still walked funny after that groin strike) pressed a button on a remote, which caused the overhead trolley to lower the cage to the vat. The girl screeched into her gag as the bottom of her enclosure disappeared into the acid. She leaped into a side split with her sneakers pressed against bars to her right and left.

"I'll kill everyone in your family," roared the Mafioso. "Starting with your whore grandmother."

Trevor let the bottom of the cage linger in its submersion. Then he nodded to the tall man, who pressed a different button. The cage came out of the acid, stopped and hovered over it.

Greenish-brown fluid oozed off the cage. The metal that had been dunked looked discolored and weakened. Entire chunks were gone, leaving jagged edges. The girl tentatively lowered her foot to stand on the bottom of the cage, but she stabbed through, sending pieces of metal into the vat below. "You can keep threatening me," said Trevor. "Or you can tell me what I want to know."

Provenzano grumbled. "It don't matter anyway. They're all dead." He hesitated, glanced at Frank, then Trevor. "Marcello, Trafficante, Rosselli and Giancana wanted Bobby gone. He went after them as AG. It would've been the end of them if he moved into the White House."

Rip's research covered this too. Carlos Marcello, Santo Trafficante, Johnny Rosselli and Sam Giancana were the most powerful mob figures of their day. They targeted Robert Kennedy when he was the U.S. Attorney General because he prosecuted them with a vengeance. People had long speculated they also killed President Kennedy in order to stop Bobby's investigations. "Tell us something we don't know." Everyone looked at him. And he looked at the caged girl. *What am I doing? Am I a part of this madness?*

"Hoffa, working for Marcello and Trafficante, took out contracts on Bobby in '62, '67 and again in '68," said Provenzano. "Did you know that?"

"Yes."

Trevor gestured to the tall man, and the cage slowly resumed its descent. The girl again screamed into her gag, trying to climb higher up the bars, having little success.

"Issa!" Provenzano slid forward in his chair, gripping the railing of the staircase.

Trevor halted the cage with another gesture. "Issa is short for Marissa? I like that."

The old man looked at Frank. "Are you gonna let this happen, *Deputy District Attorney*?"

"I quit the DA's office when they arrested my mother for a crime she didn't commit."

"Didn't commit?" Provenzano scoffed, but concern for his favorite great-granddaughter outweighed his desire to debate. He ground what was left of his teeth. "Frank Donneroummas was the go-between for Johnny Rosselli and Sirhan Sirhan."

Frank knew his shock over the old man's revelation showed, but he didn't care. *That's a direct link from mobster Johnny Rosselli to RFK's killer. Rosselli and Sirhan already shared a lawyer, Grant Cooper, who defended them at the same time in two unrelated cases in 1969.*

"Pull that thing up," said Provenzano. "She can't hold on forever."

Trevor shook his head. "Not till we hear more about Johnny Rosselli."

Sasha crept up to Frank. "Maybe you shouldn't participate in this." Her glare was as accusatorial as any he'd ever received.

"Handsome Johnny was Momo's man in L.A. and Vegas." Provenzano's voice grew hoarser by the moment. "Like all of them, he had a hard-on for the Kennedys."

Momo was a nickname for Sam Giancana, just as Handsome Johnny was for Rosselli. It was more information from Rip. He wondered what his friend would do in a situation like this. Would he let this innocent girl suffer at the hands of his son if it served the cause of justice? "No," he yelled at Trevor. "We have enough. That Donneroummas stuff can cast serious doubt on Nana's culpability."

"How?"

"The mob put Sirhan up to it. It's a straight line of conspiracy. Nana's no mobster."

"This wrinkly fossil has more to tell us."

The girl in the cage slipped and caught herself. She cried into her gag, blinked rapidly against the fumes emanating from the vat beneath her.

He needed to act quickly, or the girl would perish. Her death could easily become the catalyst for a mob war on the streets of L.A. "I can tell you what you need to know about Johnny Rosselli. He had the same lawyer as Sirhan at the same time. The lawyer was Grant Cooper, and while he was defending Sirhan for murdering Kennedy, he was put under indictment for obtaining stolen grand jury transcripts in Rosselli's trial."

That surprised Trevor. Others looked similarly surprised. A few laughed.

"I'll explain it to the grand jury," he added. "Frank Donneroummas could be our ace in the hole, connecting Sirhan to Johnny Rosselli and the Chicago Outfit."

"Is Donneroummas still alive?"

"I don't...this is the first I've heard of him." He looked at Provenzano.

The Mafioso's posture changed to one that bore fresh confidence. "I ain't seen him in a long time. But I know where to start looking."

"How 'bout you tell us where?" said Trevor.

The girl slid toward the acid, and she howled into her gag.

"Move her now," said Provenzano.

The girl whined loudly as she slid again. Eighteen inches separated her from the bottom of the cage, and it was less than a foot beyond that to the deadly acid.

"Use your head," Frank told his son. "If Donneroummas is alive and we can get him to testify, we can exonerate Nana. You don't have to hurt Marissa."

Trevor's indecision lingered. He obviously wanted to drag this out, and that said a lot about him. But with the girl nearing the end of her resistance, he turned to the tall man.

A female voice shrieked from the back door. "Frank Donaroma is dust. Ashes to ashes."

Trevor spun, and Frank turned. All eyes went to Charlotte as she rolled into the room, followed by her overweight guardian. "I'm sorry," said The Bus. "She sweet-talked me."

"Nana." Trevor spoke with a softened tone. "What do you know of Donneroummas?"

"We had fun, Diamond Joe." She looked at Provenzano. "You and Dona were crazy grease balls. Remember riding ponies bare-ass on that dried up riverbed?"

"I think you mean bareback," said Trevor.

She shook her head. "Naked as the day we were born."

The lawyer in Frank wanted to muzzle his client. But as a son, he needed to hear her out. Time outside the warehouse had transformed her. No longer a quivering mess, she was self-confident, bold even. Was schizophrenia a side-effect of ibogaine intoxication? More upsetting, however, was what she said. She put herself with the mobsters, riding ponies. Did they also ride with Sirhan? That could very well make her a conspirator.

"I told you she was a whore," said Provenzano.

Trevor started for the old man again, his fists like hammers. But a gagged scream from Marissa changed everything. She lost her grip, and her right foot slipped. She fell, hitting the corroded bottom of the cage with the side of her hip.

"Issa!" Provenzano stretched out of his chair, over the rail, reaching with both arms.

Frank shot forward, hitting the vat with all the force he could muster. Acid splashed, and the vat jolted. It moved. His legs kept churning. Marissa crashed through the bottom of the cage, still screaming. He heard her coming at him. He had to move the vat out from under her, but it was heavy. It didn't slide so much as it tilted.

An instant before the girl made impact, he felt a force rock the vat. It was a force that could only come from a man of Trevor's size and strength. It drove the container past the tipping point. Marissa landed on Frank, and they collapsed to the floor. Momentum toppled the vat into the mobile staircase, which rolled back. The sudden jolt to the stairs threw an already off-balance Provenzano over the railing. His yell was brief but loud as he landed in the world's most corrosive acid spilling from the top of the overturned Teflon vat. There was nothing the elderly mobster could do to avoid taking the plunge. He wailed. He writhed. Trevor clung to the vat, looking disoriented.

The frantic girl leaped off Frank, and Sasha pulled her to safety. He couldn't waste any time either. The splashing acid was about to reach him. He scrambled to his feet. All around him,

Provenzano's fate threw the mobsters into a self-saving frenzy. They fled the toxic bath with all the speed they could muster. Even The Bus managed to move his oversized bulk. Trevor found safety by staying atop the overturned Teflon vat – the only object immune to the acid's appetite.

Frank saw his mother slipping back into her disorientation. He rushed up and spun her chair so fast she almost fell out of it. In a full run, he pushed her out the door. He heard shouts, crashing and the cries of old Provenzano behind him. He hoped Sasha got out, but he didn't look for her because…well…he couldn't help but feel this was all somehow her fault.

CHAPTER 14

Griffith Park, Los Angeles, California. July 1967

Chasing Francis is a full-time job now that he's discovered bipedalism. And Charlotte is starting to think it wasn't such a great idea to have their first family outing be at a love-in. The boy's latest object of interest is a hipster in a military jacket. The man is the embodiment of a cartoon character with plastic toy planes on the epaulettes of his jacket, homemade medals and an Army enlisted service cap. Pete intervenes before he can reach the man, scooping him up, but it puts him toe-to-toe with the hipster. "What kind of abomination are you?" he asks.

"General Wastemoreland at my service."

"At *your* service?"

"That's right, soldier."

"I am a soldier," says Pete. "California National Guard. General *West*moreland is the U.S. commander in South Vietnam, a man of honor."

They talked about this – she and Pete, and he promised he wouldn't get into it with war protestors. Now she has to get involved. Reluctantly, she leaves Bobbi on the blanket (which she tie-dyed for this occasion) to squirm between Pete and the protestor, who smells of whiskey. "Thank you for keeping us safe, General." She tugs Pete's arm, but he's too big to move.

"Flower power is fine and dandy," says Pete. "But we *respect* our leaders."

"Daddy wants to ruin family time," she tells their son.

Pete ignores her, his eyes still on the false general, so she takes the boy from him and marches back to the blanket. "I don't know how much of this I can take. I really don't."

No sooner does she plant Francis when Bobbi finds her own pretend general. This one is middle aged and dressed like Wastemoreland with a military jacket adorned with replica medals, toy planes and plastic missiles. He chants, "World trade, not world war!" Noticing Bobbi, he whips a chocolate bar out of his pocket. "I'm General Hershey Bar. What's your name?"

Charlotte rushes toward them, but the blanket trips her up, causing her to nearly collide with the general.

He pulls back. "There's no acid in my candy, young lady. You'll have to move along."

"This is my daughter."

A slow smile forms on his wrinkled face. "Love the world. Don't bomb it." He hands her the candy bar, makes an about-face, and he marches off.

His march resembles a waddle, making her chuckle. He's harmless, but she tosses the candy anyway. She takes Bobbi by the hand and leads her back to the blanket. But she stops before reaching it, staring in dumb amazement. Pete and Wastemoreland walk away from her, peacefully, to a tent where hippies dance, shake maracas and puff away on happy herb. *Is he going to spark grass with them? Johnny Law getting high with anti-establishment hippies?* She can't believe his hypocrisy, but isn't that why she insisted they come here? Love-ins are about putting aside differences. It's what she asked him to do. *Good. Good for him.* She watches Francis hobble after his daddy. And a little flame of pride lights her up. *This family thing…it's a groovy thing.* She and Bobbi plant their butts on the blanket.

Her warm and fuzzy feeling doesn't last long. Beyond Pete, Francis and the tent crowd, she sees an odd occupation in the tree-line bordering the park. It looks to her like a couple dozen pigs – not the oink, oink kind. They're aiming their binoculars at the Beautiful People, and they have wagons ready to haul everyone to the pokey. Pete must've told her a thousand times that the fuzz only wants to keep the peace, but it doesn't look like that's what these "peace-keepers" have in mind. *Things are about to get weird, not the good kind of weird.*

She swiftly realizes that it's even worse than she imagined. Matthew is with the pigs. Matthew! She watches him go from cop to cop, talking to them like they're old friends. He's fifty yards away, but there's no mistaking it's him. Did she enter *The Twilight Zone*? Matthew's gone all law and order while Pete is out on the hippie fringe? Do-do-do-do. Do-do-do-do.

"What's the matter with her?" Pete appears only feet away from her. How did he arrive without her seeing him? He's pointing at Bobbi while a chick in a slutty outfit stands beside him, holding Frankie's hand.

She didn't notice until now that her daughter is crying beside her. Matthew must've really thrown her. "Nothing. Uh, it's nothing. She's hungry." As she digs into her bag for a spoon and applesauce, she gives the slut a look over. "Who are you?"

"Rose."

Pete smiles, and he points at Francis. "We considered naming him Rosey."

"Did we?" She slides a spoonful of sauce into her daughter's mouth.

Ignoring her question, he explains, "Rose has a lead on some work for me."

"I have a lead for you, too. Go back to the garage."

He frowns, turns to Rose. "I'm more than a greaser. I mean...I know good rubber and all. I make an engine purr, but my skills are –"

She'd love to hear him make an ass of himself in front of the floozy, but she can't stop glancing at the tree-line. The love-in is going to go south quick. It'll be worse for her because of Matt and Pete and all that. What's his game? Beach barker to establishmentarian, he's a mystery she's got to figure out. He's complex where Pete is a lunkhead, loveable at times.

"I have a friend," says Rose. "Who has a friend who has just the right job for you."

"Char, are you listening?" Seeing that she's not, he moves closer to Rose.

"Hunky and brainy." Rose gives his bicep a squeeze. "Diamond Joe will put you to work real fast."

Charlotte stands. "Diamond Joe?"

"You *are* listening." His inebriated tongue lingers on the *s* sounds in his words. "She says the man handles everything from imports to racetracks."

"I know of him." She steps up to Rose, takes Francis's hand from her. The woman's patchouli is a tad too much. "What name do you use on stage? Little Egypt?"

Pete's eyes widen on his new female friend. "You're a hoochie coochie girl?"

Rose starts to defend her honor, but she loses out to the sounds of a gagging child. Spinning around, Charlotte finds the spoon's handle sticking out of Bobbi's mouth. The utensil is partway down her throat. Like flags on an airstrip, the child waves her arms. And Charlotte makes an emergency landing on the blanket, tilts Bobbi's head back and grabs the handle.

Pete is swiftly by her side. "Not too fast, too hard. You'll hurt her." He reaches to help.

"I got it." With all care possible, she tries to ease the spoon out. But it catches. Bobbi chokes as her throat makes horrible slurping sounds. Slimy spit coats Charlotte's fingers. The saliva has nowhere to go but to puddle around the spoon lodged in her throat.

"She's turning colors," Pete yells. "She can't breathe!"

In the pool of spit in the back of her daughter's mouth, she can see the neck of the spoon touching the flap of flesh that guards the entranceway to her throat. The child's eyes are wide, filled with water and desperate, but pivoting. "Hold on, baby!" She pulls more forcefully.

Whistles shriek from the tree-line. Rose yells, "Cops!" Engines bawl as they're called to action. Angry men yell.

The sounds of alarm cause her to jolt, and the sudden movement jerks the spoon out of Bobbi's mouth. No flesh comes with it, but there's blood – lots of it, and it mixes with the puddle of saliva. The child belches onto the blanket. She turns her coughing daughter toward her. "Are you okay? Are you hurt? Say something."

Pigs and paddy wagons swarm out of the forest while clubs swing through the air. The cops bark commands to hippies. They're called *blue meanies* for a reason. They show no patience and no compassion as they neuter the flower power. The scene is like a John Wayne flick with a wrathful cavalry raiding a village full of peaceful Indians. It takes only moments for everything to become violently furious.

Pete yanks Bobbi from her mother's embrace, holding her to his chest as she shakes with fear and hacks from her choking. "Grab our stuff." He stands, takes his son's hand. "Let's go!"

Charlotte sets to work on the blanket, rolling it up. She snatches their bags. The ground rumbles, and she hears the sounds of disarray grow louder as they come toward her. Looking up and looking around, she sees a stampede of hippies. People are zigging and zagging. They're nothing short of erratic. Her family's belongings are just that, she realizes – belongings. *Forget it.* She abandons the things, runs after Pete and the kids.

Pete walks/runs toward the park exit with Bobbi in one arm and Francis's hand in his other hand. He's trying not to alarm the kids, but alcohol and grass have compromised his balance. She maneuvers between him and their son, steadying him while taking the boy's hand. As a family, they move together, toward safety and away from the madness of Griffith Park. But Pete stops abruptly.

"What are – don't stop!" She follows the direction of his gaze, and she feels her heart sink. *Oh no.* His eyes lock on no one and nothing but Matthew, who grabs Wastemoreland by the jacket and flips him to the ground while a pig beats him with a baton.

Everything around them may be fast and chaotic, but Pete turns to her slowly. "What is *he* doing here?" It's more of an accusation than a question.

#

2018

Frank's Camry turned out to be both his escape pod and his torture chamber. He loaded his mother and her chair into the car and fled the madness of the warehouse. They hopped on the Ten (Interstate 10). When it brought them to State Route 62, they took the opportunity to head toward Joshua Tree National Park. Then his torture started. Charlotte's body tremors came back, and he couldn't stop them. Her good eye wandered around like it was lost, and she struggled to swallow in a sort of gagging reflex. Where could they go, and to what doctor could he take her when law enforcement *and* Provenzano and Calessi mobsters searched for them? There was also Trevor, who was unpredictable in all things except the certainty that he'd want his beloved Nana back. As much as he wanted to believe otherwise, he knew Trevor was in charge back there. He would've had to have been in the mob for quite some time for that to happen. And it was the *Calessi* mob. Was Trevor, the mobster, now stepping up to fill Vincent Calessi's vacated position?

State Route 62 was less populated than the Ten, though neither was too active at five in the morning with the sun threatening to rise. Basing his calculation on what Sasha said, he figured about thirty-four hours had passed since Charlotte's drugging. That left him another forty-two hours – almost two more days – to worry about her intoxication turning fatal. In the faint glimmer cast by the approaching dawn, he could see her trying to speak but managing to only mumble. Rather than tax her with questions about Trevor's mob activities or the RFK assassination, he concentrated on the road leading them into the Little San Bernardino Mountains. All around them, nature encroached upon civilization. He thought it a nice departure from the opposite encroachment he found in the city. He hoped it would bring her peace.

Then there was Sasha. He had no peace when he thought of her. There was a real possibility that she, like Trevor, was a part of the Calessi crime group. If so, it wasn't a coincidence that she started dating him while he was the lead prosecutor in the Vincent Calessi trial. Could Mr. Calessi's lawyers use that as a basis for their appeal? Perhaps, though his relationship with Sasha didn't affect the outcome of the original trial. Vincent was still convicted. But it would severely tarnish Frank's reputation – any more than his son now leading the mob (*that* was grounds for an appeal) or his mother being arrested as an RFK conspirator? He felt a migraine coming on, though he'd never had one and didn't know what they felt like.

Charlotte's mumbling grew louder, more understandable. "Its dissentahs ah silenced, not praised. No expenditah is questioned. No rumah is printed. No secret is revealed." She paused, but like a recording playing on a continuous loop, she resumed. "We ah opposed around the world by a monolithic and ruthless conspiracy that relies primarily on covert means fah expanding its sphere of influence. Its mistakes ah buried, not headlined. Its dissentahs ah –"

His phone sounded off from his back pocket. He didn't hear it initially. Then he did. His first thought was that it was Trevor. Second thought was Sasha. He wouldn't answer in either case, but a look at the face of the device told him he was wrong on both counts. He answered, "I guess you're wondering how it turned out."

"I don't have to wonder," said Rip. "The DA called me, and the media is all over it. Are you okay?"

He hesitated, wondering how much he should say. And he tried to tune out Charlotte's repetitive recitation.

"Redlands P.D. caught Calessi soldiers fleeing the scene of the crime." Rip paused. "And the crime scene…did you see it?"

"Did I see the crime scene?"

"Joseph Provenzano with a vat of acid dumped on him. There was just enough of his face left to make a positive identification. Did you see them do it?"

"I think this is a case of the less you know, the better."

"Oh, I told you. Wait. What is that? Do you have someone with you?"

He pressed the phone to his chest, turned to his mother. But it wasn't like he could shut her up. She kept saying the same thing with the same accent, oblivious to everything around her.

"That's Charlotte," said Rip. "You got her! Are you going to bring her in?"

No, I'm not. Questions like that made him hesitant to give Rip back his complete trust.

"What's she saying?" asked Rip. "Give her the phone. I want to hear what she's saying?"

Because he couldn't give Rip back his complete trust, something else occurred to him. This call, monitored by Marco, could be pinpointing his location. "I can't talk to you right now."

"Hold on. I recognize it. She's reciting a speech President Kennedy gave a few months before his assassination. Conspiracy buffs have been referencing it for years."

His eyes became saucers, but all he said was, "Look after Tippy, will ya? I might be gone for a while."

#

Sasha didn't consider herself a princess, but the flophouse they fled to was below her standards. Rent-by-the-hour rooms and carpets that smelled of urine and other foul aromas, she didn't want to touch anything for fear of catching a disease that even penicillin couldn't cure. Glen, on the other hand, didn't seem to mind their surroundings. He was more interested in the phone call he made while sitting on the bed.

She opened the door to air the room out and inserted a metal chair from the table under its handle to hold it open. She stepped out onto the balcony. At least she could breathe from there. The sun started the day behind a haze, but she didn't see anyone responding to it. She counted only seven vehicles in the parking lot, three of which were motorcycles. There was mostly dust, dirt, sage brush and tumbleweed across the road from their motel. She guessed they were somewhere between Anza and La Quinta, though she couldn't be certain because they fled the Redlands warehouse in the dark of the night. And she rode bitch on the back of Trevor's bike with the wind buffeting her face and no helmet or facemask to protect her.   As she thought about it – and she'd been doing that a lot, she couldn't decide which pained her more: Frank implying she hurt his mother or him blaming her for not doing enough to help her. *I saved her, you jerk. And I didn't have to give you those drawings.*

She saw Trevor burst forth from the top of a flight of stairs to arrive on the balcony. He stormed toward her at a pace that made her want to run away from him. But she had nowhere to go and no way to get there unless she stole his bike. His course took him into the room. As he passed her, he said, "Come in here." He pulled the chair away to let the door close.

"It stinks." But she followed him because he didn't seem in a mood to argue.

He immediately went to Glen, yanking the phone out of his hand. "They could be tracking our phones." He threw it on the floor and crushed it beneath his heal.

Fury flashed across Glen's aged face. His bum hip kept him on the bed, but he still stood up to the big man by wearing a defiant look. "That was The Clipper."

Trevor's body language spoke a thousand words of surprise. He stepped back, looked at the destroyed phone, and he looked back at Glen. His skin turned a shade paler.

"Who's The Clipper?" she asked.

"The man who wants to meet you," said Glen. "I was making the arrangements." He had nothing but rebuke in his eyes as he looked back at Trevor.

CHAPTER 15

Twentynine Palms, California should have been called Twentynine Murals. Every street seemed to have a building with a mural painted on it. Frank saw his mother's body tremors decrease in proportion to how much she concentrated on the works of art. He'd take her to a motel later where they could hide until he decided what to do next. Until then, he enjoyed the positive effect the drawings had on her. That didn't mean his fears subsided. Why did she recite an ominous speech made by President Kennedy before he died?

He noticed two overweight men sitting outside a pizza joint across the street, watching them with more than casual interest. Maybe it was his recent issues with the mob and them being outside an Italian eatery while looking Italian, but they made him nervous. He rolled his mother's wheelchair into an empty lot to get away from them. It was dried and dusty, with a military mural painted on one of the neighboring buildings. The artwork paid tribute to Operation Iraqi Freedom, but most of the scenes it depicted looked like they could have come from any modern American war. He thought his mother liked it as much as he did until he saw her shaking. He rushed around the chair to face her. With her head jerking about, her good eye refused to leave the painting, and her normally misbehaving eye went along for company. "The dominos," she said. "We can't let the dominos fall."

He turned to the mural, but the only thing he could see

falling was the statue of Saddam Hussein when the U.S. military captured Baghdad. "What do you mean, Mom?"

"China, Korea, Viet-Nam, Laos…the dominos."

"Are you talking about the domino theory?"

"My brother is in Viet-Nam," she said. "His guts spread over an acre."

He stepped back. "I didn't know that."

"You don't know anything." She used her feet to turn her chair away from the mural.

Sasha said they gave her ibogaine to make her relive the past, and in one of her episodes, she described what she saw well enough for someone to draw sketches of the people she envisioned. If she was back in her past now, maybe she could identify the people in the drawings. He pulled the sketches out of his pocket, where they'd been since Redlands. The first drawing depicted a man with a fat face, hair parted on the side, horn-rimmed glasses and a thick beard that hugged his jawline. "Who is this?"

She avoided looking at it.

Moving the paper so it would be before her eyes regardless of where her head went, he pressed on with his questions. "Is this your brother? The one killed in Vietnam?"

"Big mouth in the Monkey Trial." She waved her hands to get the sketch out of her face.

The only monkey trial he knew of was the 1925 Scopes Trial in which a high school teacher was arrested and tried for teaching evolution in a public school. He couldn't imagine it had anything to do with the RFK case, so he moved on to the next sketch. It featured a man with an oval face, high forehead and bushy brows. "How about this man?"

"Pastor Pimp. I don't want to play this game anymore." She turned more to the left, her back now facing the military mural.

He followed her. "Pastor Pimp is a preacher? Was he…is he a pervert? Did he use religion to get girls to sleep with him?"

"My head hurts."

"I know." He could see pain even in the slack side of her face, which he found strange considering it was stroke-paralyzed. "But you have to try, Mom. This is important."

"Leave me alone." She swatted him away. In the motion, her hand punched through the papers, tearing them in two, severing the sketches.

"No!" He inspected the damage, desperately trying to put the pages back together. They were the only potentially useful things her memory produced thus far. The sketch he hadn't yet shown her, which depicted a bald man with hair semi-encircling his head, fared better than the other two. Its rip was along the side. The others had been split through the center of the drawings. "Do you want to be convicted? Tell me, and I won't waste any more of my time."

"You always waste time."

"They're going to go federal with this," he told his mother. "Your only hope is to tell me what you know."

She put her head in her hands, groaning.

He'd seen her do that before – often times, when he was young and she found him irritating. "Okay, Mom." He returned the papers to his pocket. "Fine, just fine."

She rubbed her temples, still groaning.

"At least tell me this. You said you went horseback riding with Joseph Provenzano and Frank Donneroummas. I need to know if Sirhan Sirhan was with you. Do you remember that? He was a little man training to be a jockey. He loved horses."

"He was a stable boy."

"That's right. Did Provenzano and Donneroummas introduce you to him?"

"Don't be stupid. Everybody knows he shoveled horse shit. It's on the news."

"That's not stupid. Stupid is thinking I can patch things up with you when we've never had anything to patch up." He spun away from her. He'd regret that outburst later. He knew it. But he had more to say – like how he put his life on hold to help her when she's been nothing but dismissive of him, like she always has been. He was about to unload on her again when he saw the Italians coming toward them. The sweat on their faces told him they weren't out for a casual stroll, and they made a beeline to him and his mother.

Charlotte groaned louder, her hands moving around her head as she tried to find the right spot to massage. Her body tremors were more intense. She squeezed her good eye shut, a tear trickling out of it.

It happened sooner than he expected, but he now regretted snapping at her a moment ago. Gently, he lifted her chin. He could feel her spasmodic twitches and her throat gagging on her uncontrollable swallowing. Her pain was…her pain hurt him. He knew he had to get her away from the approaching men, but he'd never be able to wheel her away fast enough. He turned to confront them, putting himself between them and her. Maybe they weren't with the Calessi or Provenzano mob. Maybe. He was about to find out.

#

It was risky for them to leave their desert flophouse with the police and/or Joseph Provenzano's men looking for them, but what could Sasha do? Trevor gave the order. Glen supported him, and two heavily-armed men enforced his command. That was forty-five minutes ago. The ride was, thankfully, uneventful. Now she sat in a dark and musty Palm Beach hideaway that looked like it belonged in the 1920s. There was an ornate bar along one wall with a smoky back mirror. Two taxidermy owls, perched at each end of the mirror, faced inward as if watching over the bar area. A red, crushed velvet sofa and two matching chairs occupied space along the back wall and provided seating for some shady-looking men. The walls displayed memorabilia from long dead Vaudeville entertainers. A glass display case built into the far corner of the room contained a packing chest, milk can, and straightjacket supposedly used by the great Harry Houdini. The only modern object, standing twenty feet from the display, was a pinball machine. But it was a Houdini: Master of Mystery machine – much in keeping with the theme of the place. It stood out as being odd, more so when she remembered that Frank also had one in his house. Were pinball games still popular?

Trevor spoke with the men on the crushed velvet furniture. She tried to hear them from her seat at the bar, but the pinball machine loudly invited would-be players to see if they could become the next Houdini. She didn't recall Frank's game talking like that. It was creepy.

"I know you have questions," said Glen as he took the seat beside her.

"Questions?" She gestured around the room. "What are you into?"

"I think it's better if he explains it."

"Who? The Clipper? What kind of name is that?"

"It's not a name," said the man behind the bar. "It's a title." He resembled an old-time bartender with black suspenders, white button shirt, black bowtie, and a clean, pressed apron wrapped around his waist. He wore a boutonniere of white bell-shaped flowers pinned to the left band of his suspenders. In his mid to late seventies, he had tan skin, a well-groomed white beard, hair of the same color and powerfully blue eyes. He strained a concoction into a highball glass full of ice and topped it off with a splash of club soda, a lemon slice and a cherry. He placed the lightly clouded drink before her. "Tom Collins is one of my favorites."

Glen indicated she should drink it, but she rejected his suggestion and let the glass sweat. "People don't drink these anymore."

"Sirhan Sirhan would if you could sneak one into his prison," said the bartender. "He used to like his Tom Collins."

The mention of Robert Kennedy's assassin brought Trevor to the bar, where he refused to sit or even lean against it.

She slid the beverage away from her. "That's a good reason for me not to drink it."

The bartender laughed. "I've had my eye on you for

a while." His comment made Glen sit up. She saw it, but the bartender acted like he didn't. "You're wondering why. You're a divorced woman without much of a résumé. The high mark of your education is an online certificate from the San Luis Obispo Institute of Wellness. I don't usually waste my time with unaccredited individuals."

Someone needs to tell this old timer everyone gets divorced nowadays. But that wasn't what upset her – not really. Unaccredited had been a hot word for her since she first looked into going back to school after a judge finalized her dissolution of marriage. Her life choices, including poor study habits in high school, prevented her from enrolling in any notable institutions of higher learning. The best she could do, particularly with her work schedule, was the Institute of Wellness, and she was well aware of its lack of renown. "I don't have to listen to this." She turned to Glen, hoping he'd support her, but he showed no intention of leaving with her. *Why are you so in awe of this guy?*

"But you managed to do what no one else could," said the bartender.

She knew where this was going. It was about Charlotte. "How long is 'a while'?"

"What? Oh." He smiled, showing perfect teeth – and they weren't dentures. "You've been on my radar since –"

"Since I started working with Charlotte Caron."

"I knew her as Charlotte Remy."

She turned to Glen, who fidgeted beside her. "I'd like to know what you're thinking."

"The Clipper runs the website I told you about." He addressed the bartender. "Why have you been watching us? For how long?"

It wasn't us he said he was watching. Rather than correct Glen, she thought she'd let things play out, see where they went. But she did ask the bartender, "What do you clip?"

The man smirked as if mildly amused by her question. "The website helps us get our message out, but it's hard to be taken seriously amid all the sites looking for conspiracies behind every murder or under every meteorite that falls from the sky."

"Your message?"

"Why the Kennedys were killed, and Martin Luther King," said Trevor. "Why the Twin Towers fell and why we went to war with Iraq when Al-Qaida was in Afghanistan and most of the 9/11 jack-offs were Saudi."

"You lied to your father?" She watched Trevor's face twist with confusion. "You said in the warehouse it was so he could build a defense for Charlotte. Now you're saying that's not true? You tortured a girl and killed her grandfather for government conspiracies?"

"That's not what I said."

She turned to The Clipper, aka the bartender. "I don't understand what any of it has to do with his grandmother. And I don't understand why I'm here. I'm unaccredited, remember?"

The Clipper gestured to Trevor. "He's looking at the big picture, of which his grandmother is one of those people painted into the background."

Riddles. I hate riddles. It occurred to her that the one person most equipped to help her decipher this mess was Frank. She wondered what he'd do if he were here. And she remembered how pissed she was that he kicked her to the curb. Not in reference to the relationship. They'd barely started on that. She resented him rejecting her offer. *We would've worked well together.*

"My Nana is a victim of circumstance," explained Trevor. "Thanks to you, she could take the fall for what the faceless men did. I want the truth to get out so she doesn't take the fall."

Something about that didn't ring true, she thought. There was more to why Trevor tortured the old man and the young girl than just to get information to absolve his Nana. She returned to The Clipper. "You're conspiracy theorists hiding behind a website, recruiting people to expose the truth as you see it, even if that means an old man has to die?"

"Joseph Provenzano was far from innocent of anything, but from what I understand, he died accidentally. It happens. I'm interested in exposing the rest of them. You set this in motion when you hypnotized Charlotte. With your help, we can get the others."

She could see why Glen fell for conspiracy theories. He served with her dad in Vietnam – proudly, even though they later learned their government lied about the war. And he was ignorant about computers and the internet, which made him more apt to believe these people. She, however, would need more convincing. "How long have you known Charlotte was the girl in the polka-dot dress?"

Trevor cleared his throat, but he didn't say anything.

"You should be proud of yourself," said The Clipper. "In fifty years, no one else has gotten it out of her." He took her untouched Tom Collins and dumped it in the sink. "In 1968, some skillful men programmed both the assassin and the assassin's handler. Five years earlier, they would have simply killed the two after the job was done. But Dallas, the Warren Commission's investigation and all subsequent analysis by investigators and the public taught them it was better to keep the killers alive, locking away their memories so they couldn't implicate anyone else. And they were right. After half a century, only one person was ever arrested, tried and convicted in the murder of Robert Kennedy."

"Two people were arrested," corrected Trevor. "And Nana didn't *kill* anybody."

"I still don't see what you want from me," she told The Clipper. "It's not like I'll ever get a chance to hypnotize Sirhan."

"Anything is possible." He untied his apron. "I like to seal my partnerships with a game of pinball. It's my version of a handshake." He gestured to the Houdini game. "Care to play?"

It was a strange – and vague – offer, but he had an even stranger way of sealing it. She really wished Frank was here, if for no other reason than to play pinball with this weirdo. The blinking lights and shiny toys of the pinball machine didn't tell her anything about what a partnership with The Clipper would look like. What was in it for her other than a chance to hypnotize Sirhan? *Can you imagine?* She wouldn't need Dr. Fitz or anyone else to mentor her then. She could hypnotize America's most famous living assassin? Frank might've been right. She would write a book, and it would be a bestseller. As she turned to play The Clipper in a silly game for a potentially serious arrangement, she noticed the subtitle on the machine. And it made her hesitate. Underneath the name *Houdini,* it read *Master of Mystery.* It seemed oddly prophetic.

CHAPTER 16

Redondo Beach, California. October 1967

Charlotte watches the cab pull up, and Frankie is out the door before she can stop him. *Francis*, she reminds herself. Pete calls him Frankie, so to her, from now on, he'll be Francis. Bobbi is less adventurous since almost fatally gagging on a spoon. People say her voice will stop sounding like a croak, but it's been three months. According to Pete, it was her fault. That's one of the reasons he has a Dear John letter waiting for him on the kitchen table.

Her bags aren't heavy, but they're cumbersome, bouncing down the stairs and nearly taking little Bobbi with them. "I could use some help." But the driver just sits in the car, not even looking at her. She manages to stumble up to the vehicle, pounds the trunk with her open hand.

The driver opens the door, seemingly with great reluctance – and she sees why as he rises to his full height. *Oh, shit. How did this happen?* Pete is the driver. "I was surprised when dispatch said someone here needed pick-up." Francis runs around the car, into the street, grabbing his leg. And he lifts him up. He glances at her luggage. "Is this a one-way trip?"

"You said you were working for Diamond Joe. Another lie?"

He carries their son around the back of the car, closer to her. "You can say I'm a lot of things, Char, but a liar ain't one of 'em. I've been supporting this family with two jobs. How many do you have?"

She points at Francis then touches the top of Bobbi's head. "I'm tired of being Suzy Homemaker when you're painting the town with Rosey."

"I haven't seen *Rose* since she made my introduction to Joe. Is that what this is about? You think I'm dipping my stick somewhere else?"

"I don't care where you dip it. I'm Splitsville."

"Why?"

She looks down the street, over the broken sidewalk littered with trash, graffiti and bullet casings. The spics are out, as they always are, cat-calling white chicks. Blacks are out, too, staring at her like hungry dogs eyeing a slab of meat in a butcher shop window. She can't tell him anything she hasn't already said. *When you don't feel safe in your own neighborhood*...she frowns. That's the real reason for the Dear John letter. "Call me another cab."

"You're not taking my kids."

Her frown hardens – as hard as her resolve to do the exact opposite of what he said.

#

2018

Sasha appreciated the restaurant's dark setting and the sounds from the kitchen that muted her approach. She hoped the man she came to see wouldn't fit her with cuffs upon arrival, assuming he carried them and assuming he did that sort of thing himself.

The Clipper said a waiter named José would seat her at the district attorney's table even though the DA liked to dine alone. As he slid back a chair to allow her to sit, he said, "Your lamb birria will arrive shortly, señor." He turned to Sasha. "May I bring you a beverage, señorita?"

Marco Diaz's eyes grew to twice their size when he saw her, but he simply swallowed his Dos Equis and lowered the glass.

"Sangria, por favor." She waited for José to leave them.

Her heartbeat pulsed in her ears. She found this man intimidating under normal circumstances, but more so since she betrayed his trust. Now she also interrupted his meal. The first thing she expected him to say was *where is Charlotte?* He might also want to know who put her up to taking her, given her prior relationship with Charlotte's son. But the 800lb gorilla of a question was why she did a one-eighty. She alerted him to Charlotte's conspiracy only to later spring her from custody. That sort of behavior demanded an explanation. "I protect my patients above all else," she said. "I consider it abuse to feed them a drug against their knowledge, even worse if the drug is illegal in the United States."

He raised his eyebrows.

"You might say I should've trusted you the way you trusted me when I came to you and asked you to look into Charlotte, but –"

José returned, setting a glass of fresh sangria before her. "A few more moments on your food, señor."

Mr. Diaz kept his eyes on her.

The waiter lingered. "And señor?"

"Yes, I heard you."

"I want to thank you."

Mr. Diaz glanced at him.

"Thank you for opening the case against Senator Kennedy's killers."

What the hell? She looked up at him. The Clipper said José would get her before the district attorney. He didn't say anything about him joining their conversation.

Mr. Diaz perked up. "The grand jury indicts. I just bring it to their attention."

"You are too modest." José lowered his voice. "I was a busboy at the Ambassador that night. I shook his hand. I was young, but I knew he was a man of peace who hated hate. He had courage. Above all, Señor Kennedy was love. Do you know what he said as he lay dying on the floor? He asked if everyone else was alright. That is love." His lower lip quivered. It looked like he had more to reveal, but he simply said, "I will check your food."

    Mr. Diaz took several moments to consider what the waiter said. She, however, wondered less about the content and more about the purpose of José's interruption. The Clipper promised to arrange this meeting as a condition of her agreeing to work with him. She wanted to smooth things over with the district attorney, get him to see her side of things and drop any charges he'd prepared against her. José's remembrances were not part of that deal.

    "That's what people don't understand," said the DA. "Frank doesn't understand. America is full of hate, but now and then, our brighter angels pierce the darkness. When they're gunned down before they can do what they're meant to do, it's a tragedy that robs us all. That's why I trusted the testimony you brought to me. Justice demands we find every conspirator in this crime no matter how much or how little they were involved, or whose mother they are." It sounded like he was on the stump, making a campaign speech, until he brought it back around. "The waiter seated you against my wishes, and he hasn't asked you to order food. Why are you here?"

    She could see he wanted it straight. That was fine – normally, but she hadn't yet offered enough contrition. *Why do I feel I have to explain my actions? Why not just apologize?* She saw José returning with a steaming bowl of lamb birria. It was time bought, she realized, a chance to reset the conversation while the DA enjoyed the meal set before him. Reddish-brown and garnished with leaves of green, it smelled of heavenly spices. The meat looked tender, succulent and had undoubtedly come from the finest cuts. Mr. Diaz stirred it with his spoon.   J o s é didn't leave. "I have learned things since that terrible night. No police were stationed at the Ambassador Hotel. None. There was a fifteen-minute blackout on police communications immediately after the shooting. And the LAPD destroyed the evidence."

    Mr. Diaz looked like he wanted to get to his food. And she wanted the waiter to get the hell out of there. *What is he doing?*

    "Ceiling tiles, doorjambs, a center divider – all had bullet holes," said José. "The police took them from the hotel and destroyed them."

"That's standard procedure after a trial," said Mr. Diaz. "Particularly for materials too large to store, like tiles and doorjambs."

"It also meant there would be no evidence for a retrial or if Sirhan appealed." José looked at her for the first time since bringing it all up. "They also destroyed a gun they used for sound tests, the left sleeves of Señor Kennedy's coat and shirt, and the report that measured the metal and chemical content of the bullets they recovered."

Why are you telling me this? It seemed like he wanted to convince her more than he did the DA. She still wanted him to leave but a little less now.

"With my own eyes," continued the waiter. "I saw two policemen come to the hotel the day before the assassination. They tried to get white kitchen workers jackets."

"Why?" she asked.

"That is what I would like to know. If the police had no officers at the hotel the night of the shooting, why did they want kitchen workers uniforms the day before? Keep this in mind, señorita. They shot Señor Kennedy *in the kitchen*."

"I'll be raising those questions," said the DA. "I'd like to eat now."

"Oh, sí señor." José didn't move, though – not until he added, "I believe you will do your best to find justice for the great man." He looked at her one more time. Then he left them.

Okay. That was set up from the beginning. It was The Clipper, she realized, making his pitch to the DA and using the waiter to do it. Master of Mystery, she should've known he'd put more into this meeting than he promised her. Was that what she had to look forward to from now on? Maybe she shouldn't have agreed to play that "handshake" game of pinball with him.

"This is where you offer me your services?"

"What?"

Mr. Diaz cut the lamb portion of his birria. "I know you

don't have Charlotte."

"How do you know that?"

"Because I know where she is, and I know who she's with."

She knew who was with Charlotte too, but she didn't know where they were. How did the DA know? She decided it didn't matter. What did matter was that Frank was in trouble. Harboring a fugitive was a serious crime. Then again, helping that same fugitive escape imprisonment – which she did – was just as serious.

The district attorney waited to see that she got it. And he said, "I accept your offer."

"I didn't know I made one."

"We'll retrieve Charlotte either way, but it'd be easier with your help. You have a bond."

"What do I get if I –"

"It's what you don't get: an orange jumpsuit and two roommates in a nine by twelve cell." He returned his attention to the birria. It was an authoritative return that said her intrusion was now unwelcome, and staying any longer would only sour his offer.

She stood. José glanced at her from across the room. In that look, she saw him for the pawn he was. She imagined he saw the same in her – and it was now doubly so.

CHAPTER 17

Frank watched the Italians' necks, transfixed by their gross thickness and matching jowls that swayed like curtains in a breeze when they spoke. And they'd been speaking for ten minutes. He finally cut off Ben, the elder of the two. "I'll say this again. My mother doesn't remember you, and she never worked in a pizza parlor."

"It was a destination bistro," said Ben. "Luigi's Italian Eatery. I was head chef. She was a waitress. Luigi fired her because the guys who knocked her up got in a fight in the dining area."

He perked up, looked around, but no one else heard him. They were blessedly alone in the back pool area of the desert motel from which he and his mother rented a room. "What do you mean?"

"Don't get your feathers up. All I want is to see an old friend." Ben glanced at the other Italian, named BJ – his son. "Your momma wasn't the only waitress I...uh...schlooped."

"I know, Pop. The way you talk about Cha Cha."

Ben smiled at him then turned to Frank. "Truth be known, 'til we met, I thought I might be your daddy, but you ain't got my size. And that's a honker you got on your face, bigger than your momma's."

Truth be known. He scoffed. The truth had been as elusive as his mother's affection. But one thing about which he felt reasonably certain was that she would not have *schlooped* this

overloaded plate of linguini, even in her wild youth. He wanted
to get back to that shit about guys knocking her up, though –
guys, as in plural!

"We came all this way," said BJ. "Why won't you let us
see her?"

"You came from downtown, two miles away. And I don't
understand why you want to see her at all." He pointed at Ben.
"Him, I understand, but why you?"

"Truth?" asked BJ.

He shrugged. "Why not."

"I'm a conspiracy guy – aliens at Roswell, that sort of thing.
I saw her picture on my news feed. When Pop said he knew her,
I thought, hell, I gotta meet her."

His nerves ignited in a spontaneous combustion. *That's
how they knew about us. This isn't a reunion.* He glanced at the
motel, where Charlotte was inside, suffering another headache.

"And we came from a lot farther than Twentynine Palms,"
said BJ.

"Are you Calessi?" The question nearly choked him on its
way out.

"Calessi?"

"No," said Ben. "We're from Pomona."

"We heard them on the police scanner, talking about
finding you."

He jumped out of the lounge chair at the same time his
thoughts leaped to Rip. His friend probably wasn't to blame,
but his phone call was. Someone from the DA's office must've
traced the call, as he predicted. *Shi – it.* It didn't take Sherlock
Holmes to find them in Twentynine Palms. He left the goombahs
to charge the motel, hoping to get to his mother before it was too
late. Behind him, BJ shouted, "Is she really the girl in the polka-
dot dress?"

The quickest route from the pool area to the front of their
building was a slope of reddish-brown dirt sprinkled with a few
hardy, barbed plants. He wished he didn't wear the bathing suit
or the flip flops he bought in the lobby when he booked the room,

but he would've raised needless suspicion at the pool dressed in the dirty pants he'd been wearing for days. Running in flip flops wasn't fast or easy, and his claw-curled toes struggled to keep the flops on his feet.

He turned a sharp corner around the side of the building, and his left sandal blew out, sending him tumbling into the dirt and onto the sidewalk. Scratches, dust and a couple raspberries marred his body, but of greater concern to him were the two police cars with flashing lights and a blue van parked in front of the building. The van resembled the one that took his mother from Brookside upon her arrest. He kicked off his other sandal and hobbled over the broken blacktop. If only he was in better shape and younger, but he had to make do with what he had, which in this case was legal knowledge. "Cease and desist, officers. This is unlawful –" The argument he intended to make ended with a swinging baton that barely missed his head. "Hey!" A second baton followed the first, and this one didn't miss. It went butt-end into his solar plexus, dropping him to his knees. His breath left him. He couldn't retrieve it. He was like a fish out of water, but he didn't have the energy to flop around. He toppled onto his side, straining for air. His eyes bugged out as the fear of suffocating became real. And in his terror, he saw two men in plain clothes push Charlotte and her wheelchair out of the motel. A short senior citizen trailed them. He had a reddish-purple goatee, silver hair and a face that looked wax-like without wrinkles.

Lacking air in his lungs, he could only manage to squeak. But he rose to his knees then onto all fours. He lifted his head in time to see them load Charlotte into the van. She looked confused. Her motor skills were still beyond her control. He could tell she was afraid. He found the strength to roll back onto his heals. Oxygen began its merciful return to his body, slowly and at abbreviated levels.

"Dr. Fitz wants the son to stay," said one of the cops. He had a blond, flat-top haircut with frosted tips that looked like sparkling silver in the sunlight.

The strange haircut caught his attention, but he cared more about *Dr. Who? Who's that? Why does he want me to stay?* A kick hit him between his eyes, snapping his head back and making him forget about his questions and the dude with the flat-top. Another kick slammed his chest, hurling him onto his back. No sooner did he land when fists started pummeling him from what seemed like everywhere. Each blow inflicted its own unique pain, and stars exploded like white fireworks in his field of vision. He tried to ward off the attack by flailing his arms, kicking his legs, even spitting – that didn't do much good. The beating lasted only a minute or two, but he thought it went on forever. When the men felt they had administered enough brutality, they dragged him by the arms to the open door of the motel. Thin flesh atop his feet scraped on the blacktop, adding more injury to his growing collection.

He didn't know why they beat him. It seemed personal. As the flesh around his eyes began to swell and limit his vision, he saw his surroundings change from exterior to interior. The motel room appeared to be undisturbed, indicating his mother didn't resist when they took her.

"Oh my God! What have you done? Is he –"

"Get away from him."

They dropped him onto the carpet, which was thin and without padding. Air left his lungs again. He saw low heel pumps and legs clothed in a woman's pants. As he rolled onto his side, his view travelled up the legs, arriving at the woman's face: Sasha. She looked worried for him and angry at the men who beat him. She tried to reach for him, but the cop with the strange haircut stopped her. She condemned the men, and they snapped back at her, but the words came to Frank as if from inside a closed-off room. A hazy fog began to invade his already compromised view. Unconsciousness was on its way, but...but...*I have to know what she's doing here. Why is she helping the police?* The last thing he saw was her grabbing the sketches drawn from his mother's memory, the ones he left on the table after changing into his bathing suit. She looked back at him. Whatever she said next, he didn't hear it.

He didn't hear anything.

#

It was three hours later, and Sasha still couldn't stop giving Dr. Fitz the stink eye for what went down in Twentynine Palms. She really shouldn't have been surprised, given what they did to Charlotte back in Castaic. What did that say about District Attorney Marco Diaz? He had to know what kind of people he hired to carry out his wishes.

She didn't trust The Clipper either. By his own admission, he'd been monitoring her since she first started working with Charlotte at Brookside. That alone sent his creep factor to level ten. She didn't like how Glen revered him though he barely knew him. And that game he played with José, the waiter, only made her more suspicious of him.

The District Attorney and The Clipper were two men with seemingly opposing agendas, and each thought he had her allegiance. For her, it was a lesser of two evils situation. What tipped her over to The Clipper's side was Frank. She was mad as hell at him, but she couldn't forgive that savage beating the DA's men gave him. And they made her leave before she could see if he survived it. So before getting into the van with its signal blocker, she sent The Clipper a text telling him they were leaving with their cargo and where they were going.

The van was full with seating arrangements similar to when they took Charlotte to Castaic. Dr. Fitz occupied the front passenger seat. Sasha sat behind him with Flat-top to her left and Charlotte in the back. They drugged the old lady again. This time Dr. Fitz claimed it was a sleeping pill. Other cops loyal to the district attorney took the remaining spots in the van, including the driver's seat. And most of them had sore knuckles from when they pounded Frank. They had a two car police escort: one cruiser in front and the other behind them.

She may have debated which evil to choose, but she had no doubt she had made the right decision to take those sketches from the motel room. The man who drew them was a tattoo artist, and he based them on what Charlotte described seeing during an ibogaine-induced hallucination. Since everyone wanted to know what Charlotte held in her memory, it stood to reason that the sketches would be important. And Frank didn't deserve them. It was in a moment of weakness that she gave them to him in the first place. Was she seeking his approval? Did she think he'd reconsider making her his partner after seeing the evidence she could produce for him? She hated when she didn't feel worthy. It made her do things she'd have to correct later.

Momentum made everyone lean forward as the driver of the van applied pressure to the break. "What is this?" he asked.

That woke everyone but Charlotte from their thoughts. They looked out the front window, at where the driver looked.

Flat-top turned to her with a glare that said he'd rather punch her than talk to her. "Is this your doing?" It wasn't a surprising accusation. He'd been complaining since Dr. Fitz told everyone the DA wanted her back on the team.

What had their attention, and the reason for Flat-top's question, was the large object that blocked the road up ahead. It appeared to be a felled tree or perhaps a telephone pole laying on its side – hard to tell in the night's encroaching darkness. Whatever it was, it stretched across both lanes. Distant lights suggested a jam of cars that would otherwise be headed their way.

As the driver phoned the escort cruiser ahead of them, Dr. Fitz spun around to look at her. The intensity in his eyes said he thought it *was* her doing. He didn't intimidate her, but she did regret what this would do to the potential rekindling of their working relationship. *Who am I kidding? I don't regret that. Ha!*

One by one, vehicles before them flashed red brake lights. Their van began to slow. The cops traded indecisive glances. A couple of them prepared their weapons for activity. Still on the phone with someone in the car ahead of them, the driver said, "I dunno. Go check it out."

The passenger side door opened in the first cruiser, and an officer in civilian clothes stepped out. His body movements were tentative. He looked back at them. He scanned the heavily shaded woods on his side of the road.

"Tell the others to go with him," said Dr. Fitz.

Flat-top kept his stare on Sasha, damn near burning her with it. She turned to meet him glare for glare. She was over his snide remarks. Looking at him, *actually* looking at him, she saw pain. That was a surprise. Then she remembered slamming the door on his hand and the sound it made. With everything going on, she'd forgotten about that. As she glanced at his hand resting in his lap, she saw it wrapped in a bandage. She also saw him pointing a gun at her. "If anything goes wrong," he said. "You'll be the first to get my bullet."

Energy drained from her limbs. She'd never faced the business end of a gun, and she'd never had anyone threaten her like that. She could tell he meant it. The driver stayed on the phone with someone while Dr. Fitz continued to belt out orders – to the driver, to other cops in the van. To her, it was nothing but yammering. Flat-top's gun could blast its projectile straight through her. She envisioned a small entry hole in her chest and a gaping exit wound in her back. Nothing would stop the bleeding or prevent her insides from spilling out of her.

"Hallelujah," yelled Charlotte. "Hallelujah!"

Everyone shot the old woman a curious look.

"There," yelled the driver. He pointed at the left side of the road, where people moved in the brush. "And there!" He threw his finger to the right. More people moved over there.

She didn't forget about the gun pointing at her, but she ventured a few looks outside the van. She saw people emerging from the woods. She recognized some of them as men who were in the warehouse when that old man died. Many others were *not* Trevor's friends. She knew that because they dressed differently – in camouflage with bullet-proof vests. Some had combat helmets. They sported enough weaponry to start a small war. She didn't regret placing the text that made this happen, but she feared Flat-top would punish her for it.

Charlotte spanked her on the arm excitedly. The sleeping pill had either worn off, or she never swallowed it. "T-dog," she said. "He's come to save his Nana. He'll save you too."

She glanced from the old woman slowly back to Flat-top. Despite all the excitement, he hadn't stopped looking at her. And his gun remained as undistracted as his eyes.

CHAPTER 18

Frank knocked on the front door of the Spanish Colonial style home with a snow-white stucco exterior, causing pretty hands with manicured nails to move the curtain away from the window. The face that peered back at him belonged to a stunning woman with bronze skin, gray eyes and sleek black hair. "Go away," she said. "I'll call the police."

"Mrs. Diaz?"

"My husband is a very important man."

"I know."

He heard a man and a woman bicker inside the house, but it didn't last. The door opened, and Marco met him casually dressed and looking irritated. "Jesus, Frank." He stepped onto the porch, closing the door behind him. "You have a lot of nerve coming here looking like that."

He turned to give any of the neighbors who cared to look a full view of his appearance. He resembled *Rocky* after his worst cinematic beating: swollen eyes, split lip, cuts scabbed over, welts and a nose even bigger than he had before. "It's funny that you're not offering to help me. You don't even look surprised by my appearance."

"Let's go out back."

Porch lights dropped a hazy glow on a teak swing and a pair of matching rockers to his right. He chose the swing, its support chains creaking as he made himself as comfortable as possible.

Mr. Diaz shook his head while looking around for curious neighbors.

"I wonder if I'll bleed into this wood."

"You should go to the hospital."

"Is that where you took her? I hope so, because she needs it."

Marco sat on the chair furthest from him, but he didn't say anything.

"Did you know ibogaine's side effects when you ordered it fed to my mother? Nausea, dehydration, lack of muscle coordination, seizures, tremors, irregular eye movement, and trouble swallowing...those are the manageable side effects." He glared at the DA. "My mother already has cardiovascular problems. And with what you gave her, death is now a possibility."

Mr. Diaz still didn't comment.

He wasn't normally a violent man, but he had a powerful urge to grab the bastard by the throat and squeeze until his windpipe collapsed. "When it works – in *healthy* people – ibogaine enables users to relive events from their past. I assume that was your intention when you gave the order. Maybe you knew the harm it would cause her. Maybe you didn't care. But I guarantee you'll care about one side effect I haven't yet mentioned."

"Pretending I know what you're talking about...what are you talking about?"

"Memory loss." He could see that caught the DA's attention. "Ibogaine acts as an accelerant for people in her condition. The trip you want to take down her memory lane can't happen if you speed up her dementia."

A contemplative look lingered on Marco's face until he decided to leave his chair and open the front door. "Come inside."

As much as he wanted to remain a spectacle for the neighbors, he decided to follow Mr. Diaz into the house. It was, after all, what he came for: to confront the man on his own turf. Once inside, he encountered a palace of sorts, kept too beautiful to be lived in. The floor was white marble, polished, with fudge-like swirls. Two intricately woven wrought iron staircases led to the upstairs from where little feet made scampering sounds. Swollen as his nose was, he could still smell lilac and lavender scents in the foyer. The DA led him to a room off to the right, but as he passed a mirror, he saw Mrs. Diaz's reflection watching him the way a miser would regard a bum seeking a handout. He made sure to show her his face. *Look what your husband did to me.*

Marco closed the door after they entered his study. It was smaller and more personal than his downtown office, with family photos, athletic trophies and plaques for civic accomplishments. The books that filled two wall-to-ceiling cases were less about the law and more a reflection of his personal interests: biographies, spy thrillers and every Tom Clancy novel ever written. He sat behind his sturdy but antique desk. His computer was already on, requiring merely a touch of the keypad to awaken it.

There was one couch – leather, of course. Frank sat on it before his host could tell him not to. "I don't think people know how unlike Kennedy you are. Denying an old woman due process, drugging her and having me beaten up aren't the acts of a profile in courage."

Marco didn't bother to look at him, eyes on his monitor. "Is her memory gone?"

"Not yet. She shared a thing or two with me – things that would help you look where you *should* be looking if justice was what you sought."

"Which is?"

"Which *are* available to you in exchange for immunity."

Marco laughed. "Providing material support to terrorists makes an immunity deal unlikely."

"It was never federal. You know that. Sirhan is Christian, and killing Kennedy wasn't a Jihadist act."

"There's no immunity deal in a Kennedy assassination. How about that? The best way to help her is to get her talking while I'm listening from the other side of a two-way mirror." Marco leaned back in his chair. "But we'll need to find her first."

He slid to the edge of his seat. "You lost her?"

"There was an ambush. They took your mother and your

ex-girlfriend. What you're saying concerns me. It sounds like Mrs. Caron needs hospitalization."

"Sasha." The name crawled out of his throat like a tapeworm. It was one thing – and a bad thing at that – for him to believe she betrayed the patient/hypnotist trust by giving Charlotte up to the district attorney. But she also had something to do with the beating he recently took, *and* she stole the sketches. "I don't care what happens to Sasha, but my mother –"

"It was your son."

"What?"

"Your son led the ambush and injured two of my men."

"They injured me." He tapped his swollen face. "Eye for an eye."

"I don't know anything about that." The DA turned the monitor so his visitor could see it. "Charlotte Lucille Oppenheimer. According to her birth certificate, that's your mother's name."

He *was* thinking about how great a liar the DA was…until he saw the computer screen displaying an old birth certificate with a baby's footprints stamped on its upper left and upper right. His middle-aged eyes wouldn't let him read it without approaching the desk. He approached it reluctantly, with discomfort and curiosity. The document was official, issued by a hospital in his mother's hometown of Crete, Nebraska. It stated her birth date (March 28, 1944), her first name, her middle name and Oppenheimer as her last name. It had to be a mistake.

"I'm guessing you didn't know you were Jewish." Marco smirked. "But this is more interesting." He tapped a few keys. He didn't have to look at the monitor to know what it summoned: a black and white police sketch depicting a young woman in her mid-twenties. She was Caucasian with a large, hooked nose and frizzy hair, a ponytail on the side of her head.

Frank knew the image was supposed to be his mother when she was young. Who else would it be? He felt his knees growing weaker, and he wished he was back on the couch.

Marco said, "On June 7, 1968, a traveling salesman named John Henry Fahey described this woman to a police sketch artist. He claimed to have met her at the Ambassador Hotel the morning before Senator Kennedy was shot. She acted manic and paranoid. He thought she might have been drunk or on drugs, but for whatever reason, he allowed her to tag along on some of his business meetings. He said she was nervous. She asked him to help her get away from people she believed were following her. He didn't take her seriously until a gray-haired man in a blue Ford started following them. They lost the Ford, but a dark blue VW replaced it. They lost the VW, only to have the Ford resume the tail. The girl told him the cars communicated by radio. Mr. Fahey offered to take her to the police, but she refused."

As much as he didn't want to, Frank envisioned the scene with his mother playing the part of the girl. Worry bubbled in the pit of his stomach – worry that the story could be true.

"Fahey said he dropped her off at the front entrance of the Ambassador Hotel at approximately 7:30 pm. She told him Kennedy was 'no good' and she invited him to the campaign reception so he could 'watch them get Kennedy'. When he refused, she became angry. She jumped out of the car and slammed the door."

"Allegedly."

The DA produced a sardonic smile. "He described the young woman as being in her early to mid-twenties with big blonde hair, a pronounced nose and Middle Eastern features."

"The artist drew her as white."

"Sandy Serrano was a key witness. I assume you read her testimony."

He did – with Sasha. The memory made him snarl, which cracked the crusted seal on his split lip.

"According to Ms. Serrano, the girl in the polka-dot dress was five foot six, between the ages of twenty-three and twenty-seven. She said she had brown eyes, dark brown hair and a 'funny nose' that was turned up."

"Sandy Serrano has credibility issues." Almost as soon as the words left his mouth, Frank regretted them. Ms. Serrano had credibility issues only because she recanted her testimony after a veteran cop brow beat, intimidated and scared the hell out of her.

Marco acted as if he didn't hear him, turning the monitor back to face him and clicking a tab. He slipped on a pair of glasses that gave him a distinguished look – as if he needed help in that department. And he read the screen. "Two witnesses claimed to see Sirhan, a young man and a young woman between the ages of twenty-two and twenty-five enter Kennedy Campaign Headquarters in Azusa days before the shooting. They identified Sirhan from his mug shot. The woman, they said, had a 'prominent nose' and brown or blonde hair. Other witnesses saw this trio trying to enter a restaurant in Pomona where Senator Kennedy attended a luncheon. They didn't say whether or not the woman had a pronounced nose, but their descriptions matched other accounts of what she looked like."

Pomona? Didn't those fat Italians, Ben and BJ, say they were from Pomona?

The DA removed his glasses. He struck another key and turned the monitor to his guest. Once again, it showed the 1968 police sketch of the girl. "Mr. Fahey said this young lady gave him aliases, saying she couldn't state her real name because people were watching her. She finally told him she was Gilderdine Oppenheimer, and she said it so convincingly that he believed her."

He watched the DA strike another key. He thought he needed to sit before, but the next thing he saw on the screen made it official. He landed less-than-gracefully on the couch, but his eyes never left the monitor, which showed a split screen. The sketch of the girl Fahey met was on the left. Beside it, on the right side of the screen, was a pre-nose job photograph of his mother. It was impossible to miss the resemblance shared by the two images: highly distinctive noses (like his) and frizzy hair, which was shorter and touched with gray in the picture of the older woman. The faces and eyes also looked alike, adorned with wrinkles and age spots in the latter image. This had to have been what Alex Logan meant when she said the DA had Charlotte on eyewitness testimony. "Have you...uh...have you compared these through facial recognition?"

"That's what brought us to your mother, among other things."

"Sasha brought you to my mother. Whatever she told you will be thrown out of court. She hypnotized an elderly woman with dementia. It won't make it past the grand jury."

A smile crawled up Marco's cruelly handsome face. "Okay. Here it is straight. I've never trusted your ex. You shouldn't have either, but that's your business. I don't need her to build a case against your mother – obviously." He gestured to the computer with its side-by-side images. "But the girl in the polka-dot dress isn't the big fish. I want the big fish."

He'd negotiated enough plea-bargains to know where this was headed. In his experience, the person making the offer usually had the upper hand. An immunity deal was out of the question, and he got that. It was, after all, a Kennedy assassination they were talking about. "You want the big fish," said Frank. "You want the headlines?" He paused – another negotiation tactic. "I think I can get my mother to tell me what she knows about the assassination, *without drugs*, while you're listening from the other side of the glass."

The district attorney wore about as good a poker face as he'd ever seen.

He'd been mulling over this next part since Charlotte refused to let him check her out of Brookside. She had the right to make the final decision on that, able to check in or out on her own, but he couldn't allow it with her health issues. And – oh, how it hurt him to acknowledge this – it looked increasingly more likely that she *was* guilty. He couldn't hide that fact. *This is why I stopped defending criminals and started prosecuting them, but I never expected it to be my own mother*. He took a deep breath, and that was no tactic. "If Charlotte gives up names and assuming she was party to the conspiracy – big assumption, by the way – I want your assurance that she'll serve her time in a country club facility, approved by me, and she will receive top-notch medical care, the best available. After all, you're largely responsible for her deteriorating condition. I'd hate for the press to get the scoop on that."

Marco's poker face couldn't hide his surprise. It was a good offer. It gave him everything he wanted: Charlotte punished *and* the names of other conspirators, particularly the ring leaders. "You're certain you can get her to talk?"

Frank nodded. He was far from certain, but he'd never show that in a negotiation.

"It's not enough."

"Are you crazy? I'm giving –"

"You have to work this case with me. You have to prosecute your mother."

Frank's head dropped a tad – an acknowledgment that he was essentially already prosecuting his mother. All he could manage to do was slowly close his swollen eyes.

"Okay," said the district attorney. "Now let's find her."

CHAPTER 19

Hermosa Beach, California. December 1967

Charlotte is in love with her pad – *Matthew's* pad. Two stories tall, directly on The Strand, which is a boardwalk without boards, it's out of sight. One of the best beaches in the state lies beyond The Strand, with the Pacific's majestic blue waters lapping its sand. Her arms filled with Yuletide acquisitions, she lumbers up the stairs to the guest room. The storage closet is mostly full. She doesn't remember buying that many gifts, but she did go a little wild when Matt opened his billfold for her. It's nice to be with a guy with dough for once.

"Francis Whalen, get your derrière back here!" Yvette, her friend and the children's sitter for the moment, is outside with her wards. She speaks with a shrill sounding French accent.

Looking out the window, she sees her son take a nosedive in the beach sand. Yvette scoops him up as he cries, but he's okay. Bobbi is nearby, watching reflectors on bike spokes whirl past her. *If I knew life could be this good, I'd have left Pete a year ago.*

She has some time before Yvette and the children track sand through the house. That means she can decide between gifts she'll wrap now and those she'll save for the twins' second birthday. Returning to the closet, she examines the first box she sees. It's a battery-powered toy vacuum cleaner. The banner across the front of the box says *Little Girls Love to help clean house.* Matthew must've bought it for Bobbi. She's a little put off by it. It's the kind of thing Pete would've bought if he had the money, not Matt. One of the things that brought her here was Matthew's non-conformity. She hopes he'll pass it on to the kids, but not with presents like this.

The next few gifts are from her: a Lassie plush toy, Matchbox cars, and a Pull-A-Tune Xylophone. She can't wait to see them tear through the wrapping, going from one box to the next. That would never happen if she stayed with Pete. He's all talk and bravado, little else. What did he do when he learned she planted roots here? Nothing – like he always did. She moves aside a pair of knickers hanging in the closet, and she finds a pop-up book she doesn't recognize. It's entitled *Empire Builders: A Boy's Guide to the Past, the Present and the Future.* It's a curious piece of literature, intended for Francis, bought by Matthew, and several years premature because the boy can't speak coherently, let alone read. She opens it. The first word to jump out at her is *kike,* riding high atop the book's first pop-up image.

She has to read this, warning herself not to go ape. Kike is just a word. She sits on the floor with the book, but as she gets into it, she realizes it contains more than just one offensive word. The first few pages and pop-up illustrations spin a twisted yarn about brilliant Egyptians who built the greatest empire in the ancient world despite Hebrew workers who undermined them with trickery and deceitfulness. Her palms are dampening, so are her pits. She's Jewish. No one on the West Coast knows that because she changed her name from Oppenheimer to Remy when she left Nebraska. Her life is so much easier if she pretends not to be what she really is.

Written simplistically with rhyming words, the book isn't merely anti-Semitic. It's harsh on coons, red men, and slant-eyes too. It is history from the perspective of empires. Ancient Egypt to Modern America, it portrays masters as enlightened and the masses as mindless sheep in need of a shepherd. The message is hard to miss, even for a child.

A door opens downstairs. "Charlotte à la maison?" asks Yvette.

She considers hiding the book, but someone has to help

her make sense of it. "Up here."

Yvette soft-steps up the stairs but can still be heard. "I am bringing your mail." She enters carrying envelops with a flyer on top. Her tan skin and blonde bob are dusted with sand.

"Have you seen this book?"

Yvette trades the mail for the pop-up. It takes but a second for her to recognize it. She laughs. "Matthew is so ambitious. It will be three years before Francis can read this."

"Have you read it?"

"My dear, I helped create it. I made the movable – how you say pop-ups? It is why I was in Prague, to learn the craft from Vojtěch Kubašta." She sits on the edge of the bed and crosses her legs, proudly flips the pages.

"It looks like something Nazis would give their kids."

"No, few similarities to that. Has Matthew not shared with you what we do?"

She knows Yvette works with Matthew. It was through him that they met. But she knows little beyond that. "Can I tell you something? Our situation isn't *Leave it to Beaver*. He's got a change-the-world vibe that I'm into, but I still don't know why he was in Griffith Park with the wardens. I don't know the name of the company that's paying him to have all this. He was a penniless beach barker when we met."

"Company is a misnomer. It is like a service organization. I believe I will not betray his trust if I tell you the name. In the States, it is called 8F. It has other names in other places."

A crash downstairs sounds upstairs. Something broke. A shriek from Francis accompanies the noise, but that's not unusual. He shrieks at everything. Charlotte stands, but Yvette is on her feet and out the door in a dart. "Wait," says Charlotte. "What about 8F?"

"Francis H. Whalen!" Yvette descends the stairs, her exclamation trailing behind her.

The boy doesn't have a middle name, or a letter. The *H* is probably a curse, like *Jesus H. Christ*. And Yvette is wrong about the last name too. Charlotte puts the mail on the bed. Again, the book catches her eye. *Is this the history I want my kids to learn?* Actually, it's not the kids. The book is for boys. The vacuum cleaner is for girls.

Francis's shriek becomes a steady cry. The child has lungs. She'll give him that.

She sees a flyer sitting atop the mail, addressed to her. It advertises stock car races at Lions Drag Strip in Long Beach. She's about to toss it when she notices something circled in the funny car section of the advertisement. It reads, *Pete "The Heat" Caron driving Dodge Destroyer*. The race date is tomorrow. Funny cars fire up their engines at 8 p.m.

#

Lions Drag Strip, Long Beach, California. The next evening.

The stands are beginning to fill as the PA system barks an announcer's discussion of cars and the men who drive them. Charlotte searches for the Dodge Destroyer. The program she bought at the gate says funny cars are quick accelerating dragsters built onto altered wheelbases. They have tilt-up fiberglass bodies over custom fabricated chassis. That tells her Pete is behind the wheel of a weird-looking, super-fast car with a flimsy body. She knows he's short on dough, but driving a souped-up speedster for pay is like trading your life for a handful of dimes.

A little hand sweats and squirms in her grip, meaning Francis is as nervous as her, but for different reasons. The machines are frightening. The noises they produce are deafening. She holds him tight. The last thing she needs is for him to scamper into the action or into the crowd watching it. He already has stitches on his scalp, under his hair, where yesterday's lamp broke over his head. Yvette acted quickly, washing it with liquor, sewing it shut. And she felt like a terrible mother for not taking his shrieks seriously. That's why she won't let go of him now.

"Is this bench racing?" asks Yvette as she holds Bobbi by the hand. "Sitting on a bench to watch a race? Bench racing?"

"Bench racing is when guys sit around arguing over who has the faster car."

"Oh." Yvette chuckles. "It is boys comparing les zobs...

their cocks."

Her concern for Pete won't let her laugh, but she does smirk. It's funny. She doesn't care if the kids heard Yvette. She says worse things in front of them all the time. The rocket cars blast off the starting line. She sees clouds of black smoke and one of the cars fishtailing. Francis yells at the racers with his eyes as wide as Frisbees.

"Fine machines. You know most are from the Midnight Auto Service."

It's a voice she knows well. She turns to see Matthew holding the flyer that alerted her to the race – the flyer she threw in the trash. She looks at Yvette, who leans forward to rid Bobbi's cheek of something that isn't there.

"By Midnight Auto Service, I mean stolen," says Matt.

"I thought you weren't coming home until Monday." Again, she looks at Yvette. "Did a little birdy tell you what I found in the closet?"

The crowd cheers as the race winning car farts a parachute to slow its speed.

"I wouldn't give him that book if you didn't approve."

The PA reminds her of the *Wah Wa Wa Wah* sound made by the teacher in the latest Charlie Brown special. "You were supposed to be one of the Bright Eyes who spit in society's face. But I can see you're the Establishment."

He looks around as if realizing he is in a place he doesn't belong.

Four attention-grabbing words escape the uninteresting prattle produced by the PA system: *Pete "The Heat" Caron.* She spins around to face the track. Her eyes dart over the faces of the men doing all manner of whatever. Two cars roll up to the line. The one on the spectator side of the track is purple. It looks like a dragon with orange-red flames painted along its side. It's the kind of dragster Pete would drive. The other car is a red Mercury two door.

"I thought you were digging my enlightenment," says Matthew.

She strains to see if the driver of the purple dragon is wearing a helmet, but track lighting glares off its windshield, obscuring her view.

"You want to know about 8F?" Matt turns her to face him. "I'll tell you, but –" He looks around at the dirty faces and the racing fans with missing teeth. "Not here – not among these –"

"Sheep?"

"Suiveurs," says Yvette. "Followers."

Matt gives Yvette a shake of his head.

Charlotte moves her son in front of her – putting herself between him and Matthew.

The announcer on the PA says, "This is Pete Caron's debut race, driving CJ McCaffrey's Dodge Destroyer. Y'all remember CJ. God rest his soul."

Matthew steps closer to her, mouth to her ear. "I know you're Jewish, but it's our secret."

She turns sharply, nearly hitting his nose with hers.

"It's okay." He smiles. "My Bright Eyes don't see race, religion or skin color in *individuals*. Those are constructs by which to manipulate the masses."

Engines roar, and her thoughts leap back to the man in the purple car. *Get out of that deathtrap. If this is about a payday, I'll get you bread.* She turns to Matt. "Are you a commie?"

"The exact opposite. Communism as a philosophy is egalitarian."

"English."

"Communism says everyone is equal. I'm not talking about the Soviet bastardization of it, which is the Politburo, General Secretary Brezhnev, and the rest."

Her hand on her son's chest, she can feel his little heart pounding as the cars on the track race their engines and burn their tires, preparing for the green light.

"I oppose communism because everyone is *not* equal," says Matt.

It's too late to stop the race. All she can do is brace for it and pray it doesn't end the way she fears it might.

Matt continues. "My philosophy…the 8F philosophy… comes from Alexander Hamilton. 'The people are turbulent and changing. They seldom judge or determine right.' That book is about raising children to become the enlightened leaders of the new century – the next century."

She hears him, but her eyes are glued to the purple dragon, her heart pounding like her son's. It's exciting. *Does Pete get a purse if he wins? How much?* He has to win. *Wait. How did this happen?* She glances at the people in the stands. They are young and old, guys and gals wearing nice threads and rags. They're everyday people, turbulent and changing – like her. She snatches Bobbi from Yvette. "You don't raise a leader by teaching her to push a toy vacuum."

The burning tires produce a sound that says they've been freed to race. She twists back to the track, clutching her babies and screaming as Pete passes her at a hundred and sixty mph. She realizes her children are screaming too – not out of fear, but for the same reason she is. Do they know their daddy is driving the dragon car? Yes, she decides, they know, and they love it.

CHAPTER 20

2018

The bullet missed Sasha by less than an inch, and she had the hole in her top to prove it. Fortunately, she had someone to thank for making Flat-top's shot go awry. He wore camo, like most of the others who staged the ambush. Unlike them, he had a white and rusty beard that made him look like a dirty Santa. He even had a matching belly. His name was Ernie Tolliver. He was a member of something called The Minutemen Revisited, whatever the hell that was. He pulled the van's side door open as Flat-top squeezed the trigger. It was enough of a disturbance to throw off the shot, and he thrust the deadly end of his AR-15 into Flat-top's forehead to prevent any further action. That was four hours ago.

They escaped to a hideaway in the hills, which was well-stocked. Their rescuers ate their fill upon arrival. It amazed her how much twenty hungry men – plus or minus a few – could consume, but she figured they earned their appetites. Stopping a police convoy and absconding with a high value prisoner without firing a shot was no simple feat. Charlotte was now in a back room with her grandson and a few others. She had no idea what condition she was in. She seemed rejuvenated in Trevor's presence when she last saw her. The larger question – at least for Sasha – was what did they intend to do now? She couldn't learn anything from her phone because, predictably, it had no signal. It seemed everyone was using signal blockers these days. She decided to power the device down to save its battery.

She saw Ernie step away from his companions. It was the opportunity she'd been looking for: a chance to thank him in person, in private, and maybe make an ally of him. She had a feeling she'd need it. As she made her move, the door to the back room opened. Trevor filled the jamb with his obscene size. His eyes instantly went to her, and he gestured with two fingers for her to come forward. She looked at Ernie. He looked back at her. The expression she read in the part of his face not hidden by whiskers said he was glad he wasn't her.

#

With the phone set to speaker and held at arm's length away from his face, Frank listened to it ring and ring and ring and ring. It was the least personal way for him to make the call he didn't want to make. Trevor was the best chance he had at finding his mother. He didn't really expect him to answer. He could've pinged the phone to see if it was active and find its location, but he didn't do that. Though Marco didn't say anything about it, he was sure they were looking for his son in connection with the death of Joseph Provenzano. The last thing he wanted to do was help them with that when he was already helping them build a case against his mother. He shook his head. *I'm doing the right thing. I'm doing right by her.*

Trevor's voice came through the phone. "I guess you're calling about Nana."

He nearly dropped it in surprise, and he stammered a response. "I...you...what are you doing? You can't think this is going to help her."

"Not the way *you* think."

"Her condition is serious. She needs medical care. She needs to be in a facility."

"We tried that, remember?"

"She won't survive on the run. You won't either. They'll find you. They always do." That didn't start the argument he thought it would. In fact, all he got back was dead air that made him think the call dropped. "I struck a deal for Charlotte – Nana."

Trevor replied coldly. "What deal?"

"She needs expert medical care. I can get it for her. Without it, she'll suffer. She might die. The DA wants the ring leaders. You know she knows who they are. She said as much in the warehouse. If she names names...well, that's the deal." He received more silence from the other end of the call, but this time he didn't think it dropped. He imagined Trevor talking it over with whoever helped him snatch Charlotte from police custody. His guess was Sasha.

Trevor returned. "You're working with the district attorney? Is there a trace on this call?"

"No – no, I wouldn't do that. Working with him is the only way I can get this deal. They won't mistreat her if I'm involved."

"Right." Trevor paused. "She didn't do it."

"Explain to me how she knew Joseph Provenzano *and* Frank Donneroummas? Ask Sasha there with you about what the witnesses said. Ask her what Sandy Serrano said when she described a girl who was with Sirhan before the shooting and fled after the shooting, saying, 'We shot Kennedy'. The description she gave matched Charlotte down to the big nose that's our family trait." He could feel himself snarling, his nostrils flaring as he glared at the phone. Admitting his mother's culpability out loud was painful. And his son forced him to do it.

Trevor delayed his reply. It sounded like he put his hand over the phone to muffle a conversation he had with someone else. Sasha? He returned after a few long, uncomfortable moments. "I'll meet you tomorrow night. I'll text you the place and the time."

"You'll bring Nana?"

The call ended.

#

Glen kept his voice low. "You have to be careful with questions like that around these people."

Sasha asked him several minutes ago about this nameless group's intentions with her, with Charlotte, with the whole RFK situation. She expected him to make some rah-rah statement about how they would do big things. She didn't expect him to give her a warning.

All anyone else in the room (except Charlotte) seemed to care about was Trevor's call with Frank. With that call now ended, Trevor addressed The Clipper. "Who's to say he won't arrest me as soon as I get there?"

"Does that mean you don't know?" she pressed Glen. "Or is it something you're in on?"

The Clipper glanced at her then turned to address Trevor. "We're holding the cards. And I don't only mean her." He pointed at Charlotte. "So long as we feed them a steady diet of the good stuff, they'll have to play by our rules."

Sasha jumped into their conversation. "What's the good stuff?" she asked The Clipper. She knew – particularly by the look she received from Glen – that the wise move was to stay silent and observe. *Too late.*

The Clipper seemed amused by her question, and he gestured to Trevor. "We can start with his maternal great-grandfather. Right Charlotte?"

The old woman's working eye shifted to him, but briefly. She returned to a vacant stare as she sat on the couch – the only object upon which anyone could sit, and she was its sole occupant. It was the only sign of engagement Sasha had seen from her since entering the room.

Trevor growled. "What about my great-grandfather?"

"Maternal," stressed The Clipper. "He was an Iranian spy." It was like a current shot through the room, eliciting a reaction from everyone. Charlotte flinched, but only Sasha noticed. Trevor looked like he wanted to kill The Clipper for making such an inflammatory claim. The Bus, who stood watch over Charlotte, threw an expression of shock at Trevor, as if he expected him to explain his genealogy. And Glen looked like he was about to piss his pants.

"Your grandmother's father was Khaiber Khan," continued The Clipper. "He worked for the Shah of Iran, British Intelligence and the CIA. He helped the CIA overthrow the Iranian Premier in 1953 and install the Shah as a puppet ruler."

Trevor shook his head violently. "No way."

"He named his daughter Shirin. After sixty-eight, Shirin started going by Sherry. Sometime later, Sherry became Charlotte. Shirin Khan had no social security number. Does your grandmother?" The Clipper turned to Charlotte. "Did you ever get a social security number?"

"This is nuts," said Trevor. "Of course, she has one."

Sasha watched Charlotte for more signs of engagement, but all she saw were her lips moving, no sound coming out.

The Clipper added, "Days before Robert Kennedy's assassination, witnesses saw Khaiber Khan and Sirhan Sirhan visit the senator's campaign headquarters together, trying to learn his schedule. They made several visits, and Shirin accompanied them on the final one – a day before the assassination."

Everything Trevor knew about his identity now appeared in question, but he didn't look lost. He looked – what was it? Curious? Excited? And Sasha found it offensive. "They were stalking their victim," she said. "She *was* the girl in the polka-dot dress."

Glen tugged at her top, shaking his head and trying to be subtle about it. But he wasn't.

"The dress was a tool for Sirhan's hypnosis," said The Clipper. "The dots triggered his mental programming. All she had to do was say his instigating words: *port wine*."

"How do you know that?"

The Clipper ignored her question, continuing his lesson. "Sirhan was an insecure little man. It took someone like Khaiber Khan to befriend him, to woo him into his confidence, both being from the Middle East – a heritage Sirhan embraced. It was something he was proud of. Then they brought in Shirin's boyfriend, Michael Wayne. I don't know how close they were. Free love and all, but he completed the team."

Her thoughts went to the Sandy Serrano testimony she read with Frank – and which he just referenced in his call to Trevor, who had it on speaker for all to hear. Ms. Serrano claimed

Sirhan Sirhan, the girl in the polka-dot dress and another young man passed her on the fire escape going into the Ambassador Hotel. And only the girl in the polka-dot dress and the young man came back out. *Could Michael Wayne be the young man she described?*

The Clipper continued. "Witnesses saw Khaiber Khan and Michael Wayne arrive at the Ambassador Hotel together on the night of the shooting. Other people saw Wayne casing the hotel, talking to an electrician about where Kennedy would be standing. Seconds after the shooting, witnesses said they saw Wayne run out of the pantry carrying a rolled-up poster and something shiny and metallic in his hand. A bystander tackled him, and a security guard handcuffed him. But the LAPD let him go, believing he was just a collector who wanted Kennedy to sign his poster. The man who tackled him later said he saw Michael Wayne with Sirhan in the lobby before the shooting. He said a girl in a polka-dot dress was with them."

It was as if The Clipper read her thoughts about the Serrano testimony. But if someone tackled Michael Wayne and a security guard handcuffed him, he couldn't have been the young man Sandy Serrano saw running out of the hotel after the shooting. She glanced at Charlotte and saw that she was now fully disengaged, repeating what she repeated after ingesting ibogaine. Hadn't the drug worked its way through her system by now? Why was she still reciting those words? Sasha wondered if this discussion triggered her the way the polka-dot dress and *port wine* were supposed to trigger Sirhan. And something else occurred to her as she watched Charlotte: she didn't look Middle Eastern. If her father was an Iranian, she wouldn't look as white as white bread. Maybe The Clipper's story was bullshit.

"The LAPD wasn't *entirely* negligent when it came to Michael Wayne," added The Clipper. "They didn't find anything shiny or metallic in his possession, but with the poster, they also found him carrying Keith Gilbert's business card in his pocket."

"Who is Keith Gilbert?" she asked.

"A Minuteman and a Neo-Nazi who the feds arrested in

1965 with fifteen hundred pounds of dynamite he planned to use to blow up Martin Luther King. After the cops inexplicably let Michael Wayne go, they followed up with Keith Gilbert. And they found him in possession of Michael Wayne's business card."

"You've got Minutemen out there." She pointed at the door. "Working for you."

"Working for us," corrected The Clipper. "Everyone here has an interest in the investigation. And now that you know –"

Now that I know? Sasha felt Glen lean into her.

Glen tried to keep his voice down. "That's what I was trying to tell you. I was wrong about them. They're not just mobsters, bikers and Minutemen. We need to get out of here."

The Clipper acted as if he didn't hear him – maybe he did, and maybe he didn't. But Trevor clearly did, even though he stood further from them than The Clipper. "8F," he said. "That's what we're called."

CHAPTER 21

Frank watched a Jeep enter the alley between an industrial building several years past its prime and a three-story office complex that looked underutilized. Moments later, his son appeared. It was 11:30 pm, the appointed time of their rendezvous. He'd never known him to be so punctual, and he didn't recognize the Jeep. Most importantly, he arrived alone. "Where's Nana?"

Trevor hit the worn metal door of the building with the meaty side of his fist. It took but one strike for a man to open it, releasing humming machine sounds from inside out into the night. He had stumpy legs, short arms, a round torso and glasses with a black frame. His hazel eyes looked everywhere but at them. "You're late." He opened the door wide enough for them to enter, but he closed it quickly after they did. And he locked it.

The facility was dimly lit, with a massive offset printing machine occupying over sixty feet of floor space. The machine was busy expelling the noise of its labors. A bin attached to the printer collected copies of the latest issue of *Vanity Fair*, fresh off the press. It seemed a testament to the diminishing popularity of print media that a major periodical like *Vanity Fair* tried to cut costs by printing in such an outdated facility. And where were all the workers?

"We agreed on eleven." The man looked at the clock on his phone.

Trevor towered over him. "Eleven-thirty."

"No. I specifically said eleven –"

"Who is this?" Frank asked his son, ignoring the impatience of the other man. He had to raise his voice to be heard over the machine. "Why are we all the way out here in Bell Gardens?"

Perplexed by his questions, the stubby little man threw his eyes at Trevor.

"Is it quiet in your office?" asked Trevor.

The man's head wobbled from side to side. "Quiet*er*."

Trevor acted as if he owned the place, leading them up metal stairs to a catwalk. The catwalk took them to a half metal/ half glass room that overlooked the workspace below.

How does he know his way around here? Rather than voice the question, Frank followed his son and the stumpy man into the office. He wouldn't get an answer anyway.

"There's forty-five minutes between when the last truck left and the next one picks up. And the midnight shift starts *at midnight*." The man closed the office door, cutting out a considerable amount of noise. "You leave me ten minutes to dump thirty minutes of information. Thanks." He didn't bother to remove the empty candy wrappers from his chair before sitting on it. "I want to make this clear." He directed his words at Trevor but glanced twice at Frank. "This is not a deposition. I won't testify to what I'm about to say, and you can't use my name."

Again, Frank looked to his son for answers. Again, he got none. The office had a long desk abutting the wall of windows. The desk supported two computers with monitors, a printer, assorted books, junk food wrappers and twelve to fifteen recent issues of *The New American*. He spent enough years as a prosecutor to know *The New American* was the primary publication of the John Birch Society, a far-right group with limited government and anti-communist views.

"So…there I was, tortured over what I learned for a piece I wrote." The man moved several magazines aside to find the one he wanted. He showed it to Frank while pointing at the title of an article featured on its cover. "Then the DA arrested your mother, and I'm like, *oh, shit*."

This time he made it more obvious, turning his whole

body to face his son.

Trevor simply read the words on the cover indicated by the man. "*Illuminati and the Founding Fathers* by Garrett Delany."

"That's me. I'm a Bircher, but most of all, I'm a patriot. That's why what I learned bothered me."

"You're –" Frank looked through a window at the hard-working printing machine. The John Birch Society was a potent fringe group in its heyday, at the height of the Cold War, but it no longer had enough members to justify high volume print runs of its magazine. The copies of *Vanity Fair* in the bin suggested this Bircher contracted for larger publications. That might've explained his skittishness. If his bosses weren't Birchers like him, they wouldn't appreciate him printing copies of *The New American* on company time. Then again, the place was so old and understaffed that the owners might not have cared what came off the press as long as it was something. "What did you learn?" he asked him.

Trevor gave his father a slight look of appreciation for playing along.

"I wrote an article that traced the history of the Illuminati, starting with their link to a small band of founding fathers. But I cut it short when I saw where it was going."

"Where was it going?" Frank heard the flat tone in his own voice. All conspiracy theories seemed to lead to the Illuminati, as if it was a big boogie man. And they lost their validity when they did so. *If this is a distraction by Trevor to keep me away from Charlotte, it won't work.*

"They confuse us by using different names, y'know. I found Illuminati who were also Freemasons, Odd Fellows, Skull and Bones, Bilderberg Group, 8F. They've been charting America's course since the days of George Washington."

"What course is that?" He glanced at Trevor, trying to read *his* thoughts.

"For the last century or so…communism. That's when I got nervous. We're talking *real* communism, not the Soviet variety that Steinbacher and Hilder exposed."

"Steinbacher and Hilder?"

"John Steinbacher and Anthony Hilder, Birchers. They were the first to reveal the Illuminati conspiracy to kill the Kennedys."

Trevor seemed legitimately interested in this. It made Frank think of when his son was a kid, very young, when he revealed to the boy the world's greatest mysteries, like the difference between *Godzilla* and a typical T-rex dinosaur. But the vision vanished as fast as it appeared. In its place, he saw what his boy became: a tatted, street battle-scarred, steroid-inflated man with a connection to the mob and an interest in murder conspiracies.

The Bircher continued. "Steinbacher wrote of a plot to control the world that began in Bavaria and grew to become an international Communist conspiracy. By the 1960s, it included the Rothschild banking family, the Rockefellers, Freemasons, the Zionists and such mystical societies as the Rosicrucians and the Theosophists."

"Let's focus on the Kennedys," said Trevor.

"The Communist conspiracy was obvious with the hit on JFK. Everyone knows Oswald was a Marxist. He lived in Russia for a time. He took orders from Soviet and Cuban handlers."

Trevor pressed him. "And Bobby?"

"The day after Bobby Kennedy was shot, Steinbacher and Hilder announced the Illuminati were responsible. The mainstream press mocked them, but it turned out they were right. When police later read Sirhan's notebooks, they found that under hypnosis, he wrote about the Illuminati and Master Kuthumi, who founded the Theosophical Society. Sirhan, by the way, was a Rosicrucian, and that's where he was first exposed to hypnotism."

"You getting this?" Trevor asked his father.

He almost didn't hear him. What the Bircher said made him think of the material Rip gave him. It covered Sirhan being a Rosicrucian. Of course, he already knew plenty about Sirhan and hypnotism. He also knew the young assassin filled his journals with automatic writing while hypnotized, but he didn't know those journals included references to the Illuminati or the founder of the Theosophical Society. "Yeah," he said. "I'm getting it."

"Fortunately, Steinbacher and Hilder had powerful supporters like Patrick Frawley, CEO of the Schick Safety Razor Company. And more than two thousand Los Angeles County cops were loyal Birchers back then."

"You said you ended your article when you saw where it was going," he said.

Garrett looked through the glass at the door leading outside. "Did I lock that? Yes, I did." He glanced at the desk clock, opened a drawer and extracted a Butterfinger. "I used to get really pissed when people claimed Birchers killed the Kennedys."

"Did you come across something when you researched your article?" He got a nod from Trevor. They were on the same page. Great – but not really. What was his son up to?

"I'm getting to that." Garrett took a big bite of the candy bar, his eyes rolling pleasurably back in his head before returning to his explanation. "My dad was in Desert Storm, but I can't serve. Bone spurs. I'm a patriot. I think I said that already. As a patriot, I can't get behind anyone or any group that would kill a commander-in-chief or a politician no matter what their policies."

"What did you find?"

Garrett finished his Butterfinger. He sat up to check the outside door. "Is that handle turning? It looks like it. You should get out of here."

"We're not leaving until we hear the rest," said Trevor.

"Of course. They told me to tell you everything. But that requires more than ten minutes." He looked askance at Trevor.

"Who told you that?" asked Frank.

Garrett ignored his question. "Thomas Valle was a Bircher, right? They arrested him in Chicago with a trunk full of weapons and plans to kill JFK exactly the way they killed him three weeks later in Dallas. But he was also an ex-Marine, like Oswald. And he had mob ties. I could attribute his involvement in the JFK plot to him being in the mob, not because he was a Bircher."

"Okay."

"Then I dug up stuff on John Martino, another Bircher with mob ties. He worked for Santo Trafficante and Carlos Marcello."

"Mob bosses."

"That's putting it mildly. They were two of the three most powerful bosses in the country. The other being –"

"Sam Giancana."

Garrett nodded. "Martino told a reporter from *Newsday* he was involved in the JFK plot. Not as a gunman. He said he made payments and organized things. I put him in the same category as Valle. He was acting as a mobster, not a Bircher."

"The district attorney has no interest in John F. Kennedy's assassination unless it relates to Robert F. Kennedy's assassination," said Frank.

The Bircher shifted in his chair. "'Some white patriot will splatter Robert Kennedy's spoonful of brains in public before the snow flies.' That's a quote from Westbrook Pegler, one of our members, written before Bobby's assassination. Is the district attorney interested in that?"

"Possibly. Was it a threat or an incitement to commit murder?"

"Two months before RFK's murder, the Birch Society mailed an LP record to congressmen. The cover of the album depicted Nelson Rockefeller at the precise moment an assassin's bullet smashed through his skull. Eight years later, a member of our society tried to assassinate Vice President Rockefeller. There's only so much I can justify. Know what I mean?"

He *did* know, and he nodded to show it. The First Amendment protected free speech, but not when it instigated a crime. Robert Kennedy's brains *were* splattered, as Pegler predicted. And a Bircher tried to kill Rockefeller as per the LP's artwork. "Tell me more about Pegler."

Garrett's paranoia, it turned out, was well founded. His back went straight as the front door opened, allowing two men to enter the work area below. He shot to his feet. "Time's up. You gotta go. No one can see me talking to you."

"Why not?"

The Bircher looked at Frank like he was the dumbest person he'd ever met. "Did you hear a frickin' word I said?" He opened the door. He tried to push Trevor out of the office but wasn't successful, so he took Frank by the sleeve and pulled him out onto the catwalk. "I'm implicating Birchers. It doesn't matter if they're dead or if what they did was fifty years ago. It gives the organization a bad name. Get it? What with your district attorney launching a new investigation and all –" He stopped and turned to him. They were now only a few feet from a staircase that led to the back of the building and, presumably, a rear exit. "Why are *you* working on this? Do you hate your mother or something?"

Trevor caught up to them. "Good question."

"Delany," shouted one of the men. He had a powerful and angry voice that rose above the noise produced by the printing machine. "Get your fat ass down here!"

"Dope." Garrett shook his head. "He can't find the pallet I plastic wrapped for loading. I gotta do everything, including point out the obvious. At least I can get time between shifts to myself. I gotta go. You can take the stairs down to the back door."

"Wait." Frank grabbed Garrett's arm. It was squishy to the touch, like a jelly filled sponge. "Those groups that make up the Illuminati, I've heard of most of them, but what's 8F?"

The Bircher tried to pull his arm free, but he held firm. More interesting than that – what most caught his attention – was the expression that crossed his son's face. No longer approving of his participation, he looked downright alarmed by the question. *Why does that bother him?*

Again, the Bircher pulled his arm. Again, he failed to get free. "Let me go."

"Delany! Where is that toad?"

Trevor reached to break Frank's grip on the Bircher. "We got what we came for."

He moved out of his son's reach but still maintained his hold on the Bircher. *What don't you want me to know?* His ice blue eyes drifted from Trevor to Garrett. "8F? What is it?"

"A consortium of the most influential and well-known politicians, businessmen, religious leaders and mobsters in America," said Garrett. "They named themselves after a suite in the Lamar Hotel in Houston: the 8F suite, where they often met."

Trevor moved faster than a man of his size should've been able to move, surprising both of them. He broke Frank's grip while also shoving the Bircher backward. "I told you –" He pulled his father down the stairs.

Garrett must have felt the same way about Trevor's suspicious behavior (and abrupt shove) as Frank did because he elaborated where he seemed disinclined to do so a moment ago. "They'd been running the country since December 7, 1931 – ten years to the day before the Japanese bombed Pearl Harbor. That was when Texans took over the federal government, becoming Speaker of the House and chairmen of five of the most influential committees. They held the real power in America. They didn't start calling themselves 8F until the sixties. By then, the group included such notables as Lyndon Johnson, Richard Nixon, J. Edgar Hoover and –"

Trevor leaped back up the steps he descended and threw his fist. If he intended to shut Garrett up, he succeeded. He also hit him hard enough to make his nose splatter like a stomped, ripe tomato. The Bircher landed backside-first, bounced and slid about a dozen feet. He was out cold by the time momentum stopped carrying him away from the point of impact.

Frank's eyes went to twice their normal size. He'd seen his son hit men on many occasions, but he always anticipated it. The disagreements seemed predictably destined to end with Trevor's ever-ready fists. This, however, surprised him. And he sought an explanation while continuing to watch the event unfold in real time. *He brought me here to get information I could use to absolve Charlotte? He brought me, but someone told him to do it. Not Sasha. It was someone else…someone he didn't want talked about – someone connected to 8F?*

Trevor spun to face his father. "Look what you made me do." He seemed troubled by the damage he inflicted.

That was something new. Never before had he seen his son show regret. *Why now...over just a single punch?* And Trevor didn't seem to know what to do next.

"I don't have time for this." The voice of the most vocal newly-arrived man now sounded closer. He had apparently ascended to the catwalk.

"He probably went for take-out again," said the other man, sounding equally close and equally irritated.

"His head's gonna roll if he did."

Trevor gave the unconscious Bircher a last glance. It was a quick one. He grumbled and snarled, shook his head. His departure wasn't hasty, as if he had nothing to fear from the men looking for Garrett. But he did go. As he passed Frank on the top of the stairs, he gave him a shoulder check that sent him into the wall. "If there's blowback for this, it's on you." His heavy feet took him down the staircase, and he added, "There's no 8F. Not anymore."

While watching his son disappear into the darkness of his descent, Frank heard, "What the hell happened here?" He turned to see both of the men standing over the still and bloody Bircher. One of them pulled a box-cutter blade and pointed it at him. "Don't you move, you son of a bitch."

CHAPTER 22

Los Angeles, California. April 7, 1968

In the four months since Charlotte left Matthew, the country has become a cauldron of flammable fluid. And the crowd now swarming around her says the match is about to be struck. Hell, it's *been* struck. Martin Luther King, Jr. is dead. There have been riots all around the country because of it. And she's here because of Matthew's stupid pop-up book for little boys.

She watches thousands of people cross Figueroa Street, heading toward Memorial Coliseum, where a celebration of life for the slain Civil Rights leader is about to take place. No white person would dare provoke them at this time – no one except Pete. He already hit the horn once, and he's about to do it again when she catches his fist before it can land. They're in a convertible, which offers no safe barrier between them and the hard-looking Negroes walking past. It's a brand-new olive green GTX, beautiful and covetable. Pete is bouncing like a live wire because he knows they all want to get their hands on it. And it's not his. It belongs to the dude he's working for – that guy named Provenzano, who he's supposed to pick up in twenty-five minutes. He yells, "Out of the way, Casabooboo."

"Do you want to get us killed?"

A congestion of jaywalkers forces the car to stop. He checks on Bobbi and Francis in the back seat, then he turns to her. "This is madness. You're mad."

"Drop us in front of French Dip." She points to the diner in the corner of a red brick building that's also a hotel.

"They're honoring a commie and an agitator. He was nothing to you."

"Just pull over." She watches the swarm separate to accommodate the car as it pushes ahead, creeping to the corner. She turns to the kids. "Stay with Momma and hold my hand the whole time. You dig?" Bobbi nods while her brother keeps looking around.

Pete brings the car to a rest beside a lamp post. "They're crazy in grief over Martin Luther Coon. You think you'll be safe here? Really?" He doesn't notice – or doesn't care to notice – the coloreds who whipped their heads around to look at him when he said *coon*.

"We're here to pay respect to a man who tried to find a better way." She gestures to the kids. "They'll see no one should be on the low end of life because of the accident of their race."

"At two years old do you think they'll remember this? You're changing."

Again, that pop-up book flashes through her mind. "I'm *trying* to change." She throws the door open, almost hitting the lamp post he parked too close to.

"Watch the door. Hey –" He grabs her arm. "Listen to me. You don't want to do this."

He's acting macho, but she can feel the nervousness in his quivering grip. "This isn't Watts," she tells him.

"It could be much worse."

"If you wanted to stop me, you wouldn't have driven us here."

"What could I do? You're – you'll just call another cab."

That's her thought exactly. She's kinda happy, sort of emboldened, knowing he knows she'll leave with the kids if she has to (returning to Matthew, he thinks). He has the big muscles, but she has the power. "We'll meet you here when it's over. Five o'clock?"

He sucks on his lips and shakes his head, but he says, "No later."

#

Charlotte all but declared Pete is the twins' father when she moved back in with him. She shouldn't threaten to take them from him whenever she wants to get her way – not if they both own them equally. *Own them – ha! They're my kids because I birthed them. I know what's right for them. I won't feel guilty over doing what I have to do for them. I won't.*

It's a cool day, but their little hands feel slippery in hers. Do they know the coloreds have been burning cities across the country for three days? She squeezes them tighter, remembering they're far too young to get what's going on. Someday, she hopes. Someday they'll understand kikes, blacks, spics, chinks and other slurs aren't the dirt under a W.A.S.P.'s feet. "Matthew is an asshole." Bobbi looks at her. *Did I say that out loud?*

A woman behind her says, "There's talk they're gonna give Watts a new name. They're gonna call it King Town. I like the sound of that."

A nearby man groans. "Na – I don't 'prove. Ya name them slums and ghettos after him, and that's all Honkey will eva' think ah the black man."

She doesn't dare join the conversation, but she'd like to. *They need a dose of what Robert Kennedy told those black leaders. Take responsibility, and you'll get respect. Who cares what they name the slums?*

"Who ordered the vanilla?" A young man with wide sideburns has his dark eyes fixed on her. "What'cho doing here with us, woman?" He and the Negroes with him are all dressed in black: leather jackets with turtleneck shirts and berets. Several also display firearms in holsters.

She knows who they are. How can she not? They've been haunting White America on the evening news for a while. They've been more visible lately and more menacing since Martin Luther King's slaying. She tries to maneuver herself and the kids away from the young man, but the throng is thick, making it hard to move.

He stalks her. "These aren't your people. He wasn't your

Martin."

She can't go back, and she can't go left. She and the twins can only shuffle forward.

"I think you're having fun with us," he says. "Look at the crying Negroes."

She'd love to tell him he's wrong. She wants to say *I'm enlightened. I'm down with what you're doing.* But silence is her best course. She quickly checks her kids even though she's holding their hands. They're okay, but they're scared. They can probably feel her fear. Damn that book she wouldn't let Matthew give to her son. Pete was right. They shouldn't be here.

A grandmotherly woman with curly white hair speaks up. "Let her be. We're all hurtin'."

Her fretful eyes shift to the old woman, feeling relief, but even the kindly grandmother looks at her like she doesn't belong. *Where's the white section? There have to be other whites here besides me...whites who get it.* She doesn't see any, but she does see the young man's friends coming to back him up. They maneuver like a military unit. She moves away from them like the mother she is, with two small children.

Unhindered for the most part by the crowd, the young man manages to place himself smack in front of her. She swallows her breath. His manner and his attire are more threatening in person than on the television. His face is as hard as obsidian. He has a stainless-steel firearm in his hand, ready for use. "I don't like bein' made fun of."

Her heart runs wild in her chest. She can't stand up to him, and she can't flee with the kids' hands in hers. *This is why Honkey thinks what he thinks of you when he thinks of you at all.* Again, silence is her best option when thoughts like that are in her head.

"You heard Mother May," says a woman. "She ain't causin' no harm."

One by one, others agree with the woman. Charlotte looks around in bewilderment. These people aren't unfriendly toward her. The guy with the gun is, but not the rest. It's a legitimate surprise. It shows she was right to come here. She wishes Pete stuck around to see this.

"Martin spoke of black boys and girls joining hands with white boys and girls like they was brothers and sisters," says an older black man with deep wrinkles. "Brotherhood."

The young man frowns and slowly shakes his head, tapping the gun against his chest. "Yeah, Martin said that. Then Whitey took him out. We don't need to be holding no white children's hands. We need to take care of our own, build *our* schools and feed *our* people."

That's what Kennedy said. Oh, if she could just tell him that.

"Nonviolence is to live weak and die like a lamb," he adds. "I'd rather live strong and die like a lion."

The crowd musters other comments, but they're becoming contradictory while competing to be heard. "King's way is *the* way." "Give us action, not words!" "Follow Martin's dream." "By any means necessary!" People shout out many more opposing slogans – so many that she gets dizzy, turning her head to see who said what. She finally returns her eyes to the young man, who never stopped looking at her. His black-centered eyes wilt her with their ferocity. She tries to move away from him but is even less able to do so now. With every phrase shouted, the crowd seems to close in on her. Voices calling for her expulsion from the gathering grow louder and more numerous than those arguing on behalf of her and her children.

She can't find any warm faces. She looks for the police, who are supposed to protect innocent whites from violent blacks. They're there. She sees them, almost a dozen of them, standing like hookers on Figueroa Street. They look like they'd rather be somewhere else. They don't even know she's there. "I'm here to honor King," she says weakly.

Hard black faces twist as the people who own them try to decide if she's telling the truth.

The little wet hand held by her left slips free, but she's quick to grab Francis by the arm before the crowd swallows him. "Don't move!" Her bark startles the already agitated boy. He looks like he's about to cry. She turns to Bobbi, who is already crying.

Someone yells. "This ain't no place for Black Panthers!"

"Go back to Oakland," says someone else.

She likes what she's hearing. Maybe the crowd is turning. Is that possible? If she has learned anything today, it's that these people are not homogeneous. Who'd have thought there'd be diversity within the Negro race? Matthew's pop-up book doesn't say anything about that. The Panthers appear defensive in the face of people disapproving of them. For some unknowable reason, the crowd begins to move again, making its way toward the Coliseum. Its pace is slower than she prefers, but maybe it's enough to get her and the kids to safety. She only needs about ten tightly packed bodies between her, her kids and the Panthers. If she gets that, she'll beat feet with the children straight for Figueroa. She learned a lesson today. She can explain it to the twins when they're old enough to understand. It's not *that* important that they pay their respects to King. Pete was right about that.

"Martin Luther *Coon*," says the young man.

A hundred heads turn to him, or it seems that many. The hope that buoyed her up a moment ago retreats. She feels herself sinking, knowing why he said that. She concentrates on looking straight ahead. The dream of their escape keeps her moving, pulling the kids, but the congestion, she realizes, has returned. Her momentum slows. She's getting stuck again.

The young man moves his gun like a bouncing ball. "I heard her call him Martin Luther *Coon* when she was up there on the street, sitting in a car no honest black man can afford."

She and the children are stopped – no moving right, left or forward. If she goes backward, she'll be face to face with the Panther again. And he has his wall of friends behind him. "I didn't say that." She's talking, but it's as if the words come from someone other than her. "He's lying." She nervously runs her hands through her tangled hair. In so doing, she releases her children. She has to think quickly and smartly. The blame for the *coon* comment belongs to Pete, but would anyone see the distinction when he brought her here? "I'm a Jew," she blurts out. "My people were slaves. I'm like you."

Reactions are immediate and not at all what she expected. Her truth should be their truth. It doesn't matter that the masters of her descendants were Egyptians and theirs were American. It doesn't matter that thousands of years separate their people's servitudes. Why can't they see that she and they are one? She hears some hisses sizzle in the crowd. Most of her neighbors look upon her with astonishment – and not the good kind. She feels the air growing thin.

Where are my kids? Bobbi? Francis? She reaches for them, blindly at first. Then she whips her head left and right. She can't see them. Where are they? They're lost in a hateful mob. They can't both be gone, yet they are. Did someone take them? These people would love to get their hands on some pure white, innocent children. "Bobbi? Frankie?"

Her calls are lost in a new fierce murmur developing in the crowd, growing louder by the second. She doesn't care what's causing the building din, focused as she is on her quest for her children. But she's attuned to any words that might point her in the right direction – words like *white*. She hears the angry young Panther use that word in the process of calling for the destruction of her race. He adds other phrases like *white devils* to his monologue. He pumps up the venom, trying to incite the crowd. And it seems to be working.

She can feel the tension squeezing her like a vice. She shouldn't have said *slave*. That was a poor choice, but was it as inflammatory as *coon*? Does it matter? She sees Bobbi. *Oh, thank God!* The little girl is crying in her fear and confusion, searching for her mother amidst the tall and tightly packed people around her. She pushes to get to the child when she hears a high- pitched voice scream, "Momma!" A small body wraps around her leg, squeezing, and she realizes Francis is clinging to her with all he's got. She feels relief roll over her like a heat wave. She found her kids – both of them. She tries to lift him up, but the little bugger holds on tightly.

Crack! The sound that explodes beside her is both

recognizable and unspeakable. Screams accompany it. She spins around at the precise moment her beautiful Bobbi falls to the ground, convulsing. A wound in her head spills blood onto the pavement. She dives for the child, partially slowed up by the other child still holding onto her. Where she lands, there are legs hidden by black pants and dark shins covered by stockings beneath black dresses. They're scrambling and running, seeking safety for themselves. The people's screams sound like a frightened chorus that won't shut up. All she wants is to get to Bobbi – *her* Bobbi. And the boy is like an anchor attached to her leg. She sees the flash of something shiny and steel amidst the fast-moving mass of black skin and dark clothing. It's the weapon that shot her daughter, still smoking in the hand that squeezed its trigger. She connects eyes with the young Panther as he releases his hold on the gun. The look on his face is one of shock, saying this was a supremely tragic accident. But she doesn't care. Her baby girl is…is…is she still breathing?

#

2018

Sasha had the freedom to explore her confines – how nice of her hosts. She felt the warmth and appreciated the light cast by the morning sun upon the hills that surrounded her and the out-of-date town through which she wandered. The tranquility was nice, but it did little to assuage her troubled thoughts. *And what's with this place?* She counted thirteen 1970s-era buildings. They stood on each side of the main street – the only street, and they were in various states of dilapidation. Actually, they were mere shells of buildings with no structure inside them. Grass stretched tall all around them, and bushes that used to be manicured now grew wild and misshapen. She knew California, the filmmaking capital of the world, had many retired film/television lots, but most were made to resemble Western towns. She had never heard of an abandoned 1970s film lot. Yet here she was, *wherever* it was.

To further complicate her time warp, she saw three men fiddling with modern motorcycles and that dirty Santa Ernie Tolliver working on a Corvette, a year or two old by the looks of it. *Minutemen*, she thought. It wasn't a good group to be a part of, but she didn't know any more than that because she couldn't look it up on her phone. She saw The Clipper walk out of the primary building, which actually *was* a building, and approach the motorcycle men. She marched toward him, passing Ernie Tolliver. He waved to her, wrench in hand, but she didn't wave back. Why would she? A Minuteman from the sixties intended to blow up Martin Luther King, Jr. with fifteen hundred pounds of dynamite. Who could join a group with members like that? What atrocious acts did Ernie Tolliver commit as a Minuteman? *But if Minutemen are in 8F, and I'm in 8F, I joined a group with members like that.*

She reached The Clipper feeling sick from her associations, and she didn't bother to hide it. "I want to leave."

He tilted his head to the side without replying. Maybe he didn't hear her over the loud bikes. He was also at the age where people had impaired hearing.

She raised her voice. "I need to get back to Brookside where I'm needed."

"How do you know your partner isn't already there?"

"Is he?" That would explain why she hadn't seen Glen all morning. "It doesn't matter," she said. "The place needs both of us to run properly."

The Clipper gave the nearby bikers a glance. They silenced their motors and left without question or comment. *What's he got that makes everyone obey him like that?*

"You stole their Golden Goose," said The Clipper. "Do you really think law enforcement won't be looking for you?"

The hills and all the vastness around the pseudo-town began to close in on her. She wobbled on her feet. Why hadn't that occurred to her? The district attorney wasn't stupid. He had to know she coordinated with Charlotte's abductors, especially since she stole the old woman from him once before. "I'm a fugitive."

"And now that you know." A smile crept up The Clipper's tan, mildly wrinkled face. "The hardiest plants grow in the shadows. It's where I've chosen to live most of my life."

"It's not where I want to live mine." Her eyes dropped to the little white bell-shaped flowers attached to his lapel. They seemed to be always with him, pinned to some part of his clothing. And she thought how impossible it'd be for them to grow in a shadow. *This guy's full of shit.* "You're not interested in getting her to tell us what she knows about the assassination."

"No?"

"You're –" She stopped. He had a way about him that made calling him out a lot harder than she expected. She averted her gaze and found Ernie Tolliver looking at her. He seemed acutely interested – or noticeably worried – as he watched her.

"You're about to call me Houdini?" The Clipper laughed. "I perform slight-of-hand tricks in the shadows of my speakeasy?" He shook his head, still smiling. "Houdini is just a pinball machine. I'm interested in reality and in exposing the truth."

"Someone did something to Charlotte." She tapped her temple with her finger. "If you don't know who, I'm betting you at least know how to help her. That's what I'm interested in." It was the best ultimatum she could think to give him. She spun on her heals and marched off. She felt him watching her. She felt Ernie Tolliver doing the same – and to him, she returned the look though she wasn't sure why. He didn't seem as foreign to her as everyone else around there did. But, she reminded herself, he was a Minuteman.

CHAPTER 23

Frank figured someone, perhaps a nurse or an orderly, would inform him if Garrett Delany was ready to see visitors. It was just a punch – a helluva punch, but a single punch nonetheless. It didn't seem likely that he'd still be messed up over it. Maybe by milking an injury, the Bircher was able to avoid the exposure that so worried him back in the printing warehouse.

It didn't take much to convince the deliverymen someone other than him knocked Garrett out. That probably should've insulted him – them so readily accepting that he couldn't have produced such a powerful punch. But thoughts of his son consumed him then just as they did now, some twelve hours later. From the hospital waiting room, he scoured the internet for information on 8F, hoping to read something that gelled with what he knew of his son. Was Trevor in 8F *and* the mob? Were they one in the same? Or were they smaller subsets of a larger, dangerous, international entity like the Illuminati? It seemed preposterous, but he'd heard so many wacky things lately he knew he couldn't dismiss any of it. He needed to have a follow-up conversation with Garrett because the internet told him next to nothing.

The man or the woman sitting across from him, at the opposite end of the waiting room, made a noise that caused him to look up. He didn't get in their business, but he surmised they waited on a child undergoing surgery. And it was touch and go. In looking up, he saw Rip Reed enter the room. His friend caught his glance but hesitated when he noticed the frightened, nervous couple. A look of sympathy – earnest sympathy – crossed his face, but he didn't speak to them. It didn't seem appropriate, given his status as a stranger.

"Took you long enough," he said as Rip sat beside him. "I left that message at three."

"Three *a.m.*" Rip frowned. "Some people sleep. And Tippy is fine. Good of you to ask. My grandchildren have been pulling on her ears and wrestling with her tail."

"I hope they know she'll be coming home once I've – when this is all behind me…which brings us to the other thing I asked you about."

Rip shook his head, his eyes going to the other two in the waiting room.

"They don't care. We're not talking national security here."

"Are you sure about that?" Rip kept his voice low, just above a whisper. "You asked me about 8F, Lyndon Johnson, J. Edgar Hoover and Richard Nixon. And you left it in a voice mail."

Frank studied the seriousness imprinted on his friend's face. He really didn't think it was a big deal. Fifty years ago – more than fifty years – with all the principals dead, why would anyone now think it a threat if he asked about it? "Okay. It was late. I was tired. I couldn't stop thinking about it. I should've been a little more discreet."

"Yeah." Again, Rip looked at the couple. They weren't listening. They couldn't hear him even if they tried. And they clearly had other concerns. Nevertheless, he kept his voice down. "Johnson, Hoover and 8F, I need more time for that. But I got some stuff on Nixon you might find interesting."

"Like what?"

"On November 21, 1963, the day before JFK's assassination, Richard Nixon attended a meeting at the Dallas home of oil millionaire Clint Murchison. Murchison was an 8F higher up. When the FBI later asked about the strange coincidence of him being in Dallas at the time of the president's assassination, Nixon told them he was there *two days prior* to the killing. Truth in point, he flew out of Dallas only three hours before the shots rang out."

"History has Nixon down as a liar, but –"

"Probably not directly involved, but he stood to gain from JFK's death. And he stood to gain more from Bobby's. There's an odd connection between Richard Nixon and Sirhan Sirhan."

"Another strange coincidence?"

"You tell me," Rip replied. "Nixon was a close friend of Haldor Lillenas, the most important gospel hymn writer of the 20th Century with over four thousand compositions to his credit. Their friendship dated back to when Nixon was a student at Whittier College. In the fifties, Mr. Lillenas and his wife were the primary sponsors of the Sirhan family's immigration from Palestine to the United States. And they continued to influence the Sirhans well into the next decade."

"That *is* a coincidence."

"In March of sixty-eight, Nixon was campaigning in Portland, Oregon, when he saw Robert Kennedy declare on television his intention to seek the Democratic Party's nomination for president. His aides later stated on and off the record that Nixon shut the television at that point, stared at the blank screen for a long time. Then in a deeply haunting voice, he told them, 'We've just seen some very terrible forces unleashed. Something bad is going to come of this.'"

Frank didn't say anything, but he was sure he wore as serious an expression as Rip wore only moments earlier.

"With Nixon, you have motive and means," Rip continued. "He lost one of the closest elections in history to John Kennedy in 1960. Eight years later, he likely would've faced Bobby Kennedy in the general election. He had the influence and the dubious connections to pull it off. In particular, he had a friend in the man who exerted great influence over Bobby's assassin."

He continued not to say anything then finally shook his head. "It's hearsay and conjecture at best. Knowing someone who sponsored Sirhan's family to come to the States more than a decade earlier isn't a crime. How many other families did that hymn writer sponsor over the years? And as far as what Nixon said when Bobby joined the race...with all the violence of the times, including JFK's assassination, I'll bet a lot of people said the same thing. Robert Kennedy had a bullseye painted on his back the moment he announced his candidacy."

"I thought it was the job of a prosecutor to look at any and *all* suspects."

"I am. And I'll do you one better. Proving someone as prominent as Nixon was involved would take all the attention off my mother. The Hottest Place in Hell."

"What?"

"What was the quote you gave me in RFK Park?"

Rip thought for a moment, then he answered, "*The hottest places in Hell are reserved for those who in times of moral crisis preserve their neutrality.*"

"Exactly. You accused me of –" He hesitated as he saw a woman in a white doctor's coat coming down the hallway toward the waiting area. She had news for someone, probably the nervous couple sitting across the room from him, and her expression indicated the news wasn't good. He had to finish talking before she arrived. It would be rude to do otherwise with them suffering over a bad report. "You said I take the path of least responsibility. That would be putting the blame on a prominent person, facts be damned. Everyone wants to see those headlines. But I'm following the path of justice regardless of what it does to me or my family."

Rip looked like he wanted to believe him but couldn't quite get there. "What about your son? You said he –"

Seeing the doctor enter the room, he silenced Rip with a raised finger. But she only glanced at the worried couple on her way to him and Rip. "Mr. Caron, I –" She paused, showing sadness but not too much emotion – the mark of a veteran doctor with a well-developed bedside manner. "I was told you're Mr. Delany's friend. You came in with him...I'm sorry."

"You're what?"

"He took a blow to the head. I can't imagine what kind of force that was. We tried to control the hemorrhaging, but that coupled with brain swelling, which we couldn't control, he expired some –" She checked the clock on the wall. "He passed six minutes ago. I'm very sorry."

Frank's eyebrows rose up his forehead to reach their highest point, and they stayed there. *It was just a punch. It was – Oh God. Two people are dead at Trevor's hands, and those are only the ones I know about.* He glanced at Rip, wondering what he was thinking, wondering if he wanted to remind him of what he said about following the path of justice regardless of what it did to him or his family. *No. He doesn't know Trevor did this. Does he?*

"Do you think you could help us locate his next of kin?" asked the doctor.

He nodded to her but thought, *I have to locate my own kin first.*

#

At night the faux seventies village had a ghost town feel. Sasha decided that wasn't so extraordinary since most people who'd been in their prime in the seventies were now dead or close to it. The only light came from spillage through the windows of the main house and from the moon and stars overhead. If the place was abandoned, as she assumed, where did the power for the main house come from? She didn't see or hear any generators. Someone had to pay the electric company to keep the lights on.

The Clipper said she was free to roam wherever she wanted, but that wasn't true. She couldn't leave because no one would give her a ride out of the pretend town. She didn't know how to hotwire a vehicle. And – lest she forget – she was a fugitive from the law. She just hoped no one had eyes on her now as she crept along the main street's broken sidewalk. She slid the phone out of her pocket. That no one confiscated it or even once mentioned it since she arrived only meant they knew she couldn't use it – at least not for its usual purpose. She powered the device up and hugged it to her chest to prevent its start-up from attracting attention. Forty yards from the main building, she figured she'd gone as far as she needed to go.

The building frontage to her right was that of a

neighborhood convenience store with featured items priced according to the decade they represented: milk $1.35 per gallon, eggs 62¢ per dozen, bread 73¢ per loaf, etc. She took a detour down the alley separating the store from a bicycle repair shop called The Spokesman. It was so dark in the alley she didn't see the wall that cut the space short until she bumped into it, producing a hollow thud sound as it was plywood made to look like brick. This was the spot, she decided as she rubbed the sting from the impact out of her cheek. She had one ace to play – well, three actually: three sketches taken in that brief time when ibogaine opened Charlotte's closed memories. They were in her pocket, where they had been since she stole them from Frank and Charlotte's motel room. She wasn't sure what The Clipper would do with them if he got ahold of them, but they were what he professed to want when he said he sought the truth from Charlotte. That, of course, was a lie. They'd been in the seventies-era hideaway for several days now, and he had yet to seek her assistance in accessing Charlotte's memories. What he really wanted was to put her and Charlotte on ice while the DA conducted a new investigation into RFK's assassination. That was her assumption anyway, and it was why she escaped into the alley with the sketches in one hand and her phone in the other.

She looked around again to confirm her solitude. Then she hit the flashlight icon on her phone. With its illumination as her guide, she crouched low and laid the sketches flat on the ground. To her surprise, they were ripped. She didn't remember doing that. Damn! To make things worse, there was a slight breeze which she only now noticed with the fluttering of the papers. She did her best to piece the pictures together, but the moving air tormented her. She finally had to kneel on the first two sketches. Tucking the two halves of the third drawing under her arm, she touched the phone's camera icon. She squared up the image on the screen with the first sketch. Its tear was on the side of the page, so she felt confident in the rendering's clarity. Click. She took two more photos to be sure. She moved on to the next sketch, but she stopped. Something made a noise outside the entrance to the alleyway. It sounded to her like footsteps or shuffling feet. She waited, frozen stiff.

Nothing came back to her – no more sounds and no movement. She went on to sketch two. It was imperative that she photograph the drawings. They were her only insurance policy against whatever The Clipper had in store. But in doing so quickly, she was also unsteady. The breeze didn't help either. She stuffed the pieces of the first sketch between her legs while holding the second picture in place with her left hand and right knee. The rip went through its center, so she couldn't quite align the pieces. The best she could manage with Mother Nature's blowing was something that looked like the drawing of a deformed man. It would have to do. Click. Click. She went to the third rendering.

She thought she saw something move in the alley entranceway, but she couldn't be certain. It was so dark. Rendering #2 quickly joined #1 between her legs, and she pressed the pieces of the third on the ground. Even more unsteady now, she fought to control her shaking hands. And – what an odd thing to think at that moment – she wondered if Charlotte shook from fear, like her, rather than from the effects of ibogaine.

The halves of #3 proved more cooperative than the others, and she felt more confident about this one as she lined it up for the picture. Her thumb hovered shakily over the white button that would take the photo. Just as she thought she had the image ready for capture, the nuisance wind split the halves. Click, click and click. She didn't know what the pictures looked like, and there wasn't time to check her work or do a retake. She heard more strange sounds.

She kept the flashlight on long enough for her to assemble all the pieces into a single stack. Then she killed it. The return to darkness was supposed to bring comfort with its ability to hide her, but it didn't. Again, she thought she saw movement in the front of the alley. Much to her frustration, the moon and the stars didn't help her see anything definitively. She had to assume someone was there. It would be to her detriment *not* to assume it.

She plunged the phone into her back pocket. All along,

she had intended to destroy the originals so they wouldn't fall into The Clipper's hands, but she wasn't sure if she'd be able to do it when the time came. Her captors hadn't yet discovered them. Maybe they wouldn't. But now, with someone watching her, she had no hesitancy. She ripped, and she tore. She shredded the precious papers until they became a collection of tiny pieces. If it was The Clipper that came for her or one of his henchmen, he'd get nothing from her but a fistful of confetti.

She fed the paper bits to the wind, but they only went far enough to fall back on her like snow. She hastily wiped them off. She took the bold step of walking *toward* the person who'd come for her. He'd find her but not the papers, unless she failed to wipe off all the pieces. In the dark, she couldn't tell if she got them all. She wiped some more, aggressively, but she didn't want him to see her doing that. So she stopped. She took a deep breath to fortify herself to boldly take on whoever came after her. His outline appeared first in the darkness, confirming her assumptions that he was there. It was a big and imposing outline. Did she expect otherwise? He appeared to have no hesitancy as he stalked toward her. Her mouth felt dry. The breeze blew harder, colder. Maybe it would scatter the confetti. She dared to hope so.

"I see you," he said. "What are you doing here?"

At that moment, it occurred to her, and she wasn't sure why it hadn't occurred to her before then, but *he could be a predator. He could be a rogue horny sicko wanting to have some fun with me when no one is looking.* "I'll scream," she said.

He stopped.

"That's right. I'll –" She noticed that the patch of darkness under the outline of his head was a beard. His shoulders and his arms weren't as large as she originally thought, but his belly was larger. She strained to see him more clearly.

"I wouldn't do that." He had something in his hand, and it lit up. He raised it before his chest, and with his other hand, he poked at parts of it. "I don't think he'd want me to show you this." He turned the lit object toward her. It was a rectangular screen – a cell phone.

She breathed a bit easier, realizing the man who followed her into the dark alley had been her white knight once before: Ernie Tolliver. Her eyes went from his face, which began to fill out before her, to the illuminated phone. "You have reception?"

"Do you want to see this or not?"

As she stepped closer and he pressed play, she realized his phone contained a pre-recorded video. He didn't need to have any reception to show it. The action that played out on the device occurred at Brookside in the light of day. The sounds that accompanied it were chaotic and confusing: screams and shouts, whistles and threats. It was like something she'd seen on television – clips of those police shows she never liked to watch. It was a raid of her place of business. Officers with uniforms, badges and batons charged through Brookside at the command of supervisors, one of whom she recognized as Flat-top. Employees and residents she'd come to think of as family resisted, but they couldn't stop cops from evicting them from the building. She searched for Glen in the footage but couldn't see him. Where would their residents go? Did the authorities even bother to find another facility for them? Her guess was no.

"A friend sent this to me," said Ernie. "On orders of the District Attorney of Los Angeles County, your place of business is now out of business."

"He can't –"

"He can, and he did. This video is from earlier today."

"Where's Glen?"

He cleared his throat. He shifted his weight from his right to his left, suggesting uncomfortableness. "That's the other reason I came looking for you."

CHAPTER 24

Redondo Beach, California. April 9, 1968

Charlotte feels alone in a house filled with sorrow, there yet removed, floating along the ceiling in a sort of out-of-body experience. She hears Beverly talking as if at a distance though she's only ten feet away. "She hogged a joint before the funeral," says Beverly. "But it's the ludes and acid that launched her into space." The beach bunnies are in a circle around her. Everyone came for the burial and its after-party encore, except Matthew. He was the one person she wanted to see before she got high. Now, who cares? Mr. Provenzano paid for the funeral and arranged for it to take place so soon after the murder. He's been inexplicably good to Pete. She has the feeling he's familiar with swift and efficient burials. Again, who cares? She has also come to realize that her son Francis is a bit on the stupid side. He hasn't a clue where his sister is or why everyone around him is so bent. Worst of all, he doesn't know it's his fault. He distracted Mommy, giving the Negro an opportunity to cold blood murder her precious Bobbi. But she still loves him. She has to. He's all that's left. As he waddles up to her, she drops a limp hand on his shoulder. It's not enough for him, and he tries to enliven her. *Let me be.* She removes her hand.

"Geeze-us, Cha Cha." One of the bunnies picks him up. "There, Frankie."

A scurvy dude says, "Let her fly, babe." He was the one that gave her the most potent pill. He *claimed* it was the most potent. We'll see.

Someone somewhere turns on the box. What's a party without tunes? She'd prefer the blues, but what she gets is *Puff the Magic Dragon*. A kid's song, it won't due. She tries to stand, but her body won't do much while her spirit is floating. And *what the – whoa*. There's a dragon gliding along the ceiling. The song must've summoned it, or the acid. It flaps fierce wings that send her out-of-body back into her body. She jolts as if convulsing.

Beverly is by her side in a flash, helping her to sit upright. "You're tripping. It's okay."

"What's wrong with her?" Pete arrives from nowhere. He has puffy red eyes – fire red.

She stumbles to her feet – now she can, with her spirit intact. "Get away. It wasn't my fault. Don't turn those burnin' peepers on me." He's got the dragon's wrath. The only way to save him – to save any of them – is to mute the infernal song that gives life to the flying lizard that no one but her can see. Somehow, for some reason, the tune is louder now. And the press of people between her and the radio reminds her of the black mob that witnessed Bobbi's killing. She screams a sound that's incoherent even to her, and it must've offended the dragon because the beast dives for her. She ducks. "Look out!"

Pete wraps arms the size of boa constrictors around her. "Get a grip."

She thrashes. He has scales on his arms – like dragon scales. "You're turning. No!" The soaring monster opens its jaws, about to devour them. She can't dodge it. She can't escape because Pete is too strong, holding too tight. He's always holding her, she realizes, preventing her from realizing her potential. She snaps her head back to hit his face, but he slips the blow.

"Get your shit together." He throws her back into the chair she previously occupied.

"Take it easy, fella," says a dude with a handlebar moustache. "We just buried her baby."

"*My* baby." Pete turns this way and that way. He's not sure what to do.

Beverly steps up, cups his tear-dampened face in her hands. "He didn't mean anything."

Somewhere within the cluster of people, the music box becomes silent. Someone must've received the message Charlotte put out and shut the damn thing.

Pete responds to Beverly, "I told her – God knows. Now there's a hole in my heart."

"There's a hole in her heart too."

He grunts. "All I been seeing from her is strung out." He flicks on the boob tube. "This'll occupy her 'til she comes down." He spots a guy holding a beer. "I need a drink."

Just like that, the dragon disappears with the song. Now Charlotte can resume her quest for the numbness that helps her cope. She stares at the television screen. It is mind-numbing technology, and it's a good place to start. She tries to block out the people and their chattering, but it's not so easy when a little boy waddles into her field of vision, coming toward her. With the television behind him, it looks like he's walking *out* of the screen. He resembles the girl they've come to mourn because he's her evil twin. "Get away from me!" She sits up abruptly.

The beach bunny named Louise swoops in, grabbing and lifting Frankie, swinging him out of the reach of his erratic mother. The boy squeals as he soars.

She watches Francis and Louise meld into the wall of chatterboxes. *I'll love him later. I will. Let me have this moment.* She returns to the television. It's her only friend, and it shares her sorrow by showing her people dressed in black. There are thousands of them, filling the screen. *That's how I feel. Give me black. Make it all black. Wait – what, no.* She realizes the clothes *and* the skins of the people on the boob tube are black, most of them. Where has she seen that before?

"What the hell is she watching?" says a voice she doesn't immediately recognize.

Beverly replies, "Looks like King's funeral in Atlanta."

"They're televising it?"

"He did more than Kennedy, and they televised his funeral

stuff for four days."

A famous face appears on the screen. It's the other Kennedy – the one with a cowlick that flops onto his forehead, the one now running for president. She stands in a rush, but she feels slow in doing it. She's off-balance. Someone comes to steady her – Beverly, she realizes. She takes the help. She needs it, but it barely registers with her. She can't take her eyes off the television and Bobby Kennedy, who's the star attraction at Martin Luther King, Jr.'s funeral. His pale face bobs in a black sea as he talks to everyone, shakes hands and looks sad. The darkies treat him like a friend. A Negro woman falls into him, crying into the lapel of his suit coat. And he hugs her.

She drifts toward the television, as if pulled by it. The crowd in the house moves blurrily in her periphery, continuing its chatter, but the only noise she cares about is that which comes from the broadcast. She gets close enough to the tube to turn the volume knob up. A black preacher fills the screen with his thick body and heavy voice, saying, "We give thanks to God who gave us a leader to heal the white man's sickness and the black man's slavery."

"Chrissakes, shut that off!"

She turns her swimming head to see Pete returning to her, slowed by the people packed in the house. She goes back to the television, and there's Bobby Kennedy again. Of the thousands of people at the funeral, the camera likes him best. He's huddling with black leaders, and the video shows him saying, "You have to pick up the cross of the fallen hero and carry it on."

Her mind may be confounded by chemicals, but she knows she heard America's next president correctly. He told a violent minority who believes the white man is sick to carry on. Carry on in their hatred. Carry on dealing vengeance for their enslavement. Carry on shooting little white children. She turns to find Pete – to seek his comfort in this madness. He's coming, but another man is closer. She's seen him a few times, never spoke to him, and she didn't know he was here today: Mr. Provenzano. He's a tall, lean, well-dressed, 100% Italian. He seems to be someone who should not be crossed, and he looks at the television as if something or someone on the broadcast did exactly that.

"Martin's gone," says a voice from the T.V. She throws her eyes back at the screen, finding it filled with the face of a young black man, intense and sweating in the heat of the moment, the heat of the day. "We only have one hope left," he adds. "That's our soul brother with blue eyes. That's Bobby Kennedy."

Pete's hard arm shoots across her line of sight. He pinches the power knob, turning off the television. "That's enough of that shit."

Mr. Provenzano shifts his gaze to him without moving his head. It's hard to tell whether or not he approves of ending the television's broadcast because he turns and he departs. The crowd parts obediently to make room for him.

#

2018

Frank felt his patience tested by the teddy bear wearing a flower dress that hogged the sofa chair he sat upon. He couldn't remove it because someone sewed it to the seatback. That was the purpose, of course: testing whoever sat there. The man sitting across from him in a bear-free chair made a career of evaluating people. His opinion could put someone in a mental institution or help to absolve a suspect of a crime by reason of insanity. It wouldn't look good for him to fight with a toy bear while a man like that observed him.

Dr. Issur Fierstein had the appearance more of an orthodox rabbi than a highly-respected psychiatrist. He wore a bushy, clavicle length beard and small round glasses. His office was a testament to the unconventionality of his practice. Instead of a couch, he had a beanbag chair. A contour inversion table occupied a corner of the room. There was also the teddy bear.

"Thank you for making time for me."

"Well, you said you're working with the district attorney." Dr. Fierstein forced a smile. "It's good to keep someone like that happy."

"Just to be clear, District Attorney Diaz didn't send me. He doesn't know I'm here."

Dr. Fierstein paused, showing nothing with his expression. "What can I do for you?"

Frank had an attaché bag at his feet, crammed full of notes. He hoped he wouldn't have to use it. The less he revealed about their case, the better, especially when the DA didn't sanction this meeting. "A few years ago, Sirhan Sirhan's attorneys called for a second evidentiary hearing. They claimed he was programmed to cause a distraction in the pantry which allowed a second gunman to shoot Robert Kennedy from behind. They alleged that an unidentified woman wearing a polka-dot dress lured a hypno-programmed Sirhan into the pantry as part of a plot."

"The evening news said that woman has been found."

That was a poke, wasn't it? The doctor had to know she was his mother. Everyone was talking about it. He cleared his throat. "The attorneys based their claims on the testimony of a memory expert who spent sixty hours over a three year period interviewing Sirhan."

"Daniel Brown from Harvard. Why aren't you talking to him?"

"I thought I'd consult someone who wasn't hired by defense attorneys." He squished the toy bear only to have it spring back to its original size. *How annoying.*

"When you said you were working with the district attorney, I assumed it was different sides of the same case. I assumed you had to share what you learned. What's that called?"

"Discovery – if it goes to trial. This is just a hearing."

"Right. You're not defending your mother?"

"I'm working for the State," Frank snapped. "What...uh... what can you tell me about the Manchurian Candidate theory? Is it plausible?"

Dr. Fierstein was slow in answering. "Did you see the original *Manchurian Candidate* movie starring Frank Sinatra?"

He shook his head, and he elbowed the bear. *This thing is seriously getting on my nerves.*

"The night before his assassination Robert Kennedy stayed

at the home of John Frankenheimer, who directed *The Manchurian Candidate*. What a crazy coincidence."

"I'm interested in the facts of the case."

"Are you familiar with the 1954 case of Palle Hardrup?"

Frank's eyes dropped to the attaché bag. It contained material on Palle Hardrup, but he already knew the story. "Hardrup was supposedly hypno-programmed to rob a bank and kill people while committing the robbery. The Danish high court convicted the person they believed programmed him."

"Bjorn Nielsen," said the psychiatrist. "Closer to home, and closer to the time of Sirhan's crime, you get Charles Manson, who served a life sentence for programming his followers to commit multiple murders."

It felt like the teddy bear swelled to take up more of his chair. He squirmed to reclaim the seat space he lost. "My mother's not a hypnotist, hypno-programmer, whatever it's called."

"Your mother?"

"That's what we're talking about, isn't it? That's what –" He pinched the hem of the bear's dress and shook it. "This stuffed animal represents my mother?"

"Why do you say that?"

"The flowers on the dress look like polka-dots."

Dr. Fierstein let his words hang in the air, like fruit ripening on a vine. Finally, he said, "A hypnotized person requires a trigger as well as something to keep them programmed."

Why did I say that? He had to ignore the flowers on the bear's dress that *did* look like polka-dots. He had to get back on track, be a pro. "*Port wine* triggered Sirhan. With four Tom Collins cocktails in his system, he fixated on the dots on the dress to maintain his programming."

"In the seventies, Washington finally got around to investigating CIA abuses," said the doctor. "They uncovered the MKULTRA Project, which CIA Director Allen Dulles personally created with the intention of behaviorally engineering human beings."

The bear played another game as it sat beside Frank. He

got a vision, albeit brief, of the teddy bear Trevor clutched the day he brought him to Charlotte because he was in no shape to raise a kid at that time. *Dr. Fierstein is screwing with me. Did he call the DA before I arrived? Did Marco tell him to do this? He knows Trevor killed two people.*

"The CIA employed doctors who used LSD, heroine, morphine, mescaline, psilocybin, scopolamine and other powerful drugs to turn innocent people into lab rats," continued the doctor. "They destroyed most MKULTRA files. Those that weren't destroyed had entire pages edited out. Still, investigators determined that CIA doctors *did* manipulate human behavior."

"Did they create assassins?"

"That evidence has disappeared."

He leaned to the right, putting as much space as possible between him and the bear. *Focus. Two can play this game.* "Without evidence, the Manchurian Candidate Theory lacks credibility. But the Hardrup and Manson cases establish precedence."

"Let's consider motive. For Manson and Sirhan, it was ideological. Manson's goal was anarchy by way of a race war. I believe Sirhan wanted to stop Israel from killing Palestinians with American-made bombers."

The papers in his bag covered that as well – papers he didn't want to take out for fear of playing into the hands of Marco and the doctor. "You're referring to the transcripts made public after Sirhan's trial in 1969? Prosecutors claimed Sirhan shot Kennedy because he saw a televised documentary which outlined RFK's intention to send fifty jet bombers to Israel if he became president. As a Palestinian who saw Israelis slaughter his people, it was too much for Sirhan, so he resolved to kill Kennedy. And he wrote about it in his diary."

"I understand they used the diary against him in court," said the doctor.

And who would've told you that? I knew you knew more about this than you let on.

"Most people don't realize how malleable the human mind really is," Dr. Fierstein continued. "Consider the happily married man who joins the military in a time of war."

"That's patriotism."

"Mind control on a national scale. He wasn't there when the Japanese bombed Pearl Harbor or when terrorists hit the World Trade Center. But he believed the hype and killed his country's enemies. When it was over, he went back home only to become friendly with Japanese and Muslim neighbors because his government told him to do so."

"The documentary programmed Sirhan the way media coverage of a terrorist attack might make a happily married man become a soldier? Is that what you're saying?"

"Propaganda can turn anyone into a warrior defending his sacred tribe, but it is far less personal to kill as a soldier than as an assassin. Only five percent of the population is susceptible to the kind of deep hypnosis that makes *that* possible. I've never had a session with Sirhan, but I know psychiatrists who have. They're convinced he's among that small percentage."

Frank saw Dr. Fierstein's eyes drop to the dress-wearing bear then snap back up to him. It was a tell that seemed uncharacteristic for a professional like him.

"Propaganda alone won't program at that level," continued the doctor. "It takes a skilled hypnotist to make someone do what they normally wouldn't – to become what they are not. Media influences, like that documentary, and the drugs I mentioned, are tools to help the programmer."

Frank dove into the attaché bag. After that tell, he was no longer worried about revealing too much to the psychiatrist. It seemed Marco had already told him plenty. He pulled out a page with a headline that read PROBLEMS WITH THE PROSECUTION'S CASE – 1969. "That documentary didn't help anyone program Sirhan." He scanned the page until he found what he wanted in the third paragraph. "The journal entry where Sirhan first recorded his obsession to murder Robert Kennedy was dated May 18, 1968. But the documentary that supposedly inspired his obsession didn't air in Los Angeles, where Sirhan lived, until May 20. And the documentary said nothing about

Kennedy sending American planes to Israel or even supporting the Israeli state. It wasn't until May 26, eight days *after* Sirhan wrote the diary entry, that Kennedy announced his intention to support Israel with American bombers."

"Hmm."

He felt like he delivered a strong blow to the programming argument – the argument made against his mother – and all he got back was hmm? He re-read the paper. *What did I miss?*

"I don't think that matters," Dr. Fierstein finally said. "Look at the doctors who worked for the government. If you can connect Sirhan and *your client* to anyone from MKULTRA, you have a solid case for a Manchurian Candidate."

"My client is the State."

The psychiatrist chuckled. "Yeah, and I won't be billing you for this session." He leaned forward, and he picked up the bear. It was apparently *not* attached to the chair.

CHAPTER 25

Frank's eyes snapped open as his phone beeped from the nightstand. The clock beside the phone said it was 2:13 a.m., not surprising to him because he'd been watching the numbers change for the last three hours. He had too much on his mind to sleep: what happened in Dr. Fierstein's office, what his son was up to and why his every attempt to reach him since the Bircher's death failed. And there was his mother – always his mother. He swept the phone into his hand. Tippy lifted her head from the floor. Even in the dark, he could see her ears up, like satellite dishes searching for whatever signal he sent out.

He dared to hope it was Trevor reaching out to him, but the phone told him it was a text message from Sasha. That folded his brow painfully, thanks to the soreness he still felt over the beating he took. Rip assured him he hadn't been able to get any signal from Sasha's phone since she abducted Charlotte for a second time – or a third time if he counted when she helped Marco's men in Twentynine Palms. How could she send a text if her phone didn't put out a signal?

He tapped the message icon, and three pictures appeared on the phone. He felt his eyes grow wide with the surprise the images brought to him. He knew them well, though they were now ripped with their pieces not fitting tightly together. He also knew why she had them, having seen her take them from their motel room moments before he blacked out. They appeared over-exposed, as if someone had put a spotlight on them before photographing them. One was a tad blurry, but they were all decent enough to be useful – especially if the right computer program analyzed them. He saw that she added a message: *This isn't about you and me. Find out who these men are. I'll be in touch. I'm taking care of Charlotte as best I can.*

What did she mean by that? How bad was Charlotte? He typed, *Bring her back.* He started to type more but knew anything else would just make it *about you and me.* He hit send. "She won't respond to that. Bitch."

He could see Tippy didn't approve of him calling her that, but she *was* a bitch. Why would she send the sketches now after giving them to him then stealing them back? He tried to look at things through her eyes. For her, it all started with hypnosis. He sat up abruptly, causing Tippy to jump to all fours. "Hypnotism," he realized. "Dr. Fierstein said hypnotists programmed Sirhan *and* my client. My client –" He returned to Sasha's text, enlarging each image to study, then shrinking it to go on to the next one. Back and forth he went, sliding his thumb up and down the screen to move the pictures before his eyes.

Tippy barked at him.

"No walk, girl. False alarm." He stared at Sasha's name at the top of the screen. "This isn't what you intended, but – thanks." Exiting out of her message, he scrolled through his contact list to find the number for Marco Diaz. He glanced at Tippy. "She's still a bitch, though. You don't know her like I do."

Tippy laid back down, evidently disappointed.

The phone rang twice before Marco answered, "Frank? What is it?"

He frowned. The DA didn't sound even a little bit groggy, and he so wanted to wake the bastard out of a happy slumber. "You need to hypnotize me."

Marco hesitated, but only for a moment. "I was thinking the same thing."

I doubt it. But there was no time for him to waste arguing the point. He needed to make another go at pinging Sasha's phone, and he was afraid Rip wouldn't be so easy to wake up.

#

Sasha wheeled Charlotte down the center of the only street in the pretend town of their strange captivity. The sun in her eyes prevented her from seeing much of the seventies-era façades they wandered past, but she was already sick of them. The past was the past. Her mind was on the present, particularly what became of the text she convinced Ernie to send Frank using her phone so he'd know it came from her. Dirty Santa refused to take her with him, but he did take the phone. That left her without one, but what use was it to her here anyway? *Where is he now?* She wondered if she was right in trusting him. Since she turned the pages into confetti, her phone contained the only copies of those sketches. And there was another promise she extracted from him. He said he'd look for Glen. She *really* hoped he'd deliver on that one. Glen liked to do his own thing, often without telling people ahead of time. But he left after warning her they needed to get out of there. That was a reason for her to worry.

Her musings came to an abrupt stop when Charlotte flipped the brake lever on her wheelchair. She nearly dumped the chair and the old woman onto the blacktop. "Charlotte!"

"I'm gonna die here." Charlotte tapped her temple with her finger. "But I'm taking this with me when I cross the Styx River."

She looked for eavesdroppers, but it wasn't necessary. Unless they had a long-distance microphone aimed at them, no one would be able to hear them. "You have your secrets, I know."

Charlotte laughed. "My boy will splinter them into a thousand pieces and scatter them to the wind."

Is this real, or more of her game playing? Whatever it was, she knew she had to tread carefully. Her total alone time with Charlotte over the past four days amounted to probably half an hour, and The Clipper was always somewhere nearby. She wondered if Charlotte was in a mood to talk now that he wasn't there. She stayed behind her chair so as not to spook the old woman if she *was* in a sharing mood. "Did you and Frank plan something?"

"I have secrets. *He* has deadly ones."

Her stomach dropped, which reminded her how much she'd invested in Frank. She wasn't trying to reignite their romance when she begged Ernie to send him that text. She wasn't even trying to make nice. She needed him to use the sketches to identify the men hidden in Charlotte's repressed memory. And she needed him to give her due credit for the assist. It was the only way to clear her name and put an end to her life on the run. "What do you mean?"

"What do you care?"

She exhaled exasperation, and she shook her head.

Charlotte still moved like a Parkinson's sufferer, and she appeared to be scanning the faux buildings on the side of the street. "You left my Frankie, I think. I know you two were one."

"I told you we were dating. What do you mean when you say he has deadly secrets?"

"What do I mean when I say he will splinter them into a thousand pieces and scatter them to the wind? President Kennedy said that. I am repeating him."

Game playing it is. We're back to riddles.

"Only those that stay get to know the secrets," said Charlotte. "Do you know why?"

"Why?"

"President Kennedy didn't stay, so he didn't get the secrets. Little Kennedy either."

"The secrets you're taking across the River Styx?"

Charlotte said, "The ferryman is coming for me. I've seen him."

It seemed the right time to risk moving around the chair to face the old woman. "Would you like to share those secrets with me before he comes for you?"

Charlotte studied her with that good eye of hers. The other eye remained as unanimated as the half of her face it inhabited. "I mean for you to stay with Frankie. He's too alone."

Her stomach reacted again – this time performing a summersault. Did the old woman actually care about her son?

She had never acted like it before, which made her wonder why Frank bothered. As far as she could tell, it was about atonement – him trying to make up for something he'd done. The deadly secrets, perhaps? She doubted there were any.

"Eight effin pieces." Charlotte dug for something on the seat behind her.

Did she say 8F in pieces? Or was that eight fucking pieces? Pieces of what?

With her good eye, Charlotte looked over Sasha's shoulder. "Get your things."

"I don't have any things here."

"It's time for you to go."

She turned to look where the old woman looked. All seemed normal at first glance: the face of a two-story home between similar façades with a severely overgrown front lawn and the shell of a Chevy Nova in the driveway. Then a shadow moved across the top of the Nova. A forearm poked out from behind the faux building. It was a forearm as big as her thigh.

"Is this your *thing*?"

She twisted around to see Charlotte holding her phone, but there was a major difference between how it looked now and how it looked when Ernie took it. It was now broken in pieces. Eight pieces? She didn't bother to count because there was something even more disturbing about it. There was dried blood coming off the phone in flakes. "Where did you get that?"

"Dead." Charlotte tossed it to her.

It bumbled back and forth, right hand to left, before she caught it, like it was too hot.

Trevor stepped out from behind the pretend building, but he didn't step far. He looked around cautiously. "I'm your only chance out of here."

"Wha – what?" She had a million questions. But Charlotte had already turned her chair, making her way back to the main house.

"Let's go," said Trevor. "I won't say it again."

CHAPTER 26

Frank was into his second consecutive sleepless night, but this time he entered it purposefully. It was part of the process that prepared him for hypnosis. No sleep, no food and no drink weakened his body and made him most open to hypnotic suggestion. That was how the man in charge explained it – not Marco, but the man Marco put in charge of Operation Hypnotize Frank. His name was Dr. Fitz, a strange-looking aged hippie. He had no illusions about who the doctor was or how bad he was. He remembered seeing him from a distance the day they pulled Charlotte out of Brookside, taking her into custody. He probably also gave her the dreaded ibogaine. Frank would deal with that in the future – he *definitely* would, but now he needed to get his mind to a place where his suppressed memories from 1968 could resurface. He needed Dr. Fitz to do that.

He had to put Sasha out of his mind (Rip still couldn't get a signal from her phone), but he needed the sketches she texted him. He spent the day with them, hoping they'd summon his memories from a conscious state. They didn't, so he passed them on to Marco, who'd put them through the rigors of analysis at some point. Right now, for this exercise, Dr. Fitz had them. Maybe they could summon memories from Frank's subconscious.

Location was another important part of the process. Dr. Fitz called it immersion hypnosis. The district attorney's researchers, which may or may not have included Rip, determined Charlotte lived in Redondo Beach prior to RFK's slaying. Local newspapers reported a fatality at that address on April 21, 1968. It also happened to be the date in which family and friends celebrated Frank's second birthday. The place was abandoned shortly thereafter, the building was condemned and later demolished. Not surprisingly, his mother never told him about that.

"Every breath takes you deeper," said Dr. Fitz. "As you go deeper, you feel better. As you feel better, you go deeper." He'd been calmly repeating phrases like that for hours.

He inhaled long breaths, as he'd been doing since the doctor began. The things that would have distracted him, such as a curious crowd, police and noise produced by an active community, failed to do so now. In fact, he didn't even see or hear them. Nor did he see the moon and stars overhead, vehicle headlights or lights in the windows of nearby buildings. He stood in a litter-specked house lot, breathing salty air as it drifted off the nearby ocean.

"Your mind and your body are loose. There is nothing but peace here. You are relaxed. Easy and calm. Let your thoughts wander back to the last time you were here."

The willingness to let go, along with the deprivations, handicapped the ego and super-ego parts of his personality. His id began to open up.

"You are relaxed and calm. Calm and relaxed. Nobody wants anything, needs anything. There's nothing you need to do but relax and let go. Breathe."

He felt himself drifting. Images appeared to him as if imprinted on a transparent veil.

"There are people in your house." Dr. Fitz's monotone continued. "There are lots of people. It's a birthday celebration. It's your birthday."

The images fluttering in his vision became slowly more recognizable, blinking in, then fading out, blinking back in. He saw green shag carpeting that looked like indoor grass. Bare feet trod the carpet along with feet wearing sandals. Tie-dye wall hangings and window coverings decorated the place which he now seemed to occupy. He smelled patchouli. And he smelled something else. It crept out from deep in his olfactory memory. It was sweet, heavily floral and honey-like with a wisp of suave balsam.

"What do you see?" asked the doctor.

#

A fog of sweet smoke fills the house, absorbing all the Beautiful People. Francis doesn't know who Mary Jane is, but Mama says she's the one bringing all the happy smoke. It's been a bad year, she explains. They need to get back to the good times. Pop surprises him, scooping him up off the floor. He smells like honey and pine, and he wears funny little flowers that the boy fingers. "Don't touch them," he says with a smile. "We've got something else for you."

Francis likes to be in his arms, but he squirms to get out because, on the other side of the crowd, Yvie is holding a leash connected to a brown dog with thick, gangly hair.

Mama swiftly steps between Francis and the pooch. And she yells at Pop. "No dog."

"Oh, lighten up."

"Oui, Charlotte. Lighten up." Yvie seems proud of her use of an American-ism. "Le boy needs a playmate now that –" She doesn't finish, but everyone knows what she was about to say.

"I don't know what makes you think you're welcome here, Yvette." Mama throws her fiery face at Pop. "Can't you go anywhere without her?"

"She's a friend."

"A friend you mount?"

Pop shrugs, taking her question in stride.

"No dog, Matthew." Mama points at Francis. "His father is allergic."

#

Frank couldn't see Marco Diaz or anything else that wasn't part of his hypnosis. He also couldn't hear what Marco said in a conversation with Dr. Fitz, but he heard the doctor, who sounded to him like someone talking from the far end of a tunnel. "He won't see the drawings," said Dr. Fitz. "I could hold them in front of his nose, and it wouldn't matter." There was a gap with no noise coming from the doctor. Then his voice came through clearly, speaking directly to him. "Frank, you see a man. He's a big man. He wears horn-rimmed glasses with black frames. He has sandy blond hair and a beard under his chin but not on his face. It's called an Amish beard."

#

Mama is in the bathroom with some beach bunnies, sharing hash that came from Oceanside. She's done arguing about the mutt, which means Francis gets to keep it. For now. A hodad calls it Alley-Oop, after the song. It's as good a name as any.

The boy follows Alley-Oop, who follows Yvie into a back room. On the other side of a beaded entranceway, they find four men sitting around a poker table, but they're not playing cards. Three of them look blurry, as if hidden behind a haze. But Francis sees the biggest one. He's a big tuna with black glasses and a hairy neck, naked face. He's dangling a gold pocket watch. Pop is against the wall, whispering into Yvie's ear. His spiffy threads make him stand out as cool and all-knowing. Francis is in awe of him, and he gets a wink for his admiration.

The big tuna waves the watch before a fella with a face Francis can't see, but the fella wears duds that look like he spent last night sleeping under the pier. "It's not hypnotism," says the big tuna. "It's magic. It's the power to influence events with mysterious forces."

#

Frank heard Dr. Fitz as if in a tunnel again. "I don't know what that means. Now – okay." The doctor let out an audible breath. "Mr. District Attorney, your interruptions aren't helping." A moment later, he sounded like he stood just over Frank's shoulder. "Frank, you see another man. Most of his head is bald but for hair on the sides and in the back. He has a sharp, pointed nose."

#

The haze hiding the man to the left of the big tuna disappears, and Francis watches his face take shape. It's fierce, narrow and focused. It's like a bird's face, and he has a chrome dome. He says, "The mysterious forces are in Eddie's mind."

Pop says, "Looks all show and no go to me."

Afraid of the chrome dome, Francis hides behind Pop's leg. But he peeks out at the man.

"You can't hypnotize someone to do something that goes against their basic moral code," says the big tuna. "That's why you give 'em a high moral purpose."

#

Again, Frank heard Dr. Fitz at close range. "Frank, there's another man. Do you see him? He's pudgy, with a high forehead. He has thick eyebrows and a double chin."

#

The fourth man at the poker table comes into focus, sitting to the right of the big tuna. Francis steps out from behind Pop's leg to look at him. He isn't as intimidating as the chrome dome with the bird face. He is in his middle-aged years with a full face, broad shoulders and a round gut. "Yes sir," he says. "An eye for an eye, like the Good Book says. Everyone agrees with that."

The man with the chrome dome replies. "This isn't about revenge, Curly. In most cases, the subject doesn't know the target."

The big tuna says, "When I worked on The Manchurian Candidate with Frank Sinatra –"

"We know," snaps Curly. "Can't we go an hour without you mentioning it?"

"'Scuze me."

"Meanwhile, back at the ranch," says Pop.

"All I'm sayin' is it can be done. If I have a man's trust, I can put him deep." The big tuna looks directly at Pop. "But he needs to be able to go to level five."

"Level five?"

"Where he can see things that aren't there."

"Don't forget a high moral purpose," says chrome dome. "And a trigger."

Beads in the entranceway tinkle as Mama awkwardly enters. Her threads are disheveled. Her movements are herky-jerky. Her eyes look like cloudy ice on a frozen pond. "Where's my last birthday baby? There he is. Come to Mama."

Francis slinks further behind Pop's leg.

"What did you do?" asks Pop.

Mama's manufactured smile drops. "What'd I do? Having a time is all. Fat City, right? Celebrate the death of one and the birth of the other."

Pop turns to Yvie. "Take him out of here."

Mama ignites like the wick on a stick of dynamite. "Why's she get the assignments?"

"Charlotte."

"You think I don't know? I don't make pop-up books, so I don't know?" Mama points at the men at the table. "I know him and him. I don't know him." She stumble-walks up to Pop, making Alley-Oop uncomfortable as he moves out of her way. "I read The Profound Revolution, y'know. Three times I read it cover to cover. International bankers – international Jewish bankers – are making a New World Order. I'm a Jew, and I want in." Her face sags as if gravity tugs at her cheeks. "You think mothers can't be revolutionaries?" She looks at Francis, hiding but watching her. "I'm only half a mother now."

Yvette gasps. "Oh mon Dieu!" She throws her hands over Francis's little ears while scurrying to get him out of the room.

CHAPTER 27

They called a helmet's padding a pillow, but to Sasha, it felt like Trevor's huge hand squeezing her small jaw. And with Bluetooth technology, he spoke to her while pushing the bike's acceleration beyond her comfort level. "Hold tighter," he said. "I'm not stopping if you fall off."

She couldn't see much through her helmet's tinted visor in the dark of night on a rural road without streetlights, but she did manage to catch a glimpse of a roadside sign with the word *Wisteria* on it. And she knew three 8F bikers raced after them. It was why Trevor had their Harley going over a hundred mph and climbing. She squeezed him tighter, and she imagined it was probably what it felt like to hug a giant sequoia tree. "Help me understand. We're *not* leaving 8F? Why are they chasing us?"

"I'm not. You can do what you want. I never thought you really joined anyway."

"That doesn't tell me why they're chasing us."

"I'm guessing their orders are to keep you and Nana on property." He leaned the bike left to accommodate a gradual bend in the road. It would've been gradual if he wasn't speeding.

She leaned opposite of him, afraid the bike would tip if she added her weight to his. She probably didn't need to do that, but – hell, she didn't know. "Why are you doing this for me?"

"It's not for you. They're hypnotizing Frank –"

"Your father?"

He answered her by turning his wrist. The engine roared

louder and more aggressively.

She had to squeeze him tighter as the odometer jumped into dangerous digits.

"Nana says you have to be there, so you're going."

She couldn't consider what he said when all that came to mind was a vision of her splattered on the road if the front tire hit a rock, or he lost control, or whatever. "Slow down!"

#

Francis is outside on the porch, his young heart pounding as he watches Mama through the screen, yelling over the noise of the party. Yvie tries to comfort him, but no one can block Mama out. She's going off on anti-Semitism, Rosicrucianism, Illuminati, and – smack!

Yvie turns him toward her. "How would you like to stay with me? We can make baguettes and les crepes avec brown sugar filling. Doesn't that sound delightful?"

Mama took a hard slap to the face. He tries to see who did it, but Yvie holds him in place. She's strong – stronger than him. She's about to say something else, but Daddy's home! Francis jitters with excitement, making her look where he's looking. They watch Daddy drive a car owned by Diamond Joe into the yard. Nowadays, he's always behind the wheel of a Diamond Joe car. This one is a new Camaro, tomato red, with thick black racing stripes on the hood and the trunk. Yvie lets him go this time, and he charges down the steps to meet Daddy. Lug nuts and wrenches, hub caps, headlights, fenders and bumpers are obstacles for him to navigate. They lay about the yard, items in Daddy's auto parts cornucopia. He even has a jalopy up on blocks.

He reaches the car as the door opens. Too young to be able to correctly judge distance, he runs smack into it. His head bounces. His body, too, depositing him on his rump in the dirt. He's not really hurt. Nothing is broken. But the shock drops his mouth, wets his eyes. He'll cry when he catches his breath. Daddy leaps out of the car, and the boy reaches for him.

It's impossible for Daddy not to see him, but that seems to be the case. He's captivated by the far-out scene taking place in and around the house. His big chest puffs up while the veins bulge in his arms as he squeezes his fists. He sees Mama walk onto the porch, rubbing the side of her face. Pop follows her, yelling at her backside. Some of what he says carries into the yard. "Why I can't trust...strung out since your daughter died...get clean and maybe –"

With the car running and its door open, Daddy darts toward Mama. Francis is stunned when his father passes him. His arms are still outstretched, and the water show starts – beginning as a cry, quickly becoming a full-blown wail.

Daddy takes the stairs in a single bound like Superman, and he lands before Pop. The barks fly from Mama's mouth, but there's no telling if they're hostile or appealing. She puts hands on him. Again, her intention is any observer's guess. If she's trying to move him, he's too big, too powerful and too angry to accommodate her. The wails coming from Francis shrink to a whimper as he watches the adults on the porch. Daddy yells, "Again, Char?" She screeches a response that's lost in the noise of hippies emigrating from the house to see a fight. Her face wears a red handprint. She points it out to Daddy, who turns on Pop with his fists up.

Francis sees a man nonchalantly kicking an oil can as he walks away from the house. He's round, and he looks like he once had muscles. He's the dude who sat to the right of the big tuna in the back room – the one they call Curly. He looks down at the boy then glances back at the porch. "'Be not drunk with wine, wherein is excess.'" He pats Francis on the head, groaning as it's not easy for him to bend over. "Someday, you will understand why men do what they do. It's an imperfect world." He notices the foxy Camaro running with its door invitingly open.

Daddy's words yelled at Mama drift across the yard. "If I put him through the wall, you'll only invite him back. Won't you, Char? Who do you want? You can't have us both."

"Gotta split, son." Curly bags Diamond Joe's wheels, but he pauses to drop one more line of wisdom on the boy. "'At the hand of every man's brother will I require the life of man.' So sayeth the Lord." He climbs in, closes the car door.

Francis watches the Camaro back out of the yard with Curly at its helm.

"Don't you use that," says Daddy. "You been coming and going 'tween us long before Bobbi passed."

Pop addresses Mama, staying clear of Daddy. "For once, I agree with him. It's time for you to put up or shut up. The opportunity is there if you want it."

#

Sasha alternated between feeling like she'd soon vomit and feeling as if the high speed at which she traveled pushed her insides down into her southernmost body cavity. Between those sensations, she managed to contemplate what Trevor said about his grandmother. She combined that with what Charlotte told her earlier that day about her not wanting Frank to be alone. *This escape is an attempt by a mother to protect her son,* she decided. *Why does she want to protect him now? And from what?* "How do you fit into this?"

"What?"

"Charlotte said Frank is going to break 8F into a thousand pieces. I'm wondering how you fit into that if you're still in 8F."

Trevor took his time in answering, and he used that time to avoid a strip of tire retread lying in the middle of the road. She didn't see it until they swerved around it, inhaling in sudden surprise. "I don't know about that," he said. "But I trust Nana. She brought me into 8F after my career in the Octagon flamed out. It gave me a purpose, and I believe completely in our mission."

There's so much to unpack with that. Where do I start? Coming from behind them, the beam from a headlight swept the road to their right, then it disappeared in the soft shoulder. One of the pursuing bikes was closer than she thought. She squeezed Trevor more tightly.

"You're right to be nervous. They're plenty pissed right now."

"This isn't making any sense to me."

He laughed.

"I'm serious. What are you doing?"

"Obeying orders."

"Right." She looked for more evidence of their pursuers closing the distance. She caught glimpses of light on sagebrush and earthen mounds. Their speed was so great she couldn't tell if the light came from heavenly bodies overhead or headlights behind them. "If you're loyal to 8F, like you say, you obey The Clipper, who wants me and your grandmother to stay hidden. But you're obeying Charlotte, who wants me to stop Frank from being hypnotized."

"She doesn't want you to stop it." He navigated another bend in the road. This one caused a screeching skid sound to come from the rear tire. "She wants you to put it on track. That DA and his doctor are on a witch hunt, and Nana is their witch. You need to get Frank to remember the truth. That's what she wants you to do."

That wasn't how hypnotism worked, and Charlotte should have known that. There was no point in arguing it with Trevor, so she stuck with stuff he did know. "How can you believe in the mission of 8F but disobey The Clipper?"

"The Clipper isn't 8F. He's just the leader – *a* leader. It's much bigger than him."

There was another question. She intended to ask it earlier, but the distractions of their frightening escape prevented her. Now she had the answer without having to ask why he didn't bring Charlotte with them. His grandmother wouldn't have left even if he tried to make her…not while she was trying to manipulate 8F from within. "It's a power grab."

"By Nana?" He laughed again – mockingly. "That's what Frank would say."

"Am I wrong?"

"She can't grab a spoonful of soup and bring it to her mouth without dumping it on her lap. What makes you think she could grab hold of a global society, wealthy and hidden for almost a century with influence in major governments and institutions?"

She had nothing to say to that. He'd spun her head a few times since their escape began, but this was the first thing he told her that made her forget the peril she faced – even as bugs splattered against her visor, inches from her eyes. She also didn't notice the beams from two chasing headlights illuminate the road beneath and beside her.

#

Let's Spend the Night Together *is too upbeat to be background music for a front porch quarrel. But it's playing, accompanied by yelling, bickering and accusing. Beach bunnies and ditzy dudes have joined the squabble. Francis can't take much more. The jalopy seems to be a good place for him to hide, but before he can reach it...well, lookie there. He sees the sun, golden yellow. The tear gloss in his eyes blocks much of its intensity, though it seems pretty close. It reminds him of the big tuna's watch. Everyone around the poker table liked that watch. Pop liked it too. If he can pluck the timepiece from the sky, he can give it to Pop, make him smile. Smiles are like colds. Everyone catches them – Daddy and Mama too.*

He stumbles on chubby legs to pursue the golden circle in the sky. The noise of the yelling adults continues. One voice he hears louder than most is Mama's. He always feels like he is her inconvenience. It might take more than a watch to please her. He trips over a groove in the dirt where Daddy always parks, but he doesn't fall, just staggers. Alley-Oop barks from deep in his throat – a powerful sound that makes him look back. The dog is barking at him, but he hasn't known him long enough to understand what he's saying. He goes back to trying to pluck the yellow orb from the sky. The closer he gets, the further it is. Frustrating.

Rubber squeals against pavement, jerking his head around. He's in the road now, and a candy apple red Mustang with a chrome horse on its grill gallops toward him. It's coming fast. At first, he thinks Curly is returning Diamond Joe's Camaro, but that one and this one are not the same, and they're different shades of red. Alley-Oop's barks are mostly drowned out by the car's radio. The driver of the Mustang opens wide eyes, and he makes the horn roar. Neither action slows the vehicle or removes Francis from its path.

The car paints tread on the road. Francis sees the horse-decorated grill prepare to devour him. Too frightened to scream, he stares at the raging monster. He sees Alley-Oop barking a frantic warning, and he gets it now. He understands the dog's message, telling him to get out of the road. And Mama – he hears Mama screaming along with the dog's chorus. But there's a louder noise than them. It's coming from

the Mustang, nearly upon him and bellowing a demented wail from its
radio. He does the one thing he knows to do, dropping on his rump in
the middle of the street. The Mustang's headlights are eyes glaring at
him. The grill's teeth shine with hunger. Tires screech scars upon the
road. He closes his eyes.

Slam! He's hit with a force that rocks the brain inside his skull,
disorients him. The world becomes a spinning top with him at its center.
He catches a flashing glimpse of Mama in the space he occupied a
moment earlier. She staggers from a head-on collision with the boy, but
she has to get it together. The untamed Mustang can't stop its gallop,
inches from her.

Francis sticks his arms and legs out, trying to get his spinning
tumble under control. The road scratches a bloody rash upon his skin
and impregnates it with gravel. He finally arrives at a sliding stop, and
real pain enflames his little body. Tears have begun to make his world
blurry again, but before completely losing clear sight, he sees Mama
lying motionless atop the dark skid left by the Mustang. And the out-
of-control car isn't done yet. It rages through the yard, clips the jalopy,
knocking it off its blocks. It finally comes to an abrupt and violent stop
against the house's concrete foundation. The crash hurls people off
the porch. The Mustang's face squeezes like an accordion on impact,
heaving the engine and all its guts onto the driver, who dives into the
windshield.

#

Civilization presented a stark contrast to the dark, relatively quiet
wilderness they had only recently escaped. And it gave Sasha a
whole new anxiety. She still feared for her fate if the 8Fers caught
them, but the city brought the realization that she might soon
have to put Frank's hypnotism *on track* – to use Trevor's words.

Trevor's helmet turned toward his right mirror. "Looks
like they're falling back."

"Good."

"I don't think so." He had already reduced their speed
when they entered the urban area, and he did so again now – by
another ten to twelve mph.

"You're slowing down for them? I thought the objective

was to get away."

He slowed even more to make the turn off South Broadway onto Torrance Boulevard.

How does he know where he's going? How did he – and Charlotte – know about Frank being hypnotized? She twisted to see if the 8Fers took the same turn as them. She saw a pick-up truck continue straight on South Broadway, but no one followed them. Mystified, she went back to facing forward. There wasn't as much traffic on this new road as there had been on the last. That probably had something to do with the time digitally displayed on the Redondo Beach Savings and Loan building to her right. It was 12:26 in the morning. Some pedestrians prowled the sidewalk, a few of whom appeared intoxicated. She heard the GPS come to life in her helmet. That meant it also played in Trevor's. The Bluetooth linked to his phone, which he had mounted on the bike behind the windshield. That answered her question about how he knew where to go. The device said, "Continue west on Torrance Boulevard point seven miles to Coral Way."

"How does it work if they're already in the middle of it?" he asked. "Can you jump in?"

"I can't do what your grandmother wants me to do." She felt his back stiffen against her chest pressed against it. "A hypnotist can only make suggestions. I can't control what comes out of your father's subconscious…who he blames for the assassination. He had to have seen something, and if he did, that's what would come out."

Trevor didn't respond. She knew he didn't like what she said, but he didn't know enough to argue against it. The movement of his helmet left to right meant he kept checking his mirrors for their pursuers. His phone rang into the Bluetooth of their helmets. She couldn't see who the call came from, but the flat tone with which he answered suggested he could see it. "Hello."

"I'll make this quick." It was The Clipper, colder than she'd ever heard him sound. "Come back with the girl. You know what I'm capable of. So does Charlotte." He ended the call.

It was over before she could ask about Glen. She wanted

to know about Ernie too, but since Charlotte handed over her phone, she was probably best suited to answer that question.

Trevor further reduced his speed. He didn't say anything, but he also didn't turn around.

She imagined him mulling over his predicament. What did he expect? The Clipper was going to find out. Again, she considered Charlotte's decision to stay behind. It wasn't just a stupid decision. It was...*it's what someone completely irrational would do.* "I don't think you should be taking orders from your grandmother anymore."

He brought the bike to an abrupt stop in the middle of the street.

Her first thought was that a car would rear-end them. Sitting in the bitch seat meant she'd get the worst of it. Then she realized he stopped in the turning lane, and he deployed the left blinker. She lifted her visor. The electric lights of a city beginning to go to sleep took some of the edge off her anxiety. The air she inhaled tasted of salt. She couldn't see the ocean, but she guessed they were only blocks from the beach.

"Go down that street." He pointed to a road called Coral Way, which ran perpendicular to the boulevard they now occupied. "Halfway down, take a right. You'll see where Nana, Frank and the family lived in 1968. It's an empty lot now. You might be too late for the hypnotism."

"I'm not getting off here in the middle of – what are you going to do?"

"I'll do what he told me to do...*without the girl.* Some shit needs to be sorted out."

"He's going to hurt her."

"Not when he knows what *I'm* capable of. Now go down there and tell them everything you know."

There was nothing more to debate, and getting off in the street wasn't so bad when the street was sparsely populated. She gave him the helmet and stepped off the bike. The weakness of her legs surprised her. They tingled, still feeling the vibration effects of the racing bike.

Trevor didn't linger. He turned the front wheel and sped off. He had shit waiting for him.

Watching him go, she wondered if her legs were too weak and tingling too much to carry her all the way to that empty lot. And she wondered if she *should* go. She now had the freedom to go anywhere, or so it seemed.

CHAPTER 28

Coming out of hypnosis, Frank felt like he floated in a brain fog purgatory between a conscious and subconscious state. And it was chilly. No one told him the place between places would be cold. It wasn't when he entered it. Gradually, the real world took shape around him. It was dark, but not as dark as the tone of the place he had just left. He remembered the party, the fighting and the crash. Oh, yes – he remembered. He also remembered his mother saving him. *Holy shit.* It hardly seemed possible. If only there was some sort of fact check he could apply to it. When had she ever put herself out for him? Bobbi – yes, but him?

"Put her in the back of my car," Marco told a police officer.

Frank had no idea how fast or slow he turned his head, but in so doing, he saw three cops handle Sasha, who they had handcuffed. They guided her into a maroon SUV that looked black at night. He remembered it was the vehicle he arrived in, along with Marco, Dr. Fitz and two officers, who acted more like thugs than police. "When did she get here? Where are they taking her?" He watched Marco walk away from him, toward other cops trying to disperse the small crowd that had gathered.

"You should rest." Dr. Fitz was to his left, looking happy with himself. "My guy will take you home." He waved to catch the attention of one of the cops handling Sasha.

"I'm cold. I'm shivering, and I'm sweating."

"That's normal. You'll also experience disorientation, which is why you should rest."

"My mother didn't sweat and shiver after Sasha – where are they taking her?"

"I haven't had the opportunity to treat your mother." Dr. Fitz gestured to the SUV, which now contained Sasha. "I suppose that's why they're taking her into custody."

His brain fog wasn't so thick that he didn't get his meaning. Sasha kidnapped Charlotte before the doctor could interrogate her – twice. At least he could appreciate *that* about her.

Dr. Fitz continued. "From what I know of your mother, she's had years of work done. You see, the more one is hypnotized, the easier it is to pass into and out of it. Eventually, after taking the journey enough times, the subject's mind blends the real and the envisioned. They begin to live in a pseudo-reality of their own making."

Pseudo-reality. What he remembered wasn't imaginary. His imagination wouldn't dare to spin a yarn about his mother saving him from certain death while risking her life to do it. The rest of him would've found it simply too unbelievable. Did she really do that?

Dr. Fitz added, "What I mean to say is Charlotte would be an interesting case study given what was done to her all those years ago and how she managed to live with it for so long."

The cop joined them, answering Dr. Fitz's summons. It wasn't his arrival that surprised Frank. It was his familiarity. The brain fog kept him from remembering where he'd seen the man before, but he sensed it was an occasion that didn't end well for him. The cop was stocky, in his late thirties, and he had a most memorable haircut. It looked like it belonged in the 1990s and on the head of a teenage boy: a flat-top with frosted tips.

"Hopefully, with Ms. Frye's assistance, we'll soon have Charlotte back safely."

He threw his eyes back at the doctor – not because of what he said but because he remembered the last time he saw him. "You're the doctor who – you're Dr. Fitz."

"I thought we already made our introductions."

With the flat-top cop now standing so close, he re-experienced the pain of his Twentynine Palms beat-down. The baton into his solar plexus that robbed him of air, the punches and kicks, the boot between his eyes: all re-imagined as body memories. He bent over, feeling the pain return. And Dr. Fitz was there.

"What do you want?" asked the cop of the doctor.

"This experience took more out of our friend than I expected." Dr. Fitz gestured to Frank.

"What's wrong with him?" asked the flat-top cop. "He looks messed up."

Frank formed a fist. He could snap out of his folded form and strike like an uncoiling cobra, but he wouldn't get a follow-up shot. The cop had a gun and other officers to assist him. And Frank lacked his son's strength, his youth, his tolerance for pain. He envied Trevor's ability to put someone out with one punch. Then he remembered what his punch did to Garrett Delany.

Dr. Fitz said, "Take him home while we go to the precinct." The cop's hard expression indicated he had other plans, so the doctor added, "You'll get your time with her. I promise."

He obviously meant Sasha. The thought of this violent thug-cop getting alone time with her while she was caged in a cell hit him in the heart of his lawyer sensibilities. He'd been a defense attorney all those years because he wanted to protect people against abusive authority figures like this guy, like Dr. Fitz, and like District Attorney Diaz.

The cop reached for him. "Come on."

Frank rose to his full height. His age and his stature may not have allowed him to look imposing, but he felt it. That was all he needed. "I'm going wherever she's going."

The doctor and the cop traded glances, unsure how to handle his defiance.

He took the first of several dozen steps that would bring him to Sasha. He didn't know how she arrived at this place or why. He didn't know the extent of her legal troubles. He didn't know what she did with *or to* his mother. He also didn't know how much he could believe her. But he couldn't just hand her over.

"Go home, Frank." Marco walked back toward them. "You did what we came here for. You did it well. Now it's my turn."

"As her lawyer, I insist."

"You can't be a prosecutor and a defense lawyer at the same time. Pick your side." Marco stared at him, and his look said what his words couldn't with other people listening in. They had a deal. If Frank broke it, his mother wouldn't last a week locked up in general population.

"Big shot lawyer." The flat-top cop took him by the arm. "Let's go."

#

This wasn't the first time in the last couple of hours that Sasha questioned her decision to walk that half mile to the empty house lot. They arrested her without listening to a word she said. They took her on a nerve-wracking, mostly silent, hours-long ride to a police precinct. She didn't know which precinct because it was in an area she didn't recognize. They entered through the back of the building, skipped processing, and went straight to lock-up, where they put her in a dingy, single-occupant cell. Now she sat at a table in an interrogation room facing a wall-sized mirror while Marco Diaz paced behind her with a notepad in his hand.

"Wisteria," he said. "That's all you have for me?"

Without a clock anywhere in sight, she didn't know the time, but she felt like she'd been saying the same thing for hours. "That's what the sign said. Do you know anywhere else around here where Wisteria grows? Sierra Madre is called Wisteria City."

"I know that." He walked around the table to stand in front of her. "And I know there's an abandoned film lot near there."

She made the motion of throwing something invisible up in the air. She couldn't move too much because the chain connecting her wrist restraints ran through a steel loop atop the table.

"Emphasis on *abandoned*. The Sierra Madre Police, Arcadia Police and The Pasadena Police are scouring the lot and surrounding area on my orders. They tell me the only inhabitants the place has seen in twenty years are rodents and coyotes."

"I don't know what else to say. Trevor told me to tell you everything, and I am."

"Trevor," he spit the name out as if he found it distasteful. "We suspect him of two murders – so far. Care to help us with that?"

She shrugged and shook her head.

The nod he gave back to her said he expected a response like that. "You're telling me it's a hodgepodge of outlaws. They're bikers, militia and mobsters united under one umbrella called 8F. They take their orders from an old man they fear who goes by The Clipper. By the way, a clipper is a ship. Nothing you've said so far is nautical. 8F checks out, though. Know why? Because it's on Wikipedia. Isn't that where Glen Pierce first learned of it?"

Glen was still on her mind – a lot. She couldn't imagine him dead. It was easier to imagine Ernie that way, maybe because she barely knew him.

"Do you know what we found on Glen's computer?"

"Nothing. And you raided our business, shut us down. You'll hear from my lawyer."

He laughed. "I hope you don't think that's Frank."

Her face dropped. *He's the only lawyer I know.*

The DA read off his notepad. "We found files on his computer: 8F histories going as far back as 1931. My investigators are still going through it all. You're shaking your head?"

"Glen is computer illiterate."

"You said he learned of 8F by filling out an online questionnaire."

"At the library, with someone's help. He doesn't have a personal computer."

"Well –" He looked at the notes again. When he looked back up, his eyes were colder, his expression darker. "This material *was* on a computer at your work."

If that was true, she'd need a lawyer for more than suing them over the Brookside raid. *Why won't Frank represent me?* She knew that answer before she even thought of the question.

"Let me share with you some of what we found on that computer," said the DA. "The Kennedys – both of them – died for business. President Kennedy signed National Security Action Memorandum 263, which pulled America out of Vietnam by 1965. When he signed it, war in Southeast Asia seemed likely. And war is a big money maker for well-connected people."

"That was in the movie."

"Movie?"

"*JFK*," she said. "With all this going on, I thought maybe I should watch it. It's not my kind of movie, but I learned a lot."

He smirked in a disturbingly unkind way. "Okay, well, something else they touched on in the movie: Lyndon Johnson was a member of 8F in good standing. But we learned more about that from what's on your computer – the *work computer*." The DA flipped a page in the pad. He had to squint to read the print. "Two other members of 8F were George and Herman Brown, owners of the engineering and construction company Brown and Root. In 1962, their company became part of the Halliburton Corporation, which became a subsidiary of RMK-BRJ. Other members of 8F created RMK-BRJ in order to obtain lucrative defense contracts."

She followed what he said, but most of her thoughts circled around how that material got on a Brookside work computer. She knew she didn't do it. And, of course, neither did Glen. That brought her to Ernie. *How did he get that footage of the raid he showed me on his phone?*

Marco continued, "Ninety-seven percent of the construction work done in Vietnam was contracted to RMK-BRJ. From 1965 to 1972, the Halliburton Corporation alone generated $380 million from its contract work in Vietnam. Then there was the Bell Aircraft Corporation. Lawrence D. Bell, the founder of the company, was a prominent 8F member. His company was the primary supplier of helicopters to the US military for the entirety of the war. They generated hundreds of millions of dollars in sales during combat years in Vietnam."

Still, she thought about Ernie. He, or one of his guys, could have put that information on their computer, but why? She also had no way of knowing if he sent Frank those sketches.

"Michael and Ruth Paine sponsored Lee Harvey Oswald and his wife when they left Russia and settled in Dallas," said the DA. "Michael Paine was an engineer for the Bell Corporation. His stepfather was Arthur Young, who invented the Bell Helicopter – the chopper that made the company so much money in Vietnam." He looked squarely at her, lowering the papers. "This would be circumstantial if I presented it to the grand jury. But if hard evidence could be found connecting Oswald to members of 8F, it would answer the question of motive."

"I thought you were doing Robert Kennedy."

He smiled. "That's where what we found on your computer really proves valuable."

"It wasn't *my* computer."

He dismissed her comment with the wave of his hand. "8F killed President Kennedy because he refused to commit to a full-scale war in Vietnam. Five years later, their war was in full swing, and it was a lucrative war. Robert Kennedy promised to end it if he became president, but that wasn't the main reason they killed him. He told his closest advisors he would use the power of the presidency to launch a new investigation into his brother's murder. How long do you think it would take him with those kinds of investigative powers to learn who really killed his brother? He'd ruin them."

She put Ernie on the back burner – for the moment. She didn't need to be a lawyer, a district attorney or a cop to know money was a popular motive for murder. And the more money at stake, the less it mattered how high profile the victim was, even a president and a presidential candidate. But the kicker was Robert Kennedy's intention to use the presidency to identify and prosecute his brother's assassins. That was the most compelling reason for them to kill him.

The district attorney removed three sheets of paper from the middle of the notepad. He placed them on the table, spread them out, and he slid them toward her.

She sat up with her spine as straight as a rod. She reached

tentatively for them but stopped short of actually touching them. Her photographs of the sketches. The last time she saw them was when she put them in text form for Ernie to send. Slowly, her eyes rose to the DA. "He sent them to you? That explains a lot."

"If by *he* you mean Frank. Yes, it explains that he's not your lawyer."

She actually meant Ernie, but she now saw that he did what she begged him to do. He sent the sketches to Frank. It was Frank who gave them to the DA. It still could've been Ernie who planted incriminating 8F material on a Brookside computer, but it now seemed less likely. "I'm not saying any more until I see Frank."

A shadow crossed Marco's handsome face. His eyes dropped briefly to the sketches.

You want me to tell you about them? Oh. There's my leverage. And she realized *maybe I don't need a lawyer – Frank or anyone else.*

CHAPTER 29

Santa Ana, California. May, 1968

Charlotte is in a sweet cherry ride. Her whole family could fit in the back seat, but she doesn't have a whole family anymore. Pete is wherever, and he's doing whatever. She supposes she's still with him, but…eh…who knows? Yvette is watching Francis today. That was Matthew's call. He's gone and gotten himself some *real* authority, which is why Pete's been backing off. She's not privy to what they worked out, but she is a part of whatever this is. As a reward for her involvement, Matthew places a pendant with a silver necklace into her hand. *It's beautiful. Put it on me.* A year ago, she might've said that, but she's insecure around him now. She watches him walk toward a broken-down house on the bank of a dried-up river bed. They're supposed to meet someone there. She's about to look more closely at the pendant when the outhouse beside the main house shakes. She hears a man inside it clear his throat.

Matthew gives her a glance then storms the shithouse. He pounds on the door.

A man answers. "Go away. Me and the Lord are talking."

"Curly, open up. It's Michael Wayne."

Who is Michael Wayne? An alias? She shouldn't be surprised. He's been one big enigma lately. The outhouse door opens, and a man walks out. He has a Bible tucked under his arm while adjusting his belt. She's seen his bulbous nose and puffy face several times, most recently at the abomination that became Francis's second birthday party. She's still dealing with the soreness and the bruising from when that out-of-control car clipped her. At least she saved her son. What was he doing in the street anyway? He's not a bright kid.

The man from the outhouse extends an open hand, and Matthew fills it with a rolled-up wad of cash. She's surprised, but the man is more surprised – not by the cash, but by the amount. He flips through it, his excitement growing the higher he counts. As they walk toward the car, she realizes the outermost bills on the man's roll are thousand-dollar notes. There's got to be thirty or forty thousand dollars in that collection.

"Curly," says Matthew. "Meet Shirin."

She throws a look at him as if to say *What are you flappin'?*

Curly smiles at her. "Pleasure, ma'am."

Disinclined to elaborate on the strange introduction, Matthew checks his watch. It's the third time he's done that since their arrival. And he casts a gaze down the dirt roadway.

"We met already," she says.

Curly gives her a noticeable but silent rebuke.

I shouldn't say that? Oh! She looks around for a quick distraction – something to remove the awkwardness that just fell upon them. Half a dozen ample sized turd piles bake in the sun, and she sees hoof tracks. "I…uh…I rode horses when I was little."

Curly brightens. "I give free pony rides to any boy or girl who can memorize a Bible verse."

"Where are the ponies?"

"Wild Bill's is four blocks upriver. I keep fully grown horses there too. Ever ride a palomino, Shirin?"

"Call her Sherry," says Matthew. "Makes it sound like you're familiar."

"Would you like to go riding with me, Sherry?"

Matthew seems annoyed by Curly's question. He looks down the road again.

"Uh…what d'ya say we raincheck till after it's done?" Curly suggests.

"After what's done?"

Unsure of how to proceed, Curly looks to Matthew for guidance.

"Go ahead. Tell her."

Curly buries the bills in his pocket. "After we stop the senator from stopping the war. If the war stops, you see, the North Vietnamese will enter the United States through Honolulu." He shakes his Bible before her. "That will summon the Almighty's wrath, and He'll send a tidal wave that will sink California."

She can't believe – *what?* It's the only word that comes to mind. *What?* She turns to Matthew, hoping for a clarification that makes sense.

To her surprise, he nods. And he adds, "There are reasons enough to go around."

Curly hugs the Bible as if he's afraid of losing it. "What are your reasons, Sherry? Did the Lord speak to you too?"

How am I supposed to answer that? And what are we doing that I have to have a reason for? Matthew has found what he's been looking for on the road. She whirls around for a look, and she sees a convertible darting toward them, kicking up dust. It carries three men. She realizes the one driving it is Pete's boss, Mr. Provenzano. *Matthew and Provenzano know each other?*

The car arrives in a skidding stop with dust rolling over them like Curly's prophesied tidal wave. From behind the wheel, Mr. Provenzano says, "Don't you know nothing, preacher?"

"What?"

"Wet the dirt so it don't cloud up on us." Provenzano climbs out of the convertible. He wears a gray suit that appears to exceed the value of Matt's threads. He coughs in the dust.

"If the Lord wants wet dirt, He'll make it rain."

"Did the Lord tell you he wants you to steal my Camaro?" Provenzano glances at Matthew. "Tell him it ain't a gift, *Mr. Wayne.* I ain't that generous."

Matthew turns to Curly, who tries to form words but trips over them before he can say them. That brings a smile to Provenzano's thin lips. Then he notices Charlotte.

She tilts her head to him, puffs up in her seat. "Mr.

Provenzano."

"Isn't this interesting." Again, the Italian looks at Matthew.

Matt isn't biting whatever Provenzano is serving. He turns to her and makes a show of pulling a necklace out from under his turtleneck to display it over the front of his shirt. The message is clear. She is to put hers on. Hers is identical to his, except his chain is gold, where hers is silver. Each pendant depicts an inverted triangle with a cross in its center and a red rose in the middle of the cross. It takes her a moment, but she realizes Rosicrucians wear the same pendants when they prowl the beach looking for converts. He impatiently waits for her to put it on. She's lucky to be included. She knows that, so she does as he wishes. She is no sooner out of the car when he takes her by the hand. She can feel nervousness coursing through him, but he tries to act cool as he leads her up to the convertible. A wop with a pompadour sits in the front seat, and a kid who looks like a Tijuana beggar is in the back. "Donneroummas," he says. "Who's your friend?"

"This is Joe." Provenzano walks up to join them. "Or Pedro. We'll go with Pedro."

Matthew addresses the kid. "I hear you're a stable boy."

The kid nods, but he has eyes for Charlotte's chest – way out of bounds. She kinda likes it, though. It's nice that someone notices all the primping and pushing up she did this morning.

"Pedro was training to be a jockey until he took a spill at a ranch in Corona," says the wop named Donneroummas. "He's been unemployed on disability, bouncing around ever since."

Matthew steps closer. The kid's eyes go to his pendant. She looks down at her pendant, resting upon her breasts. *That's what he's looking at.* She frowns over her disappointment.

The kid shifts from Matthew to Charlotte, back and forth. He appears to study them. "I see you at Bryton's Bookstore in Pasadena?"

Matthew shakes his head. "HQ."

The kid's eyelids disappear into his eye sockets. "San Jose?"

Matthew nods. "Office of Imperator."

"I...I'm sorry. I couldn't pay my dues. Four dollars is a lot when you can't work."

We're supposed to be Rosicrucians? How do I pull that off? She tries to remember how they acted, what they said, as she watched them on the beach.

"You've been keeping up with your studies?" asks Matthew.

"I read for free at Bryton's. I'm a corresponding member of the Supreme Grand Lodge. I...um...I've been learning white magic. You can do anything with your mind if you know how." The kid looks at Donneroummas, Provenzano and Curly. "Some people think it's queer, but I know thought transference."

Matthew nods like he understands.

"I can put my hand in boiling water, and it feels cold," says the kid. "I don't get burned."

Curly speaks up. "That's the power of the Lord. Praise be."

Matthew is quick to explain that, saying, "Curly is a reverend."

"I own horses too." Curly pulls out the wad of cash. The money captivates the kid. It also attracts Provenzano and Donneroummas, who look like they have every intention of claiming it.

Matthew clears his throat, breaking the money spell. The Italians each look elsewhere, with Provenzano finding Charlotte. And he seems to like what he finds. She's seen that look on men before, usually in her old neighborhood. "My boyfriend is your muscular mechanic." She keeps Matthew in her periphery, hoping he'll react to her comment. But he doesn't.

"Course he's got muscles," says the kid. "Girls laughed at Charles Atlas when he looked like me. But they'll stop getting off on me someday. Everybody will."

Curly seems desperate to bring the talk back to him. "The stable hands over at Wild Bill's do too much cowboying around. I'll pay good money to anyone who can break my horses."

That catches the kid's attention.

"I pay money that can change lives." Curly teases the top

thousand-dollar bill.

The kid goes bug-eyed right quick.

"He wants experience," says Matthew. "Someone who understands animal life-waves."

"I'm experienced." The kid scurries out of the car. "And I've been making a study of life-waves, human and animal." He steps up to Curly. "Sirhan Sirhan. I can break your horses."

Curly shifts the wad to his left. He thrusts out his right, grabbing and shaking the kid's hand. "Let's call you Pedro."

"Joe will do," says Matthew.

The hiring of Sirhan had Charlotte's attention, so she didn't notice Provenzano gliding up to her until he fully arrives. "There ain't nothing sexier than a woman riding horses bareback and bare-assed," he says. "Have you ever done that with your mechanic?"

Matthew looks at her. It's not a happy look. *That's what it takes to get his attention?* She turns to the Italian, raises an intrigued eyebrow. "I can't say that I have, Mr. Provenzano."

#

2018

Sasha expected the hostility she received when Flat-top gruffly marched her through the local FBI field office on Wilshire Boulevard, Suite 1700. The DA likely let everyone know she was on the wrong end of his high-profile investigation into the RFK murder. What she didn't expect was the coldness Frank gave her in the private office of Assistant Director in Charge Bill Harris. Fortunately, Flat-top stayed behind in the main area.

"I'm not your lawyer." Frank glanced at Marco then back at her. "But I'll give you some free legal advice. Help them identify these men, and they'll go easier on you." He gestured to the monitor on the wall to her right. Three sketches filled its screen – the sketches she sent him.

"The FBI has the best facial recognition software in the world and the largest database." Marco moved toward her. "But you were there when Charlotte dreamed up these men. I'm hoping you can tell us what the computer can't."

My leverage was her first thought, but Frank dominated the rest of her thinking. He wasn't her lawyer – okay, but he didn't even appear to be her friend. *To think I really liked you once. And everything I did for your mother.* Her eyes narrowed on him.

"Are you willing to help?" asked Marco. "Or should I send you back to lock-up?"

She gave his questions a solid sixty seconds of consideration just to keep them all in check. Of course, she'd "help". She wanted to see what the FBI's computer came up with as much as they did. Finally, she shrugged like a disinterested teenager saying *whatever*.

Marco nodded to an agent sitting at the desk, operating the computer. The woman made a series of keystrokes then looked at the monitor on the wall. The three sketches on display dissolved into a split screen. The left side of the split screen showed one of the three sketches – that of a man with a full face, tall forehead, unkempt brows and a sly grin. He looked like he was probably in his sixties, but the picture showed a tear down its center, which somewhat distorted the image. The right side of the monitor displayed a checker board of smaller photos changing rapidly as the software performed its search.

"The program examines eighty distinguishable landmarks found on a person's face," said Assistant Director in Charge Bill Harris.

She couldn't help but look at Frank, who glanced back at her. He seemed afraid of or at least deferential to the DA. He was a lot of things, but she never thought he was spineless.

The changing checker board found one image among many and enlarged it to match the size of the ripped sketch on the other side of the screen. It was a black and white publicity photo of a husky man with a plump, smiling face and a Bible in his hand. It wasn't identical to the sketch, but it was close. "Ninety-one percent accuracy," said Assistant Director Harris.

While everyone studied the two images on display, Frank appeared the most affected. His blue eyes bore into the monitor, shifting back and forth between the two pictures. "Who is he?"

The agent on the computer minimized the images to bring up a page of text with the publicity photo in its upper left corner. "Oliver B. Owen," she said, reading from the computer. "He was an itinerant preacher, among other things. People called him Jerry, Curly or The Walking Bible. They say he could recite any Bible verse from memory."

Marco turned to Frank. "Do you know him?"

Why would he ask him that? Is he – she looked at Frank a little differently, wondering if the DA put him in the same category as her when it came to this investigation. *What's the term they use? An accessory?*

The assistant director stepped closer to the monitor to ease his reading of the text on the screen. "He passed away in 1993. He had a peculiar arrest record that spanned three decades and numerous states. Most of his legal troubles concerned 'disorderly conduct involving morals', illicit relations with underage girls, child support suits, pray for pay schemes and arson. He allegedly burned his own church to the ground and tried to collect insurance money five different times, in five different states."

"Pastor Pimp." Frank said it so low he almost couldn't be heard, but she heard him.

Assistant Director Harris quickly roamed the text, finally finding what he sought. "Robert Kennedy's assassination," he said. "It's about two thirds down. See? Nine hours after the shooting, Mr. Owen paid the LAPD an unsolicited visit."

"Nine hours?" asked the DA. "The next morning?"

The assistant director nodded. "He told them that on June 3, 1968, he picked up a hitchhiker he later learned was Sirhan Sirhan. He gave him a ride to the Ambassador Hotel, where Sirhan told him he needed to 'see a friend in the kitchen'. After stopping at the Ambassador, the two made plans for Owen to sell Sirhan a horse. They met a few hours later to complete the transaction, but Sirhan said he wasn't able to raise all the money. He gave Owen a hundred dollars and promised to pay the remainder when Owen brought the animal to the rear entrance of the Ambassador Hotel the following night at eleven p.m."

"The night of the assassination," said Marco.

"Owen told police he couldn't make that meeting because he had a preaching engagement in Oxnard, about seventy miles away."

"Did they verify that?"

"The LAPD dismissed Owen as a publicity whore who inserted himself into the investigation in an attempt to capitalize on a national tragedy. The interesting part of Owen's story was what he said about the people who accompanied Sirhan. He said Sirhan was hitchhiking with another man when he picked them up. When he stopped at a red light, they got out, conversed with a man and a woman standing on the corner. Then Sirhan got back in the truck and spent the rest of their time talking to him about horses."

Marco looked perplexed. "Why is that interesting?"

"Owen claimed that when Sirhan gave him the down payment, he was accompanied by the same two men and woman he'd been with earlier that day. The LAPD never followed up on whether or not the woman in the story matched descriptions of the girl in the polka-dot dress."

Marco addressed Frank with a tone and body language that threatened confrontation. "Do…you…recognize him?"

Frank shook his head. The DA's suspicious gaze lingered until he at last looked away. And Frank's eyes shifted to her.

In that look, she found…a kinship? She wasn't sure about that, but one thing she was sure of: he *did* recognize the man in the publicity photo.

"Give us the next picture." Marco now wore his impatience like a disheveled suit.

The agent put her computer through a checkerboard search that appeared on the right side of the wall monitor while the left side displayed the sketch of a man with a plump face, black horn-rimmed glasses, and a bushy beard on his neck but not his face.

"I believe Dr. Fitz called that an Amish beard." Marco eyed Frank expectantly, getting no reaction from him.

Frank saw these people in his hypnosis, she realized. *And the DA knows it.* She looked back and forth between the two men. *Why am I here?*

Once again, the checkerboard gave way to a single image that shared the monitor as a split-screen with the ripped sketch. This image was a black and white photograph of a heavyset man with an Amish beard and dark horn-rimmed glasses wearing a subtle smile. His suit was the wide collar plaid type fashionable in the late sixties.

Assistant Director Harris said, "Dr. William Joseph Bryan, Jr. Ninety-four percent accuracy. That's as good as it gets. The program rarely claims one hundred percent. Too many variables…and with a torn drawing."

The agent at the computer left the pictures onscreen, this time not replacing them with text. "Dr. Bryan had a hypnotherapy practice on the Sunset Strip," she said. "He claimed to be the world's leading expert in his field. Apparently, he wasn't the only one to think so because producers hired him to be a technical advisor on the Frank Sinatra film, *The Manchurian Candidate.* But his real claim to fame was the Boston Strangler case where he hypnotized Albert DeSalvo and got him to confess to multiple murders."

Marco sparked up as if he grabbed a live wire and couldn't let it go. "Sirhan Sirhan practiced self-hypnosis in the weeks leading up to the assassination. He scribbled his automatic writing in a notebook while he was hypnotized. On one of the pages, he wrote, 'God help me…please help me. Salvo Di Di Salvo Die S Salvo.'" He looked at Assistant Director Harris. "That stood out when I read it. You don't forget that – not as a prosecutor, you don't. When the investigators later asked him about it, he said he didn't recognize the name or know where he would have heard it."

"Dr. Bryan was a colorful character," said the agent at the computer. "He had two obsessions: sex and religion. He was an ordained priest in a radical sect called the Old Roman Catholic Church. He called prayer a form of hypnotism, and he made sex an integral part of his hypnotherapy practice. In 1969, the Board of Medical Examiners gave him five years of probation for sexually molesting women patients he put under hypnosis."

Sasha's eyes jumped to the pictures on the monitor. How many times had she heard of hypnotists (almost always men) abusing the trust put into them by their patients (often women)? It was one of the reasons people refused to consider hypnotism a legitimate treatment for mental illnesses. To them, it was a trick used by guys who couldn't otherwise get laid.

The agent continued. "Dr. Bryan also worked for the United States Air Force during the Korean War, top secret. He was in charge of their brainwashing program. After the war, he became a consultant for the CIA in the MKULTRA program."

Marco turned to Frank. "I believe you're familiar with MKULTRA."

Frank looked particularly perturbed by that comment, as if he took it as a taunt. But he directed his question to the agent. "Was he related to William Jennings Bryan?"

"The presidential candidate at the turn of the century?" asked Assistant Director Harris. "And secretary of state?"

"The prosecutor in the Scopes "Monkey" Trial in 1925."

The agent nodded. "William Joseph Bryan was a descendent of William Jennings Bryan from the famous Monkey Trial."

Frank let that hang in the air, looking nowhere but at the monitor. Finally, he said, "My mother called him Big Mouth in the Monkey Trial."

Her jaw didn't drop, but it felt as if her cheeks lost whatever it was that gave them color. *Why would he admit that when he said nothing about recognizing* Pastor Pimp?

The DA all but jumped out of his skin with excitement. "You knew him as Big Tuna?"

"Yes," answered Frank sadly, defeated-like.

"We're finally getting somewhere." Marco twisted to her so fast it startled her. "We had everything we needed all along. My officers will take you back now."

She almost couldn't reply – mystified as she was by Frank's transformation. "You, uh, you didn't identify the third sketch of the bald man with the sharp nose."

The agent at the computer brought up the final sketch. Ripped on the side, it offered the clearest of the three representations. It depicted a middle-aged man with a pointy nose and hair wrapped around the sides and back of his head. "This is Reverend Xavier von Koss, the Los Angeles hypnotist who met with James Earl Ray prior to the assassination of Martin Luther King, Jr. He ran the International Society of Hypnosis with an office on Crenshaw Boulevard."

Marco glanced at Frank. "Also known as Chrome Dome?"

Frank nodded.

She watched the DA turn to her. Whatever leverage she thought she possessed, Frank had managed to make it vanish.

CHAPTER 30

There was so much revealed and so much to weigh on his mind.
It was so much to play with Frank's emotions, but he couldn't let
his feelings about his mother, her guilt, or Sasha muck up what he
decided he had to do. He had to stay on course for the thousands
of listeners who tuned in to hear Alex Logan's satellite radio
show. The DA had his ways of shaping public opinion going into
the grand jury hearing. This was Frank's.

He brought Rip to this interview but not as some kind
of cold shower counter to his attraction to Ms. Logan. This
time he needed his friend to keep him focused. They sat side
by side on the couch in Ms. Logan's apartment/studio. Frank
wore headphones and a microphone attached to the broadcast
computer by a spiral wire. Rip was a headset-free observer, and
he shared that distinction with Mittens, who lay on the desk
beside the computer.

As before, Alex was behind the computer, performing for
her audience through a microphone. "Some might say," she said.
"They *are* saying that you've traded your integrity for a ride on
the DA's coattails. Is there a job in Sacramento for you if he's
elected governor?"

"No."

The host expected him to say more. When he didn't, she
added, "We're trying to understand why you're helping the
district attorney build a case against your mother."

"I'm doing my job."

She smiled in an exasperated sort of way. "You don't expect us to believe that – not after the things you said the last time we had you in here."

"This might be hard for you or some of your listeners to accept, but –" He glanced at Rip, knowing he'd like what he was about to say next. "The truth is the truth regardless of who it implicates. That's my oath, my promise to the citizens of Los Angeles County."

Ms. Logan laughed. "Now it sounds like you're campaigning. Is that what this is, Mr. Caron? You want the DA's job when he moves on to bigger and better places?"

"We're a week away from meeting with the grand jury, and we're scrambling to put the pieces of this case together." He could see that caught both Alex and Rip by surprise, as he expected it would. "If we can't convince them of a larger conspiracy to murder presidential hopeful Robert Kennedy –"

"They won't recommend a trial, the DA will have egg on his face and –"

"Forget Sacramento. He'll be lucky to keep the job he has." He caught a look from Rip that asked *are you sure you want to go this route?*

Like the last time they met, Alex let dead air interrupt the interview.

The silence didn't bother him like it did before because he knew how she used it. He was about to use it the same way. But first, he paused to appreciate the host's beauty. She had the same platinum highlights, and they still sparkled like polished silver under overhead lights. Her almond eyes and extended lashes, her full lips both firm and soft at once…she was…she *wasn't* as beautiful as Sasha. *Where did that come from?* There wasn't anything more beautiful than a woman who needed him as much as he needed her. Without him, Sasha might face charges of kidnapping, criminal conspiracy, aiding and abetting a fugitive, impeding an investigation, withholding information vital to an investigation…it was a long list. Without her, he couldn't relate to his mother. He also…nope, that was it, he decided. He didn't need her for anything other than help with his mother. He didn't need anyone but his loyal dog. Oh, and from time to time, his friend who now sat beside him. He looked at Rip. *That's why I brought you here.* He smiled. *Thanks for the focus.* Rip looked back at him like he thought his mind was all twisted up.

"If I'm hearing you correctly," said Ms. Logan. "And I think I am – are you saying District Attorney Diaz and his team have failed to make a case against your mother?"

"You know I can't comment on that." Again, he glanced at Rip, knowing he would *not* like what he was about to say next. "What I can tell you is there are individuals we are looking at other than my mother."

"Other than or in addition to?"

"Other than."

#

Sasha knew what the district attorney wanted when he had her brought back into the interrogation room and left alone with a radio tuned to the Serious News satellite broadcast. She also knew he and several others – likely including Dr. Fitz – were on the other side of the two-way glass, watching her. They expected her to be so unnerved by Frank towing the party line in public that she'd give them what they wanted on 8F. They believed she still held out on them. It was the only way they could explain finding nothing when they searched that abandoned seventies film lot. Of course, they were wrong. She told them everything she knew. But if it worked to her advantage to play coy, that was what she'd do. It was the only play she had left.

Speaking through the radio, Frank said, "There was a cotton farmer from Delano, California named Roy Donald Murray. He was a heavy drinker and a big gambler."

She couldn't see or hear anyone on the other side of the glass, but she tried to imagine how they saw what Frank said as towing the party line. To her, it sounded the opposite of what the DA would want people to know. Wouldn't he want the public to hear Charlotte's son talk about the strong case they had against his mother? It'd be a master stroke of publicity.

Frank continued. "In April 1968, Mr. Murray pledged two thousand dollars to pay off a contract to kill Senator Robert Kennedy."

"Two thousand dollars to kill someone of Kennedy's notoriety seems a paltry sum," said the show's host. "Even when you consider inflation."

Another voice spoke from the radio. It was a man's voice. "That's not…uh…that's best left for the grand jury to interpret, don't you think, Mr. Deputy District Attorney?"

She perked up, listening more closely. Her reflection in the mirror showed a furrowed brow and a tilted head.

After a slight pause, Frank continued as if the other man never spoke. "Murray was adding *his share* to the contract."

"What was the contract?" asked the female host.

"It was half a million to three-quarters of a million dollars to kill Senator Kennedy if it looked like he was going to win the Democratic presidential nomination. California was considered the point of proof that he would win."

She stared at the glass, trying to see through it, trying to see the DA on the other side throwing a fit over what Frank said. She'd never been a legal junkie, but she knew it was unheard of for a prosecutor to give specifics of his case to the media before a trial or a hearing…especially if those specifics were not in keeping with the central theme of the case. *Is Frank trying to make up for what he divulged in the FBI field office?*

"Why would an alcoholic, gambling cotton farmer from California put money toward a hit on Robert Kennedy?" asked the radio show host.

The other man on the radio tried to interrupt. "Okay. We've gone far enough –"

"Kennedy supported the grape pickers strike in Delano," said Frank. "He humiliated the Kern County Sheriff, who arrested strikers for no reason. He supported César Chávez, the UFW. He pushed for federal protections for farm workers, better schooling for Latinos."

"He was bad for business," said the host. "I get it. Did

other farmers kick in on the contract? That's a lot of money to put together in two-thousand dollar increments."

"No – no. Roy Murray was a gambler, connected to the Vegas mob. He was a close friend of Johnny Rosselli. It was a mafia contract."

She saw her reflection in the glass light up. She imagined it was what they wanted, but she didn't care. The old man in the warehouse talked about Johnny Rosselli when Trevor tortured his granddaughter, or great-granddaughter – whatever. He said Johnny Rosselli was a mobster out of Las Vegas and Los Angeles who had the same lawyer as Sirhan Sirhan at the exact same time. The old man also mentioned a mob contract on RFK. It had to be the same contract Frank now tied to Roy Donald Murray and Johnny Rosselli. There seemed to be a lot of disparate elements of the plot: mobsters, lawyers, farmers, contracts and government hypnotists. Each on their own did not explain what happened, but if something or someone could be shown to have pulled all those elements together, a clear picture could emerge. And where had she already seen disparate elements united under one banner? 8F.

The door opened, and her stomach dropped as Flat-top came into the room. She pushed her chair back and shot to her feet – glad they didn't chain her to the table this time. But he stepped aside, allowing District Attorney Diaz to charge up to her. "What aren't you telling me?"

It was an odd choice of words, she thought. He didn't ask what she wasn't telling *them*, the representatives of the people of California. He wanted to know what she didn't tell *him*. It might have been a mental slip, but it told her everything she needed to know about the district attorney's mindset. *This is about him.*

#

Ambassador Hotel, Los Angeles, California. June 4, 1968

Charlotte is *no way with RFK*. He caters to the coloreds, meaning there will be race wars for sure if voters put him in the White House. Matthew hasn't told her much, but she's been watching and listening. She's fairly certain he'll use Kennedy's love of minorities to embarrass him tonight at the hotel. The Rosicrucian kid, who looks like he's from Tijuana, will freak out in front of all the cameras. He'll scream every anti-Kennedy thing they've taught him over the last three weeks. And with the miracle of television, the world will see minorities are opposed to Bobby's Kumbaya Coalition as much as whites.

She's been casing the Ambassador all morning, not entirely sure of her role in the disturbance. She decided to wear a neutral tan long-sleeve top, skirt and leggings. Her flats are basic brown. There's nothing flashy about her outfit. She thinks Matthew will want it that way, but...oh, hot hell. Why is Yvette here? She's supposed to be watching Francis.

Dressed in pretty paisleys, Yvette marches up to her, takes her by the arm.

"Where's Francis?"

Yvette walks her along a wall lined with red velvet paper and smoky mirrors, opens the bathroom door. Two ladies are there doing touch ups in the mirror. One is a brunette. The other is reddish-blonde. They're more spiffed up than a morning would expect them to be. "Add some blush," she tells Charlotte. She sets her purse down, checks the stalls but doesn't find anyone else. The brunette leaves, giving Yvette a smirk on her way out. The air is heavy with perfume and anticipation. Even Helen Keller could see something is afoot. "Blush. Hurry up."

She didn't notice it before, but Yvette no longer has a French accent. "What gives?"

The other woman speaks under her breath as she walks past Yvette. "Three minutes. Do it quickly." Out the door, she goes.

That sounds downright frightening.

Yvette charges up to her. Charlotte jerks back, throwing her hands into a defensive position. The Frenchwoman who's not French opens her purse, ruffling through its contents.

What's she gonna do in three minutes?

Yvette pulls her fists out of her purse, and they're filled with liners and brushes, tubes, tweezers and scissors. She attacks

Charlotte, forcing her to back into the far wall. "Hold still."

"What are you doing?" She squirms the way a child would in such a situation.

"You're too pale. You have to look exotic." Yvette tries to paint her face, but she gives up. "Ah...I need more time." She flicks Charlotte's nest of hair. "What can I make of this?"

"Have you lost your marbles? Where is Francis?"

"He's with his father."

"Which one?"

Yvette looks at her queerly. "Did you not see Michael this morning? Did he have the boy? Do you honestly think I'd bring a child to this?"

"Who's Michael?"

Yvette exhales her impatience. "Shirin."

That name again. Charlotte runs through events of the last three weeks – since she acquired the strange alias. She, Matthew and the Rosicrucian kid met with doctors of the mind on the Sunset Strip and on Crenshaw Boulevard. She got the impression they also worked on the kid when she and Matthew weren't around. There was a trip to the Santa Ana Mountains where the trio shot guns at tin cans. Matthew told her it was to boost the kid's confidence, pretending he was Wyatt Earp. They also visited Kennedy campaign headquarters in Azusa in an attempt to learn the candidate's schedule. They snuck into a luncheon in Pomona where Kennedy spoke to supporters. Each incident seemed innocent as it happened, but looking back she realizes there was more to it. "He made me call him Michael when strangers were nearby."

"And you were Shirin."

"How could I be so stupid?"

Yvette acts like she doesn't get the question, but she startles when two girls enter the powder room – two girls she apparently doesn't recognize, one wearing an RFK campaign pin. She thrusts the make-up tools into Charlotte's hand, forcing her to wrap her fingers around them. "Do it yourself," she whispers. "Remember, Shirin is a Middle Eastern name." She looks at the girls uncomfortably and exits hastily, leaving Charlotte to figure the rest out on her own.

#

Charlotte slides the letter into a pre-addressed envelope, and she licks it closed. She figured it out. Oh boy, did she figure it out. She wants to hand her correspondence to the concierge, but he's busy with a man wearing a Styrofoam Kennedy campaign hat. A million eyes seem to be on her, so she walks away with the letter securely pinched between her fingers. Her other hand holds the purse Yvette abandoned in the bathroom. Coincidentally – or *not* coincidentally – it matches her outfit perfectly. She did what she could with her face in the bathroom, as Yvette ordered. She now wears a complexion she'd call lightly Arabic. She also wrestled her wild hair into a side ponytail, but she couldn't do anything about her nose. It's as prominent as ever.

Matthew/Michael sent her to the hotel because he wants her to be noticed. That's what she's come to realize. It's that pop-up book all over again. When the events of today have run their course, he expects the blame to fall on people of color and the Jews – not to forget the Jews. He wanted witnesses to see her casing the hotel this morning when she looked like a Jew. He wants them to see her now as a Middle Eastern woman. She's playing two roles, implicating two races. And she's certain she was wrong about what she thought the disturbance would be.

She can't go that far with him. She needs to split, but to where and how can she get there? Maybe she can wait things out in an inconspicuous corner of the hotel. She turns left and right, searching for that corner. First, she needs to send out the letter, but the front desk clerk is busier than the concierge. He has more lights around him too. There are lights everywhere and crews setting up cameras, running cables. She's afraid Yvette is lurking nearby, watching her. Yvette's on-and-off lover, Lee, could be as well. She knows Diamond Joe Provenzano's boys are there. She's seen them with their black leather overcoats out of place in the June heat. Through a sea of campaign supporters and everyday hotel guests, she notices the Ambassador Coffee

Shop. It's reputed to be a happening spot where celebrities often mingle with regular folks. A joint like that sounds like it would make an ideal inconspicuous corner.

"You can stop lookin', hon. I'm here."

Her heart beats the drum of fear against the back of her breast bone. She pivots to find herself face to face with...it's not Matthew. That's a relief. "Who are you?"

"John H. Fahey." The man's smile could be either contagious or infectious, depending upon perspective. He's clean-shaven with crow's feet creeping out from the corners of his brown eyes, and his straight dark hair is sprinkled with gray. Judging by his blue suit, Italian shoes and stylish watch that pokes out from under his left cuff, he has enough dough to live a comfortable life. "Do you need help with something?"

"Do you know where the post office is?"

"I didn't know the hotel had one."

Well, he's not a manager. She has no time to waste, so she leaves him, passing two, three and four people at a time. She has to get her message out. *Someone must know where the post office is.* She hears a reporter and a cameraman discussing where Kennedy will stand later this evening. She could run up and give them the scoop of a lifetime. She knows they'd flip for her story. She also knows it would be her last act on earth.

Her fingers are moist with sweat, soaking into the letter. She checks to see that the handwriting on the envelope hasn't smudged. She addressed it to Pete, but she wrote it for him *and* their son. He is their son, by the way. That's what she decided. Henceforth and forever, Matthew will have no claim to the boy. In case she doesn't make it back to them, she wants Pete and Francis to know the part love played in her decision to be here. Her love for Bobbi made her grow to hate her daughter's namesake. Her love for Francis made her buy into Matthew's plan to build a brighter future. Her love for Pete...that's harder to explain. Can he accept that she loved two men at the same time?

Another shock hits her system – sudden and visual. It chills her blood, but she can't look away from it, away from him.

His skin is dark now. He appears to have come from someplace faraway, maybe a region around the Mediterranean Sea. His hair is more black than usual, with a style that's long on top, combed straight, shorter on the sides. Despite the alterations, she knows him to be Matthew/Michael.

It's more imperative than ever that she beat feet to someplace else. But a force like a powerful wind yanks the letter from her hand. She spins around, and there's Lee. The scent of his foreign cologne swims up her nostrils. He wears an earpiece that makes him look like a government agent. "What's this?" He reads the front of the envelope. "To Pete Caron."

She grabs for it, but she's too slow. "I...I want to make sure he's taking care of Francis."

"You could've called him." He opens the letter, his hazel eyes travelling over her writing.

And...she bolts. It's better for her to sacrifice the letter than herself along with it. She may not believe in God, but she can thank him for the lobby crowd. It absorbs her, provides her cover. But where can she go? Where...where indeed? There's the coffee shop, looking like it did moments ago, with Mr. Fahey sitting at its squiggly-shaped counter. He's sipping a hot brew and looking rejected. It's time she changed that. *Yes, you can help me, Mr. John H. Fahey.*

CHAPTER 31

2018

Frank left his car in a busted-up parking lot littered with drug paraphernalia and signs of gang activity. Keeping a lookout for any and all threats to his person, he crept past exposed girders, broken concrete, and disconnected window frames. Glass shards sounded like popping corn as they crunched beneath his shoes. As he neared a set of rusted double doors, he heard a wail that stopped him short. He heard a wet smack, like something hitting meaty flesh.

"What am I doing?" He was far less suited for this than his friend Rip would've been. He didn't even have a gun. But after his surprising revelation on Alex Logan's satellite show, he doubted he'd be able to get his friend to do anything other than walk Tippy.

It was all according to his plan, though. Long before the satellite show, he used his slow-healing bumps and bruises to evidence his claim that the DA's men were taking license with their boss's orders. And he told Rip he had no reason to believe Marco had anything to do with his men drugging Charlotte. Thinking these rogue men might jeopardize the investigation, Rip honored his request to install a GPS tracker on the van Dr. Fitz and his thugs used to carry out the DA's wishes. In the process of installing the tracker, Rip found and also disabled a signal blocker someone installed in the van to thwart phone traces. But there was one aspect of the plan that concerned him:

Rip informing Marco of the GPS tracker. His way around that was to tell his friend the less Marco knew, the less he could be implicated in what his men did in his name. Rip seemed to buy that. He may not have been able to understand Rip's steadfast loyalty to Marco, but he found a way to work it to his advantage. Or so he thought. Maybe Rip was smarter than that. Maybe he saw through Frank's manipulation. Hopefully, not.

And he knew Marco was spiraling. They sped toward the date of the grand jury hearing with, at best, a circumstantial case. After hyping it in a months-long media blitz and publicly arresting an infirm, dementia-suffering old woman, the pressure was on for the DA to produce something solid. Frank said as much in the interview, knowing it would rile Marco.

With there being a possibility that Marco would do something desperate, he followed the tracker to where the van sat parked outside the Junípero Serra Elementary School gymnasium. Located half a mile from the Hollywood Freeway (aka the 101), the school had been abandoned for years and slated for demolition. It seemed the ideal spot for a desperate act.

He opened one of the two doors on squeaky rusted hinges, surprised that it opened at all. Darkness fell over him, but not so dark he couldn't see it grow lighter the further he went into the building. As his eyes adjusted, he saw a dilapidated gymnasium take shape: broken and missing floorboards, hoops without backboards and backboards without hoops. He saw the dark swirls of graffiti on the walls and broken bleachers barely able to support their own weight. The wail and the smack he heard moments ago didn't repeat themselves, but he detected scampering sounds. He thought he saw shadows shaped like men disappear around a corner. And a door closed.

He crept toward the muted light that fell onto the basketball court from broken windows high up in the walls. He took his phone out, his finger hovering over the camera icon, but he didn't dare turn on its flashlight. Though he couldn't see any, he had the feeling eyes were upon him. He didn't know what he expected to find. He thought maybe he'd interrupt a document shredding or a paper burning. He smirked at his own ridiculousness. Marco's men were in the evidence gathering phase, not destroying. He'd seen too many espionage movies.

Though he approached the light, he kept to the shadows. A wall-mounted backboard with missing glass called to him. The closer he got to it, the thicker the air felt. He didn't venture too close, but he saw a puddle glistening beneath its rusty basketball rim. Not clear like water, it was dark. He didn't have to touch it to know it was blood – a substantial amount of it. A chain dangled above the puddle, from the rim. It had four off-shoots with a manacle at the end of each. He also saw clearer fluid on the floor, which he thought might be sweat, piss or both. From the smell, he guessed all the bodily liquids were freshly deposited. *This goes so far beyond beating me up.* They couldn't be torturing people, could they? He saw all he needed of that in the chemical warehouse with Joseph Provenzano. Didn't anyone know there were easier and more humane ways of obtaining information?

"Get your hands off me, you mother fu –" A smack abruptly shut someone up. Heavy objects made toppling sounds, as if a person or an object crashed into them – likely a person. The noises came from a room adjacent to the gymnasium, perhaps a locker room.

He fumbled with his phone, trying to find the video record feature. Photographic evidence was good, but video evidence was better.

A roar from a gruff voice escaped the far side of the gym, becoming an echo in the open space. He stood upright despite his desire to stay hidden.

"Mr. Kentworth Lee." That came from a voice he recognized and expected to find. The sounds of struggle followed, grunting and cursing, someone being manhandled.

For his own safety, he knew he should leave, but if this was what he thought it was, how could he go? *The Hottest Place in Hell, right? Rip would be proud of me.* He snuck cautiously closer to the action, none of which he could yet see.

"Former CIA agent Kentworth Lee," said that same voice.

"Do you know how long we've been looking for you?"

"Screw off, you dandy-boy hippie freak," shouted a man who sounded out of breath.

Frank escaped the openness of the basketball court by shimmying close to the wall, beneath the bleachers. But they posed their own dangers with jagged, exposed metal and barely functioning support beams. It wouldn't take more than a bird to perch on the stands, he thought, and they'd collapse, crushing him.

"Let's see – strap him in! His leg. Get his leg. Okay, where was I with this? Sources say you worked out of the JMWAVE station in Miami in the early sixties – the JMWAVE that coordinated Operation Mongoose, our government's thirty-three part program to rid Cuba of Castro."

Oh shit. If the remains of torture he found under the backboard were any indication of what to expect, he knew the man they held – this Kentworth Lee – was in for a world of hurt. It was far darker under the bleachers than anywhere else in the gym. Because of that, he couldn't look anywhere but directly in front of him. As if to remind him of that, a steel rod scratched his cheek. He stopped, eased back from it. *Did it draw blood? When was my last tetanus shot?*

"You were in Vietnam for much of the war, trying to make Charlie talk. Thank you for your service. They say you perfected The Bell Telephone Hour, an interrogation tactic used by field operatives. By all accounts, it was very effective."

Here I'm worried about tetanus, and they're about to – what the hell is The Bell Telephone Hour? He forced himself to keep going, and only two steps later, he felt and heard something crunch beneath his shoe. It looked like a hypodermic needle, but he couldn't be sure. It made noise though. He was sure of that.

"Question number one – and feel free to elaborate to make this easier on everyone – was there a connection between Operation Mongoose and Bobby Kennedy's murder?"

A gap between bleachers gave Frank his first unimpeded view of the torture. And it was far worse than he imagined. Naked but for a pair of boxer shorts, Kentworth Lee was an eighty-plus year old man with a torso shaped like a barrel. His chest, stomach and shoulders wore a carpet of gray hair saturated with perspiration. Canvas straps held him to a metal chair, the front two legs of which stood in a kiddie pool filled with water. His bare feet were in the water, his ankles strapped to the chair legs. Metal clamps squeezed his bleeding nipples while copper wires connected the clamps to an EA312 military phone resting on a nearby table.

"So you know that we know – and to move this forward – Operation Mongoose had a six phase schedule. It was coordinated by Attorney General Robert Kennedy, and it involved political, psychological, military, and sabotage operations designed to destabilize Castro's government."

Frank had to move to the left about a foot to get visual confirmation of what he already knew. The interrogator was Dr. Fitz, a sweaty sheen on his skin, his hair a mess and his body jittering with excitement. He had four heavily-armed men assisting him, none of whom were the cop with the flat-top haircut.

"Take these pinchers off my tits," hissed the torture victim.

Dr. Fitz continued. "The plan was supposed to culminate with military intervention in Cuba by October of 1962. But the Missile Crisis happened in October of '62, and President Kennedy changed his mind about Operation Mongoose."

The prisoner fought his restraints, looking at the clamps on his nipples. "Fuck!"

"Tell us about the agents who worked on Operation Mongoose," said the doctor.

Mr. Lee shook his head – maybe as an answer, maybe from the pain.

Dr. Fitz feigned disappointment. "JMWAVE had five hundred operatives and thousands of anti-Castro Cuban exiles on its payroll. I'll throw some names at you to refresh your memory. You tell me if they were JMWAVE. Okay?"

Frank started recording. It was to catch them in the act,

though, not because he wanted to hear what the prisoner had to say. *Right?* He had to remind himself. *UNCAT – The United Nations Convention against Torture says this is an international crime.*

"Thane Cesar?" asked Dr. Fitz.

The prisoner didn't acknowledge his question.

"Dr. William Joseph Bryan?"

They just discussed him in the FBI field office, he remembered. There was no way Marco wasn't behind this. *If only he'd show his face for the camera.*

"Everette Howard Hunt," continued the doctor.

There was no response from the prisoner except to struggle with his pain. It looked unbearable.

"Come now," said Dr. Fitz. "You must remember Hunt. He served thirty-three months in prison for participating in the Watergate cover-up, but before that, he trained Cuban exiles for the Bay of Pigs Invasion. Your memory needs some incentive." He settled into the chair beside the table housing the military phone. He gave the phone several hard cranks. Electricity rode the wires from the phone to clamps on the prisoner's nipples, and Mr. Lee writhed. Water splashed as his chair bounced in the pool, his feet kicking as much as they could in their restraints.

"I'll see you behind bars," Frank hissed to himself. He kept his camera aimed, wishing he could add better lighting to it.

The prisoner spoke hoarsely. "Hunt was one of the tramps arrested in Dealey Plaza after they shot President Kennedy." His chin fell to his chest, and he sucked air into his taxed lungs.

Dr. Fitz seemed to give that consideration. He even glanced at one of the thugs standing nearby. "Hunt admitted that in a deathbed confession he recorded for posterity. Tell Mr. Caron something he doesn't know."

Frank froze. He felt all his energy drain from his body, into the floor. On the face of his phone, he saw Dr. Fitz turn slowly to look at him.

"Come on out." One of the thugs wasn't very big, but he didn't need to be. His gun was plenty big enough, and he aimed it at Frank from outside the bleachers.

He slid along the wall, avoiding the dangers of the stands to meet a weapon that could tear him to shreds with the press of a finger. The thug grabbed his arm and pulled him the last eighteen inches out of his hiding place, pushed him toward the site of Kentworth Lee's torture. "How'd you know I was here?"

Dr. Fitz laughed. "You need a stealthier vehicle."

He now had a closer view of the suffering prisoner. The man's chin was on his chest, and blood from his nipples mixed with sweat to trickle over his round belly, catching in patches of his hair. "You're breaking so many laws here."

The man who extracted him from the bleachers snatched his phone. As quick as he did that, he also threw it into the kiddie pool of water, where it promptly sank.

"Let's get you up to speed now," said Dr. Fitz. "After all, we're doing this for you – for the argument you're going to make."

"You're not doing this for me. I don't want to hear any –"

Dr. Fitz waived his protest away as if swatting at a fly. "Our previous informant, who you just missed, was an FBI agent who worked closely with Director J. Edgar Hoover."

"You're calling torture victims informants now?"

It was hard for emotion to show on Dr. Fitz's heavily worked upon face, but a smirk managed to creep through. "Our informant said J. Edgar Hoover admitted to knowing Robert Kennedy's assassination was a CIA operation, but he also admitted there was nothing he could do about it. CIA operative Robert Maheu was the go-between for the CIA and Johnny Rosselli and the Chicago mob when they plotted to overthrow Castro. And Maheu was an intimate of Ace Security guard Thane Cesar and much of the upper ranks of the LAPD. I assume you're familiar with Thane Cesar."

How can I not be? Cesar's name was all over the assassination because he was the security guard who took the detour, leading RFK into the kitchen pantry. He also stood closest to RFK when the shots rang out.   But Frank offered no reaction – nothing to encourage Dr. Fitz.

"It seems likely that Robert Maheu was the architect of Bobby's assassination," said Dr. Fitz. "But he needed an assassination specialist to pull it off. That's why Mr. Lee is here. He's going to tell us which of the CIA's assassination specialists carried out *this* assassination."

"You're too stupid to know what you don't know," roared the prisoner. "The agency doesn't meddle in domestic affairs. That means I got nothing to tell you."

Dr. Fitz shook his head. "Lumumba of the Congo, South Vietnamese president Diem and Trujillo of the Dominican Republic – those assassinations originated with the CIA, specifically E. Howard Hunt, David Atlee Phillips, and –"

"And they were in *other* countries," hissed the prisoner.

Dr. Fitz turned to the thug to his right. "We have a hostile witness here."

That was apparently a command. The thug set his gun on the floor outside the pool and stepped into the water. Frank saw that he made a point of grinding his heel into the submerged phone, creating cracking and crunching sounds. In one swift yank, he pulled Kentworth Lee's boxer shorts down to his ankles. Lee bounced in his chair. "What are you – you sick fuck. What are you doing?" The man removed the clamp from Lee's left nipple. He washed it thoroughly in the pool's water, being sure to get it nice and wet. Then he pinched the wet clamp onto Lee's scrotum, just above his testicle. The scream that caused the prisoner to emit had no match in the natural world. But he wasn't content to simply put the squeeze onto Lee's vas deferens. He dampened the second clamp and sank its teeth into the head of Mr. Lee's fear-shrunken penis.

Dr. Fitz seemed to get off on the prisoner's shrieks. "Hunt organized assassinations all over the world, always on orders. Those orders came from as high as CIA deputy director Richard Helms. Who else in those days carried out assassinations for your agency?"

The prisoner bounced more in his chair, and he wrestled with his restraints. Water splashed. His voice grew hoarser as he continued to wail.

Dr. Fitz turned the crank over once, twice, a third and a fourth time. He fed off the new sound it inspired – a cross between a screech and a roar, made by raw vocal cords. The prisoner's pain was off the charts. His body went rigid, muscles flexing. He bent his head back and threw his extraordinary cries at the ceiling.

"This is crazy," Frank yelled. "Let him go."

His breathing heavy with glee as well as from exertion, Dr. Fitz repeated his question. "Who performed assassinations for the CIA in the 1960s?"

Mr. Lee stopped screaming, but his body remained as stiff as if he had rigor mortis. He breathed even heavier than Dr. Fitz. "It was Hunt and Phillips. That's all. All done overseas."

The doctor cast a glance at Frank, frowned.

Not again! He shot forward to stop Dr. Fitz, but the man who extracted him from the bleachers stabbed his gun into his chest.

Dr. Fitz went back to work on the phone – harder and faster than his previous efforts. He found his stride, but he wasn't young. It took some real effort to crank that thing. Even with the hoarse, otherworldly noise it brought from the prisoner and the adrenaline that coursed through his body, he had to stop sooner than he apparently wanted. Sweat coated his brow, the beads of which rolled down to his Botox frozen cheeks. "I can…I can do this all day."

I doubt it. But Frank didn't try to move, stilled by the man's pointing gun.

"Now," continued Dr. Fitz. "We have Hunt and Phillips, but they're both accounted for in April through June of '68." He looked at Frank. "Remember, Robert Maheu might have been the architect, but he needed an assassination specialist. That specialist would have been in the country, probably even in L.A., when the hit on Robert Kennedy took place."

Once again, Frank had the déjà vu feeling that he'd already been here when Trevor tortured information out of

Joseph Provenzano – information he wanted Frank to present to the grand jury. "I'm not revealing any of these facts to anyone unless you let him go right now."

That seemed to throw Dr. Fitz, and he looked at a nearby door that had a window with a latticework of wire within it.

Who's watching from behind that door? Is it Marco? Is Marco behind that door?

Oblivious to all but his own pain and suffering, the prisoner responded to Dr. Fitz's last inquiry. "Carlos Marcello and Santo Trafficante, it was them. They recruited Cuban exiles from Operation Mongoose."

Frank closed his eyes, knowing that despite his efforts to stop it, the captive just earned himself more shocks. Mob bosses Carlos Marcello and Santo Trafficante helped the CIA train Cuban exiles for Operation Mongoose, so they would've been in a position to recruit the exiles for an assassination plot, but –

"The mob didn't have the resources to commit high profile killings and cover them up," said Dr. Fitz, putting voice to Frank's thoughts. "Only the CIA and the FBI could pull it off and cover it up. The CIA was experienced in assassinations. Who in the CIA killed the Kennedys?"

Slowly, with what appeared to be great effort, Mr. Lee turned to look at Frank.

"For God's sake, tell him," said Frank. "Stop your suffering."

The prisoner couldn't completely shake his head, but he managed to move it enough to give his answer.

That was all Dr. Fitz needed. He went back to cranking the phone. "I'll electrocute it out of you if that's what it takes, but you *will* tell us." He built up speed on the military phone, the rotations becoming too numerous to count. He looked mad, but he was far from it. His eyes kept shifting from the prisoner to that door, the prisoner to the door.

"Marco," Frank yelled at the door. "I know you're back there. Stop him!"

Mr. Lee's raw voice found new ways to express his

pain. He writhed and rocked. Each shock created a different spasm, violent and traumatic to his system. His chair hopped so forcefully it broke the kiddie pool. Water spilled onto the floor, making haste to get away from the tortured man. But the canvas straps wouldn't let him go, cutting into his straining body.

Frank screamed at the doctor. "You'll kill him. Give him a chance to answer."

Dr. Fitz didn't seem to care about that. The permanently frozen part of his face was like a perspiring doll, but the rest of him put every effort into manifesting his physical exertions: grunting, snarling, spitting, sucking air, gritting teeth. His unkempt hair became more unkempt.

There were minutes – possibly only seconds – remaining in the prisoner's endurance. The place smelled of burnt flesh, and smoke floated up from his genitals. He faced the darkness above and the ceiling rafters, opened mouth as if to scream, but his voice had no sound left to expel. He was going to expire like that: gape mouthed and eyes heavenward.

Frank couldn't stand idle while another man died. He shoved the thug's gun aside and ran to the broken kiddie pool, jumping in. He reached for the first clamp. He had to remove it gently, but with the screams and the shocks, all he could think was that he wanted to stop the torture. And he forgot about the water in the pool beneath his running feet in shoes with little traction. His hand found the vas deferens clamp, but his feet slid out from under him in the same moment. As he fell, he tore the most precious part of the man's anatomy off in the mouth of the clamp. Mr. Lee's voice found a new type of scream, and he sent it up to the rafters. But he was alive – clearly. Frank scramble-slipped up to a kneeling position and removed the second clamp. Blood from the man's genitals washed over his hands, and it wouldn't stop. There was so much blood.

CHAPTER 32

Sasha wasn't two steps from the now opened door of her cell when Flat-top grabbed her by the arm and pulled her out. She stumbled but didn't fall. She'd already done enough looking around the last few times they took her into and out of the cell to know there were no cameras recording what would happen next. And what *would* happen now that she'd given Marco Diaz everything? She couldn't bluff the DA after he saw her reaction to Frank's radio interview through that two-way glass. She told him what the elderly mobster said about Johnny Rosselli, Sirhan Sirhan, and a mob contract on RFK. She told him about the Minutemen and what she thought about 8F uniting widely disparate elements under one banner. She even made another pitch for her helping him with his case. It was all for naught.

As she tried and failed to pull her arm free of Flat-top's grip, she realized the DA had given her over to him. His hand seemed fine *and strong* now, but he wanted revenge for what she did to it back in Castaic. She wondered if he'd rough her up the way they did Frank in Twentynine Palms. Or would she get it worse? That wasn't her being terminally dramatic – not at all. She'd seen too many of the DA's dark tactics. No one at the precinct processed her upon arrival, so there was no record of her being there. She also had no lawyer. She couldn't forget that. "Where are you taking me?"

Flat-top pulled her past empty cells (no witnesses) toward a back door, barely visible in the shadows that surrounded it.

Her imagination ran unrestrained through her mind. She didn't remember the area behind the building because it was dark, late, and she was tired when they first brought her there. She wondered if it had a grimy alley with a dumpster that could fit a body. That seemed unlikely so close to a police station. But she could imagine an unmarked car with a plain-clothed driver waiting to take her and Flat-top to a remote place. Or maybe Flat-top would throw her in the trunk and take her to some killing place on his own. "Frank," she yelled. It was a word – the one name – that brought some relief to her raw and terrified emotions, though it only bounced feebly around the dark, empty space of the precinct's lock-up.

#

Pacific Coast Highway, California. June 4, 1968

Charlotte's white knight – Mr. John H. Fahey – said *you can trust me. I'm for McCarthy.* He seriously miscalculated if he intended to put her at ease with a comment like that. He said it after she confided that they were going to get Kennedy at tonight's rally. Who makes such a blasé response after hearing such a frightening claim? He essentially told her *I don't care if they kill Kennedy. I'm voting for McCarthy.* Now she sits in the front passenger seat as he cruises across lanes to drift the car out onto a scenic headland. It's a headland, by the way, that ends with a drop off a cliff. She's like one of Francis's bouncy toys as she throws her head to and fro, looking at the dark boulders they pass and the thorny bushes. He stops at the most picturesque spot of the promontory where the Pacific stretches out as far as she can see, boats bobbing lazily upon it. He lets out a relaxed sigh and says, "The Mamas and the Papas should sing about this."

"Are you off your rocker?" She checks the side mirror. "They're following us."

He shifts into park. His easy smile shows his coffee-stained teeth.

"Are you forgetting the old fogey in the blue Ford?"

"Lost him in Malibu."

"And the dark blue VW?"

He rests his arm on the seatback behind her, cool as a cucumber.

"They're really after us," she says. "I think they're using radios to communicate."

He laughs. "They're my competitors is all – playing games."

He's a bird brain. No one in their right mind would take being followed so lightly unless they're in on it. And they *have* been followed – ever since leaving the Ambassador. *If he's not in on it,* she wonders, *does he intend to rob me?* That's his plan? She has money. She found it in the purse Yvette abandoned in the hotel bathroom.

As if trying to dissuade her of that notion, he gives her ponytail a little twirl. And he has a new look on his face – a bedroom look. *Oh,* that's *what he wants.* The price for him escorting her out of L.A. is a hump in a parked car? She should've realized it earlier. It's the currency most men use…or hope to. She considers paying it but abandons the thought when she sees a disturbing reflection in the side mirror. The Volkswagen is back, and this time the driver steps out of the car to stretch. He's stocky, and he has dark hair with bronze skin. He looks like he could pop off a person's head with little effort. "Are your competitors Provenzano men?"

Mr. Fahey looks back, and his bedroom eyes disappear. If he doesn't know this man, he certainly knows the Provenzano name. "Who are you?"

"Alice. I told you."

"And you said you were Jean."

"Betty. My name is Betty."

The Italian climbs back into the VW. He could ram them with his car, pushing them over the embankment. He could leave them, but he probably won't do that because he's been on their trail for miles. He most likely intends to box them in, waiting for reinforcements to arrive.

She hears gravel popping under tires. Her mirror shows what's happening, but she turns to get a better view through the back window. Rather than creeping ahead, she sees the

Volkswagen roll backward to disappear behind a large boulder. "Burn rubber," she screams. "Go now!"

Mr. Fahey yanks the gear column into the *R* position and gasses the car. At least he recognizes the seriousness of their situation now. Their backward-spinning tires spit rocks against the undercarriage. They soar past the boulder, able to see the Italian watching them from the front seat of the VW. A horn roars as they back into the road – a Mack truck coming at them without any apparent intention of slowing. Mr. Fahey wastes time by looking in his rear-view mirror then turning to peer out his back window to be sure the mirror isn't lying to him. "Shit!"

The Mack is nearly upon them. Its horn rattles her heart in her ribcage. In the horror of her eminent death, the last thing to catch her eye is the Italian in the VW. And she sees him smile. *Goombah. Dago. You want me dead so you can pin the assassination on me?* She jerks the gear shift to *D*. "Floor it!"

Mr. Fahey obeys her command. As the Mack truck leaves fishtailing streaks of black on the road, a new obstacle comes at them from the other direction. It's a Woody in its own lane, and it doesn't seem inclined to give up its ground.

Mr. Fahey jerks the wheel hard to the right. His crying tires paint squiggly artwork on the road, but they manage to find their lane moments before impact with the Woody. He glances at her with eyes that are wide and wet. His death white hands choke the steering wheel as he continues to feed gas to the engine. "I'm a taking…we're gonna go…I gotta get you to the cops."

"Take me back to L.A."

"You're out of your mind."

"My real name is Gilderdine Oppenheimer. You need to take me back because…Kennedy may be no good, but he doesn't deserve what they're going to give him."

"Even if you're dealing the straight dope this time, what are you gonna do about it?"

She shrugs – her eyes on the road and her mind in L.A.

"We have to go to the police."

That word – his last word – triggers a memory, which visits

her with all the disjointed unreality of an acid flashback and none of the pleasure. She recalls Matthew plotting with police before they beat the brains out of love-in devotees in Griffith Park. It was a shock when she saw it happen last year, but it's a revelation as she re-views it now. "I think the police are in on it."

#

Mr. Fahey took Charlotte to Oxnard rather than straight to L.A. Once there, he skipped his sales meeting, turned the car around and took them on a leisurely drive back down the coast. He even stopped to grab a bite to eat in Santa Monica. His behavior made no sense unless he thought that by acting casual, they'd go unnoticed. She didn't know because they didn't discuss it. She could've left him at any time, but that would only make her vulnerable to whomever or whatever came next. She had to trust him to get her back to L.A. and to the kid who looked Mexican. It's all about him now.

"I'm staying on Kenmore near Olympic," she says as they creep through the L.A. sprawl. She's not really staying there, but the Rosicrucian is. They put him in a flophouse where Matthew's men can tighten the final screws in his head in preparation for his date with destiny.

"Koreatown?"

She nods, wondering how she can best intercept the kid between the flophouse and the hotel. She's risking her life, but she has to try to stop them. Killing another Kennedy is not acceptable in her book, regardless of what she thinks of him. The Rosicrucian won't walk or drive himself to the hotel, so who will take him? She knows Donneroummas is in Vegas on business. Diamond Joe won't get his hands dirty like that. *Oh, God, no.* Pete still does most of Joe Provenzano's driving. If they didn't tap him earlier, the letter she wrote that Lee intercepted might make him get the call now. Who'll raise Francis if *both* his parents take the fall for this?

The city outside the windows looks strange to her. She hasn't seen the Kenmore area of Olympic Boulevard in years, but she knows it's in decline. That's not the case with the homes and businesses she's viewing right now. They have fresh paint. They're solidly constructed. The streets are clean. "Where is this? Where are we?"

Mr. Fahey doesn't answer her, and he doesn't have to. They're coming up on an unmistakable structure. The property is immense. Canopies cover the sidewalk. And meticulously manicured grounds lead to the front entrance of the Ambassador Hotel.

She spins to face him, eyes as wide as saucers.

"It's been...uh...interesting," he says. "Good luck to you, whatever your name is."

"Gilderdine. It's Gilderdine. I told you. You can't leave me. They're gonna get Mr. Kennedy here – tonight."

He stops the car. His expression is hard and cold. His eyes urge her to get out.

"Come...uh...come to the reception with me. You can ditch the ride and change your threads. We still have time. Meet me in the lobby in an hour. Say eight thirty?" She puts both imploring hands on his forearm. "I need your help."

"This is the end of our trip."

"No."

He looks everywhere but at her. His eyes seem drawn to the canopied walkway.

And her eyes turn from saucers to slits. In her mind, she hears his words again. *You can trust me. I'm for McCarthy.* Her extremities turn cold, and she slides her hands off his arm before they freeze to it. Whirling around, she yanks the handle and heaves the door open. She springs from the seat. Outside the car, she has no desire to ever see him again. She slams the door.

Apparently, he has no desire to see her either, peeling away fast enough to mean business.

She's unsure of where to go or what to do, but she can't stand stupidly by the curb. Outside alone, she's more noticeable than inside among the many. The coffee shop was good to her once. Maybe she can return to it and spot the Rosicrucian as he enters the hotel. Beginning her long but hurried trek to the entrance, she smells flower perfume floating in the breeze. She tries to put Mr. Fahey's behavior out of her mind. He could be in on it. Or he could be a coward acting weird out of nervousness.

Hands come out of nowhere – probably the nearby bushes. They grab her arms while a third hand covers her mouth, absorbing her scream. Her captors drag her off the canopied sidewalk, into the thick vegetation. Branches scratch her. She loses her right shoe, and her foot squishes in the planter's soil. She flails wildly and uselessly, bites the hand on her mouth. It only squeezes her tighter. A darkening blue sky crosses her field of vision, as do gnarly black branches with green leaves, shadows, hands, and thick fingers with short nails. She sees black polka-dots on white fabric. Her abductors abruptly drop her like a sack of trash. Scrambling to sit up, she finds she's surrounded by three Provenzano muscle men, the brunette and the reddish-blonde woman she saw in the bathroom and Yvette. Each lady wears a polka-dot dress. The brunette's dress is yellow with brown dots. The reddish-blonde wears green with yellow dots. Yvette's outfit is white with black dots and a bib collar with a small black bow. It's the latter outfit that brings her up to a kneeling position. "That's my dress. You're wearing the dress Matthew gave me." He gave it to her the day they went shooting in the Santa Ana Mountains. The cowboy stuff was for the Mexican kid. The dress was for her. "How did *you* get it?"

Yvette waves a paper like it's a flag at Lions Drag Strip. She looks disappointed.

It's the letter Lee snatched from her earlier in the day. And it's about as damning as it can get. She sits back. The dress now worn by Yvette was as much a gift to her as was the Rosicrucian necklace. *I'm so stupid.* She shakes her head. "I didn't name anybody but myself."

"You talk about your love for Matthew."

Again, she looks over the dress. "Love is why I thought that was mine." Something clicks behind her. She has little experience with firearms, but she knows it's a gun. Her heart pumps wildly as she turns to face whoever is about to shoot her. At least she won't go out a coward. To her surprise, she finds Matthew instead of the killing end of a gun. He looks Mediterranean for tonight's adventure, wearing dark pants, a gold cardigan sweater over a light shirt, and a boutonniere of tiny flowers pinned to the inside lapel of the shirt.

He has no emotion as he looks upon her – not cold, not hot, no affection and no disdain. It's more disturbing to her than if he'd explode with fury. He speaks in a slow and methodical voice. "The day you speak a word of this will be the day our son dies." His eyes shift to Yvette. "Release her." He turns, walks between shrubs. And he's gone.

He's not our *son.* But she's smart enough not to say that under the circumstances.

Yvette awakens a Bic lighter. She touches the flame to the letter, and a fire begins the work of devouring the explanation of love Charlotte had written upon it.

#

2018

Sunlight burned Sasha's eyes, and she recoiled away from it while regaining her balance. That backed her into Flat-top, who blocked the rear doorway through which he just threw her. She bounced off him. The lot behind the precinct – where he deposited her – contained no officers, but she saw police cars, marked and unmarked. There were motorcycles. Civilians mulled around outside the police lot, doing average things on an average day. *This place is too conspicuous for an execution or abduction. What is he planning to do to me?*

His eyes were hard on her and unforgiving. "Don't give me a reason."

A reason to do what?

He drifted back into the building, moving almost like an apparition, and he pulled the door closed with him. It sealed with a slam.

She jumped from the noise. "You're letting me go?" Of course, the shut door had no answer for her. Gradually, the sounds of the city returned her to reality. She wasn't aware until then that she had blocked them out. *It can't be this easy.* She'd been in this situation before, she realized. It wasn't exactly the same, but it was close enough to what Trevor did when he left her in Redondo Beach. He just left her. He did instruct her to tell the authorities everything she knew. *No instructions this time? I'm supposed to do what? I can't go back to The Clipper and 8F if that's what you want. I don't even know where they are.* She wondered if Frank had anything to do with this peculiar release. It warmed her to think he looked out for her despite what he said in the FBI field office. Even if it wasn't true, she liked the thought of it.

The thought didn't last, though – not when confronted by her reality. She was more vulnerable on her own than she'd been sitting in an anonymous lock-up. In the jail cell, she could see if danger came at her. Not so here on the outside. She'd never see 8F come for her *if* they came for her. And wouldn't it be convenient for the district attorney if she died in a random accident before she could tell anyone what she knew of his less-than-ethical (illegal) tactics?

She had to get to someplace safe as fast as possible. She didn't have money or a credit card with which to pay a cab fare. She didn't have her phone with its Uber app. She doubted she could count on the kindness of a stranger. The neighborhood outside the police station looked sketchy at best. She noticed something else as she surveyed her new environment. There was a yellow Corvette idling thirty yards away from her. It was too rich for the neighborhood, and it probably wasn't an unmarked cop car because it didn't have a backseat for them to place an arrestee. Its tinted, driver-side window slowly lowered, providing an unimpeded view of the driver. He looked back at her. It took her a moment to recognize him without his dirty Santa beard, but she choked on her own gasp when she did.

Before she could speak his name, Ernie Tolliver said, "Want a ride?" His eyes wandered over the lot. "It's not gonna do either of us any good to stick around here."

CHAPTER 33

Outside the courthouse, spectators, protestors and attention-seekers tested the limits of police barricades. They had much to say, pumped up by many months of media coverage and internet debate, but their opinions couldn't permeate the walls. Four bailiffs stood watch inside the courtroom. They were silent reminders of the official nature of the hearing, assisted by a transcriptionist who kept word-for-word records. No judge presided over it. There were no defendants or defense attorneys, only the prosecution. It was their job to bring a solid case to twenty-three impartial, randomly selected residents of the County of Los Angeles, California.

Frank took a deep breath before approaching the grand jury. He glanced at the seal affixed to the wall behind what would've normally been the judge's bench. *California Superior Court, County of Los Angeles* ran along the outer edge of the seal. He exhaled. He didn't look back at the prosecution table, afraid it would anger him too much to do so. Marco sat there, looking as self-righteous as ever. Two obedient assistants, one male and one female, accompanied him. "You've been given evidentiary packets summarizing our case," he said.

Some of the jurors looked at their thick collection of papers. Several flipped pages.

He had a script in his hand to keep him on track, written by someone on Marco's staff. But it didn't tell the jurors what they wanted to know. As much as they were supposed to ignore the media, they couldn't shut their ears to tantalizing talk of a son prosecuting his mother in one of the most high-profile cases in recent California history. He wondered how he could inform them of the deal he struck to get Charlotte the best medical care in a country club prison. How could he tell them Marco blackmailed him by threatening to implicate him in the torture and attempted murder of former CIA agent Kentworth Lee, now comatose in an undisclosed, allegedly federal facility? He couldn't – not yet, maybe not at all. So he followed the script. "The Fifth Amendment to the U.S. Constitution specifies that charges for capital and infamous crimes are to be brought by an indictment from a grand jury. Robert Kennedy's assassination is one of the most infamous murders in American history. It was a state crime committed here in Los Angeles. That was why they originally tried it in a state court. Over the years, new evidence and testimony came to light indicating other individuals besides the shooter were involved in the murder. We have finally reached a point where there is enough compelling evidence to formally bring the case to you, a criminal grand jury, in the hopes you will indict those individuals, be them alive or dead."

The jurors seemed conscientious and ready to do what the state asked of them.

He continued. "We are not seeking to exonerate convicted shooter Sirhan Sirhan, but to bring to justice those who conspired with him to commit this heinous crime. You must return either the true bill or a bill of ignoramus. You must decide if there is probable cause to bring this to trial. Robert Francis Kennedy was murdered five decades ago, but I'm asking you to remember that there is no statute of limitations for murder cases, especially ones with far reaching consequences for our state and our nation."

It was a simple enough opening statement. He returned to his seat, as the script demanded. He knew it looked like he was Marco's lapdog, selling out his family for his boss's ambitions. If it didn't look like that, it certainly felt it. And his slouching shoulders said as much.

The script called for Marco to take over. For the next two

hours, he laid out the State's argument for the grand jury. He showed crime scene photos and referenced transcripts from Sirhan's original trial in 1969. He played the audio recording made by Stanislaw Pruszynski, explaining how it prompted his office to re-examine RFK's murder. Of course, he skipped Charlotte's hypnotism and Sasha telling him about it, which really inspired his investigation.

With the jury seemingly on his side, Marco proceeded to take issue with the ballistics report from the 1969 trial. He explained that between August 12, 1970 and January 12, 1971, a criminologist with impeccable credentials named William W. Harper examined all the physical evidence and autopsy photographs of the case. That was *before* the LAPD destroyed all such evidence. Comparing the rifling angle of two bullets recovered from the crime scene, Mr. Harper concluded the bullets came from two different guns. The first had been removed from the abdomen of William Weisel, a news director who survived the shooting. They recovered the second bullet from RFK's neck. Reading a sworn affidavit from Mr. Harper dated December 28, 1971, he said, "'Since the rifling angle is a basic class characteristic of a fired bullet, it is my contention that such a difference would rule out the possibility of those bullets having been fired in the same weapon. Two guns were being fired concurrently in the kitchen pantry of the Ambassador Hotel at the time of the shooting.'"

He reminded jurors that Sirhan's gun held only eight rounds. He then accounted for the bullets retrieved from the crime scene. The July 8, 1968 report filed by the LAPD claimed doctors removed seven bullets from the bodies of the six victims: two from Robert Kennedy, and five from the victims who survived. The police claimed an eighth bullet travelled through Kennedy and was lost in the ceiling interspace. That would have been the maximum Sirhan could've fired. Then Marco introduced an official police photograph identified as A-94-cc, which showed two LAPD sergeants pointing at a hole in a doorjamb of the pantry that was made by a small-caliber bullet. "Nine shots make a conspiracy," he told the jurors.

Following along in their packets, jurors listened as he said Sirhan Sirhan came at Senator Kennedy from the left front. According to witnesses, Sirhan was never closer than one foot from Kennedy. Many claimed the distance between the shooter and his victim was as great as three feet. But the wound that killed RFK entered the back of his head from behind his right ear. 1969 testimony from Los Angeles County Coroner Thomas Noguchi, who performed the senator's autopsy, stated that three bullets hit Kennedy from behind, and the fatal shot came from one inch away. The coroner cited powder burns behind Kennedy's right ear as evidence of his claims concerning the direction and proximity of the gun that fired the fatal shot.

At this point, they broke for a forty-five minute lunch. Frank was the first to leave the courtroom, eager for fresh air, eager to stop feeling like he betrayed his mother.

#

Sasha followed Ernie up the stairs. He had more than twenty years on her and a belly that looked like a beach ball, but she found herself sucking more wind than him. She attributed it to her recent lack of physical activity: a captive in the seventies-era town and a prisoner in the DA's private lock-up. His condition she attributed to him being on the run from 8F since agreeing to send her text with the sketches. He developed stamina where she built fear. It was time for her to change that. It was time for her to stop worrying and stop expecting Frank to save her ass.

Interestingly, Frank was why they were where they were, taking the stairs as fast as they could to meet him on the fourth floor when he stepped off the elevator. And, though Ernie refused to confirm her theory, she figured Frank was the reason the DA let her go. The larger question concerned the relationship between Frank and Ernie. How did they even have a relationship? Did she inadvertently put them together when she convinced Ernie to send her sketches text? She couldn't imagine how that was possible when the phone he used was her phone, and it came back to her in pieces with his blood on it.

He stopped at the fourth-floor door without opening it. "Don't let him see you."

A perplexed look transformed her face.

"As far as he knows, I sent you safely off into the sunset. This thing could blow up if he knew you were here."

"He *did* get me released?"

Ernie opened the door. "Stay here."

"Wait." She grabbed his shirt. "What thing? What are you up to?"

His eyes dropped to her hand and stayed there until it opened to release him.

"Why did you bring me here?" she asked.

"You insisted. Besides, Frank Caron has his plan, and I have mine." He stepped through the door, looked back at her one last time. "Remember. Don't let him see you."

She watched him hustle down the corridor as the elevator bell announced Frank's arrival on the fourth floor. For a busy courthouse with hundreds of people gathered outside, reporters and police, she was surprised to see no one but Ernie in the hallway. She took half a step after him, and she kept the door open with one arm in case she had to disappear behind it. She wouldn't abuse his trust and blow up whatever *this thing* was, but she had to get some idea of what was going on – especially if he intended her to be a part of his plan. Unfortunately, getting close enough to hear them would also make her visible. The corridor offered no place for her to hide unless she entered one of the offices that opened into it. And those offices, she saw, belonged to the superior court judges who heard cases in the courtrooms on floors below this one. With the grand jury hearing already well underway, what business did Frank and Ernie have with any of these judges? Maybe she could take a few more steps into the hallway.

#

All shook up was the best way to describe Frank, but it had nothing to do with the song of that name. He barely knew Ernie Tolliver, but he had to trust him to deliver on what he promised. He also had to trust Trevor, who vouched for Mr. Tolliver. The overall plan was his, but this part was all Trevor – pitched to him at the last minute when his son called from out of the blue (good thing he maintained a land line at his house). Now, with everything in motion, the superior court judge Trevor arranged for him to meet wasn't there. His office door was locked, and calls to his cell went unanswered. What else was he to think but that Trevor was screwing him again?

He returned to the courtroom a little weaker for having skipped lunch and a little dizzy for all the worry that twisted him up inside. Then he saw what they did to the courtroom during the recess. "What the –" In his absence, Marco's staff reconfigured the room with props and cardboard cutouts to make it look like the kitchen pantry of the Ambassador Hotel on the night of RFK's shooting. As he weaved through the maze of new objects, he saw some of the men he'd come to associate with violence – assholes who beat him up in Twentynine Palms and helped Dr. Fitz in that abandoned school gymnasium. He looked for Dr. Fitz but couldn't find him. Marco knew better than to bring *him* to court. He did see Marco, though, smirking as he saw him recognize the violent assholes. Without commenting on that, the DA handed him a paper and moved him to the center of the room. "You'll be Kennedy. Read your line when I point to you."

"We're re-enacting the crime?" He didn't get an answer from the DA, who went to coordinate the seating of the audience, aka the jurors. "Who's playing Sirhan?"

Jurors looked excited for the show to begin as they took their seats. They nudged one another. They whispered while pointing at props and various actors. The room's overhead lights dimmed enough to silence the room. The DA pointed at Frank. It was his cue. He saw it but didn't take it...not until Marco loudly cleared his throat and pointed at him more emphatically. Finally, reluctantly, he read from his paper. "Now it's on to Chicago, and let's win there."

The DA took over, reading aloud from a revised script Frank hadn't yet seen. "At 12:14 a.m., June 5, 1968, Robert

Kennedy concluded his speech after winning the California Democratic Primary. Assistant maître d' Karl Uecker led him into the kitchen pantry, and security guard Thane Cesar joined them, taking Kennedy's right elbow. They passed through the pantry on their way to a press meeting in the Colonial Room."

Two of the DA's thugs grabbed Frank – one at each arm – and he again flashed back to the beating they gave him in Twentynine Palms. He squirmed as they led him through the set with its cardboard props. He was sure no one handled RFK so roughly fifty years ago.

"Amid all the congratulations and glad-handing from the crowd, Kennedy turned left to shake hands with porter Jesus Perez and busboy Juan Romero."

He did as the DA narrated, happy to pull away from the thugs. He shook the hands of two actors he didn't recognize, and he thought they squeezed his hand with unnecessary firmness.

"The banquet supervisor summoned Uecker, who pulled Senator Kennedy toward the Colonial room. Meanwhile, Sirhan Sirhan reached across Uecker's left shoulder and smiled as if he wanted to shake hands with Kennedy. But he was pointing a .22 revolver at Kennedy's head."

Frank's heart jumped as he saw the actor portraying Sirhan surge forward with the barrel of a gun pointing at him. It seemed horrifyingly real, and his hands flew up to protect his face.

"Two quick shots rang out."

Jurors startled as the gun held by the Sirhan actor made two loud cracks.

"Uecker lost his grip on the senator," said Marco. "Kennedy jumped. His hands rose to the side of his face. He stumbled backward and fell to the floor as more gunshots followed. Witnesses said it sounded like someone lit 'a string of firecrackers.'"

He didn't have to pretend for this part. It was as if the Sirhan actor *really* wanted to kill him, so he dropped to the floor.

"The police report claims Ace security guard Thane Cesar ducked and lost his balance. He fell against an ice machine. When he looked up, Kennedy was lying on his back with blood coming out of his right ear and pooling on the floor."

The man portraying Cesar stumbled against a cardboard prop and pulled his weapon.

"'Put that gun away!'" yelled Marco. "That's what Senator Kennedy's bodyguard Bill Barry shouted when Thane Cesar drew his pistol. Meanwhile, others restrained Sirhan."

The man pretending to be Sirhan lowered his gun and moved close to the cardboard cutouts, which were supposed to represent people trying to restrain him. The Cesar actor stood over Frank while holding his pistol.

"Thane Cesar was a racist who believed the Kennedys handed America to the blacks," said Marco. "He owned a .22 caliber handgun like the one used by Sirhan. His position beside the senator matched the angle and distance from which the coroner claimed Kennedy was shot."

The Cesar actor seemed more anxious to harm Frank than the man who played Sirhan. Perhaps he wanted to finish the job they started in Twentynine Palms.

The DA continued. "But Thane Cesar had no criminal past. He had no advanced knowledge that Kennedy would walk through the pantry, and he was assigned pantry duty only at the last minute. He also volunteered to take a polygraph test, saying he had nothing to do with the shooting. And he passed it. He sold his .22 caliber handgun after the assassination, giving the buyer a signed and dated receipt. If he was guilty, that would have been a foolish thing to do."

Frank glanced at Marco, who he could only partially see behind the cutouts restraining the Sirhan actor. In all their planning, they never discussed this explanation of Cesar's innocence. He wondered if it came from Rip. He wondered what became of Rip. He hadn't seen or heard from him since convincing him to put a tracker on Dr. Fitz's vehicle and he called him eight or nine times, leaving messages.

Marco went on undeterred. "A person of greater interest is hotel Security Chief William Gardner, who ordered Cesar to escort Robert Kennedy through the pantry to the Colonial Room. He gave the same order to Uecker and another assistant maître d named Minasian. When interviewed by the FBI, Mr. Gardner said he was one floor below the pantry at the time of the shooting. He claimed to be with hotel guard Lloyd Curtis and Ace guard Willie Bell, but Curtis and Bell said Gardner went upstairs to the pantry area about fifteen minutes before Kennedy was shot. Could Gardner have been one of the guards who witnesses saw pull a gun in the pantry?"

He hadn't considered the hotel's head of security. He also saw nothing that connected his mother to the man. Maybe that was good for Charlotte. He figured he'd find out when they got to the part of the hearing that included her. He wished he could read ahead in the DA's new script.

"It appears Mr. Gardner was involved," said Marco. "But he would have been one piece of the puzzle. There had to be a crazy gunman firing as a distraction while someone else delivered the kill shot. For that, I refer you to Deputy District Attorney Frank Caron."

What? Shit. He wasn't familiar with the revised script or the re-enactment, but they'd always planned for him to present the most important part of the case. Apparently, that was still the plan. The problem was that he still didn't know how he'd address the role played by the girl in the polka-dot dress. The unreliability of the judge upstairs only made that more of a problem.

But Marco wasn't done yet. "You may have heard Mr. Caron is the son of –"

"Thank you, Mr. District Attorney." He stood, snatched the script from Marco and picked up where he left off, trying to project a confidence that contrasted with what he showed the jury before the break. He thought it was his best chance of downplaying his mother as a suspect. "Sirhan Sirhan was an emotionally disturbed young man with an interest in self-hypnosis as taught by the Rosicrucian Order. He was also among the five percent of the population that's most susceptible to the kind of deep hypnosis that allows for human programming."

He saw jurors squirming in their seats, looking askance, and a few even groaned. He knew it was because the programming argument sounded like something out of a sci-fi movie. "Before you dismiss this idea, consider how America's intelligence services formed the MKULTRA program in the fifties and sixties with the purpose of perfecting human mind control, part of which included programmable assassins."

Marco gave him a reassuring nod.

He ignored him as best he could. "The *men* who coordinated this plot –" It was no accident that he emphasized that word. "– found Sirhan working at a horse track. The track was popular with mobsters, one of whom was Frank Donneroummas, who befriended Sirhan and introduced him to a con man named Jerry Owen. Mr. Owen made Sirhan's introduction to Dr. William J. Bryan. Dr. Bryan was a world-class hypnotist who led the Air Force's brainwashing program and consulted for the CIA's MKULTRA program to create hypnotizable assassins."

"You will find the documentation to support this on pages eighty-nine through ninety-six of your packets," said Marco.

"The chain of custody comes together clearly. Sirhan passes from mobster Frank Donneroummas to mob-connected con man Jerry Owen to hypnotist Dr. William J. Bryan." He watched jurors flip pages in their packets, following along. Then he noticed the part of the script that dealt with the girl in the polka-dot dress. And he skipped it, leaping ahead. "There were many moving parts. It was a plot with different and diverse players, requiring expert coordination. On page one nineteen, you can see what might've motivated someone in the CIA to join the conspiracy. In particular, I refer you to President Kennedy's vow to 'splinter the CIA into a thousand pieces and scatter it into the winds.' An assassin killed John Kennedy before he could dismantle the agency, but what if a second President Kennedy came along to fulfill the promise of his fallen brother?"

The district attorney began to fidget. Frank omitting the girl in the polka-dot dress didn't sit well with him, and he wanted to take over. He stood.

But the momentum belonged to Frank, as did the jury's attention. "Please look at the sworn affidavit on page one twenty. It's from Robert Walton, who was the lawyer for a CIA agent named –" He stopped as he read the name. And he looked at Marco with shock on his face. *This is the name Dr. Fitz tried to torture out of Kentworth Lee. How did you get it?* He returned to the jurors, aware of how closely they watched him. "David Sanchez Morales."

The DA sat back down. He looked smug and satisfied, gestured for Frank to proceed.

"Um." There was no time for him to scan ahead and preview what he was about to tell the jury. "You can see the highlighted portion of the affidavit. According to Mr. Walton, CIA Agent David Sanchez Morales admitted, and this is a direct quote, 'I was in Dallas when I, when *we* got that mother fucker. And I was in Los Angeles when we got the little bastard.'"

More than a few eyebrows climbed up jurors' foreheads, and not from the foul language.

"Mr. Walton went on to explain, 'what he said to me was that he was in some way implicated with the death of John Kennedy, and let's go one step further, and also with Bobby.'" He looked at the jurors, wondering if they realized how big a bombshell this was. "Mr. Walton told the same story to a congressional investigator and on camera for a BBC report on Robert Kennedy's murder."

Marco may have told him to continue, but he wasn't content to sit on the sidelines. He stood as if ejected by his chair, speaking extemporaneously. "David Sanchez Morales was a classic Cold War spy. Almost a cliché, he really was a racist, hard-drinking, tough guy. He ran the CIA's anti-Castro paramilitary program in Miami in the early sixties. One of his good friends was Las Vegas mobster Johnny Rosselli. In 1954 he took part in a coup in Guatemala. In the mid-sixties, he went to Southeast Asia as part of Operation Phoenix, which targeted Vietcong leaders for assassination. He executed former Cuban leader Che Guevara in 1967. In 1973, he participated in the bloody overthrow of Chile's

Salvador Allende."

Frank was too stunned to try to steal momentum back from the DA. If the sworn affidavit from Robert Walton was true – and as an attorney, Walton knew not to lie under oath, David Sanchez Morales *was* their case. Not knowing what else to do, he returned to his seat.

Marco continued. "As his best friend for more than fifty years once told an investigator, 'When some asshole needed to be killed, [Morales] was the man to do it. That was his job.'"

So absorbed in his thoughts was Frank that he didn't see the male assistant leave the table until the already dim lights dimmed further. He saw the young man press a button on the wall, which enabled a screen to descend from the ceiling to hide the superior court seal behind the judge's chair. A buzz sounded from above, and a ceiling projector tilted to aim at the screen.

Marco said, "In your packets, you will see declassified CIA document 104-10308-10274."

The assistant returned from the back of the room, pointing and clicking a remote as he walked. The projector flashed to life, casting a floor plan of a sixties-era restaurant kitchen onto the screen. The server's line, chef's area, and dishwasher's station in the diagram appeared close to a staircase, beneath which sat a closet pantry.

"This is a diagram of the kitchen of the Montecatini Restaurant, one of Fidel Castro's favorite places to eat in the early sixties," said Marco. "He visited every month and always left his guards behind when he entered the kitchen to chat with employees." The DA moved subtly closer to the jury – a courtroom technique meant to gain their trust. "On August 28, 1962, Agent Morales submitted a plan to William Harvey, his CIA superior, to assassinate Castro in this kitchen. The plan called for an assassin to hide in the pantry. When Fidel approached, the assassin would leap out and shoot him at close range. Castro would be a sitting duck."

Soft light drifted into the courtroom from its rear. Most people, including Marco, didn't notice it as they were too caught up in the presentation and the floor diagram projected onto the screen. But Frank saw it. Two guards in the back did too. It was the door, creeping open enough to allow Ernie Tolliver and Sasha to enter. One of the guards approached them, his hand on his gun, but Ernie produced credentials that satisfied him, backing him off. The credentials came from Frank, but he didn't intend them for Sasha. He intended her to be far away from here. His eyes narrowed on Ernie, certain another one of Trevor's associates had undermined him.

"CIA honchos rejected Morales's plan citing two problems," said Marco. "The closet pantry would only be able to hold one assassin. And there'd be nowhere for the assassin to run after the shooting."

The jury may have been as into the presentation as movie-goers watching a Hollywood thriller, but Frank thought Ernie and Sasha looked anxious. She also looked nervous. *Why her more than him? What's going on?*

"His superiors scrapped his plan, but that doesn't mean Agent Morales forgot about it," said Marco. "By his own admission, he played a part in President Kennedy's 1963 assassination. Five years later, he saw a chance to get the second brother by resurrecting his kitchen pantry plan at the Ambassador Hotel. But he needed accomplices to pull it off."

Frank felt more than he heard an alarm scream in his head. It told him the DA was about to target his mother. He knew the moment would come, and he still didn't have a plan for how to handle it. He would have if Rip had returned his calls – *oh, what the...wasn't that the unspoken part of his* Hottest Place in Hell *warning? Blaming others for your failings?*

Marco continued. "It's unlikely this was an official CIA operation though its success certainly benefited the agency. The team David Sanchez Morales assembled consisted of people outside the agency who had connections *to him.* Johnny Rosselli recruited Frank Donneroummas and so forth." He gestured to Frank. "Mr. Caron already laid that out, but he stopped short of revealing the small group of intimates who prepared Sirhan to be the distraction. These intimates moved him into position and made sure he played his part."

Several jurors looked at Frank. They knew his mother was one of the intimates who supposedly moved Sirhan into position. He couldn't keep her out of the hearing, but maybe he could play down her role. With so much going on in the case, so much information, he'd throw up a distraction. He couldn't miss the irony of it: a distraction, like Sirhan provided the distraction while someone fired the kill shot into Robert Kennedy's head. He saw Ernie texting in the back of the room. That was a surprise because it was what he was *supposed* to do. They had coordinated it earlier. Could it be that Ernie wasn't undermining him? He shot to his feet. It would take a big announcement to distract the jury. "District Attorney Diaz is talking about 8F."

"No, I'm – what?"

"You won't find it in your packets," he said. "It's an organization –" The door to his left, in the front of the courtroom, flew open. *Thank God. Perfect timing. He must've been waiting for Ernie's text...as planned.* A man entered. He was in his late forties, a few years younger than Frank, with hair that was more pepper than salt. He wore the inexpensive suit of a public servant. He cast a brief glance at Ernie as he approached Frank.

"This is a closed hearing." Marco turned to the nearest bailiff. "Remove this man."

"Turn on the lights," said the intruder.

The assistant who dimmed the lights earlier froze with indecision. He stared at the newcomer, looked at Frank, turned to Marco. The DA gestured for him to do as instructed, so he did.

With the lights coming up, the newcomer spoke to Frank. "I'm Aaron Carpenter with the attorney general's office. I've been authorized to give you this." He handed over a paper that bore the seal, official letterhead and signature of the Attorney General of the State of California. "It grants you full authority to bring this case to the grand jury."

"It's *being* brought," said Marco. "This is my hearing. Let me see that."

Frank read the paper quickly. It was all there, as he hoped it would be. He handed it to Marco. It was amazing how one document could change how he felt. He had his doubts, especially with Sasha there, but he could now admit Ernie delivered on his promise to get the AG's man into the courtroom. Of course, Frank did everything else: contacting the AG, getting him to order Sasha's release – that could've been a problem, but for whatever reason, Marco never brought it up. He assumed Marco thought someone else informed the attorney general of her illegal incarceration. Once he made all the arrangements with the AG, he needed someone to keep the AG's man a secret and coordinate his entrance perfectly while *he* played the part of Marco's dutiful employee in court. He would've preferred it to be Rip, but he didn't return his calls. "Arrest the district attorney," he told the bailiffs. They promptly obeyed him, having already received their orders from the attorney general's office. Marco stopped reading the AG's paper, his head whipping left and right, as Frank said, "Mr. Diaz, you are accused of mishandling government resources, wasting taxpayer money and committing criminal acts, including torture and possibly murder, in an attempt to litigate a case for personal gain, a case that has already been litigated."

Marco's face went from dumbfounded to hard and then to deathly cold. He knew better than to fully resist, but that didn't stop him from twisting violently to frustrate the bailiffs arresting him. His thugs/actors in his play didn't know what to do, so they didn't do anything. Like him, they abused their positions. And they had to worry about their possible arrests.

At this point, the judge from the fourth floor was supposed to take the bench, but Trevor failed to deliver on that one. That left the AG's man on the scene, Aaron Carpenter. Frank expected him to step up, but someone else entered through the front door. He looked to be in his eighties, but well-kept for his age. A slight curvature of the spine bent his shoulders forward. He had a full head of hair and a nicely trimmed beard, all white, and his skin was tan. His most striking feature was a pair of piercing blue eyes. He wore a dark judge's robe that was unremarkable but for the boutonniere of tiny white flowers pinned to it. All business, he looked at no one but the man restrained by bailiffs. And he said, "Pursuant to section 925 of the California penal code, the grand jury shall investigate the officers of the county." He seemed the personification of authority as he ascended the steps that brought him to the raised perch of the judge's bench. He lifted the gavel. "Court will break to reorganize. In thirty minutes, we will reconvene to hear the charges brought against Los Angeles County District Attorney Marco Diaz." He brought the gavel down on the wooden plate, and it sounded like a thunderclap in the stunned courtroom.

Aaron Carpenter seemed satisfied, while Frank was confused. He never met Trevor's judge, but he checked enough of his background to know this wasn't him. But who was he to question when the AG's appointed representative approved of him? As the saying went, it was above his pay grade. And he had a full plate already. He had to convince the grand jury to indict a sitting and popular district attorney. His eyes drifted over to find Marco Diaz glaring at him.

CHAPTER 34

Sasha knew the arrest would come. Ernie explained it when he picked her up at the precinct, but he failed to tell her The Clipper would oversee it. If she knew that, she would've insisted on sticking to Frank's plan to get her as far away from things as possible. The shock first hit her when The Clipper entered the room wearing a black judge's robe. Now, as a bailiff introduced him as the Honorable Daniel M. Hartman, she felt outright fear. She was persona non grata in 8F. Ernie was too. With The Clipper controlling the hearing from the bench, she couldn't stop seeing herself as a pawn about to be sacrificed in some chess match she didn't understand.

After calling the room to order, the judge thanked the grand jury for participating in the RFK "ruse" (his word). He said rehashing the Kennedy murder case served two purposes: to keep the district attorney from suspecting there was an investigation into his conduct and to provide enough rope for the DA to make for himself a strong noose. *So the RFK hearing was a sting operation? At what point did it become that, and who made that decision?* Again, the judge cited the state's penal code (section 933 subsection 05 subsection E) by declaring the subject of the investigation shall meet with the grand jury. In this case, meeting with jurors meant the DA had to sit through the hearing without speaking. It was pure humiliation, which she guessed was the intention. What she didn't get was why The Clipper bothered to come out of hiding to play the role of judge. Surely there was someone less valuable to 8F who could have taken that risk. And who authorized him assuming the position of judge?

The judge handed the hearing over to Frank because the attorney general designated him the lead prosecutor. But as a bailiff swore Dr. Fitz in as the first witness, Frank did nothing. Well, he stood. He seemed incapable of leaving the prosecution table, though. *What's wrong with him?* She always assumed he was good at his job. He won the case against Vincent Calessi, after all. His paralysis was so complete that the AG's representative, Aaron Carpenter, had to step up and question the witness. "So the grand jury understands," said Mr. Carpenter. "You received a transactional immunity deal for your testimony today and in a subsequent trial, if there is one."

"Yes."

"That means you will not be prosecuted for crimes related to the subject matter of your testimony, but you *will* be prosecuted if you fail to tell this court the truth. Do you understand?"

"I understand."

Still, Frank remained by the table. She saw him turn to Ernie, who sat a few feet away from her in the fourth row of the spectator section. He seemed to want answers, but Ernie was preoccupied texting. The expression on his face said he didn't like the texts that came back to him. She leaned closer to him. "It looks like Frank didn't know this witness was going to be called. Did you?"

Ernie kept his eyes and his attention on his phone.

She didn't hear what Aaron Carpenter next asked the witness, but she heard his reply. "I'm not a legal scholar," said Dr. Fitz. "But I believe Mrs. Caron's detainment in an undisclosed location was a lawful detainment for the purposes of questioning."

She felt herself heating from within. Lawful or not, it was definitely inhumane to incarcerate *and drug* a sick, confused, elderly woman.

"How did you question her?"

Dr. Fitz cast his eyes across the room at Sasha. "I didn't have the chance. Someone broke her out of our custody before –"

"Before the drug you forced upon her could take effect." Frank shook off his paralysis to approach the witness stand. "I believe it was ibogaine. Isn't that illegal in the United States?"

"Yes."

Frank gave Mr. Carpenter a glance, as if to say *I got this.* It took a moment, but the AG's representative yielded him the floor. "Is ibogaine dangerous?" he asked. "Perhaps even lethal if the person taking it is elderly like Mrs. Caron, had a stroke and suffers from dementia?"

"It could be."

"Who told you to give my mother an illegal, potentially lethal drug without her consent?"

Dr. Fitz glanced at Marco Diaz, then he returned to Frank. "Ibogaine has many benefits. It's been known to cure powerful addictions. For those like *your mother*, who are not addicts, it can resurrect deeply suppressed memories in vivid detail. It's like a time machine that can take them back to a specific moment in their life and make them relive it, no matter how far back or how much they might have suppressed the memory."

Frank repeated, "Who told you to do that?"

"District Attorney Diaz wanted to get her talking about Robert Kennedy's assassination. He thought – *we* thought – ibogaine would be more effective than hypnosis, which can be unreliable."

This is where they call me. The witness made a dig at hypnosis, which Sasha thought was funny considering he hypnotized Frank in Redondo Beach. If this was the reason Ernie wanted her here, she was glad of it. *To correct this Yale-educated, professional...* to her surprise, Frank didn't call her. Instead, he asked his next question. "The accused ordered you to give an illegal, potentially lethal drug to an elderly woman with severe health issues?"

"I wouldn't say it was an order. The district attorney and I discussed the most effective and expedient way to get your mother to reveal what she knew of the assassination. I suggested ibogaine, which usually has minimal, if any, long term effects. District Attorney Diaz approved it based on my recommendation as a mental health professional."

"He's taking the rap 'cause he can't be prosecuted," mumbled Ernie. "He'll get his reward for loyalty later. It's what I'd do."

Is that what you did do? It would explain him and The Clipper both being in the courtroom while seemingly at odds. Again, she wondered about his plan and how it involved her.

"Let's discuss what happened at the Junípero Serra Elementary School," said Frank.

Dr. Fitz slowly exhaled. "When we tortured former CIA agent Kentworth Lee so he'd answer questions about a case for which your mother was the primary suspect?"

"I didn't –" Frank took a moment, composed himself. "Who ordered you to do that? Who watched from the next room while you put clamps on the man's nipples and his genitals then fired them with electric shocks like you were jump starting a car battery?"

Dr. Fitz's face couldn't show much emotion, but he appeared to be confused. "I didn't know anybody was watching from the next room. But I did see *you* order Mr. Lee to talk then castrate him when he didn't. It was *you* that violently tore his genitals off with a clamp."

Gasps popped like movie corn in the jury box. They weren't shy about openly speculating that Frank, not Marco Diaz, was the public official guilty of wrongdoing.

She turned to Ernie, expecting him to have some reassurance for her, some explanation.

Ernie seemed frustrated, but it was because of his phone, not what went on in the courtroom. "I'll be right back." He shuffled out of the row and hurried to the back of the room.

All Sasha could do was watch him disappear through the rear door.

The Clipper looked astonished from where he sat. And he did the best thing a judge could do under the circumstances. He pounded his gavel and declared a recess.

Frank was plainly stunned by the turn of events and his

quick loss of favor.

Sasha's natural instinct was to go up and comfort him. He seemed to need it. But could she really say for certain that he didn't torture and castrate that man? She wasn't there. She had warned him before, back in the warehouse, when they killed Joseph Provenzano. She also recalled what Charlotte and Trevor said about him. They told her he did something terrible in the past. Terrible secrets seemed to be coded into his DNA, starting not with his mother but with his grandfather, somebody named Khan (if she could believe what The Clipper said in that film lot). One thing she did know: *getting out of that relationship was the best thing that ever happened to me*. She decided to stay where she was...to not comfort him.

#

This break lasted only as long as it took to get the jury to stop thinking of Frank as a prosecutor and accept him as a witness. Nothing about any of it was typical. If it had been a trial rather than a grand jury hearing, he wouldn't have been able to go from prosecutor to witness then eventually back to prosecutor. If it hadn't been for the AG's support, he wouldn't have been able to turn the RFK hearing into a hearing on the district attorney. Unprecedented leeway came to him by way of Sacramento – probably because the AG saw Marco as a serious rival for the governor's seat in the upcoming election. He found the AG's reason less important than his own reality: if he botched it, there'd be hell to pay. Exonerated, Marco Diaz would be stronger than ever, and he'd want revenge. The AG would want to punish Frank for damaging his reputation with a failed and embarrassing hearing. He shuddered to think what would become of his mother, whether she deserved it or not. And after how he handled Dr. Fitz as a witness, a botch seemed likely.

With Frank now on the witness stand, the AG's man, Aaron Carpenter, assumed the prosecutorial duties. He asked his first question after the swearing in, to which Frank replied, "We were in the city of Twentynine Palms at a motel when Mr. Diaz's personal henchmen, some of whom played parts in that assassination reenactment we saw earlier, abducted my mother and beat me unconscious. Dr. Fitz was their leader, just as he led in the torture of the former CIA agent."

"Can you prove they did this to you following orders from the district attorney?"

"You gave his men immunity, so we can't leverage them into testifying against him." He didn't know if they all got immunity, but the deal they cut with Dr. Fitz was obviously *not* to their advantage. He glanced at Marco. Though hand-cuffed and watched over by bailiffs, he looked pleased with Frank's answer. And that only frustrated him more.

Mr. Carpenter and Judge Hartman traded glances. In a fact-based hearing, he just gave them nothing they could use.

A door in the back of the courtroom crept cautiously open, and Ripley Reed entered.

Normally, Frank would've been happy to see his friend, especially at such a critical moment. But Rip's refusal to answer any of his recent calls made him wonder if his "friend" came to support him or Marco – probably Marco.

Judge Hartman spoke up. "This hearing is not open to the public."

Before Rip could respond, another door opened. This one was the front side door of the courtroom, the one through which Aaron Carpenter and Judge Hartman originally entered. *Not yet.* Frank planned this interruption, just as he coordinated the other – again, with Ernie's help. Mr. Tolliver was supposed to place a text (as he did before) to a person waiting in the wings, but he left the courtroom before the last break without knowing when to place the text. And timing was crucial.

Frank watched his mother enter the courtroom in a wheelchair – as planned. Everyone took it as a surprise: Sasha, Marco and jurors (who recognized her from a picture in their packets). But the person pushing her chair was Ernie when it should have been Trevor.

Emotions swirled so powerfully within Frank that they nearly knocked him off the witness stand. His son failed him again, leaving someone else to do what he had promised to do. His mother hit him the hardest, though. She still shook and seemed a bit disoriented, but the worst effects of her ibogaine intake seemed to have passed – a relief for him, of course. But he couldn't bury the resentment she raised in him. He turned his world upside down to defend and protect her. In return, she was nothing but a condescending liar, and…hell, *she* resented *him*.

Of all the reactions to Charlotte's arrival, Judge Hartman had the strangest of all. His face fell while his back shot up straight. He looked like he saw the Devil herself. For her part, Charlotte locked onto the judge with her good eye. One half of her face still suffered from paralysis, but the functional side wore a look Frank had never seen before, even when he most disappointed her. *How do they know each other? Why do they look at each other like that?*

#

Los Angeles, California. June 6, 1968

"We interrupt this broadcast for an announcement from Kennedy spokesman Frank Mankiewicz at the Good Samaritan Hospital."

Sitting in the backseat between two Provenzano men, Charlotte looks over the seatback. Matthew is driving. Another Italian occupies the front passenger seat. Directly before her, embedded in the dash, is the car radio. Its keys are like the big protruding teeth of a hillbilly, but its words aren't those of some ignorant Jethro. They're important to the nation and even more important to the men riding with her. They, like her, have a personal stake in the announcement. She did nothing to perpetuate the deed for which there's an announcement, but she also didn't prevent it. For the last day and a half, she hid out in a motel. She watched the news reports, knew they got Kennedy as they planned. But he hasn't died. He's in a coma. While he lingers in that state, hope remains that he'll pull through. *She* hopes he'll pull through. She thinks of his poor mother. It's not the first time she's thought of Rose Kennedy in the last few days. To lose her son, the president, and now this…it's too much for a mother to take.

A somber voice, apparently that of Mr. Mankiewicz, says, "Senator Robert Francis Kennedy died at 1:44 a.m. today, June 6, 1968. With Senator Kennedy at the time of his death were –" Matthew turns it off.

Silence follows the click of the radio knob, allowing what Mr. Mankiewicz said to linger in the air. She drops her head. When someone who made as many waves as Bobby Kennedy dies from sudden violence, it's not an accident. It's a professional job thoroughly done. That's why she's with these men. It's time for the clean-up, especially now that RFK is gone.

The desert is the mob's favorite place to get rid of someone who knows too much. But this is the city, the Sunset Strip, to be precise. People on the sidewalk go about their business, ignorant of the conspirators cruising past them. A woman in a nearby sedan weeps over the news she must've just heard on her radio. She has a boy with her. He looks to be about a year older than Francis, but he's Hispanic. The woman is too. Kennedy was much adored by their community. What will they do now? Probably moan, cry and complain as they keep laying the bricks to build America's empire. "I didn't say anything," says Charlotte, breaking the silence. "I won't."

Nothing comes back to her.

"I know I said that before, but I mean it. You know me." She notices the body odor of the men sandwiching her more acutely than she had only a moment ago. "Matthew."

"Who's that?" asks the man in the front passenger seat.

Matthew looks at her in the mirror – and she back at him. It's an exchange that doesn't need words, that's not shared by the Italians. It tells her she *just* said something, already breaking her promise. The front passenger wasn't being sarcastic. These men know him as Michael, and they know her as Shirin. He puts on the blinker and steers toward an office building with a parking lot. She knows the place too well for her liking. Her skin feels moist, her body hot, and she realizes she smells her *own* perspiration. It has the odor of a rotting corpse. But it's not her body that will die here. This Sunset Strip office will see the death of her memories and the scramble of her mind. She wonders if she'd be better off buried in the desert. "No!" She twists and turns, but it does no good with the men on each side of her: their strength, their weaponry and their promise to do what the man they know as Michael Wayne tells them to do.

\#

2018

"I have to calm her down." Sasha glanced at Ernie, who returned to her side after settling Charlotte into the witness stand. She assumed he brought her here to help the old woman through her testimony. Nothing else made sense. Charlotte managed to give an affirmative answer to the bailiff's swear-in question, but she fidgeted. She shook in her wheelchair, vibrating the stand. With The Clipper playing judge only a few feet away from her, it was too much.

Ernie responded simply and softly. "Stay where you are."

She watched Frank approach his mother. "We're seeking an indictment against the district attorney for abuse of power," he said. "He is accused of taking the law into his own hands as he tried to build a case against you. This is about him. Do you understand?"

Charlotte nodded – maybe. It could've been more of her erratic movements.

"She never had any direct one on one with the district attorney." Sasha looked at Ernie. "She has nothing to say that would incriminate him. What are you scheming?"

"I need you to tell me you understand," said Frank.

"She does," said the judge. "Let the record show the witness nodded. Ask her your questions, but keep them limited to the district attorney and his behavior. Do *you* understand?"

Sasha saw The Clipper glance at Mr. Carpenter. In all her interactions with him, he never looked at anyone so...she couldn't quite find the word. *Tentatively* seemed to best describe how he looked at the AG's representative.

"District Attorney Marco Diaz had you arrested," Frank said to his mother. "He accused you of being a conspirator in the assassination of Robert Kennedy fifty years ago. Do you know on what grounds he based this accusation?" Getting a blank look from Charlotte, he rephrased the question. "What made him think you were the girl in the polka-dot dress?"

It took her a few long and uncomfortable moments, but Charlotte raised a quivering hand, and she pointed across the courtroom at Sasha.

She felt the heat of the old woman's accusation – all the hotter because it was true. She *was* the reason Mr. Diaz went after Charlotte. *But...but...*Without looking away from the wrinkly, pointing finger, she said, "It's not my fault the district attorney abused and drugged her. I'm not responsible for everything else he did."

Ernie didn't respond, and the reason for that was that he was once again preoccupied with his phone: this time making a call.

She knew next to nothing about courtroom propriety, but *since when do they let spectators text and make calls?* No one seemed to notice, not even the bailiffs, who should have.

"The witness identified Sasha Frye," Frank told the jury. "She hypnotized my mother then told District Attorney Diaz what she said under hypnosis. *That* was why he arrested her. But Ms. Frye's only qualification for being a hypnotist is a certificate she received for completing an online course run by a wellness institute operating out of a strip mall."

That was a blow to her most sensitive vulnerability – her lack of accreditation. It felt as if everyone looked at her with ridicule. She made a show of glaring at Frank, but the more she thought about it, as painful as that was, she had to admit he was right. *Unaccredited and inexperienced, who am I to think that after fifty years, I could unlock Charlotte's mental programming when no one else could?*

Marco yelled from his seat. "He's testifying – Your Honor. Seriously."

"You are *not* to be heard from." The Clipper's eyes were as cold as slices of a blue glacier, aimed at Marco. He shifted them to

Frank. "Do you have a question for the witness?"

"Let's talk about your illegal incarceration without arraignment in an off-the-grid location," said Frank. "Dr. Fitz tells us it was for the purpose of questioning – without your attorney present, I might add. What can you –" He stopped as his mother mumbled a cadence that gradually grew loud enough to be heard and clear enough to be understood.

In a strong New England accent, Charlotte said, "...around the world by a monolithic and ruthless conspiracy that relies primarily on covert means fah expanding its sphere of influence. Its mistakes ah buried, not headlined. Its dissentahs ah silenced, not praised. No expenditah is questioned. No rumah is printed. No secret is revealed."

Sasha looked suspiciously at Charlotte. *Is this another performance?*

Both of Charlotte's eyes locked onto something only she could see. She appeared to be in a trance. "Its mistakes ah buried, not headlined. Its dissentahs ah silenced, not praised. No expenditah is questioned. No rumah is printed. No secret is revealed." Like a recording stuck on replay, she repeated, "We ah opposed around the world by a monolithic and ruthless conspiracy that relies primarily on covert means fah expanding its sphere of influence. Its mistakes ah buried, not headlined. Its dissentahs ah silenced, not praised. No expenditah is questioned. No rumah is printed. No secret is revealed."

Charlotte's words were eerie. Their meaning, the cadence she used, and her accent that mimicked a beloved martyr, it made jurors curious and uncomfortable. They looked around, not knowing what to do. Marco appeared excited from where he sat in his restraints, supervised by bailiffs. It was as if he'd been waiting a lifetime to hear someone say what Charlotte now said.

Sasha elbowed Ernie. "That's a speech by Robert –." She didn't finish because Ernie, she saw, had his phone up, facing the witness stand. And Trevor was on the screen, FaceTiming.

"What did you say?" Frank asked Sasha from across the room.

She gave Ernie a look of warning. Then she decided *screw it. He knows what he's doing.* She threw her answer back to Frank. "It's the alarm on her mental lock-box."

"Explain that."

It took everything she had not to say *who's unaccredited now?* Her eyes shifted to The Clipper. He looked worried, and he seemed to seek answers – or maybe it was some instruction he sought – from Mr. Carpenter. The AG's representative, however, was deep in consultation with the black man who entered the courtroom only moments before Trevor and Charlotte entered. With so much going on, was it any wonder no one noticed Ernie FaceTiming the hearing with Trevor? *Why didn't Trevor come himself?*

Frank spun on the defendant. "You did this! You fed her a drug that fried her brain."

Marco pretended not to hear him. He had eyes only for the old woman on the stand.

"…conspiracy that relies primarily on covert means fah expanding its sphere of influence. Its mistakes ah buried, not headlined. Its dissentahs ah silenced, not praised. No expenditah is questioned. No rumah is printed. No secret is revealed."

The Clipper was on his own, with no advice from the AG's man, so he said, "Bailiffs, remove the witness. Call a psychiatrist. She needs to be institutionalized –." His blue eyes shot wide when he saw Ernie holding up the phone. "What are you doing? Bailiffs, arrest that man."

Trevor's voice roared out of the phone's small speaker. "Listen to her," he said. "Does what she's saying sound familiar?"

"…dissentahs ah silenced, not praised. No expenditah is questioned. No rumah is printed. No secret is revealed. We ah opposed around the world by a monolithic and ruthless –"

Sasha knew The Clipper needed to hear what Trevor said. It was an indictment – sure, but more than that, it was dissention. *And dissentahs ah* not to be *silenced*. Without really thinking of the consequences, she sprang to her feet. "Does what she's saying sound familiar?"

The Clipper didn't look at her, but he beat on the wooden puck with his gavel. "Recess. I call a recess."

Charlotte struggled while continuing to recite her words from the stand. Her aged face contorted. She lost the paralysis that crippled half of it. Her eyes, now synchronized, remained fixed on something nobody but her could see.

"Go," said Ernie.

Sasha turned to see him point her toward the witness stand. "This was your plan." She didn't need him to elaborate – and he didn't. She walked boldly down the center aisle. Her eyes stayed on the old woman, but she could feel everyone looking at her. This time it wasn't with ridicule. They wanted help and answers. They wanted her for Charlotte. The old woman's struggle taxed her frail body. Everyone could see that, Frank especially. "They programmed her fifty years ago," she explained. "They put everything she saw and did, everything she remembered about the assassination, into a mental box and locked it away. She's picking that lock now, trying to work through it."

Frank said, "Why did you ask him if what she's saying sounds familiar?"

She watched The Clipper abandon the bench to go from bailiff to bailiff. He issued orders that no one obeyed. Charlotte's endless cadence on the witness stand seemed to madden him.

"...a monolithic and ruthless conspiracy that relies primarily on covert means fah expanding its sphere of influence. Its mistakes ah buried, not headlined. Its –"

Frank whipped around to look at his mother. "Monolithic and ruthless conspiracy?"

Charlotte saw his sudden movement – both her eyes catching it. Like her facial paralysis that came and went and her misaligned eyes that now worked in unison, it was a performance.

Watching the old woman return to her recitation and her struggles, Sasha realized *Charlotte picked her mental lock a while ago. And her hypnotized confession about being the girl in the polka-dot dress was also a performance.* She smiled. She had to. The wily old woman fooled everyone.

"Those aren't Bobby's words," said Frank. "They're John's. Right, Rip? She's reciting a speech President Kennedy gave shortly before his assassination. It's a warning about –" He turned to Ernie, still FaceTiming, and he added, "8F."

The Clipper shouted at Aaron Carpenter. "You need to shut this down now!"

Mr. Carpenter looked at him with something akin to pity on his face, but he did nothing. The black man broke away from him, stalked toward the front of the courtroom. Now the eyes of the jurors went from him to The Clipper to Frank to Charlotte, around the room and even to each other. Who was in charge here?

Sasha pointed at the judge, "The Clipper." And she threw her words at Marco Diaz. "I don't know if anything about him is *nautical*, but that's who I was talking about. He's –"

"Michael Wayne." Charlotte shouted out intensely and clearly. "My handler and the assassination mastermind. He's the builder of empires."

The Clipper made a go for the side door, but the man named Rip beat him to it. With one hand, he drew a gun. With the other hand, he pulled credentials from his pocket. "FBI. You're under arrest. Bailiffs, a little help here."

Surprise gripped everyone – particularly Frank, who stared gape-jawed at the black man. People began to find their voices as bailiffs rushed across the room to help the FBI agent apprehend The Clipper. Before the noise could drown her out, Charlotte turned to Frank. She had one last thing to say, and she made sure everyone heard it. "He's your father."

EPILOGUE

The media was like a pack of ravenous wolves – once again. They kept trying, and they kept failing to breach the security line outside the precinct. Frank got it. He really did. This was the story that kept giving. But he had nothing more to tell them. His mother had been released to his custody, which meant he had to find a place for her – someplace that wouldn't hypnotize her. Trevor was in the wind, nothing new there. And he came to the precinct to get closure from the man Charlotte claimed was his father. *What does that make Pete Caron, who raised me?*

"You have some scary genetics."

He knew that was Marco before he actually turned to see him. It was as if the son of a bitch read his thoughts. "The law doesn't condemn sons for the crimes of their fathers."

"And mothers." Marco stood where the administrative area met the lock-up.

"You can't drag her through this again." He gestured to the media throng outside the front windows. "They'll ruin you."

Marco grew a smirk. "The grand jury cleared me of wrongdoing, in case you missed it. I'm still the DA."

"The FBI is onto you…as they've been since first embedding Rip in your office."

"That one fooled both of us," said Marco. "I saw the surprise on your face. And it made me wonder, of all the thousands of people working in the District Attorney's Office, why was Ripley Reed the only one to befriend you? Given your family's history,

I'd wager he's more interested in you than me." He glanced to the left and made a come forward gesture. Sasha stepped out from behind a cluster of cops, uniformed and plain-clothed. "Enough about Agent Reed," said Marco. "We have business with your father...all three of us."

Sasha glanced sideways at Frank. She looked like she had to be there but wanted to be anywhere else. Her eyes went back to the cops, where she gave her most hateful expression to the dude with the flat-top haircut.

"Okay," said Marco upon her arrival. "Let's do this."

Every precinct was different, but to Frank, the lock-up areas always seemed the same. They were holding pens, temporary storage for detainees who the cops hadn't finished questioning to their satisfaction. He knew Sasha had been there longer than most, and passing through now probably felt to her like an unpleasant flashback. Did Marco threaten her with another lock-up if she didn't come do this? Did she know it was Frank that got her out last time?

"Some ground rules," said Marco. "Don't waste my time with any daddy issues. We're here to get information on the assassination and –" He spun around. "I want to know about 8F. You get him talking about that."

You think exposing 8F will give you a ticket to Washington, D.C. and let you bypass Sacramento? Frank shook his head. The man's ambition knew no limits.

The DA resumed his trek through the lock-up area. A cell to his left held a man who looked like a male prostitute, track marks on his arms. "Hello, Willie."

Willie gazed forward with unfocused eyes. It took a moment, but Frank realized it was his testimony a few years back that broke an illegal Hollywood sex ring. Marco got some great press out of it. Frank stopped outside his cell. "What are they charging you with?"

"Misunderstanding," slurred Willie. "Wrong place, wrong time." Some of the puncture marks on his right arm had scabs. His eyes had dark rings. His hair was matted and clumped. He hadn't shaved in days, and when he did, he missed a patch on his cheek.

What brought you to this? Judging by his condition, Frank figured he likely *was* in the wrong place at the wrong time. He was probably guilty of something for which he was the only victim, which meant he needed help, not incarceration. The cops had him in here where he didn't belong because they knew they could leverage his fame from the Hollywood case to get themselves some good-ole Marco-style free press. When did the law become so much dirty manipulation? Day one, he guessed. That was when. "Can you remember my name?"

"What?"

"My name is Frank Caron, public defender. I'm willing to help you."

Marco laughed. "You think you can return to private practice?" He walked back toward him, shifting his eyes to Sasha. "Tell him why he can't do that. Tell him what you told me."

"He's a killer," she said.

Frank spun around to face her.

"He killed his son's mother," she told Willie. "But not in a way that would convict him."

Frank wasn't entirely surprised, knowing to what she referred, and it probably came from Trevor. He long ago put a sainted halo over his mother's head by attributing her death to him. "My ex-girlfriend, Trevor's mom, died from an overdose. I wasn't there. I was never there. When I was, we fought, exasperating her drug problem. For that, I bear some responsibility."

"Sounds like we could make a case for negligent homicide," said Marco.

There was no negligent homicide case, and Marco knew it. Of greater concern was Sasha. She tried to sound tough and accusatory, but he could see her insecurity and her confusion.

"Your mother...and Trevor...they said –"

He let out a long exhale. "What happened to Robyn, his mom, was horrible. I did everything wrong with her. I admit it. That's why I gave the boy to my mother to raise because I thought I'd only screw him up more. Turns out she screwed him up. Is that it? They teased that I did something unspeakable? It wasn't that." He stepped up to her. The way she looked at him: like a girl hurt by her lover's lies. She deserved to know the real reason he kept people at a distance, including why he rejected her offer to help him with his mother's *situation*.

"Then what's your dirty secret?"

The question came from Willie, reminding him others besides Sasha were there. He directed his answer to her, though. "My twin sister died because of me."

"I thought you were an only child," she said.

"That's how I grew up. Alone."

"When did this happen?" asked Marco.

"April 7, 1968."

"When you were two years old?" asked Sasha.

"We're wasting time with this. C'mon." Marco resumed walking deeper into lock-up.

But they didn't move. "When you were a young child, you caused an accident that got your sister killed?" asked Sasha.

"It wasn't an accident. A Black Panther shot her at a Civil Rights event."

"I might be high as shit," said Willie. "But this don't make no sense."

"He's right," said Sasha.

"Hey," Marco returned. "This isn't a suggestion. Now. Let's go."

Still, they didn't move. Fifty years of blame by his mother and fifty years of living with the shame rooted him in place. He heard echoes of what Rip said in Robert F. Kennedy Inspiration Park: *You spent your life taking the path of least responsibility to avoid being the cause of another calamity.* "The path of least responsibility," he said aloud.

She continued to look at him – no longer out of hurt, but with sympathy.

He couldn't recall ever seeing her look *at him* that way. It was a bit reminiscent of how she looked when she convinced him to let her treat Charlotte with hypnosis. He could now see why his mother opened up to her when she didn't to anyone else, including him. There was something about Sasha that seemed trustworthy and genuine. It made him want to unburden himself to her, as if she'd put him in a safe place where none of the nastiness hiding in his memories could hurt him. "I've never remembered getting Bobbi killed, but I've never been able to forget that I did it."

"Your mother –"

"I've been trying to make my peace with her since her dementia diagnosis. She doesn't have much time." There was more he wanted to tell her. He searched for the words, but –

"She made her peace," said Sasha. "That's what this was all about."

Police whistles shrieked from far back in the lock-up. Shrill, choppy and desperate, they filled the air. Detainees they hadn't yet met responded to the whistles with shouts and wails. They banged on their bars like captive monkeys.

A man yelled amidst the noise. "Ten fifty-six!" He repeated, "Ten fifty-six!"

Frank had spent enough time defending people in trouble to know 10-56 was the police code for suicide. 10-56A was the code for a suicide *attempt*, but he didn't hear that. He ran in the direction of the whistles, passing Marco and jail cells with erupting prisoners. The sounds of urgency summoned him, getting louder with every stride he completed. It was a full assault upon his hearing, but he couldn't retreat from it. He knew – deep inside, he knew – that the sounds of emergency blared for none other than his father. What he saw when he reached the most isolated cell in the furthermost part of the lock-up area only confirmed the accuracy of his intuition. The silver haired man Charlotte said was his father lay motionless on the floor. Two cops worked on him while three more buzzed into and out of his cell. Attempts to revive him did nothing but jar his body, but it still looked as if he left this life with little discomfort. White bubbly foam filled the space between his lips, indicating both his death and the means by which it occurred.

"No!" Marco charged into the cell. "No, no, no!"

Frank saw a few tiny white bell-shaped flowers lying on the floor beneath the dead man's left earlobe, only to be scattered unnoticed by the officers working on the body.

Sasha arrived behind him. "He accepted his fate."

He turned to her. "Was he ordered to do this?"

"He was ordered to play judge in the hearing. I know that."

"By Aaron Carpenter?" In his peripheral vision, he saw Marco turn from the body to eavesdrop on their conversation.

She shrugged. "If Mr. Carpenter gave those orders, they probably came from someone else. That's how they keep 8F going – sacrifice and replace."

His eyes went down to the dead man in the cell. He didn't have any affection for him. He didn't know him. But a mysterious heat turned his face fire-engine red anyway. He even heard the engine's alarm, though it could've been an ambulance outside called to the scene. "His grandson," he mumbled. "My son."

Marco rushed out of the cell, stopping only inches from his face. "I know you've been covering for him. How long do you think you can keep that up?"

"He didn't come to court because he knew you were on to him," Sasha told Marco.

The more Frank thought about it, the hotter he felt. It was *The Hottest Place in Hell*-kind of hot. He recalled Trevor giving orders to mobsters as well as Minutemen like Ernie Tolliver. His son arranged to have the "judge" oversee Marco's corruption hearing. Where did he get the authority to do that if not from 8F? The judge that showed up wasn't the one he promised, but that seemed deliberate, as if he set up The Clipper all along. Sasha said the old man was there on orders. A loyal 8F soldier to the end, they sacrificed him so they could replace him with the next generation. *Oh, God.* "Scary genetics doesn't begin to describe it." He glanced at Sasha. *Can I do it? Should I do it – take down my son? Or…or…* He took a deep breath, then he asked, "Have you ever considered working for a defense lawyer?"

THE END

Guy Cote spent his formative years in Sanford, Maine pretending to be an adventurer and marching up and down Main Street waving an American flag while wearing an army uniform (his youthful response to the Iranian Hostage Crisis). As his body grew and his maturity followed, Guy played sports and emulated fictional characters he saw on the silver screen. He eventually tired of living vicariously through other people's creations, so he began writing his own screenplays. He completed his first script, *The Magic of a Lifetime*, shortly before graduating from The University of Maine.

With a script and a freshly minted Bachelors Degree in hand, Guy moved to Florida to work in the Sunshine State's burgeoning film industry. In the process, he wrote five more screenplays: *Tried and True* (currently in pre-production to become a feature film), *G.I. Joe: The Making of a Hero*, *The Paper Trail*, *Soulmate* and *The Widowmaker*.

Guy's fascination with other times and other places eventually drew him back into academia where he earned his Masters Degree in history from The University of South Florida. Thereafter, he took a teaching position in a public school and dedicated himself to the creation of his first novel. *Long Live the King* is the culmination of that effort. It is Guy's hope and belief that you'll enjoy reading this novel as much as he enjoyed crafting it and he looks forward to the two of you meeting again in the sequel.

Like most authors, Guy relishes feedback from his readers. Feel free to visit and leave him a message at www.guycotebooks.com. See you there…

www.ingramcontent.com/pod-product-compliance
Lightning Source LLC
Chambersburg PA
CBHW030932260626
47169CB00002B/452